"In this beautifully read sequel to
Don Robertson's *The Greatest Thing Since
Sliced Bread,* Morris Bird III continues his advance
on adulthood even as did Holden Caulfield . . .
Funny, sarcastic, touching, and, yes, nostalgic, this is a
novel of character to be enjoyed by all ages."
—*Library Journal*

PRAISE FOR
The Greatest Thing Since Sliced Bread

"A brilliant piece of writing—a book to put on the same shelf
as *The Catcher in the Rye* and *The Outsiders.*"
—Stephen King

"Delightful . . . universal enough to send a twinge of nostalgia
through any ex-boy."
—*The New York Times Book Review*

"Purely wonderful . . . belongs on the same shelf as *The Adventures of Tom Sawyer* and *Penrod.*"
—*Chicago Tribune*

The
Sum and Total
of Now

DON ROBERTSON

BERKLEY BOOKS, NEW YORK

THE BERKLEY PUBLISHING GROUP
Published by the Penguin Group
Penguin Group (USA) Inc.
375 Hudson Street, New York, New York 10014, USA

Penguin Group (Canada), 90 Eglinton Avenue East, Suite 700, Toronto, Ontario M4P 2Y3, Canada (a division of Pearson Penguin Canada Inc.)
Penguin Books Ltd., 80 Strand, London WC2R 0RL, England
Penguin Group Ireland, 25 St. Stephen's Green, Dublin 2, Ireland
(a division of Penguin Books Ltd.)
Penguin Group (Australia), 250 Camberwell Road, Camberwell, Victoria 3124, Australia
(a division of Pearson Australia Group Pty. Ltd.)
Penguin Books India Pvt. Ltd., 11 Community Centre, Panchsheel Park, New Delhi—110 017, India
Penguin Group (NZ), 67 Apollo Drive, Rosedale, North Shore, 0632, New Zealand
(a division of Pearson New Zealand Ltd.)
Penguin Books (South Africa) (Pty.) Ltd., 24 Sturdee Avenue, Rosebank, Johannesburg 2196, South Africa

Penguin Books Ltd., Registered Offices: 80 Strand, London WC2R 0RL, England

This is a work of fiction. Names, characters, places, and incidents either are the product of the author's imagination or are used fictitiously, and any resemblance to actual persons, living or dead, business establishments, events, or locales is entirely coincidental. The publisher does not have any control over and does not assume any responsibility for author or third-party websites or their content.

THE SUM AND TOTAL OF NOW

PRINTING HISTORY
Putnam Publishing Company hardcover edition: June 1966
Berkley trade paperback edition: August 2009

ISBN: 978-0-425-23084-8

PRINTED IN THE UNITED STATES OF AMERICA

10   9   8   7   6   5   4   3   2   1

For Pat, Ray, Kyle, Sarah
and Daniel MacDonnell

As *is* the earthy, such *are* they that also are earthy: and as *is* the heavenly, such *are* they also that are heavenly.

And as we have borne the image of the earthy, we shall also bear the image of the heavenly.

Now this I say, brethren, that flesh and blood cannot inherit the kingdom of God; neither doth corruption inherit incorruption.

Behold, I shew you a mystery; We shall not all sleep, but we shall all be changed.

In a moment, in the twinkling of an eye, at the last trump: for the trumpet shall sound, and the dead shall be raised incorruptible, and we shall be changed.

For this corruptible must put on incorruption, and this mortal *must* put on immortality.

So when this corruptible shall have put on incorruption, and this mortal shall have put on immortality, then shall be brought to pass the saying that is written, Death is swallowed up in victory.

O death, where *is* thy sting? O grave, where *is* thy victory?

The sting of death *is* sin; and the strength of sin *is* the law.

But thanks *be* to God, which giveth us the victory through our Lord Jesus Christ.

Therefore, my beloved brethren, be ye steadfast, unmoveable, always abounding in the work of the Lord, forasmuch as ye know that your labour is not in vain in the Lord.

—1 CORINTHIANS 15:48–58

NOTE: *The place and the time of this book are as real as I can make them. And the baseball game herein described actually did take place. There really is an Addison Junior High, but it never had a principal named Wright M. Ludwigson, and let us pray it never does. The other Addison faculty and staff members also are fictions. The only real people mentioned here are those who had achieved fame of one sort or another in 1948. And there is not, nor has there ever been, an Ohio town called Paradise Falls. The author would like to thank Norman Wagy, of WJW-TV, Cleveland, for permitting him to reacquaint himself with* The Treasure of the Sierra Madre.

And, finally, this is no autobiography. I repeat—no, no, no, not in the slightest way, shape, manner or form.

The
Sum and Total
of Now

People were forever telling the boy that confusions were a part of Growing Up. What you did was, they said, you sifted the confusions, placed them in their Proper Perspective. After enough years of doing this, they said, then you achieved Maturity, and Maturity was oh just the finest thing a person could—

Sure. Yeah. Big deal.

The thing was, his grandmother was dying. The thing was, she hurt. The thing was, she asked him to help her. The thing was, he didn't have the time to wait for Maturity.

And anyway, how come, if Maturity was so fine and made it so you had the answers to everything, how come his mother and his father and his aunts and his uncles behaved the way they did? A lot they cared that his grandmother was dying. A lot they cared that she hurt. They were too busy behaving like Fred C. Dobbs.

A person could get sour just thinking about it. Maybe, for all the boy knew, the world was nothing more than a great big Fred C. Dobbs with oceans.

Which meant that it all was left up to him.

And so he did what he did. And did it because he loved her, respected her dignity.

And it hurt. But better the hurt than doing nothing. And besides, it wasn't that bad. He would endure.

He called on the sum and total of his personal now, and he supposed it was a long way from being good old Maturity, but what else was there for him? Everything . . . confusions, sights, sounds, odors, books, experiences, pain, laughter, even the fierce and brave and sturdy words of his grandmother, even her words and especially her words . . . was thrown into a stew pot somewhere in the region of his navel, and from this real uck of a mess came an answer.

Maybe not the right answer, but an answer.

And at least it didn't have anything to do with Fred C. Dobbs.

The year was 1948, and the month was August, and Morris Bird III was thirteen years old, and the whole world was funny in his mind. Events and people went in every which direction, and he had a hard time keeping a line on what he liked to think of as goodness.

A few years ago, this had been easy. There had been a war, and it all had been very neat. When you got up in the morning, you knew who was on whose side. The Russians were our friends, and we admired their heroism. In the newsreels, they killed Germans real good. They scattered dead Germans all across the snow, and the sight of all those dead Germans made the heart rejoice. You went yayyy, and you whistled through the openings between your teeth, and you beat your palms together in short jubilant bursts.

But now the good Russians had become bad Russians. Times changed, and big deal.

Oh sure, Morris Bird III knew it wasn't up to him to worry about the Russians. He certainly had better things to do. Still, it dug at him, made him thick in the belly. The world was so very complicated, and all the time things changed, and how were you supposed to deal with it, how were you supposed to keep it in focus?

Was everything Fake? What was truth? What was hot air? Did anything mean anything, or was it best just to go out and have a good time?

Morris Bird III wished he knew. Then maybe, among other things, his complexion would clear up.

His complexion. Some complexion. It was killing him. Especially his forehead. It put him in mind of the surface of the moon.

No one in the world washed his face as often as Morris Bird III did. Washed and rubbed. Washed and rubbed and rinsed. Ran the water from the HOT spigot until great clouds of steam rose to fog up the bathroom mirror and make visibility zero. Sloshed the soap and a washrag in the scalding water. Then, squealing, pressed the suds against the bad places. Oh it was terrible, but what choice did he have? There was this girl named Julie Sutton, and she was very pretty, and he wanted to make her his Slave *for real*, and clearly he couldn't accomplish this if his face—and especially his forehead—put her in mind of the surface of the moon.

Julie Sutton. Oh. Ah. Julie Sutton.

Already his *head* was full of Slaves. He didn't quite know what he was supposed to do with them, but there they were. He would save them. He didn't suppose it would be long before he found out. Then, and no doubt with great energy, he would take appropriate action.

But Julie Sutton was different. He was unwilling to keep her in his head. He wanted her to be his Slave *for real.* With a veil. And jangling bracelets. Dancing sinuously to the music of an oboe, like maybe María Montez.

And so he washed. Washed and rubbed. Washed and rubbed and rinsed.

Morris Bird III was thin, dark, small for his age but not so small that people took him for a midget. Still, sometimes it bothered him. It was no fun being mistaken for ten when you actually were thirteen. (There was this guy who lived on the next street. His name was Don Schwamb, and he was fifteen and very big and fat. He called Morris Bird III insulting names, and the most insulting of them all was Termite. Some day Morris Bird III would have to settle up with this Don Schwamb. Some day, just as soon as he figured out a method.)

But please don't get the wrong idea. Morris Bird III's smallness didn't keep him awake nights. There were quite a few things that bothered him a whole lot worse. His dumb name, for instance.

Morris Bird III: now *there* was a name.

Yeah, a person could die laughing.

Morris Bird The Turd. Oh how funny.

Back when he'd been a little kid and hadn't known his nose from third base, he had thought of himself as Morris Bird The Eye Eye Eye and he'd not been too bothered by his name. But times changed. Things dug. And now he had an absolute Urge to Kill whenever he thought about his idiotic name.

Who's that dark stranger just came ridin into town, Luke?

Wal now, he calls himself Morris Bird III.

You mean that handsome feller on the white horse got him a name like *that?*

Yep.

The name don't hardly go with the man, do it?

Nope.

Oh, he could see it all. The dusty little cow town, the two skinny cowboys, their hats pushed to the backs of their heads. And of course he could hear their laughter. Morris Bird III, tenderfoot, dude, sissy. Oh haw haw haw. How funny. He could even hear the hollow sounds the cowboys made as they clapped each other on the back, sending off little poofs of dust. Their laughter was dry, and it hung all around like a bored and laconic sigh. Oh big deal. Oh *great.*

And the terrible thing was, there was no one he could blame. No one living, that is. The original Morris Bird, the man who had started the whole silly business, had been dead for about a thousand years or so. This Morris Bird had lived in a small Ohio town called Paradise Falls, where he had edited a newspaper. He and his wife had had just one child, a son, and they had named him Morris Bird II. And so, when Morris Bird II had a son, naturally the son's name had to be Morris Bird III. Family tradition and all that bushwah.

The saloon doors swing open, and in comes the handsome stranger.

Brian Donlevy, who owns the saloon, is standing at the bar. He wears a black suit, white shirt, black string tie. His gunbelt has a silver buckle.

You're Donlevy, says the handsome stranger, advancing.

Donlevy's eyes narrow. That is correct, sir, he says. And who might you be?

You killed my best friend, says the handsome stranger. Shot him in the back.

Brian Donlevy backs away from the bar. He holds his arms away from his sides. But what might your name be, stranger? he asks politely. His eyes are the eyes of a boa constrictor.

My name is Morris Bird III, says the stranger.

How's that again?

I *said:* Morris Bird III.

Brian Donlevy's laughter begins somewhere in his chest. Then his mouth opens, and nothing can be seen other than teeth. From it comes a sequence of roars. Finally he has to bend double. He wraps his arms around his chest. Then, with a great happy shriek, he falls dead. The bartender places pennies on his eyes, but the grin remains. He has quite literally laughed himself to death.

The handsome stranger, the murder of his best friend avenged, makes fists, takes a deep breath.

Wal stranger, says the bartender, I guess you done what you set out to do.

Oh shut up!

The bartender snickers.

The handsome stranger presses his face into his pillow and makes a number of pinched trapped noises. His fists are all tight and pink.

Okay, okay, so maybe his name wasn't all *that* important. But, on the other hand, who in Creation was better qualified to judge? What was he supposed to do? Put an ad in the paper and call forth all the Morris Bird IIIs in the world so they could hold a convention to determine just exactly how painful the name was?

Boy. Sometimes things sure did make a person wonder.

The year was 1948, and the month was August, and the name of the city where Morris Bird III lived was Cleveland. His home was at 9106 Edmunds Avenue, on the East Side in what was known as the Hough Area. This was a neighborhood that everyone said had seen better days, and Morris Bird III could believe it. In the past year, some colored people had moved into the neighborhood, and this was supposed to be Death. I'm certainly glad we don't own this place, said his father. If we did, we'd probably have to take a terrible loss. The landlord, on the other hand, what does it matter to him? White, colored—it's all the same. And anyway, once we're driven out, he'll be able to stuff this place with colored people, split it up into little flats. He'll put twenty people in here where there's just the four of us now. Oh it'll be a great situation, oh you bet.

His father talked like that all the time. His father was very cheerful, a barrel of fun. Sure he was. So had been Hitler.

Ah now, hold on. No sense being unfair. His father had problems, and a person had to make allowances.

One of Morris Bird II's problems was the fact that he had only one foot. One real foot, that is. He wore a wooden thing that served him as a second foot. He had lost a foot in an automobile accident in 1927. Morris Bird III didn't know the details of the accident. No one had seen fit to tell him. This wasn't much of a family for people to see fit to tell other people much of anything. But this didn't mean they didn't *talk* . . . Oh there was plenty of talk, and especially from Morris Bird III's father. The man was actually *paid* to talk. He was employed by Radio Station WCCC, which called itself The Voice of Cleveland & Northeastern Ohio. He was the host of a program, *The Early Bird Show,* which was on the air from 5 to 10 o'clock every morning of the week except Sunday. It consisted of a little music, a little news, a little chatter and a great many commercials—principally from used car establishments, cutrate furniture stores and firms that manufactured remedies for headaches, heartburn and congested bowels. *The Early Bird Show* had been in existence about a year, and it marked the first time in fifteen years of broadcasting that Morris Bird III's father had a program of his own. Prior to the establishment of *The Early Bird Show,* he had been simply an announcer, a bonger of chimes, a station identifier. Not that he had been a bad one. Far from it. When it came to identifying the station, Morris

Bird III's father had been superb. His voice was enormous, reso-
nant, a thing of power and impact. When he told you you were
listening to WCCC, The Voice of Cleveland & Northeastern Ohio,
you *believed* it. As a matter of fact, back in his younger days Morris Bird III had had trouble separating his father from The Voice
of Cleveland & Northeastern Ohio. When he did bad, he never
was bawled out by a human being known to one and all as his
father; he always was bawled out by an enormous and terrifying
Voice, and it filled his head with visions of all sorts of awful
things, like volcanoes and the atom bomb and God. But that
had been a long time ago, and times changed, and now Morris
Bird III didn't know what to think of his father. When his father
bawled him out, it was just routine. He felt no terror; he saw no
visions, and in a way maybe it was sad.

There were two other members of his family—his mother,
whose name was Alice, and his little sister, Sandra, who was ten
and had a yappy mouth like a terrier and was reading *Appleton's
Cyclopaedia of American Biography,* the 1887 edition, Volume III,
GRIN through LOC. She had found it in the attic. It had once
belonged to the original Morris Bird. No one knew what had
happened to the other volumes. No one except Sandra particularly cared. She was forever badgering the rest of the family about
the missing volumes, and that was good old Sandra for you.

When Morris Bird III's mother spoke, it was as though she
had a mouthful of small pointed stones. She collected china owls.
She was skinny and she was very fond of money, and Morris
Bird III stayed out of her way as much as he could. Not that he
hated her or was *afraid* of her or anything like *that;* he just simply
stayed out of her way. Ever since the end of the war, she'd been
difficult to get along with. During the war she'd had a fulltime

job as secretary to a Mr. Thomas D. Beeler, office manager for the Cleveland Bolt & Screw Co., and each week she'd brought home a great deal of what she'd been fond of calling the Extra. But now, with no war, there was no Extra, and she sort of spooked around the house. Her china owls were everywhere. She always bought dayold bread.

And then of course there was his grandmother.

She was his mother's mother. Her name was Mrs. Elizabeth H. Jones, and she was beautiful. She also happened to be dying of cancer of the stomach. She had taken care of Morris Bird III and Sandra during the war while their mother had been off making the Extra. She had been very brave, and she'd never considered it a criminal offense to smile. She'd cooked good, too.

But Grandma didn't live in the house on Edmunds Avenue any longer. Her original home had been in Paradise Falls, and she had moved back there in the fall of 1945. She'd sold her Paradise Falls home before coming to Cleveland, and so now she was living in the home of one of her sons, a man named James N. Jones Jr., police chief of Paradise Falls and sort of a drunk. He'd once been a bigshot football star, but that had been years ago.

If you could call it living.

She lay in a big brass bed that sagged in the middle, and most of the time she hurt. Sometimes she cried. Morris Bird III had seen her cry. He and his mother and Sandra had visited her last month. She had talked quite brightly for a few minutes, but then—without a speck of warning—the crying had started up. Her face, her beautiful face, turned all wrinkled and yellowish, and Morris Bird III and Sandra were shooed from the room. He didn't like to remember it. He hoped, if he was lucky, he never saw her again.

Things changed. Things forever adjusted themselves and took new shapes. His grandmother had been brave beyond bravery, wise beyond wisdom, but now her face was all wrinkled and yellowish, and she didn't even have the strength to keep from crying in front of her grandchildren. What sort of grandmother was this? Why couldn't people (the good people especially) just up and *die* without having to *change* first? Why couldn't God just reach down and squash them instead of first having to pull them apart like maybe people were *flies* or something? His grandmother had known Virtue, and she had been a beautiful woman. She had been young for a grandmother, and there had been no liverspots on her hands. She had made Morris Bird III understand the sense in Doing Right. Often, when she lived in the Edmunds Avenue house, they had long talks in the kitchen. He had loved the kitchen in those days. It had always smelled so good, and never mind the fact that there had been rationing. To make do, to endure, to be brave: those are the important things, said the grandmother. It's very easy to make a face and throw up your arms and say Oh poor me, the world's against me, and so I'm going to give up. But, if that's the right attitude, then please tell me why people are born in the first place? So don't let me hear you feeling sorry for yourself. There are enough *important* things for you to be concerning yourself with. I don't want you to be wasting your time on something as *unimportant* as *that*.

Ah, those had been the days. Plump and soft, her unspotted hands had performed magical extravagances with stews, casseroles, meatloaves and whatever else had been available. She was the only person in the civilized world who could make a baloney sandwich that tasted like something other than Old Dead Rat. Somehow she dressed it up with lettuce and mayonnaise and mustard. However she did it, the baloney sandwich emerged tasting like something other than baloney, and praise be. After all this time, Morris Bird III still remembered the miraculous flavor of his grandmother's baloney sandwiches, and so how come she had offended God? What had she done? Why did she have to cry? Couldn't she have held it *back*? Didn't she have any strength at *all*?

Bruh. He didn't like to think about it. He hoped she would hurry up and die.

Yeah. It surely was some life. Pity him. Poor little Morris Bird III, poor little feller, boo hoo.

The year was 1948, and the month was August, and poor Morris Bird III, sob, sniffle, wasn't it too bad about him?

Nuts. Bushwah.

From time to time he sent himself little news flashes. They said: COME OFF IT. They made him grin and shrug and sort of snicker, and for a day or two everything was all right. He forgot the Russians and dayold bread and his dying grandmother and his complexion. He turned to things he could enjoy. There were a lot of them.

Like, for instance, baseball.

In Cleveland, nobody talked about anything else. The Indians and the New York Yankees and the Boston Red Sox and the Philadelphia Athletics were engaged in a struggle for the American League championship the likes of which the eyes of mortal man never had witnessed. The experts called it the greatest pennant race of all time, and who in his right mind would have denied it? Certainly, whenever the Indians played, everyone in town died about a million billion zillion deaths. Some of the games were actually too much—at least for Morris Bird III. Sometimes, while listening to the games on the little radio his Uncle Alan had given him for his twelfth birthday (it had a plastic cover, and on that plastic cover was inscribed the word SILVERTONE, and sometimes the volume control went ALL OUT OF WHACK, MAKING THE SOUND BLAST FORTH AND BRINGING ANGRY SHOUTS FROM HIS FATHER AND MOTHER), sometimes he was unable to stand the agony. So he had to shut the radio off and count to some arbitrary figure, like maybe two hundred. By that time, he figured, the crisis would be over; the suspense would no longer exist. Either Lou Boudreau, the Indians' manager and certified hero, got the hit with the bases loaded or he didn't. Either way, Morris Bird III had spared himself pain. Maybe this made him out to be some sort of ninny. If so, tough. Baseball in Cleveland that summer was a serious business; it grabbed people by the throat. The crowds at the Cleveland Stadium were the largest the game ever had attracted . . . anywhere. Sixty and seventy thousand people were showing up for some of the games, and the Indians' owner, a flamboyant and grinning fellow named Bill Veeck, considered it a bad day or night when attendance dropped below forty thousand. No fooling. Oh such a time it was, and Morris Bird III was grateful he didn't suffer from any sort of heart disorder. If he'd been the frail type, he'd already have been long gone, the late, cut-down-in-the-prime-of-life Morris Bird III, God love him, RIP.

And like, for another instance, the movies.

He went to more movies than anybody. Absolutely *anybody*. In that year of 1948, he had already seen *Golden Earrings,* starring Ray Milland and Marlene Dietrich; *The Road to Rio* starring Bing Crosby, Bob Hope and Dorothy Lamour; *T-Men,* starring Dennis O'Keefe and K. T. Stevens; *The Naked City,* starring Barry Fitzgerald, Tom Drake, Ted DeCorsia, Howard Duff and Dorothy Hart; *Out of the Past,* starring Robert Mitchum, Jane Greer and Kirk Douglas; *Call Northside 777,* starring James Stewart, Richard Conte and Helen Walker; *The Golden Eye,* starring Roland Winters, Victor Sen Young, Mantan Moreland and Ralph Dunn; *Killer McCoy,* starring Mickey Rooney, Ann Blyth and James Dunn; *Mr. Blandings Builds His Dream House,* starring Cary Grant, Myrna Loy and Melvyn Douglas; *The Pirate,* starring Gene Kelly and Judy Garland; *The Search,* starring Aline MacMahon, Ivan Jandl and Montgomery Clift; *Where There's Life,* starring Bob Hope; *Arch of Triumph,* starring Ingrid Bergman and Charles Boyer; *Key Largo,* starring Humphrey Bogart, Lauren Bacall, Edward G.

Robinson and Claire Trevor; *The Fuller Brush Man,* starring Red Skelton; *Scuddo Hoo! Scudda Hay!,* starring Lon McAllister; *The Time of Your Life,* starring James Cagney, Jeanne Cagney, James Barton, Wayne Morris, Reginald Beane and Tom Powers; *The Woman in White,* starring Sidney Greenstreet and Eleanor Parker; *Casbah,* starring Tony Martin and Yvonne DeCarlo; *The Sainted Sisters,* starring Joan Caulfield and Veronica Lake; *The Bride Goes Wild,* starring Van Johnson and June Allyson; *Fighting Father Dunne,* starring Pat O'Brien; *So This Is New York,* starring Rudy Vallee, Henry Morgan and Donna Drake; *A Foreign Affair,* starring Marlene Dietrich, Jean Arthur, Millard Mitchell and John Lund; *Easter Parade,* starring Fred Astaire and Judy Garland; *Fort Apache,* starring Shirley Temple and John Agar; *So Evil My Love,* starring Ray Milland, Geraldine Fitzgerald and Ann Todd; *The Sign of the Ram,* starring Susan Peters, Phyllis Thaxter and Alexander Knox; *Sitting Pretty,* starring Clifton Webb, Robert Young and Maureen O'Hara; *Relentless,* starring Robert Young and Marguerite Chapman; *The Miracle of the Bells,* starring Fred MacMurray and Valli; *Captain from Castile,* starring Tyrone Power and Cesar Romero; *Ride the Pink Horse,* starring Robert Montgomery, Wanda Hendrix, Thomas Gomez and Fred Clark, and *The Treasure of the Sierre Madre,* starring Humphrey Bogart, Walter Huston, Tim Holt, Bruce Bennett, Barton MacLaine and Alfonso Bedoya.

Morris Bird III loved the movies. He loved them because they made sense. Things worked out. You knew who the bad guys were, and you knew they would lose. Nothing was left hanging. For him, the only truly desirable world was the one that concerned itself with pistols and production numbers and dead bodies falling from closets and long kisses and weepy farewells and secret formulas and master conspiracies and popcorn and rattling bags and pink signs that said EXIT and drinking fountains that released reluctant little streams of lukewarm water, not to mention the hero stalking the villain down the main street of a town that likely as not was called Silver City or Dry Wells or Longhorn, not to mention James Cagney snarling at the prison priest as he is led to the electric chair, not to mention Charlie Chan telling his #2 Son that those who listen at keyholes seldom hear good words about themselves, not to mention Barry Fitzgerald, the kindly detective, sighing and telling a colleague that ah, 'tis a heavy case indeed, not to mention Clifton Webb pushing the oatmeal into the baby's face. Ah, a person could go on and on, summoning to his mind a succession of dazzling and endless delights. And, everywhere you looked, people had clear complexions.

And like, for still another instance, his gallery of Slaves.

He couldn't quite remember when it had all started, but maybe there hadn't been any specific *time*. Maybe it had simply sneaked up on him. Like a cloud of gas or whatever. At any rate, for the past few months he had been carefully recruiting members of his harem. No one knew a thing about it. He would have died first rather than tell. Why the secret recruiting program? Well, why not? He figured he'd understand his reasons soon enough. In the meantime, it was a wise squirrel that gathered its goodies. And anyway, he figured he did *too* understand his reasons. He was only kidding himself by insisting he was ignorant. Which was why he'd lately been paying so much attention to his complexion. Which was why he'd lately taken up exercises, especially pushups, deep knee bends, things like that. They wore you out, and thus they kept your body healthy. And this was what he needed—to be worn out and thus healthy. So far, knock on a redwood plank, he'd not succumbed to the various physical pressures and mental subversions that had been tap, tap, tapping and sometimes pound, pound, pounding (OPEN UP, IN THE NAME OF THE LAW OF NATURE!) at the entrance to the temple of his body. It was a terrible struggle, and it didn't help matters that he kept seeing himself as Cornwallis at Yorktown. He told himself he needed a winning attitude. He ground his teeth, punished himself with more pushups, more deep knee bends. He forced his mind to contemplate such things as buttercups in a meadow, streetcars, batting averages, the Great Steppes of Siberia. But girls and women pick buttercups. Girls and women ride streetcars. Girls and women attend baseball games. Girls and women ride in immense sleds across the Great Steppes of Siberia. So big deal. So it was some mind he had. And so he recruited his Slaves.

In September, he would be entering the 8A at Addison Junior High School. It had been the previous spring, when he had been in the 8B, that the Slave concept had come to him, like the cloud of gas or whatever. He understood nothing at all about girls and women, which was of course why he wanted them for Slaves. When a girl or a woman was a Slave, it was not necessary to understand her. You simply ordered her around. She gave you no trouble. She couldn't afford to.

Addison Junior High was at the corner of Hough Avenue and East 79th Street—about a mile from the house on Edmunds Avenue. Every day in the school year Morris Bird III walked this distance, both ways. Except when the weather was very cold, he didn't mind the walk. Not at all. There was too much to see. The house on Edmunds Avenue wasn't far from East 90th Street. Both streets were residential. To get to school, he first walked west on Edmunds, then south on East 90th. There were houses, and there were apartment buildings, and there were houses that were connected to each other in rows of three or four. Sidewalks were marked for hopscotch, and here and there they had humps. They were quite cracked, and you took care not to step on a crack. At 1697 East 90th, there was a big old wooden house that had a *television aerial.* The house was owned by a family named Goodman, and until Thursday, April 22, 1948, a boy named Benny Goodman had lived there. This Benny Goodman had been a good friend of Morris Bird III. He had been skinny, with dark hair and immense eyes and a loud happy way of talking, and he had walked with a limp, and now the worms were feasting on Benny Goodman, and not much of it made sense. Not *much?* Nuts. Bushwah. Not *any* of it. Morris Bird III was beginning to wonder if maybe he cast some sort of spell over his friends. Four years ago he had been buddies with a boy named Stanley Chaloupka, a flabby and awkward boy who wouldn't have hurt a fly if his life had depended on it, a quiet boy with a big grin and the most splendid layout of Lionel O Gauge trains in the Western Hemisphere, but on October 20, 1944, this Stanley Chaloupka had been killed in an explosion, and so big deal: two buddies, two dead—batting average: 1.000. And now, if you counted his grandmother as a buddy, he was about to make it three for three. Huh. It made you stop and think. Maybe, for all he knew, his complexion was a warning that he carried the Mark of the Black Death, or some such thing. Whenever he passed the house at 1697 East 90th, he rubbed a hand across his forehead and tried to keep from making a face.

The walk to school took him one block south on East 90th. Then he turned right on Hough Avenue, which was the main drag in that part of the city. People who didn't know Cleveland pronounced the name of this street How and Hoo and Hoof. Actually, it was pronounced Huff. His grandmother, fresh from Paradise Falls, had at first called it How, which had made Morris Bird III and Sandra laugh like the devil. One morning at the breakfast table Morris Bird III had gotten off what his grandmother had insisted was an Alltime Classic Remark.

How are you this morning? she asked him as he seated himself at the table.

I'm fine, thank you, said Morris Bird III. And huff are you?

Well, his grandmother's whoops must have been heard for blocks. She laughed so hard that she got *him* to laughing. After a time, they both were weeping. Eventually they had to blow their noses. They whickered and snorted, and then they hugged each other, and it turned out to be a very good day, with lots of sunshine and fat clouds and sweet odors.

Now, though, he didn't think it had been such a killer of a remark. A dumb kid trying to be a wise guy: hot spit.

But, anyway, Hough Avenue. To get to Addison Junior High School, he first had to walk past his kidstuff school, his old school—Hough Elementary. A lot had happened to him at Hough Elementary. He had spent six years there. Six and a half, if you counted kindergarten. It was a tall old building of brick and concrete and wood, and it was surrounded by an iron picket fence with little pointy things on top of the pickets. He remembered a great many of the things that had happened to him at Hough

19

Elementary. He hoped that, as the years went by, he would forget most of them. He didn't think this feeling was sour grapes. As far as he was concerned, he just simply didn't want to fill his mind with memories of dumb kidstuff things. Back in the days when he'd attended Hough Elementary, he'd seen things as being simple. Now, looking back, he understood that the only simple thing had been Morris Bird III, the one and only. Oh he thought about it a lot. He really did. Sometimes he saw himself as being some sort of a loony because he thought so much, but he couldn't help it. His mind was like his forehead: he was stuck with both of them. Hough Elementary: it was at Hough Elementary that he had tossed a salami sandwich, all drippy and evil with mayonnaise, against the side of an automobile owned by a Mrs. Clementine Ochs, who happened to be the principal. Mrs. Ochs was fit to be tied, gagged and carted off to the loony bin. She called an assembly and demanded that the guilty party step forward. Naturally, Morris Bird III did not step forward. A boy named Logan MacMurray, a bully with green teeth and a loud mouth, was charged by Mrs. Ochs with the crime. He made no denials, and so Mrs. Ochs threw him out of school. This all made Morris Bird III feel just dandy, and it was a long time before he was able to make his peace with the incident. He figured it was the worst thing that had ever happened to him at Hough Elementary. But there were other things that were almost as bad. The time, for instance, he dropkicked Johnny Sellers' brandnew football through an open window of an apartment building next to the schoolyard. It had been a stupid showoff trick, and he'd had to rob his Porky Pig bank to pay for the football. Served him right, and he didn't deny it. And then there was the time, away back when he'd been in maybe the first grade, when he'd gone around thinking he had a speedometer in his belly. A speedometer that showed how old he was, the way a speedometer in a car showed how many miles the car had traveled. Oh he surely had been a genius, yes indeed. Yeah, yeah, yeah, all right, he knew all about the allowances you had to make for little kids, but they didn't come easy. Embarrassments, shame, blunders, betrayals— these were not things to be spat out easily, like seeds from a grape. The word it all came down to was Courage, acknowledging his grandmother's words and coping, making do, and the word itself was easy, but the living of it wasn't. Almost four years ago now, on the day (October 20, 1944) his buddy Stanley Chaloupka had been killed in the gas explosion, Morris Bird III had behaved in a courageous manner (helping some injured people), and thus he had made it up to Logan MacMurray and had erased his early dropkick and speedometer embarrassments, but a lot of things had happened since then, and the world had revealed itself as being a lot more complicated, and Courage was a harder word to understand. Here he was, thirteen now and pocked and angry, immersing himself in baseball and movies and mournful lonely deep knee bends, and oh boy oh boy oh *boy* how things forever changed. He saw himself as a thing of now, and whatever he was, was the sum and total of his now, but the now forever changed, and he was a clamor of arrivals and departures and memories and aches and growth and rot, openings and closings, enthusiasms and rejections, and what he kept trying to tell himself was: HOLD ON NOW. YOU'RE JUST A KID. NO ONE EXPECTS YOU TO UNDERSTAND ANYTHING. LOOK, WHAT YOU OUGHT TO DO IS GO SOMEWHERE AND KICK AN OLD TIN CAN AND WHISTLE FOR YOUR DOG. ONLY YOU GOT NO DOG. AND WHAT IF

YOU KICK A TIN CAN THAT'S FULL OF ROCKS? YOU MIGHT HURT YOUR FOOT.

Things forever and relentlessly changed. Hair grew. A voice deepened. Older people, people who knew better, up and betrayed you by dying. Wars ended, and there was no more Extra, and so twice a week a skinny woman trotted to the store to buy her beloved dayold bread. Good Russians became bad Russians. Joe Gordon, who had been a villain when he had played second base two years ago for the New York Yankees, now was a hero for the Indians. Nothing resisted change. A long time ago, someone had told Morris Bird III that every twentyfour hours he was one day closer to dying, and at first the remark had seemed nonsensical, but now it didn't seem nonsensical at all. Every day something died, or something withered, or something was revealed to be Fake, and the thing he should have done was carry around a notebook. That way, he could have recorded all the dead, withering, Fake things. At the same time, he could have recorded all the things that were being born, that were growing, that were coming to him as Truth. By doing this, he would have had some line on the way the world was moving. But he had no notebook, and so he had to guess, and his guess was on the side of the dead, the withered, the Fake. All the tin cans in his path seemed to be full of stones, and from time to time he asked himself, Maybe huh I'm crazy? He hoped not, but how would he ever know for sure? He looked around, and so many things seemed to be going down the drain (his complexion, his grandmother, Benny Goodman, Stanley Chaloupka) and oh if only he could take some Bab-o or Sani-Flush or whatever and scour out his mind and heart and start all over again, reduce the sum and total of his personal now to zero. But that sort of thinking was foolish. Nothing was simple except the minds of those who wished they were. The only thing he could do was pay attention to everything, examine and evaluate, enlarge his sum and total. Which he did. Every day. Despite pain. Despite astonishment.

But, again, Hough Avenue. The walk from East 90th Street to Addison Junior High School was seven goodsized blocks. Only for Morris Bird III the blocks were getting shorter, the street narrower, the buildings smaller. Things forever and relentlessly changed, ah *yes*. His walk took him past first Hough Elementary, then a couple of frame houses that were said to be occupied by Hillbillies (and he could believe it, considering their lack of paint and the weedy condition of their front yards), then past an enormous apartment building set back from the sidewalk (a redbrick structure with a cement arch over the entrance, it was the building where Julie Sutton lived, and therefore it was hallowed, sublime), then past a row of business establishments that included Sam's Barber Shop (Morris Bird III had his hair cut there; Sam's hands were so clean they just about glowed; he always called Morris Bird III Young Man, and he talked a great deal about colored people, whom he despised), a Fisher Bros. store (the day-old bread was bought here), the Hough-89th Bar, the Turner Tavern, the Shop-n-Save Supermarket and finally Albrecht's Drug Store, which was at the corner of Hough Avenue and a middle-sized diagonal main drag called Crawford Road. Over the years, Morris Bird III had crooked a great deal of merchandise from Albrecht's Drug Store, including candybars, pocket editions of novels by Dashiell Hammett, Erle Stanley Gardner and Zane Grey, pencils, magazines and once even a city street map. He was an expert crooker, but took no particular pride in it. In that neighborhood, almost every kid was. To have taken pride in it would have been like taking pride in breathing. Crossing Crawford Road, you walked past the Red Arrow Restaurant, then a place that was simply called Bar, then a row of apartment buildings, then Skrab's Confectionery, then the Astor Theater. Most of Morris Bird III's glorious movie times took place in the Astor Theater. It was the only movie house in the neighborhood, and business there had been good for years. During the war, it had been so good that on Saturday afternoons, if you left after seeing only one show, you were given free for nothing a candybar. Beyond the theater was a fillingstation, then the Loree A. Wells Funeral Home (it had a canopy that led from the front entrance down to the sidewalk), then a little market and grocery store called Whitman's, then a couple of frame houses, then an establishment that was simply called Drugs, then a few more frame houses that more often than not were festooned with signs that said ZINGLER FOR COUNCIL and like that there, and *then*—crouched back a bit from the street— Addison Junior High. In all its, ha ha, splendor. Addison Junior High: Wright M. Ludwigson, Principal. Motto: Abandon Hope, All Ye Who Enter Here. Oh boy. Good old Wright M. Ludwigson. Some principal. There was one difference between Wright M. Ludwigson and the late Adolf Hitler. Wright M. Ludwigson wore no mustache. (He was quite addicted to wandering into the Boys' Gym and giving the classes little lectures on The Perils of Selfabuse. He had a voice that sounded like a clarinet filled with old sticks.) Morris Bird III was a member of the homeroom of a Mrs. Lydia C. Principe, who had a cast in her left eye and was seven thousand, six hundred and fortythree years old. She also had dark hair on her arms and legs. She taught algebra, and better you should have taken algebra from Stalin. On the blackboard behind her desk were written the words: BE PRECISE. She never allowed them to be erased. All in all, she was about as charming and inoffensive as a dead kitten floating in a punchbowl full of pink lemonade and ice cubes and little sprigs of mint. When she gave a test, she subtracted the Wrongs from the Rights. Her name was pronounced prin-cih-pee, and when the boys in her homeroom went to the toilet they called it Taking a Principe. Yeah, she was some teacher. She surely did make life worth living. Yeah, like mustard gas. Huh, and it was funny, but at one time Morris Bird III hadn't particularly minded going to school. He was no dumbbell. As a matter of fact, most of the kids saw him as being some sort of Brain. But in the past semester or so, his liking for school had gone someplace and hid. He could date the disappearance almost from the day his complexion began giving him trouble. In the 7B and 7A he'd made the Merit Roll (a B average) three times and the Honor Roll (a B+ average) once. But in the 8B his midsemester average had been B- and his final average a bare C+, which certainly didn't represent the true Morris Bird III functioning on all his cylinders. Ah, but a lot he cared. By that time he had too many other things to occupy his attention, and the largest of them was of course his gallery of Slaves. As far as he could recall, he began recruiting the Slaves shortly after he went to work after school as a page in the school library. The job paid 35 cents an hour, and he worked two hours each afternoon after school. His work consisted mainly of putting books back on shelves. He'd had to familiarize himself with the Dewey Decimal System, but it had been a snap. He had gotten the hang of it in about twenty minutes. Which had given him plenty of time to contemplate the world around him, and specifically the world of the Addison Junior High library. The chief librarian's name was Mrs. Evelyn Hoyt, and you could scratch *her*. She looked like Marjorie Main. You could also scratch one of her assistants, a woman whose name was Miss Laverne Tuthill. This one wore a Sonotone and her face had more fuzz than a mohair sofa and she liked to nibble like a bunnyrabbit on her fingernails. But the *other* assistant—ah, *there* was a different story! Her name was Miss Gail Beggs, and she was slender, and she was tall, and she stuck out perkily in front, and she had acres and acres and miles and miles of rich dark hair that trailed down over her shoulders in thick gentle waves, and then of course there were her legs. Talk about your Betty Grable. Whoo. Lordy Lordy. Often, when she sat down, she crossed her magnificent legs, and the resultant view—or hint of a view—was enough to make Morris Bird III want to run shrieking and flapping out into the street and hurl himself under the wheels of the nearest trackless trolley. Naturally enough, the boys at the school called her Legs Beggs and made moist salacious sounds whenever they spoke of her. And so she was ushered into Morris Bird III's harem, issued her veil and little tinklebells and put to work dancing to the music of the oboe. Since then, the roster had increased by veritable leaps and bounds. New favorites came and went, and now he was almost reduced to running them in and out of his mind in *shifts*. As of August, 1948, the roster stood at eleven. In alphabetical order, it consisted of:

ONE—*Miss Gail (Legs) Beggs.*

TWO—*Estelle Bunning*, a large 9B girl of Hillbilly extraction who was generally conceded to have the largest breasts of any female in the school, not excluding the faculty and staff. She wore purplish lipstick, and her mouth almost always was wet, and she was reputed to be seventeen years of age. She liked to wear sweaters with horizontal stripes. Her favorite phrase was Gosh Dingies Dayumm, and she hung around a lot in the candystore across East 79th Street from the school. She was seen often in the company of the odious Don Schwamb and other low types. Last semester Morris Bird III had a history class in a room that overlooked the schoolyard. In this same period, Estelle Bunning had gym. When the warm weather came, her class went outside once a week—on Thursdays—to play softball. Morris Bird III had a great view of home plate. He was especially enchanted with watching Estelle Bunning run the bases. It would have taken an attack of leprosy before he would have consented to miss school on a Thursday.

THREE—*Twila Bunning*, Estelle's younger sister. She was only in the 7A, but she promised to be, as someone once had put it, a chip off the old boob once she got her full growth. She had bad teeth, but otherwise she showed great potential.

FOUR—*Rose Estes*, age fourteen, daughter of the Honorable Dwight F. Estes, mayor of Paradise Falls, Ohio, and Mrs. Norma Westfall Estes, clubwoman. On June 24, 1946, when Rose Estes was twelve and Morris Bird III was eleven, she took him by the hand and led him into a clump of trees near the Paradise River and showed him all she had. She was quite solemn about it, almost apologetic. She was very skinny, and she had freckles and wore spectacles that were so thick he bet they could have resisted bullets. She let him look all he wanted. She took off everything except her spectacles and then she just stood there and she didn't say a word. He wasn't very impressed. Now, looking back on the incident, all he remembered was that a) he could see the outline of her ribs, and b) she had three moles on her tummy that were so evenly spaced they made him think of the Belt of Orion.

Still, she *had* shown him everything she'd had, and this was enough to gain her admittance to the harem. And the funny thing was—the older he got, the more he looked back on the incident. Maybe, if he had to go down to Paradise Falls for his grandmother's funeral, he would look up old Rose Estes. More than two years had gone by, and perhaps she'd picked up some meat.

FIVE—*Sylvia Goodman*, age twenty, older sister of the late Benny Goodman. A junior at Western Reserve University, she was a plump and cushiony girl with a voice that sounded like a streetcar going around a curve too fast. In the warm weather she wore dresses that were severely scooped out at the neck, and Morris Bird III kind of wished she were interested in softball.

SIX—*Mrs. Frances Hampl*, allegedly a Divorced Woman, teacher of English at Addison Junior High. Trim and calm, with great legs but not much of a chest, she had graying hair and a small heartshaped face. She never spoke loudly, but for some reason you always listened. Her skirts never were loose, and she made marvelous elastic rubbing whispery sounds when she moved. When you got close to her, she always smelled good. It made you feel great. Especially in the throat and midsection.

SEVEN—*Miss Veronica Lake*, the motion picture actress. Morris Bird III had been a Veronica Lake fan ever since 1942, the year she had made her debut with Alan Ladd and the verminous Laird Cregar in *This Gun for Hire*. He had liked the way her blond hair had trailed down over one eye, but there had been more to it than *that*. In 1944, when Veronica Lake had her hair cut (women all over the country were imitating her hairstyle, and some of them—those who worked in war plants—were getting their hair caught in machines; so Veronica Lake, doing her patriotic duty, had her golden locks trimmed), it hadn't made a bit of difference to Morris Bird III. He'd kept on loving her, and he still did, and so he happily included her on this roster.

EIGHT—*Mrs. Mary Ellen Mossler*, about forty and a War Widow. She was, for all Morris Bird III knew, the only War Widow on all of Edmunds Avenue, all two blocks of it. She lived across the street from his house, and she Drank, and his mother said it was a Disgrace. Maybe so, but she sure did look good. The word for her was willowy, but she would have been great at softball, too. She had a lot of Dates, and he liked to watch her come out of her house with her escort of the evening. She walked like Lauren Bacall, but she smiled more often, and her escorts always appeared to be quite pleased with themselves.

NINE—*Miss Gail Russell*, the motion picture actress. The eyes and mouth. Ah, Lordy Lordy, the eyes and mouth.

TEN—*Louise Sandberg*, a narrow and blinking girl, a member of his homeroom, with nothing to recommend her except the fact that for the past two Valentine's Days she had sent him cards signed GUESS WHO? He figured the least he could do was include her on the roster. And anyway, he wasn't so foolish that he resisted the attention. So let her giggle whenever she was around him. Let her hide her face in her hands. If it made her feel better, great. Besides, it was interesting to get a GUESS WHO? card from someone who wrote her name and return address on the envelope.

ELEVEN—*Julie Sutton*, the Golden Princess of the World.

Julie Sutton. Oh. Ah. Julie Sutton.

She was dark and fragile and silent. The few times she did

speak, she looked at you sideways, as though you were ready at the slightest sign of trouble to run off and climb a tree. She kept her hair bobbed short, and most of the time she wore dresses that had white collars. Her voice was pinched and reedy, and she had a habit of looking back over a shoulder as though maybe she thought something awful was sneaking up on her.

Morris Bird III did not understand her. He did not hope to understand her. She had great astonished brown eyes, and he had no idea what lay behind them, and of course this just about drove him out of his mind. In school, she walked the way most girls did (in a sort of dopey sloppy shuffle), but, when she was *out* of school, she skittered rather than walked, and her eyes kept looking back for something awful. In her home she kept a pet lizard. It was a very small and inoffensive lizard, and its name was Czerny. It ate leaves and things, and it didn't move around very much. She played the piano a lot. She had been studying it for years at the Cleveland Institute of Music. Morris Bird III had visited her home once. He remembered a great deal about the visit. This included the enormous pile of sheet music on the piano. Some of it was by someone named Czerny, and so he supposed the lizard's name was some sort of private joke with her.

Her health apparently wasn't very good. She stayed out of school a lot. In the cold and damp weather, more often than not she had a cough. It was a dry and embarrassed little cough, but it stuck with her for weeks. Some of the boys called her Old Croupy, but more of them called her Gunboats. This was because of her feet. They were too large for the rest of her, or at least that was what everyone *said*. Morris Bird III didn't understand this. Her feet didn't *appear* too large. They were just, as far as he could tell, feet. And, since they belonged to Julie Sutton, they were pretty feet. But then maybe he didn't know too much about feet. Still, he never would have called her Gunboats. He couldn't have. He adored her. Silent and apprehensive, skittering (big feet or no), hugging her schoolbooks to her trim little tummy and a chest that was just beginning to move out, hurrying home to feed old Czerny his leaves or whatever, she was the Golden Princess of the World, and she made him want to fall down.

And, besides all that, she was shorter than he was.

He had a good memory for dates. Whenever something interesting happened to him (and no matter whether it was good, bad or indifferent), he tried to memorize the date. He thought of it as a sort of a laying out of mileposts. The way he saw the situation, a person needed mileposts. Otherwise, how would he know whether anything had happened to him? How would he know when he moved off dead center? Things forever and relentlessly changed, and mileposts were the best measuring apparatus. Mileposts, dates, ages, statistical facts—change was measured against them, and a person could *understand* them, and they helped to keep him from capsizing. And Morris Bird III in no way wanted to capsize. There was too much he had yet to investigate.

Such as Julie Sutton. Oh. Ah. Julie Sutton. Such as over and above everything Julie Sutton.

There had been one large Julie Sutton date—or milepost—so far. It had been Friday, May 28, 1948, the day he had visited the place where she lived. It had been an accident, and it had astounded him, and it *still* astounded him. He had worked at it and worked at it in his mind, worked at it so hard that it had given him dull foolish little headaches, but he had found no answer. Still, he didn't give up. Some day maybe his mind would be large enough to produce the answer. Until then he would work at it and work at it, try to hurry his poor dumb mind along.

It had been late in the afternoon, about 5:30 or so. His job at the Addison library kept him in school until about 5. It was raining, and it was his favorite kind of rain, a proclamative rain, loud and urgent and slanted. He and the sensational Miss Beggs were the last two persons out of the library. She wore a yellow slicker with a matching rain hat, and she looked like some sort of misty and fragrant goddess. They walked down the hall together to the front door. Morris Bird III had on his raincoat, and he had to sort of trot to keep up with her. She smelled moist and profound. At the door, she smiled at him, asked him if he had a way of getting home. He told her he always walked. He said he didn't think he would melt. Miss Beggs laughed, and this was what he'd hoped would happen. Made the day worthwhile. (Her laughter was not girlish. Rather, it seemed to come from her chest, which was a good place for anything to come from. It was breathy and contralto, full of teeth and lips, and it made him feel as though the contents of about seven large pots of LePage's Library Paste had been forced down his throat.) Still laughing, Miss Beggs ran outside and scuttled around the building to the Faculty & Staff Parking Lot. He stood on the stoop and watched her run. Rainwater slanted into his eyes, but he did not blink. He might have missed something. Then, as soon as she was out of sight, he started on his way home. He could have caught a Hough Avenue trackless trolley, but fooey on that. The rain felt fine. And anyway, he needed something to take his mind off Miss Beggs. Tucking his chin against his chest and hunching his shoulders a little, he cleared his throat of the LePage's Library Paste and moved along Hough Avenue at a brisk pace. He timed his breath with his steps, felt rainwater dribble down the back of his neck. He blinked, grimaced, let it all happen. The street was gray, and the buildings were gray, and the sky was gray, but they were a *good* gray, a *definite* and *substantial* gray, and he just bet the farmers were happy. Cars and buses and trucks went *hish*. Somehow a raindrop got up his nose. He sneezed, then laughed. The sky let loose an immense thunderclap. He laughed louder. He hugged himself, looked up at the sky, told the raindrops they knew what they could do. He moved in hops and lurches, inspected the new *good* grayness. Shapes were reflected off it. This was God's own grayness, and everything was being washed. Poor shabby ramshackle old Hough Avenue, which Lord knows *needed* it, was having at least some of its encrustations floated off. Anonymous bits and drabs of paper swirled along the gutters and down into the sewers. Dog mess was carried off. Hockers came loose from the sidewalks. So did globs of gum. Rinds, pits, peels, cores—all were carried to the gutters, as were sticks, slices of tarred and greasy earth. Looking up the side streets, Morris Bird III grinned at the new damp green of trees and grass. Water rushed from drainspouts and off roofs. It had soaked through his shoes. His feet went squish. And so what? He showed his face to the sky. Come on, he told the sky, do your best. Hit my forehead with your water. Hit it all you want. I need to be clean. See my forehead. Clean it. Clean it the way you are cleaning the streets and the sidewalks. See me. Find me. I need it. Then, shaking his head, Morris Bird III made a face and told himself: COME OFF

IT. WHAT'S THE MATTER WITH YOU? YOU WANT TO BE
CARRIED OFF SOMEWHERE WHERE YOU'LL SPEND THE
REST OF YOUR DAYS CUTTING OUT PAPER DOLLS? Chuck-
ling, he gathered the collar of his soggy raincoat closer around his
throat and hurried, tiptoing and puddlejumping, toward home
and whatever undistinguished supper his mother had prepared
this time. Boy, at about 5:30 or so every night he surely did miss
his grandmother, that magician of baloney sandwiches, etc.

Then, as he was crossing Crawford Road, someone skittered
up beside him and said: "You can share my umbrella if you
want to."

His breath all went away. He stopped. Some sort of sound
came from his nose.

Julie Sutton frowned at him. "The light's going to change,"
she said. "Come *on*. We can't stand here in the middle of the
street. You want a *car* to hit you?"

"Okay," said Morris Bird III. "Sure." He leaned toward her,
and now they both were under her umbrella. He grasped the
handle above her hand. It was almost like choosing up sides. The
umbrella was pink, not very big. They crossed the street, and
then they walked along for a minute or so in silence. His heart
was full of flames and crimson gases.

Julie was the first to speak. "How come you said okay?" she
asked him.

"Huh?"

"I asked you if you wanted a car to hit you, and you said
okay."

"Oh? I did? Well, uh, what I meant was: okay, I wanted to
share your umbrella."

"Oh."

Silence from Morris Bird III. His chest hurt. He didn't look at her.

"Mrs. Principe wouldn't have liked what you said," Julie told him.

"Huh?"

"The blackboard. The BE PRECISE."

"Oh," said Morris Bird III. "Uh huh. I see what you mean."

"She's almost as fussy as Miss Diehl."

"Miss who?"

"Miss Diehl. She's my teacher at the Institute."

"Oh."

"She insists on every *note,* every *shading.* She never lets up."

"That so?"

"Yes," said Julie. "That's so."

Then they both were silent again. He took a quick look at her out of a corner of an eye. Her face had no expression. He supposed she was mad at him. He supposed he hadn't shown enough enthusiasm for Miss Diehl's fussiness. He wished he were brave enough to sag to the sidewalk right out here in the rain in front of God and everybody and kiss her Gunboats and beg her forgiveness. But that much braveness he did not possess, and all he could do was stare blandly straight ahead and try to keep his head under the umbrella. They walked past the Fisher Bros. store and the Turner Tavern and the Hough-89th Bar. The rain slanted against the backs of their necks. Then they came to the place where she lived—the enormous redbrick apartment building with the cement arch over the entrance.

"I live here," she said.

"Yes," said Morris Bird III. "I know."

"*How* do you know?"

"I just *know,* that's all."

They were standing at the place where the entrance walk to the building met the sidewalk. "You just *know?*" she asked him.

"Yes."

"But *how?*"

"I don't know. I guess maybe I saw you going in here one day."

"Oh."

He let go his share of the umbrella handle and stepped back. "Thanks very much," he said.

"I've got a lizard," said Julie Sutton.

Morris Bird III brushed rain off his forehead. "How's that?"

"I *said:* I've got a *lizard.* I keep him in a terrarium. His name is Czerny."

"Chairny?"

"Yes. It's spelled C-Z-E-R-N-Y."

"Mm."

"You can see him if you want to."

"Oh?"

"Yes. His name is Czerny Sutton. He doesn't bite or anything. Sometimes, when the light is right, his eyes look orange."

"Orange," said Morris Bird III. "Mm. Well."

"And we can talk."

"Mm," said Morris Bird III.

"And besides, you're all *wet.* You need to dry *off.*"

"I'm supposed to go home for supper."

"You can call. We've got a *telephone,* for heaven's sake."

"Uh, that's nice."

"Well, let's not just *stand* here."

"All right," said Morris Bird III. Again he took hold of his share of the umbrella handle. He wished there were a fire extinguisher handy. He would have swallowed it.

They entered the building and climbed the stairs to the third floor. The hallway was dark. He groped along behind Julie. She had closed the umbrella, and now she dragged it along the carpeted floor. She was humming under her breath. She stopped at Apartment 316 and handed the umbrella to Morris Bird III. She took a key from a pocket in her dress. "I have to use both hands to open the door," she said. "Whenever the weather is damp, it swells. The door, I mean." She inserted the key in the lock, grunted, twisted. At the same time, she leaned against the door with her free hand.

"Let me help," said Morris Bird III. He hit the door with the handle of the umbrella. The door flew open. Julie went flying across the threshold. She landed on the floor on all fours. For a flick of an instant he saw her underpants.

She looked back over her shoulder at him.

He wondered if there was someplace nearby where he could slash his wrists, or maybe commit hara-kiri like Keye Luke or Philip Ahn.

But she was grinning. "Dumbhead," she said, but she was grinning to beat anything.

"Oh," said Morris Bird III. "Oh. I'm sorry." He went to her, bent over her.

She held out her hands. "Give me a pull," she said.

He looked at her hands.

"I *said:* give me a *pull*."

He touched her hands. He almost shuddered.

She closed her hands around his.

Now he knew what people felt like when they stuck their

fingers in light sockets. A drop of water rolled inside his ear. It itched. He closed his hands into fists. Julie's hands squeezed the fists.

"Pull," she said.

Biting the soft juicy part of the inside of his lower lip, he pulled.

She came gracefully to her feet. Her skirt swirled a little. "Thank you," she said. She released his hands.

He looked down at his hands. They appeared to be the same old hands. He breathed deeply. It felt good. He did it again. Then he stuck a finger inside the itching ear and cleaned out the water.

Julie made a clucking sound. "My mother says the only thing a person should put in his ear is his elbow."

"Mm," said Morris Bird III, and he examined his feet.

"Well," she said, "come on in." Then, for no reason he could see, she let out a raspy little laugh. "Welcome to our humble abode."

Morris Bird III chewed on that same soft juicy part of the inside of his lower lip. He looked around. They apparently were in the livingroom. The shades were drawn. The furniture appeared fat and dark. Outside, the rain still was making its gray splattery sounds.

"Sit down on the sofa," said Julie. "It's the most comfortable."

He walked across the room and sat down. He sank. "Thank you," he said. He crossed his legs, cleared his throat. Then he looked down at himself. "Uh?"

She was standing across the room. "Yes?"

"Maybe . . . uh, maybe I ought to take off my raincoat?"

Julie drew in her breath. "Oh, am I forever *dumb*," she said.

"Come on. Let me have it. I'll hang it in the kitchen. And your shoes, too."

"My shoes?"

"Yes. They're wet, too. Out in the hall I heard them go squish."

"That's okay."

"No. No. I insist. Your shoes."

Morris Bird III grunted. He stood up, took off his coat. It wasn't until he started to take off his coat that he realized he still held the umbrella. Julie came forward. She was smiling. He handed her the umbrella. Then he shucked himself out of the raincoat. It was cold and slippery. He handed it to her.

"Ouuu," said Julie, making a face. "Clam*my*."

"Uh huh," said Morris Bird III. He sat down.

"Your shoes," said Julie.

"Oh," said Morris Bird III. "Oh. Oh yeah." He bent down, slipped off his shoes. They came off quickly. They were loafers. Water sloshed. He handed them to Julie.

"Ouuu," said Julie. "Now these are what I call *wet*." She held them away from her and made another face. "Be right back." She went through a doorway toward what presumably was the kitchen.

He leaned back and sighed. He blinked, drew fresh saliva, bathed the roof of his mouth. Then he looked around again. His eyes had become accustomed to the darkness. He saw the piano. It was the biggest thing in the room; it seemed almost *bigger* than the room. It was what he'd heard people describe as a *grand* piano, and the top of it held great stacks of music. He looked at it, cleared his throat, and then for some reason he nodded. "Mm," he said, giggling, "hi there, piano." He placed a hand over his mouth. He wondered if maybe worms were eating at his brain. Or maybe some of the rainwater had seeped through. Water on the brain: he bet it was more serious than water on the knee. "Bruh," he said, and his head went vigorously from side to side. He wondered what was keeping Julie Sutton. He looked at his hands, rubbed his arms. They seemed to be the same old hands and arms. Well, at least he hadn't changed into a troll. He patted his face, his chest, his stomach, his thighs, his knees, his legs, his feet. Everything was in place. He reached up and touched his teeth, kneaded his skin. He had no fangs, and no hair had grown, so he guessed he wasn't a werewolf. He nodded. "Hang in there," he said. He looked beyond the piano into what he supposed was the diningroom. It was like everybody's diningroom; it didn't appear to have been used in years. A large window was at the far end of the diningroom. It was streaked with raindrops. The rain was hitting it slantwise. It made a quiet sound, like *pit pit pit pit pit*. "Pit pit pit pit pit," he said under his breath. He crossed his legs, then uncrossed them. "Cheer up," he said. "You'll soon be dead." Again he was wondering what was keeping Julie Sutton. Maybe *she* was dead. Or maybe she had gone to sleep in her native Transylvanian earth. Then he told himself: Come *on* now. That's no thing to be thinking about *her*. You and your bigdeal sense of humor. Ha ha.

Then Julie came back into the room. She was carrying a tray. It held two glasses of chocolate milk and a platter of crackers. "I thought maybe you'd like something to eat," she said. She held the tray forward. "Here. Hold this."

He took the tray.

She went to a wall and flicked a switch. The ceiling light came on. "There," she said. "That's better. Now we have some light on the subject."

"Yes," said Morris Bird III.

Julie came and sat beside him on the sofa. The distance between them was about a foot. She had combed her hair, and she smelled faintly of soap. Good homely soap, maybe Ivory.

Morris Bird III blinked in the light. He tried to look at her without her knowing it. She was beautiful. Oh. Ah. Was she ever. The dampness had brought little glints and shadows to her hair, and for some reason her sweet little mouth was moist. She wore no lipstick, but she didn't hardly need it. He examined her dress. It was a light blue, and it was sort of crinkly, and it—wait, wait, hold on. She had *changed* her dress. The dress she'd been wearing when she'd met him in the middle of Crawford Road had been blue all right, but a darker blue. So she had changed her dress. Why? For *him?*

She took the tray from him. "I changed my dress," she said. Her voice was matteroffact. "The other one was wet."

"Mm," said Morris Bird III. He sighed as quietly as he could, what with all that wind going out of his sails.

She placed the tray on her lap. "Glass of chocolate milk?" she said, holding one out to him.

"Mm," said Morris Bird III, clearing his throat. "Thank you. Don't mind if I do." He took the glass.

She placed the tray on a coffeetable in front of them. "I love chocolate milk," she said, lifting the second glass. She turned to him. "Your health," she said, smiling.

He lifted his glass. "Same to you."

They touched glasses and drank.

The chocolate milk was cold and sticky. His tongue rubbed the roof of his mouth. He realized he was smiling.

She nodded toward the tray. "Help yourself," she said. "They're Ritz crackers. They're all I could find. Except for breakfast, we don't have our meals here, so there's never much on hand." She hesitated, then: "My mother and I, I mean. My father doesn't live here anymore. Say, did you ever play raindrop race?"

He just looked at her.

She smiled politely. "I said raindrop race."

"Mm," said Morris Bird III.

"What you do is, you race raindrops on a windowpane. First one to the bottom wins. It's a regular *game.*"

"Oh," said Morris Bird III.

"It's fun."

"No fooling."

"Yes. A lot of fun. Sometimes your raindrop gets joined by another raindrop. That makes it fatter and heavier, and it moves faster."

Morris Bird III leaned forward and took a Ritz cracker. "Uh huh," he said, popping the cracker in his mouth. He chewed slowly.

She placed her glass on the tray. "Come on. I'll play you a game." She stood up.

He looked up at her. "A game of raindrop?"

"Yes."

"Raindrop," said Morris Bird III.

"Come *on.*"

He shrugged, stood up. He followed her into the diningroom. He still held his glass of chocolate milk. He sipped at it, washing down the Ritz cracker. "Mm," he said. "Raindrop." He took another sip of his chocolate milk. "Well, what do you know."

Now they were at the window. She turned and stared at him. "You think I'm crazy?"

"No."

She smiled. "Well, sometimes *I* do."

Morris Bird III also smiled. He wished he were Errol Flynn or someone like that. Errol Flynn always knew what to say. But all the great Morris Bird III could do was smile, and it sort of made his face hurt.

Julie inspected the window. The pit pit pit pit pit of the raindrops was considerably louder than it had been back when they had been sitting on the sofa. She touched the pane, and the heat from her hand made a foggy outline. She pointed to the top of the window. "You take the one on the right. I'll take the one in the middle."

Morris Bird III frowned. There were about ninety thousand raindrops hanging at the top of the window. "Which *one* on the right?" he wanted to know.

"The *fat* one," said Julie. She pointed to his raindrop. It was globby. Then she pointed to her own raindrop. It was maybe two inches from his, and it was just as globby. She leaned forward until her nose was almost touching the pane. Her eyes flicked back and forth from one raindrop to the other. "I think yours is a little fatter than mine," she said. "Well, that's only fair, seeing as how you're a beginner."

Morris Bird III drew back a little.

"Come *on*," Julie said to her raindrop. "*Move.*"

Neither of the raindrops moved. Morris Bird III finished his glass of chocolate milk. All right, so maybe she *was* crazy. No one was perfect. He looked at her. He looked her up and down. She didn't notice. She was too busy concentrating on her raindrop. Her mouth was tight. It was almost as though she had no lips. Her chest went in and out. He enjoyed watching her chest. Then she gave a little shriek. He flinched. "Look," she said, and now she was whispering, "mine's *moved*."

Sure enough. It had. About an inch.

Morris Bird III looked at his own raindrop. It hadn't budged.

Julie's raindrop shot to the left about an inch. It was joined by a cluster of about halfadozen smaller raindrops. It wiggled down about three more inches.

Morris Bird III's raindrop still hadn't moved.

Julie's raindrop made a wriggly streak as it veered to the right and then down another inch. Now it was about six inches from the bottom.

Morris Bird III made a fist.

Julie saw him. She frowned. "No fair hitting the window."

Morris Bird III shrugged, stuffed the hand in a pants pocket.

Julie's raindrop slid down another inch, maybe an inch and a half.

Morris Bird III's raindrop was globbier, but it still hadn't moved. Some raindrop.

Julie's raindrop moved downward in the shape of an S. Now it was about an inch from the bottom. Morris Bird III supposed he was being skunked, or shut out. Oh boy, what a stupid thought. It was a stupid game, and who in his right mind cared? The raindrop game: big deal.

Yeah, but then how come he was holding his breath?

Julie's raindrop slithered sideways, but not down.

"Come *on*," Morris Bird III told his raindrop. His voice sounded thin and idiotic. Down went Julie's raindrop, then sideways. A quarter of an inch more, and the race would be over.

But then . . . and with a suddenness that made Julie give a little squeak . . . Morris Bird III's raindrop began to move. It moved straight, and it moved true, and it kept gaining momentum. Adding smaller raindrops as it slid down, it rolled in a direct line from top to bottom of the pane, hitting the bottom and spreading into a fat gelatinous shape that resembled an overweight upsidedown *T*.

"Well," said Morris Bird III, "imagine that." He looked at Julie.

She was smiling, but it was the sort of smile people screwed their faces into when they had hemorrhoids and were trying to perform #2.

"Uh," he said, "I guess I won."

"That's right."

"Well. Uh. It was. Uh. Yes. It was very exciting."

Julie nodded. She held out her right hand.

Morris Bird III's glass was in his right hand. He switched it to his left hand. Then he shook hands with her. She did not have much of a grip. As a matter of fact, she had no grip at all to speak of.

"Don't squeeze," she said. "I don't want my fingers hurt. The piano, I mean."

"Sure," said Morris Bird III. He released her hand.

She looked at her hand for a moment. "Now I think maybe we'll go into the bedroom."

He looked at her.

"Czerny's in the bedroom," she said. "You want to see him, don't you?"

"Oh," said Morris Bird III. "Sure."

"And . . . nice going."

"Huh?"

"Winning the race."

"Oh. Well, It was nothing."

"You did good for a beginner."

"Thank you."

Julie nodded. "I don't lose very often. I almost always beat Claramae."

"Who?"

"Claramae."

"Who's she?"

"Nobody."

"Huh?"

"I made her up. She's colored, and she's got big teeth, and her hair's in pigtails, and she calls me Honeychile. She's got a voice like Butterfly McQueen. You remember Butterfly McQueen from *Duel in the Sun*? The colored girl with the squeaky voice?"

"Oh. Yeah. I remember her."

"We play raindrop race a lot. I give her a drop, and I take a drop, and for some reason my drop almost always wins. But she's a good sport."

"That's nice."

"We play a lot of games. Our favorite game is the Nancy Turpin game."

"Oh? What's that?"

"We try to figure out what she's like."

"Nancy Turpin? You try to figure out what Nancy Turpin's like?"

"Yes."

"And who's Nancy Turpin?"

"She was a runnerup for Miss Ohio back I think it was in 1946."

"That's nice."

"She married my daddy."

"Oh. I see."

"I've got a picture of her."

"That so?"

"You want to see it?"

"Okay."

"It's in the bedroom with Czerny. Come on."

"Sure," said Morris Bird III. By this time, he would have been game for flying to the moon in a peagreen boat, or whatever. She led him back into the livingroom, then through the door where she had vanished with his raincoat and shoes. It opened into a hall. He could see the kitchen at the end of the hall. She took him to a door that opened to the right of the hall. She opened the door, preceded him into a bedroom that was full of ducks. He'd never seen so many ducks in his whole entire life.

"You like my ducks?" she asked him.

A hollow sound came from the base of Morris Bird III's throat. "Sure," he finally said. "They're fine."

"Some collection, huh?"

"Yes indeed."

Julie grinned. She placed her hands on her hips and looked around. Her eyes were damp, and he wondered if maybe she was going to cry. Girls and women got that way sometimes when they were proud or happy. Which made an awful lot of sense. Sure. Like trying to find the beginning and the end of a perfect circle. Oh well. Morris Bird III wasn't about to change the way girls and women behaved, so he looked around the room at all the ducks. There were six stuffed and very fuzzy ducks on the bedspread. Three were white, two yellow and one green. It was maybe the first green duck he'd ever seen. On the dresser, lined up in almost a military formation, were eight, nine, ten, eleven, *twelve* rubber ducks. Four of them were Donald Ducks of various sizes. There was a purplish mama duck and four little ducks that trailed behind her. The other three ducks were the sort seen in a baby's playpen. On the floor next to the dresser were five more stuffed ducks—four white, one yellow. On the floor by the bed was a pulltoy consisting of a mama duck and three little ones. They were yellow, and they had little red wheels. A string trailed from the mama duck's neck. Julie bent over, picked up the string, pulled the ducks forward a couple of feet. They went *wack*, and their wheels squeaked, and then they went *wack* again. Julie let go the string and straightened up. A tear was on her left cheek. She brushed it away and sniffled. Morris Bird III looked away. He examined the walls. They held five paintings of ducks in flight. He looked at them very closely. He wanted to give Julie time to put an end to her sniffles.

"I had a real duck once," she said. Small voice.

"Oh?" said Morris Bird III, still inspecting the pictures.

"Yes. My daddy gave him to me. It was when I was real little and we were living in Zilwaukee."

"Milwaukee?"

"Zilwaukee. It's in Michigan."

"Oh."

"Most people get the name wrong, what with Milwaukee being so big and famous and all."

"Uh huh."

"You going to look at that wall all night?"

Morris Bird III gave his mouth another spit bath. He turned. "I'm sorry."

She seemed all right again. At least there were no more tears. "His name was Dippy," she said.

"Oh?"

"My real duck. My daddy named him that. Dippy Duck. It was because he walked sideways, like maybe he was drunk. The duck, I mean."

"Mm."

"Then one day he sort of staggered out into the street, and that was the end of him."

"A car hit him?"

"A truck. A real big truck. A big Gulf truck. Poor Dippy. I was standing on the sidewalk. The truck sent him flying. He gave a real high squawk, and his feathers went every which way. I should have run out after him, but I guess there wasn't the time."

"Probably not," said Morris Bird III.

"I cried. My daddy cried, too. He smelled like Roi-Tan cigars. You want to see the picture of Nancy Turpin? My daddy's in it, too. My mother doesn't know I have the picture. I keep it hidden."

"Sure. If you want to show it."

"Why not?" said Julie. She went to the bed, knelt down and

lifted a corner of the mattress. She came up with a small envelope. She straightened, opened the envelope and pulled out the photograph. She handed the photograph to Morris Bird III.

He frowned at it. A tall heavyset man stood with an arm around a young girl who was wearing a bathing suit. She was a blonde, and she was mostly chest. They were standing on what apparently was a beach, and they both were squinting and showing plenty of teeth.

"Very nice," said Morris Bird III. He gave the picture back to Julie.

"Nice?"

"Well, what I mean is, she's goodlooking."

"Oh. Oh yes. She certainly *appears* to be, doesn't she?"

"Yes."

Julie slipped the picture back into the envelope, returned the envelope to its hidingplace under the mattress. She patted down the bedspread. "Uh, I've never met her."

"Oh?"

Julie turned to face him. She really was very small. "No. I never have. They just got married last month. It was the day after my mother got the divorce."

"Mm."

"My mother hates her."

"Uh huh."

"My mother talks a lot about her."

"Uh huh."

"My mother is thirtyfive, and Nancy Turpin's only twenty-two."

"Mm," said Morris Bird III. "I guess that makes a difference."

"I guess it does. It's one of the things I talk about with Claramae."

"Oh. Yes. Claramae."

"Claramae never gives me any trouble. That's the reason I made her colored. I figured she'd be grateful to be with *me* instead of all the time a lot of *colored people*."

"Well. Uh. Sure. That makes sense."

"I'll be seeing Nancy Turpin in July."

"Oh?"

"Yes. She and my daddy are living in Toledo now. I get to spend one month a year with them. The judge said so."

"Mm."

"They have a place by the lake."

"Oh. You ought to have a good time."

"I hope so. I mean, if she wants me to love her, I'll try."

"Good," said Morris Bird III.

"That's very important, isn't it?"

"Oh yes."

"Well, *I* think it is."

"I'm not arguing with you."

"My mother yells a lot."

"All mothers yell a lot."

"She calls my daddy a dirty filthy *philanthropist*."

"What's that?"

"I don't know exactly. I think it has something to do with a married man who runs around with other women."

"Oh."

"You ever read the *Oz* book?"

"I saw the movie."

"My mother makes me think of the *Oz* book. The Wicked Witch of the East."

"That's the one the house fell on, isn't it?"

"Yes."

"She must be something."

"She *is*."

"Say. About your mother. Where is she?"

"You know the Red Arrow? At Hough and Crawford?"

"Yes."

"She's a waitress there. She works from five until the place closes at one-thirty. I have my dinner there every night. With her. That's where I was coming from today."

"Oh. The food any good in there?"

"Fair."

"Funny. I've lived around here all my life, but I've never been in there."

"Well, you haven't missed all *that* much."

Morris Bird III nodded. "That's good," he said.

Julie took a step toward him, then hesitated. She looked down at her feet. "Morris? Can I ask you a question?"

"Sure."

"Promise you won't lie?"

"I promise."

"You think my feet are too big?"

"Your *feet*?"

"Don't act so innocent. I know what the kids at school say. They call me Gunboats. They think they're being real funny."

"There's nothing wrong with your feet."

"Now. You promised you wouldn't lie."

"I'm *not*."

"How can I believe you?"

"I don't know."

"I mean, is your word any good?"

"Yes," said Morris Bird III. He still held his stupid chocolate milk glass. He looked down at it. Then he looked up, and he was glaring. "You got no right to ask me a question like that."

She stepped back. "I'm sorry."

"Go sit on the edge of the bed."

"What?"

"Just do like I say. I got an idea."

"You going to hurt me?"

"No. Crying out loud. Just go sit on the edge of the bed."

"All *right* . . ." said Julie. She went to the bed and sat down.

He followed her, knelt in front of her. First, though, he had to push out of his way the mama duck and the three little ducks on red wheels. They went *wack*, but only once, and rather quietly. "Now," he said, "take off a shoe. Either one."

"Either one?"

"Yes."

"All right." She bent over and slipped off her right shoe. It was a loafer, and a penny had been wedged into the open place just behind the toes. When she straightened, her hair brushed the tip of Morris Bird III's nose. He cleared his throat, breathed through his mouth.

She wore no socks. Her foot was bony, with a thin network of veins on the instep. He placed his right hand next to the foot. "Now," he said, "which one's bigger?"

"My foot."

"Sure. But by how much?"

"I don't know. Maybe an inch."

"So all right. That proves my point."

"How?"

"What do you mean, how? It's *your foot* and *my hand*. And your foot is only an inch bigger. Now, an ordinary person's foot would be a whole lot bigger." Here Morris Bird III placed the hand next to his own stockinged foot. "Look. Look there. *My* foot's a good *three* inches bigger than my hand."

"Uh huh," said Julie, nodding. "But how come they call me Gunboats?"

"I don't know."

"I mean, don't they have to have some sort of *reason?*"

Morris Bird III stood up. He shrugged. "I don't know. I guess not."

"It's not very fair."

"A lot of things aren't very fair."

"I don't think my feet are so bad."

"They *aren't*."

"If there was only a *reason* . . ." She put on her shoe and stood up.

"Maybe there is."

"Oh?" said Julie. She moved until her chest was just about touching his.

He backed away a little. He stared at his glass. It was clouded and sticky. He wished she knew enough to keep her distance. "Uh," he said, "that's just the way kids are sometimes. One day somebody probably was bored, and so because he didn't have anything better to do he said to a buddy: You know, seems to me Julie Sutton's got big feet. Let's call her Gunboats. And that was that. The name caught on, and nobody ever bothered to check.

Like Alvin Flanagan. You know him, that 7B kid in Miss Beam's homeroom?"

"The fat one who talks with a limp?"

"Yeah. Everyone calls him Sunshine."

"So?"

"So, don't you get it? He's just a fat kid who walks with a limp. Why should he be called Sunshine? There's no reason. Gimpy I could see, or Twinkletoes. But why Sunshine? There's no reason at all. It's just a name."

"And you're saying Gunboats is just a name?"

"Uh huh."

"Thank you. You're very sweet."

"That's me. Real sweet. You know what I got stitched across my chest?"

"What?"

"XXX, like on a bag of sugar."

"You're *crazy.*"

"Uh huh," said Morris Bird III. His jaw fell open, and his lower lip flapped loosely. "That's me," he said. "The village idiot."

Julie giggled.

Morris Bird III grinned at her. He couldn't remember when he'd felt so good. His skin was all tingly, and he almost wanted to cry. She giggled so hard she had to place a hand over her mouth. His heart went all globby like his raindrop. He handed her his chocolate milk glass, then used the little fingers of both hands to pull out the corners of his lips. Then he stuck out his tongue, and the resultant face made Julie shriek. Oh. Ah. This was more like it. Julie Sutton laughing, yes indeed. Julie Sutton and her Claramae and her ducks. Oh boy, the thing to do when you felt sorry for yourself was to examine someone else. Yeah, you never had it so bad but what someone else didn't have it worse. He made a lot of faces for her, and she laughed so hard she had to squeeze her face and eyes and peek at him moistly through the openings between her fingers. She laughed until she squealed, and then she laughed some more, and finally all she could do was gasp soundlessly, and it all made Morris Bird III feel like some sort of great and golden hero. He jumped around the room, scratching his armpits like a baboon and bringing up from his chest a succession of hollow grunting noises. Julie clapped her hands, shrieked, told him for heaven's sake to stop it before she had a *heart* attack. Okay, he told her, seizing the end of the string that was attached to the duck pull toy. Dragging the pulltoy behind him, he staggered around the room. He crossed his eyes and allowed his tongue to hang out. *Wack* went the pulltoy, and *wack* and *wack* and *wack* and *wack*. He was breathing hard now, and he was sweating a little, but so what? A sound of laughter was coming from Julie Sutton, and it was a sweet sound, worth all the exertion—and more. *Wack* went the pulltoy, and *wack* and *wack* and *wack* and *wack*, and the ducks' heads nodded with each turn of the wheels, nodded in cadence rhythmic, cadence perfect, and oh boy, she *liked* him; he made her *laugh*, and ah praise the Lord, life was good. He added his own sound of laughter to hers, and he snuffled and gasped and did a little dance, and glory be, how sweet, how warm. He kept himself a safe distance away from Julie, never once touching her, but he knew (or at least he *hoped*) they had somehow picked up a closeness that had nothing to do with distance. It was all very mysterious, and it probably was the greatest thing that ever had happened to him. It was a tiny room, and it was full of ducks and laughter, and for Morris Bird III it was like maybe some sort of holy place. Laughing and chattering, he and Julie had come across something, a huge happy giggly whatchamacallit that probably had more than a little to do with the heats and juices he'd been feeling lately, and oh Lordy Lordy he never wanted to die. After a time, when their laughter had subsided a little, she asked him did he want to take a look at Czerny. Sure, he said, why not? She led him across the room to a closet door next to the dresser.

"The sides of the terrarium are low," she said. "So when I go out I keep it in the closet. That way, if Czerny crawls out, I don't have so much trouble finding him." She opened the closet door, bent down and picked up something. It looked to Morris Bird III like a dish full of dirt. She set it on the dresser. "Well," she said, nodding down, "there he is. Come look."

Morris Bird III looked down. He saw dirt, and what appeared to be moss, and a couple of leaves. "I don't see anything," he said.

"See the leaf on the right?"

"Yeah?"

"His head's under it. You can see his rear end sticking out."

"Oh," said Morris Bird III. "Oh yeah. Now I see him."

She removed the leaf. Czerny was maybe three inches long. He was as brown as the earth, and he was motionless. "He doesn't move an awful lot," she said.

"How do you know if he's alive?"

Julie pressed a fingernail against Czerny's tail. He twitched. "He's alive," she said.

"Mm," said Morris Bird III. "Very interesting."

"I bring him leaves. See this leaf in my hand? See where he's bitten out of it?"

Morris Bird III looked down at the leaf, but he really was looking at the hand that held it. "Yeah," he said, "I see." There were little gashes in the leaf.

Julie returned the leaf to the terrarium. "I think he's asleep. When he's awake, sometimes I take the terrarium to the window. When the light hits his eyes just right, they turn orange."

"Mm," said Morris Bird III.

"Funny thing, though."

"What's that?"

"Well, like you said, it's hard to tell if he's alive. He really is what you'd have to call sluggish. *But,* when he gets of a mind to go somewhere, he can really move. No fooling. Like a flash. So, when I'm not home, I have to keep the terrarium in the closet like I said. One time he got all the way out to the fire escape. It's a good thing I found him, or he probably would have fallen through those iron strips or whatever they are—those strips you walk on, I mean. As it *was,* he was sort of hanging *on.*"

"Mm."

She picked up the terrarium and returned it to the closet. "Come on," she said, straightening. "I'll play the piano for you."

"Okay."

They returned to the livingroom. He seated himself on the sofa. She had his chocolate milk glass. She asked him if he wanted a refill. He told her he didn't mind if he did. She took both glasses to the kitchen, returned a moment later with refills. The rain had stopped. He had a funny feeling there was something he'd forgotten to do. Oh well. Fooey on it.

58

She went to the piano and sat down. She placed her glass on a pile of music. "Anything special you want me to play?"

"No. That's okay. Anything you want to play is all right with me."

"A little Chopin then. I love Chopin."

"Okay."

"Good," said Julie. She flexed her fingers and began to play. She leaned a little forward, and her head and shoulders moved from side to side in rhythm with the music. It was fluttery music, running up and down music, kids playing in the street music. She smiled, and from time to time she closed her eyes. There was no music on the rack in front of her. Morris Bird III hadn't been prepared for this. The truth was, he'd been prepared to be bored. But now he was sitting up straight, and he was unaware of breath or the room or anything. The music beat at him with tiny fists, and then he was smiling (so was Julie), and he'd never heard anything lovelier. He leaned forward, propped his elbows on his knees, rested his chin on his fists. The music skittered and skipped, and the sound was like a wheel full of colors all sparkly and streaky, and it occurred to him what with raindrops and Claramae and ducks and chocolate milk and Ritz crackers and the mysterious Nancy Turpin and the dead Dippy and an insignificant lizard named Czerny—that he was having the best time he'd had in oh he didn't know how long. Not that he understood much of it, but who cared? It was enough just to let it happen. Nodding, closing her eyes and from time to time even humming, Julie sent the music cascading all around them, and finally Morris Bird III just about got to wishing he could fall down and chew on a fist. He was sweating, but he couldn't have cared less. His breath was taut and uncomfortable, so big deal. All that mattered was the music, the girl, the now. He wished he could freeze the sum and total of his personal now, keep it focused on this moment until the end of eternity, which probably wouldn't be half long enough.

She played for an hour, maybe longer. She played Chopin. She played Mozart. She played Beethoven and Schumann and Brahms and even a little Scriabin. Sometimes she used music, and sometimes she did not. She told him she had been studying the piano for almost ten years. She explained to him that *studying the piano* was a whole lot different—a whole lot more serious—than just taking dumb old *piano lessons*. She asked him did he understand the difference. He told her he thought he did. She told him the piano was the most important thing that had ever happened to her. He nodded, told her yes, he could tell. For some reason that didn't bear looking into, he felt a little jealous. But that was dumb. How could a person be jealous of *music?* After all, it wasn't as though she'd confessed to him a secret passion for Gregory Peck. Now *Gregory Peck* he would have been jealous of. But music, no. That was stupid. And besides, it gave her too much pleasure. Not only that, but who was Morris Bird III to be jealous? It wasn't as though Julie were his *girlfriend* or anything like *that*. Girlfriend? *Girlfriend?* Bruh, the thought was enough to make his bones rattle. All he *needed* was a *girlfriend*. What did a person do with one? Girlfriends were for odious fat elderly types like Don Schwamb, who at fifteen no doubt understood something of the world.

After discussing music, Morris Bird III and Julie got to talking about themselves. Julie did most of the talking. She came and sat next to him on the sofa, and the words came from her in urgent bursts, all breathy and quick, as though she had to get all of them out before some magic hour when she was scheduled to turn into a frog or a pumpkin or a hamburger patty or something. "At school, I don't say much," she told him. "I think of things to say, but they almost always seem dumb."

"So? People all the time say dumb things. Join the club."

"I couldn't do that. I don't know how. And anyway, clubs scare me."

"Oh?"

"When you join a club, it means people *expect* things from you."

"So? Big deal. So they expect things from you."

"But I got nothing to *give*."

"How about your music?"

"No. The music's *mine*."

"That doesn't make any sense. When you play the piano, *I* hear it. The music's just as good for me as it is for you. It's not something a person can hear when he's all alone—unless he's on his way to the loony bin."

"No. No. That's not what I *mean*. All I *mean* is I can't get up in front of people and do things. Lots of people, I mean. Not just you. With just you everything's fine. I'll tell you something. Monday, when you see me in school, the chances are I won't say a word to you. Maybe it's shyness, or maybe it's oh I don't know what, but the point is, my mind'll probably be like the Gobi Desert. All dead and driedout, I mean. That's the way it's always been with me. So promise me something, okay?"

"What's that?"

"Promise me you won't get mad if I don't talk to you."

"Sure."

"Say it like you mean it."

"Sure!"

Julie smiled. "Thank you."

"For nothing," said Morris Bird III. He made a deprecating motion with a hand.

"Will you be my *friend* even if I don't talk to you?"

"Sure," said Morris Bird III. Then, after a pause, he made his voice louder and more enthusiastic. *"Sure!"*

"You get along all right with your family?"

"I guess so."

"You're lucky."

"Yeah."

"No fooling."

"Okay. If you say so."

Julie studied her knuckles. She opened her mouth to say something, but then she thought better of it. Finally all she did was sort of grunt. She leaned forward a little, wrapped her arms around her waist.

"Something you want to say?" he asked her.

She shook her head no.

"Yes there is."

Reluctantly she shook her head yes.

"So okay. Out with it. The suspense is killing me," said Morris Bird III.

"I . . . uh . . . I've never never *never* . . ."

"Never never never what?"

"Never . . . uh . . . never talked so much."

"Oh," said Morris Bird III. His belly was thick. He looked away from her. His breath was heavy. It made him sort of wheeze. He looked at the piano, drew some air into his lungs. It hurt.

"I've just chattered and chattered and chattered," said Julie.

Morris Bird III didn't say anything.

She touched his hand.

He made a squealing sound.

"I'm sorry," she said. The touch of her hand went away.

Morris Bird III just about wanted to cry. "No," he said, "that's okay." He still was looking at the piano.

"Look at me," said Julie.

He looked at her. He didn't want to, but he did, and his eyes were hot.

She was smiling. Her chest was going in and out, and there was a little moisture on her forehead and in the place between her lips and nose.

Now his stomach hurt.

She moved a little closer to him. She did this by wriggling her bottom.

Morris Bird III wanted to bend double.

"I'll think about you a lot," she said. She touched his hand again.

"Me, too," he said. "I mean, *I'll* think about *you* a lot."

"Good. I'm glad."

"I'm glad you're glad."

"I'm glad you're glad I'm glad."

"I'm glad you're glad I'm glad you're glad."

Julie giggled.

Morris Bird III laughed.

"Glad," said Julie. "What a funny word."

"Teddy Karam would call it dalg."

"He still say things backwards?"

"Uh huh."

"Oh, is the world ever full of nuts."

"Present company, too?"

"Oh *yes*," said Julie. "You *bet*."

Morris Bird III sniggered.

Then there was a silence. But it was not an uncomfortable silence. It was just a silence. There simply was no reason for anything to be said. They sat there and held hands, and Morris Bird III listened to his pulse and took deep breaths, and nothing else was necessary. He looked at Julie all he wanted. Now he wasn't afraid. He looked at her and looked at her and looked at her. He smiled at her, and she smiled at him. Once she even squeezed his hand. He felt weightless, like a balloon. It was a wonder to him he hadn't floated up to the ceiling. He was fortunate to have her holding his hand. She was anchoring him. He hoped she wouldn't change into a frog or a pumpkin or a hamburger patty. He could hear her breath. Even though the sound of his pulse was loud, he still could hear her breath. He watched her chest. Her face was a little pink, and she almost was smiling. He took in the way her hair swept back from her forehead. Her skirt had hiked itself up, and he was able to see her knees. They were pale and smooth, and they made him rub his tongue against his teeth. The rhythm of her chest was perfectly even; it was almost musical. He examined her waist. It was tiny, and it looked soft. Soft and warm. He wished he could press the back of a hand against it. He could see her in a veil. He could see her dancing to the music of an oboe. His eyes became wet. He sniffled a little. He blinked, cleared the wetness from his eyes. He hoped she hadn't noticed it. When he got up to go, he said nothing. Neither did Julie. She went to the kitchen and fetched his raincoat and shoes. They were warm and dry. When she gave them to him, both of her hands touched both of his. He sighed, put on the coat and shoes. She walked him to the door. She opened it for him. Finally he spoke. He told her he had had a fine time. Same here, said Julie. He nodded, stepped out into the hall. Halfway down the hall, he turned and looked back. She still stood in the doorway. He waved at her. She waved back. She was very small. He felt like a soldier leaving his sweetheart and going off to war. This was the sort of thing old Errol Flynn was so good at. He waved again, then went down the stairs and outside to Hough Avenue. It was dark. Hot, too. Muggy from the rain. It wasn't until he was climbing the porch steps of his home that he realized he'd forgotten to telephone. His mother was fit to be tied. It turned out she had called the police. This wasn't the first time Morris Bird III had been missing from home. Almost four years ago, on the day his buddy Stanley Chaloupka had been killed in the explosion, Morris Bird III and Sandra had wandered off without authorization—and on a school day at that. It had been a funny sort of day. All sorts of things had gotten themselves screwed up in his mind. Until the summer of 1944, Stanley Chaloupka had lived in Morris Bird III's neighborhood. But then Stanley and his mother moved away—clear over to East 63rd Street by the lake, a good four miles or so from the old neighborhood. For some dumb reason that had to do with Selfrespect and Courage and all that there, Morris Bird III decided to go visit Stanley. But it wasn't enough to visit Stanley. The distance would have to be *walked*. Why walked? Well, why not? When a person walks four miles, the getting there means a whole lot more. Or something. At any rate, Morris Bird III did walk the four miles— pulling dumb old Sandra in a red wagon he'd rented from Teddy Karam, the boy who said everything backwards. It was quite a walk, and then . . . just as they got there . . . the explosion happened to happen. It came from some nearby gas tanks. The wagon was destroyed, and Stanley Chaloupka was killed, and both Morris Bird III and Sandra were burned, and by the time they finally got home their parents were just about foaming at the mouth and rolling around on the floor. If it hadn't been for the intervention of Morris Bird III's grandmother, both he and Sandra probably would have been shot at sunrise. As it was, they were restricted to the house for the next four weekends, and that winter Morris Bird III went into business shoveling snow off people's walks. The proceeds of the business were turned over to Teddy Karam's family until the wagon was paid for. The sum came to twenty dollars, and Morris Bird III would go to his grave believing he had been taken. So, when Morris Bird III didn't come home to dinner this night almost four years later, his mother and father were ready for the worst. They called the police. Then, at 9:30, when he walked in the front door, there was a commotion the likes of which the world had never seen. His mother came screeching at him, and his father (limping a little) came bellowing in his best Voice of Cleveland & Northeastern Ohio pearshaped tones, and the upshot of it was that a) Morris Bird III was spanked, b) he was forbidden to go to the movies for a month, c) he was restricted to the house for six weekends, d) he was forbidden to play shortstop that summer with the Gordon Park Berardinos of Class F, and e) he was sent to bed with nothing to eat. Oh boy, talk about your Spanish Inquisition. His mother's face had absolutely no blood, and his father's hand was like a snakeskin whip. (The spanking was the most degrading. Morris Bird III, owner of Slaves, suffering the humiliation of a *paddling!* It had been years since that sort of littleboy outrage had been perpetrated against him. Oh well, at least he didn't bawl. He supposed this was something.) Okay. All right. So the punishment was severe. But somehow the offense had been worth the punishment. He had gotten to know Julie Sutton. He had taken a ride to the moon in a peagreen boat. Raindrops, secret photographs, music, ducks, Claramae, a lizard named Czerny, plus talk of Gunboats and love and a mother who was the logical successor to the Wicked Witch of the East, plus the touch of a hand, the sight of a pair of knees, the anxious *in* and *out* and *in* and *out* of a certain very special chest. You stacked all those things against the punishment, and the equation came out just about even. So okay. All right. So for half the night Morris Bird III was forced to sleep on his stomach because his rear end stung too much. So it had been worth it. Before going to bed, he went into the bathroom and washed his face. Washed it real good. Washed and rubbed. Washed and rubbed and rinsed.

Sandra came into his room late that night. He wasn't asleep, though.

"Morris?" she said, whispering.

He opened his eyes. He had been watching his Slaves. "Yeah. I'm awake."

She came to the bed and sat down on the edge. "I had to Go," she said. "I just wanted to see how you're doing."

"I'm doing fine."

"Morris?"

"Yeah?"

"It was worth it, wasn't it?"

"Yeah."

"Like the time we went to see Stanley Chalipka?"

"Chaloupka. Yeah. Like that."

"I heard Them yelling. It was a girl this time, wasn't it?"

"Yeah."

"When They yell, They yell. I heard everything. I was supposed to be good little Sandra, upstairs in bed, but I heard every word They said. Is she a nice girl?"

"Yeah."

"Good," said Sandra. "As long as it was worth it." She came off the bed and went to the door. "That's the important thing. Well, good night." She went out.

He heard her pad down the hall to her own room, and oh *boy*, what *next?*

Sure enough, the next Monday there came not a word from Julie Sutton. She wouldn't even *look* at Morris Bird III. She bent over her books, and all he could see was the back of her neck and the top of her head. They were pretty enough, but seeing them wasn't the same as seeing all of her, or listening to her voice and her talk of ducks and nonexistent colored girls and all that.

But he wasn't mad. He was her friend. He had every intention of keeping the promise he had made to her.

So she walked, flatfooted, in that dopey sloppy shuffle, hugging her books to her chest, keeping her head down and her face blank; she walked through the halls of Addison Junior High, halls that smelled of disinfectant and perspiration and lipstick and chalkdust and sandwiches wrapped in wax paper; she walked past kids who screeched, kids who sprinted, kids who jostled each other, kids whose feet made anxious slapping noises on the concrete floor, kids who nudged and snickered and told dirty stories; she walked past rows of lockers, and all around her doors were slammed, and now and then someone dropped a book that went *thut*; she walked softly, and she said not a word (from time to time, if she was late for a class, she skittered, but mostly she simply walked), and naturally Morris Bird III kept her in sight most of the time, and naturally his pulse rang in his ears like some immense Oriental gong, like in the Charlie Chan movies. . . .

And she sat, notebook open, pencil at the ready, face pale and small, eyes looking down, always looking down; she sat without particularly moving anything except her chest; she spoke when she was spoken to, and otherwise she kept her thoughts to herself (yeah, and he could see those thoughts, thoughts that had to do with music, a lizard, a golden house on the lake at Toledo where her father and the enigmatic Nancy Turpin waited on the beach, arms around each other's waists, her father puffing jauntily on a Roi-Tan, Nancy grinning and thrusting forward her majestic chest); she sat and listened to all the things that were happening in her head and heart and whatever; she sat silently, allowing nothing to get out. . . .

And Morris Bird III was not surprised. After all, he had been warned. So all right. So it hurt. So big fat deal. He would endure. And some day maybe something would happen to change the situation.

The Gordon Park Berardino thing hurt, too. Morris Bird III had had the shortstop job all locked up. He had played in the team's first two games, and he was batting .667—four hits for six times at bat. He didn't have much power, but he did hit the ball with a certain amount of shortrange authority. And in those two games he had fielded eight chances cleanly. He moved around pretty well, and his arm was adequate if not spectacular. The team won those two games, 11–9 over the Keltners and 2–0 over the Boudreaus, and the second of the games was every bit as good as any bigleague game. The Berardinos' pitcher, Teddy Karam (known to his teammates as The Splendid Southpaw), allowed only one hit, a single to right field by some dumb kid who just happened to swing late and bloop the ball over the head of the Berardinos' first baseman, a big gunky Hillbilly boy named Jasper Reed. Morris Bird III fielded four ground balls with his usual flawless alacrity, had two singles, stole a base and scored both the Berardinos' runs. In the fourth inning he came in on a wild pitch, and in the sixth he trotted home when the Boudreaus' catcher threw wildly in an attempt to pick a runner off first base. It was a marvelous game. The Berardinos made only two errors, and the Boudreaus committed only three, and he just bet that was some sort of record for Class F. After all, in Class F almost every team had its share of Slops (the age limit was fourteen), but on the Gordon Park Berardinos the Slop quota was remarkably low. Or at least it was as long as Morris Bird III was playing. After his departure, a kid named Oscar Adams was put in to play shortstop, and this Oscar Adams was like the Black Death. Until Morris Bird III's departure, Oscar Adams had played an acceptable right field (after all, there were precious few lefthanded hitters in the league, and a clumsy guy could do little damage in right field). *But,* as soon as the shortstop vacancy was created, old Oscar Adams insisted on taking over the position. And there was nothing Teddy Karam, the manager, could do about it. Granted, Oscar Adams was the world's worst Slop in the field, but he also happened to be able to hit a baseball more than three hundred feet. He was five feet ten inches tall, and he weighed almost two hundred pounds, and when he hit the ball it went for miles and miles and *miles*. He had a voice like Sidney Greenstreet, and at fourteen he had as much hair on his chest as your average goodsized baboon, and so what was Teddy Karam to do? You didn't argue with Oscar Adams. If he wanted to play shortstop, he played shortstop. If he wanted to beat your head into the ground, he beat your head into the ground. It was that simple. He liked to sit and knead the muscles in his arms and legs, and he was someone you did not under any circumstances argue with, cross, thwart, laugh at or mess with. He called himself Oscar By God You Better Believe It Adams, and everyone believed it; everyone was afraid of him. No, change that. One person hadn't been afraid of him. Benny Goodman, the late Benny Goodman who now was food for worms, hadn't been a bit afraid of Oscar Adams. Maybe this was because Benny Goodman had worn a brace on his left leg (a polio brace), but probably not. Even though a cripple can afford to be unafraid of an Oscar Adams (Who hits a cripple? What good are muscles in opposition to the tongue of someone who walks with a limp?), the bravery of Benny Goodman had been deeper. Or at least Morris Bird III thought so. Benny Goodman . . . ah, now there had been a true & genuine Character. A tiny fellow with a build of a jockey (and the narrow hawkish face of one, too), Benny Goodman had been the only boy in Mrs. Principe's homeroom shorter than Morris Bird III. But don't for a moment think this held Benny Goodman back. Talky, always snapping his fingers and humming little dribs and drabs of unidentifiable song under his breath, grinning at everything and everyone, swiveling his head back and forth like a sparrow keeping watch for a tomcat, Benny Goodman was known as The Perpetual Motion Machine, and no one was more delighted by the nickname than he was. Yeah, he told Morris Bird III one day, okay, so I got a lot of the old zip. So what's wrong with that? The way I see it, we only got so many days, so what am I supposed to do? Sleep? Huh! Sleep! Big deal! Look, each night we sleep eight hours, right? Okay, now suppose a person lives to sixty. Do you realize that he spends *twenty years* out of his sweet life lying in the old sack making with the zzzzz, lying there with his mouth open and his tonsils hanging out? You call that *living?* People say sleep is good for you, but who are the people who say it? Old people, people who've run out of gas. Me, I sleep as little as I can get away with. I got plenty of gas—and I don't mean the kind you take Bisodol to get rid of. (You ever taste Bisodol? Bluh. Better you should stay sick.) Yeah, this was some guy, this Benny Goodman, and if you didn't like him, tough. He had what he called a Philosophy of Life, and the way he saw it, the whole business of getting through each day was pretty simple. Yeah, he told Morris Bird III, so okay, so I'm a loudmouth. But who do I hurt? (*Whom?* I think I should have said Whom. Yeah. Whom. My old man's always after me about my grammar.) Anyway, *whom* do I hurt? If you don't like the things I say, you don't have to listen. You can go somewhere else and listen to things you *want* to hear. There's nothing I can do about it. I'm just a poor helpless cripple, and I surely can't *chase* you. (Don't look at me like that. I'm *kidding.*) Okay. Now, where was I? Oh. Oh yeah. My, you should excuse the expression, Philosophy of Life. Look, every day all the

time I *see* things. And things *happen* to me. You know, like maybe
seeing a couple of mice making out with each other outside in
the driveway where the garbage cans are. Or like finding out
that Esna means Domestic Slave in the crossword puzzle. No,
not Esn*a*. So—Esna, Esne; that's not the point—the thing is: I,
Benny Goodman, this poor little cripple you see before you, get
a Large Charge out of everything that happens. Here I am, Benny
Goodman, your friendly neighborhood circumcised Bob Cratchit,
and every morning I hop to the window and I say: Good morning, world, Benny Goodman is all present and accounted for, and
buddy I ask you: What's wrong with that? I mean, everybody's
got to have a Philosophy of Life, and I kind of think mine's better than a lot I've heard of. I mean, at least I don't lie around with
my tonsils hanging out. (Not that I *got* tonsils, you understand.
They were taken out in the spring of 1939 by my father's good
friend, Dr. Leonard S. Aaronson. Ah, Dr. Aaronson. I remember
him like it was the day before yesterday. He had a cast in his eye.
Just like Old Lady Principe's.) Most of the kids in Mrs. Principe's
homeroom could take Benny Goodman or leave him alone. They
got tired of his jabber. But he did have three close friends. They
were Morris Bird III, Teddy Karam and the lumpish Oscar
Adams. Morris Bird III *liked* Benny Goodman because he seemed
to have some idea what was going on. Teddy Karam (a sneaky
Lebanese swindler and con man and usurer if there ever was
one, a seller of punchboard chances who loaned sums of up to
50 cents at an interest rate of 5 cents a day) was *interested* in
Benny Goodman because Benny Goodman had brains and
maybe some day could be helpful. As for Oscar Adams, he *loved*
Benny Goodman. This probably was because Benny Goodman
never had taken any guff from him. When it came to insults,

Benny Goodman was the best. And he admitted it, not without pride. I am, he said, what a person would almost have to call the Joe DiMaggio of the Bad Mouth. One time, while involved in some sort of minor squabble with Oscar Adams, Benny said: Oscar, I just bet you may even have a brain somewhere up in that Mammoth Cave you call your head. Tell you what, would you do me a favor? When you die, will you leave me your brain? I want to give it to the Natural History Museum. For the insect collection. Let me tell you something, Oscar old boy. You ought to file a lawsuit against God. It must have slipped His mind that people can't think with muscles. And that *face* of yours! You see that movie last year, the one called *The Jolson Story?* Well, seems Hollywood is going in big for making pictures telling stories of people's lives. That's a break for you. I mean, you ought to start saving your money now for the bus fare and get yourself out there. It's only a question of time before someone decides to make *The Bela Lugosi Story,* and you don't want to miss out on your big chance. I can see it now! Oscar Adams, otherwise known as Mr. Garbage Bag of 1948, starring in *The Bela Lugosi Story!* Oh! Ah! Such a triumph! I mean, Alan Ladd will slash his wrists! Cary Grant will enter a monastery! Gary Cooper will go into the dried fig business! Morris Bird III and Teddy Karam were present when Benny Goodman unloaded this barrage on Oscar Adams, and they almost fainted dead away when all Oscar did was laugh and sort of blush. Oh you're some talker, said Oscar, but that was as far as it went. He folded his massive arms and gave Benny Goodman an affectionate smile, and it was as though Benny had said, Nice day. Morris Bird III had no clear idea why Oscar tolerated Benny. If he—Morris Bird III—had said the things Benny had said, he—Morris Bird III—would have been minus one head, plus maybe an arm or leg or two. But the more Benny insulted Oscar, the more Oscar hung around Benny. And happily, maybe even gratefully, laughing a lot and blushing like a silly girl. Oh well. If Oscar didn't mind, no one else did. It was sort of pleasant to see the big jerk get what for. And anyway, there was too much to do to be worrying about something like *that*. Although Benny had the bad leg, he used neither crutches nor a cane. True, he walked in a sort of sidewise stagger, but they all were used to it, and anyway, he never complained. They acknowledged him as their leader, and he was just about in complete charge of their activities. Since he couldn't get around as easily as they could, he entertained them a great deal in his home. He was a great one for games, especially games based on real sports. The previous fall, he had organized them into what he had called the East 90th Street College Athletic Conference. Each of them was a college, and first they played a quadruple roundrobin schedule of Electric Football. The final standings:

	WON	LOST
Goodman Military	12	0
Bird A&M	6	6
Karam State	6	6
Adams Tech	0	12

They met every Friday night in Benny's house. The games were played in the basement on a brandnew cardtable supplied by Benny's father. Refreshments were supplied by Benny's mother. And such refreshments they were. Cornedbeef sandwiches. Pickles. Root beer. Cream soda. Little cakes. Ah, such feasts. So what if no one was able to defeat the juggernaut from

Goodman Military. There were more things in life than winning.
Like, for instance, food. Yeah, Benny was fond of saying, it's quite
something the way I fatten you guys up for the kill. He wasn't
kidding: *kill* was precisely the right word. At Electric Football, he
was an undisputed champion. In its dozen games, the mighty
Goodman Military team scored 361 points to its opponents' col-
lective 74. There was only one game that was particularly close—
a 13–0 victory over gallant Bird A&M. The other Goodman
Military triumphs were by preposterously lopsided scores, including one by 49–2 over hapless Adams Tech. Poor Oscar: he just
didn't seem to get the hang of the game. Oh well, Benny told him,
cheer up. Maybe you'll be better at basketball. After concluding
their football season, the four members of the East 90th Street
College Athletic Conference began basketball hostilities. The
game they used was called Bas-Ket. It consisted of a board with
holes under which were springs. Baskets were posted at each end
of the board. A table tennis ball was used, and the idea was to
catapult the ball from hole to basket. Four periods of seven minutes each were played. Benny used his mother's oven timer to
keep track of the minutes. Every team played every other team
eight times. The final standings:

	WON	LOST
Goodman Military	17	7
Bird A&M	16	8
Karam State	15	9
Adams Tech	0	24

As the standings would indicate, it was a breathtaking season.
As a matter of fact, Goodman Military and Bird A&M were tied

for the lead going into the last game. And what a game it was. With four minutes remaining in the fourth quarter, the score was 58–51, favor of Bird A&M, and Morris Bird III really had old Benny sweating. You could see the sweat on Benny's forehead, his arms, the backs of his hands. He was grinning and humming, but it didn't take a genius to figure out that he was scared. He couldn't seem to take his eyes off the oven timer. Yeah, he said, this is a serious situation. Almost what you'd have to call critical. Old Benny's got his work cut out for him. The table tennis ball rolled slowly, finally settled in the center hole on Morris Bird III's side. This was the easiest shot on the entire board. Even Oscar Adams almost invariably made it. Grinning, Morris Bird III pulled back the handle of the spring and let fly. The ball sailed over the basket and the backboard and clear across the room. Time was called while Oscar Adams fetched the ball, and now it was Benny's turn to grin. And mean it. He wiped the sweat off his forehead. You have just, he told Morris Bird III, made your fatal error. The rules of the game called for your opponent to take a foul shot whenever you threw the ball out of bounds. There was a special hole at each end of the board for foul shots. Benny made the foul shot. Now the score was 58–52, favor of Bird A&M. Then Benny got a center shot. *Swish.* 58–54. Then Benny made another foul shot. 58–55. Morris Bird III got a shot from his right forward position. The ball went over the backboard. Chuckling, Benny made the foul shot. 58–56. Morris Bird III retaliated with a successful foul shot of his own. 59–56. Now there was just a minute to go. The ball rolled into Benny's center hole, and *swish.* 59–58. It bounced into Benny's left guard hole, away at the back of the court. He let fly. The ball hit the edge of the rim, hesitated and dropped in. Now Benny was ahead, 60–59. About twenty seconds to go, said Teddy Karam, watching the oven timer. Morris Bird III wished Teddy had kept his big fat mouth shut. The ball rolled straight for Morris Bird III's center hole. It circled the hole, started to settle there but then thought better of it and rolled off to the side. Morris Bird III groaned. The ball slowly made its way down the side of the board, finally came to rest in Benny's left guard hole. Sorry, said Benny, and he let go a long shot that went straight in just as the bell from the oven timer began to ring. The final score: Goodman Military 62, Bird A&M (gallant to the very last) 59. When the bell stopped ringing, both Morris Bird III and Benny leaned back in their chairs, closed their eyes and made puffy hollow sounds with their breath. Oscar Adams went to Benny and clapped him on the back, and all the blood went out of poor Benny's face. Oscar then proceeded to make a great deal of noise. Benny fought to get back his breath. A little later, once Oscar had calmed down and Benny had regained his breath, they all agreed that it had been quite a game. Benny's mother came bearing one of her great feasts, and Benny grinned and hummed as he entered the game into his Scorebook. Benny's best subject at school was math, and the Scorebook was one of the greatest delights of his life. He had kept statistics on both the football and basketball seasons of the East 90th Street College Athletic Conference. All four of the member institutions had made up names for their players, and Benny's had been the most imaginative. Since his was a military school, he had named his players after generals. The twelve members of his basketball team were named Hannibal, Dwight, Eisen, Hower, Arnold, Benedict, Mack, Arthur, Bonaparte, Douglas, Grantleigh and Julius. His center, Eisen, led the league in scoring. Teddy Karam, the guy who liked to say things backwards, had a squad consisting of people named Senoj, Det, Marak, Drib, Smada, Epicnirp, Namurt, Yewed, Namdoog, Teksab, Llab and Tippit. (Naturally, Tippit was the center, and his name was the pride and joy of Teddy Karam's existence.) Morris Bird III named his basketball team after movie stars. The roster consisted of Bogart, Ladd, Cooper, Grant, Greenstreet, Lorre (a good dribbler, but weak under the boards), Rooney (a good set shot, but also weak under the boards), Hope, Crosby, Autry, Rogers and Flynn. At the suggestion of Benny Goodman, Oscar Adams named his winless team after famous losers and defeats. The roster consisted of Lee, Davis, Hitler, Mussolini, Dewey, Willkie, Landon, Hoover, York, Towne, Dunn and Kirk. All these names were recorded in Benny's Scorebook, as were the complete box scores of all the games in both sports. Benny typed out the box scores and the individual scoring statistics, and such neat typing the world had never seen. If you're going to do a thing, he told them, do it well. Otherwise don't bother. They all nodded at this. As a matter of fact, they nodded at just about everything he said. They didn't know how else to deal with him. His knowledge and his confidence made them believe him almost without question. And anyway, how do you argue with someone who lets you get in a word sideways about once every three weeks? Besides, as far as Morris Bird III was concerned, he was having too good a time. An argument might have jeopardized the Friday nights at the Goodmans', might have brought them to an end. Morris Bird III didn't want this to happen for anything. He'd never known people like the Goodmans, unless maybe you counted his grandmother. But the Goodmans were his grandmother multiplied by four, and their voices were his grandmother's voice multiplied by about ten thousand, and whenever he visited their place he couldn't get over all the laugher and palaver and flapping of arms. First of course there was Benny. Then there was his sister, the vast cushiony Sylvia with the voice like the streetcar going around the curve too fast. She looked like something that perhaps Errol Flynn would affix to the prow of a pirate ship, and she was a great one for hugging people. When Morris Bird III, Teddy Karam and Oscar Adams came to the Goodman home on Friday nights, she was almost always the one who let them into the house. She had these absolutely great teeth, and she liked to show them off along with all the rest of her. The sessions of the East 90th Street College Athletic Conference got under way at 7 sharp every Friday night, and she invariably sat in on the first couple of games, noisily and happily rooting for her brother. She would sort of jump and plop whenever he scored a touchdown or basket, and naturally she was a source of great distraction to his opponents. Not that they complained. They could have been dragged naked over hot coals all the way to Chicago and they wouldn't have uttered a peep. So what if it *did* impair their proficiency at Electric Football and Bas-Ket? There were rewards, and by far the largest of the rewards was the delicious fact that she hugged each of them. The hugs came about an hour after the sessions of the East 90th Street College Athletic Conference began. She went out on dates every Friday night, and her escorts (edgy young men who invariably had glittery eyes) arrived at about 8 o'clock. They were shown into the basement by Mrs. Goodman, and there Sylvia would introduce them to the boys. A different young man showed up each Friday night, and sometimes Sylvia laughed about this, telling the boys she guessed she just wasn't the type of girl the young men could take large steady doses of. Morris Bird III wasn't quite sure what she meant by this, but he didn't think it was quite as funny as she made it out to be. He sensed a sort of bravery—and a sort of despair—in her words, and for some dumb reason he almost felt sorry for her. Ah, but that was a lot of nonsense. Feeling sorry for Sylvia Goodman made about as much sense as feeling sorry for Mount Rushmore. If she couldn't take care of herself, no one could. And besides, what was the sense in *thinking about* Sylvia Goodman? She was to be *looked at* and *admired*. Who needed *thought?* Things of the mind were better saved for girls with flat chests. Sylvia Goodman may have had a great many faults (not that Morris Bird III had discovered any), but they certainly did *not* include a flat chest. This fact was literally pressed home on him every Friday night, shortly after the glittery young men showed up. Screeching and grinning, Sylvia never failed to hug Benny, Morris Bird III, Teddy Karam *and* Oscar Adams before leaving on her date. She always smelled like hothouse flowers, and her hugs made Morris Bird III's eyeballs feel as though the blood was about to burst from them. It wasn't really just Sylvia who hugged him; it was Woman; it was all Women, the dead and the living and the yet unborn. It was a wonder to him that her hugs didn't produce in him some sort of gasping squealing *fit*, all slobbery and twitchy and thick in the throat. Jasper Reed, the Hillbilly boy, called them Hissy Fits, and he used the phrase to describe his personal reaction to the sight of the spectacular Estelle Bunning, she of the purplish lipstick and the sweaters with horizontal stripes. But it was just as apt in connection with Sylvia Goodman. More so, in fact—at least as far as Morris Bird III was concerned. After all, he'd never been hugged by Estelle Bunning. But he *had* been hugged by Sylvia Goodman, and oh, ah, some day he just bet he would be needing an oxygen tent. Was oxygen any good to counteract a Hissy Fit? He hoped so. Ah boy, the joys of Electric Football and Bas-Ket. I'm glad to see you guys enjoy yourselves so much when you come here, Benny told them, and then he grinned, and Morris Bird III knew old Benny wasn't missing a thing. No one in that family missed much. Benny's father, whose full name was Dr. Bernard M. Goodman, was a professor of English at Western Reserve. He was tall and hairless, with bony wrists and a voice full of saliva, and his specialty was modern English and American poetry, but he was a good head: he never pressed it on anyone. Sometimes he went down into the basement and watched the members of the East 90th Street College Athletic Conference have at each other, but he never horned in. He wasn't one of those hearty professional parents who talked too much and were forever smiling for no reason. He spoke when he was spoken to, but otherwise he kept his bright remarks to himself. Benny only commented one time on his father, but his words were all that was needed to be said. The Old Man's okay, he told the others. He believes a whole lot in what he calls Dignity. To him, that means letting me do what I want, as long as I don't hurt anybody. When he talks, he's usually got something to say. Otherwise he just sort of hangs loose, know what I mean? Now don't get me wrong. I don't mean he sits in the corner with his hands folded or anything like *that*. All I'm saying is that he doesn't see anything wrong with letting me go the way I go. If I get out of line, then whappo, he's down on me real hard, but otherwise he leaves me alone. He calls it Dignity. But just don't get the idea he's some sort of absentminded professor dumbhead. You should all of you be such dumbheads. (You want to know something? If he wanted to, he could sit down right now and recite poems for oh I bet three or four hours and never do the same poem twice. And all of them full of $64 words, you know? Words that not even *I* can understand, and that's saying a whole lot.) Ah, good old Benny. In the immortal words of the great Oscar Adams, Benny was some talker. Those Friday nights, what with his palaver plus his sister's squealing plus the warm words of his mother (a stout woman with a mole on her nose, Mrs. Goodman also spent a lot of time watching the games and rooting for Benny—but joyfully, not in a way that made the other three boys angry) plus the rich salivary syllables of his father (syllables that came only in answer to a question, syllables that never had the flavor of the buttinsky) plus the comments, criticisms, outbursts, laughter and declamations of the three guests . . . well, when seven such people were gathered in one place, a good time was almost guaranteed. For Morris Bird III, there had never been such a time. He'd never really understood the pleasures of silliness and makebelieve. At his own home, now that his grandmother was back in Paradise Falls, there was no silliness. There were plenty of pearshaped tones, and there was plenty of worrying about the absence of the Extra, and you always walked softly because that way no one became angry with you, and you understood that somehow you were being cheated, and the Friday nights at the Goodmans' made the somehow perfectly clear. In all his life, Morris Bird III had never heard a kid of Benny Goodman's age talk about Dignity. He'd heard adults talk about it, and he understood something of what they meant, but to hear the words come from *Benny,* someone so young and all, well, it was a very remarkable thing. Great day in the morning, if at *thirteen* Benny knew so much, what would he be like when he grew up? The thought was almost scary. Huh, when did Benny have time just to be a kid? Whoo, you'd think that later would be time enough for all the heavy thinking. But it took all kinds, and Benny's being the way he was discombobulated not a soul. But then Benny had to go and die, and it all had to do with the fact that a colored man named Earle P. Starr had a fight with a woman, and oh boy, oh boy, all the questions that came from *that*. Questions, questions. Sometimes, as far as Morris Bird III was concerned, he wished he could drill a hole in his head and let them all dribble out, like catsup maybe, or maple syrup. The events that led to the death of Benny Goodman were directly traceable to the formation of the Gordon Park Berardinos. If it hadn't been for the team, Benny never would have been away over on Superior Avenue at Ansel Road, and thus he wouldn't have been killed. The Gordon Park Berardinos—the name was Benny's idea, and so, for that matter, was the team. The idea of the team came to him shortly after the close of the basketball season of the East 90th Street College Athletic Conference. He was having lunch with his three associates in the Addison Junior High cafeteria. Eyeing his wieners and beans guardedly (and no wonder; they had been known, it was said, to fight back), he pushed them around his plate with a fork, then made a hollow exasperated noise in the base of his throat. He laid down the fork, looked at his three associates and said: This time it's going to be for real. You follow my reasoning? They looked at him blankly. Naturally, they did not follow his reasoning. He was a great one for pulling little tricks like that. Words would emerge from his private thoughts; if you didn't understand the words, you were made out to be a dumbhead. But how were you supposed to know his private thoughts? Well, anyway, it was a little device he used to keep his three associates in their place. It was sneaky, sure, but wasn't sneakiness a part of being smart? And anyway, it wasn't all *that* smart. If it *had* been, Morris Bird III never would have seen through it. So, that day in the cafeteria, he wasn't angry with Benny. The thought would come out soon enough. His time wasn't so valuable that he couldn't afford to wait. And he didn't have to wait long. Benny laid out the thought quickly, saying: What I mean is, let's have a for real baseball team. In Class F. We got enough pretty good players right in our homeroom. Now, don't look at me like that. *I* don't want to play. Couldn't if I wanted to. But I can get things organized. I'll be the manager. How about it, huh? What do you think? Well, they thought it was a pretty good idea. As a matter of fact, they thought it was a *fine* idea. Good, said Benny, and the first thing he did was delegate old Oscar Adams to recruit players. You *bet* I will, said Oscar. He made fists as he said the words, and it really wasn't very surprising that the roster of the Gordon Park Berardinos was filled by that time the next day. In the meantime, Benny had telephoned the city recreation department and the newspaper that sponsored Class F. Leave the paper work to me, he said. It's a snap. Then he tore a sheet of paper from his looseleaf notebook and had all the players sign their names, ages, addresses and telephone numbers. They all were from Mrs. Principe's homeroom, and none of them had given Oscar Adams a bit of trouble. Late in the lunch period, Benny gathered all twelve of the players in a corner of the cafeteria, sat them down at a long table and told them: We'll practice twice a week, on Tuesdays and Thursdays. I don't want any excuses from anyone. Practices'll begin at four o'clock in the afternoon. I don't know where they'll be held yet, but I'll let you know. Bird here has to work in the library after school, but he'll get to the practices as soon as he's able. As for the rest of you, I know for a fact none of you does anything after school except mess around, so don't bother with excuses. Adams here is in charge of seeing to it that all of you show up. We're going to be the best Class F team in the city, or we're going to die in the attempt. It's only a game, sure, but it just so happens that scores are kept and winning's better than losing, and don't let anybody tell you different. I mean, I've been poor and I've been rich, and believe me rich is better. That's an old saying I picked up somewhere from one of my relatives, and it's a good thing to remember. Old Benny, when he talks you listen. He doesn't talk just to be beating his gums. The following Tuesday the first practice was held. It took place in a grassy field in Rockefeller Park not far from the corner of Superior Avenue and Ansel Road. All twelve players showed up. It was late in March, and patches of snow still were on the ground, but Benny had them work out for more than two hours. Run! Run! Run! he shouted. Show a little hustle! He leaned against a tree and clapped his hands, whistled through his teeth, whooped, hollered. Two nights later, he announced to the team that henceforth and forevermore it would be known as the Gordon Park Berardinos. Everyone except Oscar Adams protested. What sort of name was *that?* There wasn't a one of them—except Benny—who could even *spell* it. Oh sure, they knew where the name had *come* from. Johnny Berardino was a utility infielder for the Indians, and big deal. He was just a substitute. He only got in a game when Joe Gordon or Lou Boudreau was hurt, which meant he was the kind of a guy you were lucky to hear from maybe once a month. They voiced these objections to Benny, and Benny told them: Yeah, yeah, I *know,* and that's *exactly why* I chose his name. That doesn't make sense to any of you, does it? I can tell by the looks on your handsome faces. Well then, think of it this way: Johnny Berardino isn't exactly the bestknown of the Indian players, right? No, when you think of the Indians you don't very often think of *him*, do you? Well, *that's just the point*. Everybody and his brother is naming teams after Gordon and Boudreau and Bob Feller and all the other big stars. So, ho hum, should we be the umpteenth million team to be named after Lou Boudreau? I say *no*. I say we're *us*, and I say we're *different*, and I say we're going to set ourselves off from everybody else; I say the team is going to be called the Gordon Park *Berardinos*. That way, no one'll have trouble remembering us. Okay? Now then, how could anyone argue with such logic? No more objections were offered. The practices continued. The perfect attendance record was maintained. And even those players who didn't particularly like Benny (which meant most of the players on the team) had to admit he knew a good deal about the game. He quickly determined where each player was best suited, and he brooked no dissent. When Morris Bird III was installed at shortstop, Oscar Adams wasn't a bit happy. But, when he went to Benny about it, Benny didn't even give him a chance to open his mouth. Adams, said Benny, you're very valuable to this team—but not at shortstop. I know. I know. Lou Boudreau is your very favorite player in the whole world, but that gives you no big fat right to play short. You're going to play right field, and you're going to hit a lot of home runs, and that'll make you a very valuable man, so let's not hear you going around moaning like a stuck pig. Bird is the shortstop on this team, and that's all there is *to* it. *You*, you big bucket of cat whoop, you play shortstop like my Uncle Sidney, who's fiftythree and got heart trouble. So speak to me not, dear heart, about the subject. It's closed. Your friend Benny has spoken. And, nodding meekly,

Oscar Adams told Benny okay, okay, fine, if that's the way you want it. And Benny assured him it *was* most definitely the way he wanted it, and from that moment on there was nary a word from Oscar Adams about shortstop. Benny was killed at about 6:30 in the evening of Thursday, April 22, 1948. Practice had just ended. He and Oscar Adams and Teddy Karam and the third baseman, a boy named Tom Hollingsworth, were crossing Superior at Ansel. The light was with them. Morris Bird III, who had crossed on the previous light, was waiting for them at the far side of the street. The car came east on Superior. It was a 1938 Dodge, and it was on the wrong side of the street. The driver was Earle P. Starr. The next morning, the paper told all about Earle P. Starr. Seems he had had some sort of an argument with his lady friend. At any rate, according to what he told police, he went to a saloon and started drinking. After spending about five hours in that saloon, he decided to go out and drive around and clear his head. The saloon was on Central Avenue near East 79th Street, several miles south of Superior and Ansel. He got into his car and started driving and the next thing he knew he was at Superior and Ansel and he was driving on the wrong side of the street. Oscar Adams and Teddy Karam and Tom Hollingsworth got out of the way. Benny Goodman, being crippled, didn't. He was facing the 1938 Dodge when it hit him. It did not send him flying. It simply knocked him down and ran over him. There was rather a loud thump, but that was all. No screams or anything like that. The car careened around the corner onto Ansel, and Morris Bird III saw the license number: AR-303-JZ. The car did not stop. It disappeared south on Ansel. People came running from all over. Morris Bird III made a mental note of the license number. Oscar Adams was weeping and wailing. Everyone ran to the center of the street where Benny lay. His eyes were open. There was no blood. One of his jacket sleeves was torn, but otherwise nothing appeared to be wrong with him. As far as Morris Bird III was concerned, this had to be a miracle. After all, the car had run clear *over* Benny. The four boys squatted around him. A dozen adults also squatted around him. He tried to grin. He lasted about a minute, and then he died. But he did get off one final crack. Just before he died, he looked at the weeping Oscar Adams and he said, whispering: Come on, you big . . . goof. You look . . . like . . . uh, you look like you . . . you look like you just threw . . . up . . . all over your own . . . birthday . . . cake.

Morris Bird III gave the license number to the police, and within an hour Earle P. Starr had been arrested. Now Earle P. Starr was in the penitentiary, and he was doing one to ten years for second-degree manslaughter. There had been no trial. Had there been one, Morris Bird III would have been called to testify. But Earle P. Starr had pleaded guilty, and so Morris Bird III never had a chance to meet the man. Which probably was just as well. He had no idea what Earle P. Starr was like, except that he was colored, fiftysix years of age, a veteran of World War I and lived on Scovill Avenue. This information had come from the newspapers. Benny's picture was carried on the front page of all three of them. The stories had made a great fuss over what they called Benny's *courage* in managing the Gordon Park Berardinos even though he was crippled. The stories gave Morris Bird III a thick feeling at the roof of his mouth, and he bet Benny would have been made absolutely ill all over.

Benny was buried the next day in the family plot of his mother's people. The cemetery was small, and the graves were very close together. The headstones made Morris Bird III think of rushhour in a Hough Avenue trackless trolley. He did not attend the funeral (he didn't know whether he would be welcome at a Jewish funeral, and he didn't have the nerve to ask), but he and Teddy Karam and Oscar Adams did visit the grave the following Sunday. They were taken there by Oscar's father in a big fat shiny 1948 Fraser. It was a great car. You couldn't feel any bumps. It smelled good. Mr. Adams was a short dark man with a Teddy Roosevelt mustache. He owned a small Kaiser-Fraser agency on Superior Avenue near East 55th Street. All the way out to the cemetery, he talked about automobiles. According to him, the Kaiser and the Fraser were about ten years ahead of their time. He said he hoped the public would understand what a bargain the cars were. He didn't sound very optimistic. The public, he said, you got to go slow for the public. Otherwise you leave everybody behind. People sometimes don't have too much of the old imagination. But I'll tell you one thing: if anyone can sell these cars, it's Yours Truly, Charley Adams. And if *I* can't sell them, no one can.

The earth over Benny's grave was mounded, raw, a dirty sickish pale gummy brown. There was no headstone yet. It was surrounded by the graves of people named Berkowitz. They apparently were the relatives of Benny's mother. Morris Bird III and Teddy Karam and Oscar Adams stood at one end of the grave. Morris Bird III's armpits and forehead were moist. He looked at the sky. He saw nothing in particular. A long time ago his grandmother had urged him to look at the sky at least once a day. It'll help you keep things in perspective, she had said. And so now he looked at the sky. And saw nothing in particular. It was a cold and gray and weary sky, and it threatened rain, and big deal. He looked at Teddy Karam, and then he looked at Oscar Adams. Teddy Karam was scraping a toe of a shoe in the grass at the foot of the grave. Oscar Adams was sniffling. Morris Bird III sighed. They had brought no flowers or anything like that. He supposed they should have chipped in for flowers. He was cold. He rubbed his hands together. He blew on his hands. He looked around. He saw nothing much except the riot of tombstones. A few yards behind them, the Fraser was parked on a gravel drive. Mr. Adams sat inside the car. He was reading the sports section from the morning paper. Morris Bird III blinked, examined the grave again. There were no flowers on the grave. Well, maybe the Goodman family had asked that flowers be omitted. This made Morris Bird III glad. Dead was dead, and why kill flowers to celebrate the death of something else? One kind of death was enough. Now he was very happy that he and Teddy Karam and Oscar Adams had not chipped in for flowers. He looked down at his feet. His hands were shaking. He made fists. He looked off toward a tree. Now he didn't dare look at the grave. A horrible thought had gone crashing across his mind. It had to do with the thing inside the grave. He wanted to *look* at it. He shuddered. Teddy Karam frowned at him. He shrugged. Teddy Karam looked away. Oscar Adams still was sniffling. Morris Bird III closed his eyes, closed them tightly, closed them so tightly that he saw a big green balloon that grew and grew and grew like a glob of paint. Finally it faded, and then he saw little white dots that danced with the rhythm of his heart. He was happy to be seeing these colors and shapes. They prevented him from speculating on what the thing inside the grave looked like. He cleared his throat. Then, without saying anything, he moved away from the grave. Teddy Karam and Oscar Adams followed him. They didn't say anything either. They all returned to the car. On the way home, Mr. Adams discussed automatic transmissions and suspension bars.

That night, Morris Bird III walked over to the house on East 90th Street and paid a call on the Goodman family. The front room was full of people. He didn't recognize any of them. Mr. Goodman met him at the front door and took him back to the kitchen. He wasn't introduced to the people in the front room, which bothered him not a bit. He'd not come to this house to see *them*.

Mrs. Goodman and Sylvia were sitting at the kitchen table. Mrs. Goodman's eyes seemed big. A glass of something purple was on the table in front of her. She looked at Morris Bird III and asked him if he'd seen the aerial on the roof. He told her no, he hadn't noticed. She told him he really should go outside and take a look. It's really something, she said. Benny would have been very pleased with it. Very proud.

Sylvia patted her mother's hand. There, there, she said, and her voice was low, not a bit screechy. She wore a black dress, and it made her appear almost shapeless.

The television set's in the front room, said Mr. Goodman. It was installed yesterday. We'd wanted to surprise him. It has a twelve-inch screen. It's a Muntz. On my salary, a Muntz is all I can afford.

Yes, said Morris Bird III.

He loved baseball, said Mrs. Goodman.

We got it so he could watch all the games, said Mr. Goodman.

Uh huh, said Morris Bird III, nodding.

It's a good thing what WEWS is doing, said Mrs. Goodman. Televising the games, I mean.

Morris Bird III nodded.

We appreciate your being here, said Mr. Goodman.

Thank you, said Morris Bird III.

Mrs. Goodman drank some of the purple.

Sylvia frowned at her mother, then she almost smiled at Morris Bird III. It was as though she had sent him a telegram.

Mrs. Goodman licked her lips. This is very fine, she said.

The people in the front room are relatives of ours, said Mr. Goodman. I didn't think you'd want to meet all of them.

A real cherry flavor, said Mrs. Goodman.

Mr. Goodman patted Morris Bird III on a shoulder. Don't worry, he said. I won't quote any poetry.

You can if you want to, said Morris Bird III.

Mrs. Goodman burst into tears. So did Sylvia. They embraced each other.

Morris Bird III looked at Mr. Goodman and said: Well, maybe I better be on my way.

You're a very good boy, said Mr. Goodman.

I'm nothing, said Morris Bird III. All I do is stand here.

Mrs. Goodman pulled herself away from Sylvia. She wiped at

93

her eyes. She blinked at Morris Bird III and said: Don't contradict my husband.

Morris Bird III shrugged. His eyes were warm.

It could have given him a lot of pleasure, said Mrs. Goodman.

She means the television, Mr. Goodman said to Morris Bird III.

God brings things down, said Mrs. Goodman.

Morris Bird III frowned.

We don't blame the poor *schwartzer,* said Mrs. Goodman. It was God.

Sure, said Morris Bird III.

If it hadn't been the *schwartzer,* it would have been something else, said Mrs. Goodman. A bolt of lightning maybe.

Morris Bird III looked at his hands. Yeah, he said.

My wife is a secret Calvinist, said Mr. Goodman.

Morris Bird III looked at Mr. Goodman.

Never mind, said Mr. Goodman, shrugging. It's not worth explaining.

He liked you the best, said Mrs. Goodman.

Me? said Morris Bird III.

Yes, said Mrs. Goodman. He told me, he said: Mama, this kid Morris Bird III is going to amount to something. He *listens.* And then Benny told me, he said: Sometimes I wish *I* could listen, too.

Still waters, said Sylvia.

Oh *crap,* said Morris Bird III.

They all stared at him.

He started to cry.

Boy, he hated tears. They had no *purpose.* They mended nothing, brought nothing back to life. They were unmanly, stupid, embarrassing. And, when you finally got right down to it, they were kind of Fake. Standing there in the kitchen of the Goodman home, standing there and crying, standing there and balling his fists and stuffing them into his eyesockets, standing there with his chest jerking, standing there with pinched sounds coming from somewhere behind his nose, he kept telling himself: FORGET IT. KILL IT. TURN IT OFF. THIS IS A PERFORMANCE. WHO DO YOU THINK YOU ARE? PAUL MUNI OR SOMEBODY? Mr. and Mrs. Goodman and Sylvia clustered around him and made clucking noises, and all he could think of was: IS SYLVIA GOING TO HUG ME? Which she did. And so did Mrs. Goodman. And even *Mr.* Goodman. Big deal.

More or less by acclamation, Teddy Karam became the new manager of the Gordon Park Berardinos. About two weeks after Benny's death, a reporter and photographer from one of the afternoon papers came to watch the team practice. Teddy Karam talked at great length with the reporter. He said the team would try to do it for old Benny. He talked of the determination the players felt. Oh, he talked and talked, did Teddy Karam, and his words were about as honest as a cardboard battleship, and the reporter took down every one of them, for posterity or whatever. The story appeared the next day. Only one picture was carried. It was of Teddy Karam. His face was grim, dedicated. The word *courage* appeared in the story eleven times.

After reading the story, Morris Bird III almost had to run to the bathroom and york.

There was not a peep from Oscar Adams. Even though Benny was dead, and even though he—Oscar—could have intimidated Teddy Karam into moving him to shortstop, he said nothing. One afternoon in May he explained his attitude to Morris Bird III. Not that Morris Bird III had asked for an explanation. Not that Morris Bird III gave a whoop one way or the other. If Oscar chose not to rock the boat, fine.

But silence is never enough. So Oscar had to explain himself. Bird, he said, you don't have to worry about short. Far as I'm concerned, you can play short until you fall down dead. It was what Benny wanted. And I'm here to see to it that all the things he wanted get carried through just the way he wanted them. You follow me?

Yeah, said Morris Bird III, I follow you.

And am I right or am I right?

You're right.

Benny, he was smart.

Yeah.

He told me I was a good shortstop, but you was a better one.

Oh?

Uh huh. He really liked you as a shortstop a whole lot. Because, if he hadn't of liked you a whole lot, he would of picked me. But he told me not to feel bad. He told me I was a real good shortstop, good enough to play there on most any team. It was just that he said you were a *little bit* better. A *little bit*. Just a little tiny *bit*.

Oh? That so? I seem to remember he said you played shortstop worse than some uncle of his who has a heart condition.

He didn't say no such thing!

Okay, said Morris Bird III. My mistake.

That night, before going to sleep, Morris Bird III sent himself a little telegram. It said: PEOPLE WHO CHOP UP OTHER PEOPLE THE WAY YOU CHOPPED UP OSCAR ADAMS STINK. SO HE'D BUILT UP A LITTLE LIE. SO GREAT. DID YOU HAVE TO CHOP HIM UP? EVERYBODY FAKES ONCE IN A WHILE, BUT YOU HAD TO BE A BIG MAN AND GO AND CALL HIM ON IT. YOU STINK.

But then The Voice of Cleveland & Northeastern Ohio ended Morris Bird III's career as a member of the Gordon Park Berardinos. And Oscar Adams became shortstop. Which was very logical. Ah, things forever and relentlessly changed, and Benny's wish no longer had any bearing on the situation, and so Oscar Adams moved in. And, after winning their first two games, the Gordon Park Berardinos lost eleven straight. Oscar Adams made an average of three errors per game, while hitting an average of two home runs per game. Which meant that all the defeats were by scores of 17–11 and like that there. And Teddy Karam, poor Teddy Karam, he was the *pitcher*.

What Morris Bird III needed—and he admitted it—was something or someone to straighten him out. He wished his grandmother weren't dying. If she were in good shape and had her wits about her, maybe she would have been able to get his thinking on an even keel. But she was down there in Paradise Falls, and she cried a great deal, and it was only a question of time before she died, and she was no help at all. Which was great. Which was absolutely ducky. Boy, how he did ever envy little kids. In their way of seeing things, a line could be drawn through a problem, and most of the time it could be solved. For a little kid, there was no such thing as doubt. He remembered his own time as a little kid. The big words had been Bravery and Obligation and Unselfishness. He had learned them from his grandmother and a lot of other people. In those days, there had been plenty of cans to kick. He had been good old Jack Armstrong, and he'd kept his eye on the sky. Almost every Sunday his grandmother had taken him and Sandra to church—an Episcopal church with high windows and a good smell. The rector, a big booming man whose name was the Rev. Gar P. Pallister, was a particular favorite of the grandmother's. You listen when he talks, the grandmother told the children. He *cares*. He's no shouldershrugger. How do I know? Oh, I just *know*. I'm not altogether a total loss as a judge of character. And so Morris Bird III listened to the Rev. Gar P. Pallister, and one day in the sermon the Rev. Gar P. Pallister said: In the language of today, I suppose there are some people who would call Jesus a sissy. After all, we call Him The Gentle Jesus, isn't that so? We see pictures of Him surrounded by lambs, and the temptation is to say to ourselves: Ah, how sweet. But, if we assume this attitude, we miss the point. We view Jesus as a sissy, and no one likes a sissy. Jesus was no sissy. Jesus had strength. His strength was Love, and there is nothing sissified in Love. He was never One for drawing back. There is a bravery in gentleness, in patience, in offering Love where none is sought, where in fact it has been given an unqualified rejection. The world is weary, and the world is scarred, and disillusionment rules the day, but do we for one moment believe we are lost? The answer must be no. We still understand the strength of Love. We still have the capacity to indulge in it. And as Christians, not as sissies. The world abounds with fraud and evil, but it also abounds with Love—if we *allow* the Love, the abiding gentleness of Jesus Christ, to invade our souls. And proudly. Resolutely. Rejecting the spurious. The Son of God was no Milksop, and it is no disgrace to Love. Let us pray.

Yeah. Bravery. Love. Ministers. Sermons. Sure.

But what did Love have to do with a colored man named Earle P. Starr getting drunk? What did it have to do with day-old bread? How come, if it meant so much, did some people have to surround themselves with stuffed ducks and rubber ducks and little ducks that moved on red wheels and went *wack*?

And what did Bravery have to do with people who called a crippled kid Sunshine? What did it have to do with sitting all by yourself and playing raindrop race with someone named Claramae who didn't even exist? How come, if it meant so much, the brave ones (like, for instance, Benny Goodman) got squashed?

Not that Morris Bird III didn't understand a little of Love and Bravery. He did. And not that he didn't appreciate them. He did. They were warm, and they had a whole lot to do with Being Good, and his grandmother and Stanley Chaloupka and Benny Goodman and a great many other people had taught him their value.

But no one had taught him to understand Fake, and it sur-rounded him, and it was driving him out of his mind. (Okay. At thirteen maybe he was being extreme. What right did he have to let *anything* drive him out of his mind? But he felt what he felt, and so maybe things bothered him more than they bothered the next person.)

Fake had nothing to do with Love and Bravery—that much he knew for sure. Which just meant that the sum and total of a person's now had to be guided by more than those two things.

Somehow you had to separate the sheep from the goats and go on from there, take it in your stride, not make a great big federal case out of every Fake thing that came along. Okay, fine, but how much Fake could a person shrug away?

Fake was Arlene Kovacs, who lived three doors down the street and wore falsies.

Fake was Republicans.

Fake was killing off poor Sonny Tufts at the end of the picture because there was only one girl and Alan Ladd already had her.

Fake was interviewing that guy H. Norman Schwarzkopf on *Gangbusters* by means of something called proxy.

Fake was not saying what you meant.

Fake was saying what you meant, but saying it as though you were joking.

Fake was worrying about the Extra when you already had more money than about 85% of the people in the whole world.

Fake was rooting against the Indians when they were losing, rooting for them when they were winning.

Fake was going to a cemetery and feeling nothing except an urge to peek inside a grave.

Fake was using tears to give a Performance.

Fake was wearing sweaters with horizontal stripes that called attention to yourself.

Fake was saying We'll See instead of an outright No.

Fake was feeling disgusted with a poor old dying woman because she cried.

Fake was not liking Orson Welles because he had Rita Hayworth and you didn't.

Fake was lying about how good a shortstop you were.

Fake was *all* lying.

Fake was knocking President Truman when all he was trying to do was his job.

Fake was never smiling.

Fake was always smiling.

Fake was automatically disliking people you didn't understand.

Fake was going to a dead kid's house and wondering about a hug.

Fake was telling the Oscar Adamses of this world what you thought of them—but only when you knew they couldn't fight back.

Fake was buying dayold bread at the same time as you were gathering an expensive and cluttery collection of china owls.

Fake was calling someone Gunboats just because you didn't have anything better to do.

Fake was thinking Fred C. Dobbs was a great guy.

Fred C. Dobbs was the principal character in the greatest movie Morris Bird III had ever seen. It was called *The Treasure of the*

Sierra Madre, and he had gone to theaters seven times to see it. On three of those occasions, he had sat through the picture twice. Ten times watching one movie was an alltime world's record for him. His previous record was six, for a picture called *The Pride of the Yankees,* starring Gary Cooper. It had been a great picture, too. It had made him cry.

The first time he saw *The Treasure of the Sierra Madre* was in February of 1948. He and the other three members of the East 90th Street College Athletic Conference went downtown to the Hippodrome Theater on Euclid Avenue. They saw a Saturday matinee. It was Teddy Karam's birthday, and so the movie was his treat. He paid the admissions with money from his punchboards and his 5-cents-a-day loan business. He even bought candy for everyone. Morris Bird III had a Hershey bar with almonds.

The Treasure of the Sierra Madre took place in Mexico. It had to do with the adventures of three prospectors named Curtin, Howard and Fred C. Dobbs. Curtin was a young fellow, and he was a pretty decent sort of person. Howard, the only really professional prospector of the three, was a loud-mouthed old galoot with a lot of energy and common sense.

But Fred C. Dobbs . . .

Ah, that Fred C. Dobbs . . .

Now *there* was a dirty rat. The dirtiest, scroungiest, most greedy, tricky, evil, furry, hairy, dribbling, raunchy scum of the earth Morris Bird III ever had seen in his whole entire life. With Fred C. Dobbs, the big thing in life was Gimme. When he and Curtin and Howard came upon a vein of gold, this Fred C. Dobbs became convinced the others were out to get rid of him so they could divide his share. It preyed so much on his mind that he got to talking to himself. Muttering, throwing dirty looks at the other two men, lacing his words with spit and venom, he said: *If you know what's good for you, you won't monkey around with*

Fred
C.
Dobbs.

The more gold they dug up, the crazier Fred C. Dobbs behaved. The richer he became, the more worms showed up to feast on his soul. As the picture progressed, Morris Bird III sort of scrunched down in his seat and hugged his knees. He kept thinking of his mother and china owls and dayold bread.

And, finally, Fred C. Dobbs fell completely apart. He betrayed both Curtin and Howard and made off with all the gold. But did he really gain anything? No. He was jumped by a gang of Mexican bandits, and his head was chopped off.

And, the funny thing was, the gold returned to the earth. The bandits didn't know that Fred C. Dobbs was carrying gold. The only reason they killed him was because they wanted his burros and the hides that were strapped to the burros' backs. All the little bags of gold dust also were strapped to the burros' backs, but the bandits thought the bags contained only sand, and so they ripped open the bags and let the gold dust blow away.

So what did the movie mean?

Was it just some sort of big joke?

No. Not to Morris Bird III.

The thing was, he sort of cringed. The thing was, he kept seeing his mother.

Which made this, no matter how uncomfortable he was, the greatest movie he had ever seen.

The members of the East 90th Street College Athletic Conference held a spirited conversation about the picture. It took place in the Blue Boar Cafeteria, where they stopped for a snack before heading home. The food was Dutch treat; Teddy Karam had used up all his punchboard and interest money—or at least that was what he *said.* Actually, he'd probably simply used up all the money he'd *cared* to use up. Teddy Karam broke was like Mr. Kellogg being out of corn flakes.

Morris Bird III had a dish of mashed potatoes and gravy and a glass of milk. Teddy Karam had a hamburger, French fries and a cup of hot chocolate. Benny Goodman had a glass of milk. Oscar Adams, after borrowing forty cents from Morris Bird III, had a ham sandwich on rye, a dish of mashed potatoes and gravy, a glass of milk and a dish of rice pudding with raisins. It all vanished in maybe two minutes, and then he burped about seventyfour thousand times. He didn't contribute an awful lot to the discussion.

"I don't care what you say," said Teddy Karam. "That guy Fred C. Dobbs had the right idea."

"Oh?" said Benny Goodman.

"Yeah," said Teddy Karam. "I know, maybe some people would call him greedy, but I call him smart."

"Because he was a hog?" Benny wanted to know.

"No," said Teddy.

"Then how was he smart?"

"Because he thought of Number One. Because he trusted nobody."

"And where did it get him?"

"Ahh," said Teddy, snorting, "that's just Hollywood. He had to get punished. If that story had of taken place in real life, he would of gotten away."

"And that makes him a good guy?"

"It makes him a *winner*."

"And the winners are the good guys?"

"Sure. Why not? Who ever hears about losers?"

Benny Goodman shook his head.

"What's *that* supposed to mean?" Teddy Karam asked him.

Benny Goodman smiled. "It means you stink."

"Huh?"

"Don't get in an uproar. Anybody who talks the way you do *knows* he stinks."

Teddy Karam looked at Morris Bird III.

"Don't look at *me*," said Morris Bird III. He was enjoying this. He'd not forgotten the twenty dollars he'd had to pay Teddy Karam for that old wagon.

Teddy Karam's face was dark. He gave Benny Goodman a dirty look. "I don't like people to say I stink."

Benny Goodman's smile became an outright grin. "Oh come off it. You do, too. It means you're a real hard guy. The way you see things, it's the biggest compliment you could get."

A gentle belch from Oscar Adams. He shifted his position, patted his stomach. "Sometimes I eat too fast," he said.

No one paid any attention to him.

None of the darkness had left Teddy Karam's face. "And what's wrong with being hard?" he asked Benny Goodman.

"Nothing," said Benny Goodman. "You'll probably go far. Like you said, it's good to be a winner."

Teddy Karam took a large bite from his hamburger. "Yeah," he said through his food, "everybody knows that. My old man, he says: Nothing in this life is given to you. The things you want, you go out and you grab them. You take care of Number One. Everybody *else* is taking care of Number One, so there's no sin in it. It's just human nature."

Morris Bird III spoke up. "You mean it's human nature to ream everybody you think maybe is blocking you out from something?"

"Right with Eversharp."

"I don't believe that."

"Tough."

"Karam?" said Benny Goodman.

"Yeah?" said Teddy Karam, drinking some of his hot chocolate.

"What happened to Fred C. Dobbs?"

"He died. He got his head chopped off. But that was only Hollywood."

"Okay. Let's say it was only Hollywood. But what about the other two guys? What happened when they found out all the gold dust had been blown away?"

"They laughed."

"Doesn't that tell you something?"

"It tells me they were crazy."

"They weren't crazy."

"Maybe *you* don't call it crazy," said Teddy Karam. "*Me*, though, I call it *crazy*. They lost all that money, and all they did was laugh. They should of been taken off to the boobyhatch."

"No," said Benny Goodman. "Those two guys were *men*."

"Men? Sure. Big deal," said Teddy Karam.

"They *took it in their stride*. Fred C. Dobbs, the guy who was always looking out for Number One, the gold destroyed *him*."

"Hey, this is some conversation," said Oscar Adams. "Real deep and all, I mean. Interesting."

Teddy Karam ignored Oscar Adams. He swallowed, glared at Benny Goodman. "So?"

"So come *on*," said Benny Goodman. "You're not dumb. You know what I'm driving at. Fred C. Dobbs, the bigdeal always-looking-out-for-Number-One guy, was really the weak sister. He was destroyed, wasn't he?"

"So?"

"So it makes them stronger than he was."

Teddy Karam was silent.

Benny Goodman leaned forward. "You listen to old Benny. There's a whole lot more to everything than reaming everybody in sight. Old Benny says so, and old Benny knows."

"The shadow *knowwwws*," said Oscar Adams, cackling.

"Thank you very much," Benny Goodman said to Oscar Adams.

Oscar Adams shut up and looked away; his face was a little red.

"Yeah, Adams," said Teddy Karam, "please don't interrupt The Great Man when he's honoring us with his great words of wisdom."

"Thank *you*, too," said Benny, grinning at Teddy Karam. "It's good to know that my great brain is appreciated."

"Bluh," said Teddy Karam, making a face.

"Nobody gets Benny Goodman mad," said Benny Goodman.

"Life's too short. Benny Goodman's got too much to do. He can't bother himself with getting mad." A hesitation, then: "Me, I wouldn't mind living like that old guy, the one called Howard."

"Because he had all those babes fussing over him in that village?" Teddy Karam wanted to know.

"Sure? Why not? But it's more than that. He had balance."

"Huh?" said Teddy Karam.

"Balance. I mean, he never let things get the best of him."

"My old man says good losers always get tromped on," said Teddy Karam.

Benny Goodman shrugged. "A lot of people say that. But saying so doesn't make it true."

"Oh. A wise guy. He knows more than my old man."

"I wouldn't be surprised," said Benny Goodman.

Morris Bird III laughed.

Teddy Karam glared at him.

Morris Bird III laughed some more. He laughed so hard he started to cough. He washed away the cough with a gulp of milk.

"The world's full of wise guys," said Teddy Karam.

"Sticks and stones," Morris Bird III told him.

Teddy Karam made a fist.

"Come on," said Morris Bird III.

Teddy Karam just looked at Morris Bird III.

"Come on come on come *on*," said Morris Bird III.

Teddy Karam looked at Oscar Adams.

"What's going on?" said Oscar Adams.

Benny Goodman started to laugh.

"Come on," said Morris Bird III to Teddy Karam. "You want to make something out of it?"

Oscar Adams started laughing along with Benny Goodman.

Now Morris Bird III was grinning at Teddy Karam. He knew Teddy Karam pretty well. Oh, Teddy Karam was a tough *talker* all right, but no one ever had seen him *do* anything tough. He was a pretty good guy, was old Teddy Karam, but now and then you had to call him. (Not that Morris Bird III was much of a fighter. He'd had exactly three fights in his whole entire life, and he'd lost two of them. But now and then dignity demanded that he draw a line. This was one of those times, and he wasn't particularly afraid. Particularly.)

Teddy Karam looked down at his fist. He was sweating a little, which was kind of peculiar for February when he was sitting in a drafty cafeteria.

"Aw, come on," said Benny Goodman, choking. "Come on, Karam, get off your high horse. Nobody was making fun of you. Or your old man. Or anybody else."

"He's laughing at me," said Teddy Karam, nodding in the direction of Morris Bird III.

"Well, who isn't laughing at you?" said Benny. "I'm laughing at you too. So is Adams. You want to take me on too, poor helpless cripple that I am? And how about Adams? You think may you're Superman? Well, I got news for you. If you think you can tangle with old Adams here, you got another guess coming. Against Adams, you'd be like Clark Kent."

Teddy Karam abruptly opened the fist.

Morris Bird III leaned back in his chair. He spooned mashed potatoes into his mouth. They tasted gritty. He could hear his heart. It made a series of hollow sounds deep inside his head, and he wasn't particularly proud of himself.

"At a way to go, pal," Oscar Adams said to Teddy Karam. "I wouldn't of wanted to of had to cream your butt."

Benny Goodman sniggered. "Creamed butt? Hey, they ought to put that on the menu."

Even Teddy Karam had to grin at that one.

"Creamed Lebanese butt," said Benny Goodman. "On toast maybe."

"With chocolate sauce," said Morris Bird III.

"And cashew nuts," said Oscar Adams.

"Gesundheit," said Teddy Karam.

"Huh?" said Oscar Adams.

"You said cashew didn't you?"

Benny Goodman let his eyeballs roll up.

Morris Bird III made a sound like he was having a heart attack.

Oscar Adams thought it over for a moment. Then a lightbulb went on, and he laughed.

They finished their food and left the cafeteria. They headed north on East 9th Street toward Superior Avenue, where they would catch the Hough Avenue trackless trolley for home. They walked slowly, so Benny Goodman could keep up. They passed a men's clothing store, a hotdog emporium, a newsstand, and then they were in front of a place called the Roxy Burlesk. It had a lot of lights, and a lot of pictures, big pictures, tinted pink and blue. They examined the pictures. The pictures were of people named Rose (The Bosom) St. Regis and Desirée Desire and Irma (Passion Fruit) Lovejoy. The four members of the East 90th Street College Athletic Conference made whistly and snickery sounds and agreed that none of these ladies appeared to be in any imminent danger of starving to death. Benny compared Rose (The Bosom) St. Regis with a Holstein. Teddy Karam, who confessed himself to be a leg man, expressed a preference for Irma (Passion Fruit) Lovejoy. Morris Bird III and Oscar Adams remained more or less silent. Morris Bird III kept his eyes on the navel of Desirée Desire. She was a blonde, and she had a small heartshaped mouth, but those things he barely noticed. His interest was centered on her navel and her tummy. He supposed he would have to do some pushups and deep knee bends later. Well, so be it.

After they had boarded the Hough Avenue trackless trolley, they again got to talking about Fred C. Dobbs. Teddy Karam brought up the subject. He said Fred C. Dobbs' main problem had been stupidity. Benny Goodman asked Teddy what he meant. "Well," said Teddy, "the dumb jerk should of made sure Curtin was dead."

"But what does that have to do with the price of fish?" Benny wanted to know.

"Huh?" said Teddy.

"Dumb ox. It was the *bandits* who caught up with Fred C. Dobbs—not *Curtin*. Curtin didn't have anything to do with it."

"Curtin was with Howard. They were looking for Fred C. Dobbs," said Morris Bird III.

"I know *that*," said Teddy. "What I *meant* was, Fred C. Dobbs should of killed Curtin, then gone to the Indian village and fed Howard a big story about how Curtin had jumped him. He could of told Howard he'd killed Curtin in selfdefense."

Benny shook his head. "Boy, that's some mind you got."

Teddy continued. "And then Fred C. Dobbs, once he and

Howard were safe back in civilization, brought there by those Indians, old Fred C. Dobbs could have figured out some way to bump off Howard. After all, Howard was an old man. It wouldn't of been too hard."

Benny shuddered.

Teddy was pleased. "Some thinking, huh?"

"Yeah," said Benny. "You're a regular Fred C. Dobbs."

"Only smarter," said Morris Bird III.

"Amen," said Benny.

"You ain't making *me* mad," said Teddy, grinning.

"You don't get it, do you?" said Benny.

"Get what?" said Teddy.

Benny shrugged, looked out the window. There were snow and slush on the pavement. "Going to be a cold night," he said. "I don't like cold nights. They make my leg hurt."

"So take a hot water bottle to bed with you," said Teddy. "But answer my question first. What is it I don't get?"

"Never *mind*."

"No. I want to know."

"You'll *never* know. So never *mind*."

"I got you backed in a corner. You got no answer for me, so all you can say is never mind."

"Sure," said Benny. "That's right. You said it."

"Yeah," said Teddy, nodding. But he was frowning.

"You'll never *knowwwwww*," sang Oscar Adams under his breath, "just how *muhhhhhch* I love you. You'll never *knowwwww* just how much I care . . ."

"I just may throw up," said Benny, glaring at Oscar Adams.

Everyone laughed, and then the subject was changed. The rest of the way home, the four members of the East 90th Street College Athletic Conference discussed the visual aspects of Rose (The Bosom) St. Regis and Desirée Desire and Irma (Passion Fruit) Lovejoy. They chose their favorites. The voting came out: Rose (The Bosom) St. Regis 2 (Benny Goodman and Teddy Karam); Desirée Desire 1 (Morris Bird III), and Irma (Passion Fruit) Lovejoy 1 (Oscar Adams). Benny said it figured that Oscar Adams would choose a girl who had the nickname Passion Fruit. Naturally, Oscar asked him why. Because, said Benny, you're always thinking about your stomach.

That movie, *The Treasure of the Sierra Madre,* really hit Morris Bird III where he lived. If old Fred C. Dobbs had been a woman, Morris Bird III's mother could have played the part with no trouble. She wouldn't have had to act the part; she could have lived it. Every time he saw the picture, he saw his mother. This made him feel terrible, it made him want to throw himself in front of a train. He loved his mother. He always had loved his mother. But it was difficult. She was so screechy. She was always so worried about the Extra. Often (even now, at thirteen, when maybe he should have been more grownup about it) he had wanted to hug his mother, but she was not the sort of person you just willy-nilly up and hugged out of a clear blue sky. She was all strings and snap and tight muscles, and there was really no place decent you could get *hold* of her. It was like trying to hug a Gillette Blue Blade. She moved in a sort of crouch, and she was all elbows and dry skin, and every movement she made told the world: *If you know what's good for you, you won't monkey around with*

Alice
Anna
Bird.

And nobody monkeyed around with her. Not anymore. She did as she pleased, and that was that. The world abounded with china owls.

As far as Morris Bird III was concerned, there was only one person who'd ever monkeyed around with her. That person was his grandmother.

But his grandmother was a very special person. His grandmother had substance. His grandmother could recite all the verses of Edgar Allan Poe's "The Raven." She knew the difference between a crocodile and an alligator. She baked upside-down cakes that didn't taste like old undershirts. She could sing in pitch. She could dance the Charleston. She had once shaken hands with John W. Davis, Democratic presidential candidate in the year 1924. She could hook rugs. She enjoyed *Easy Aces* and *Vic and Sade* and *The Guiding Light* and *I Love a Mystery*. She liked Gene Kelly's scar. She had cried on the day of President Roosevelt's death, and she'd not bothered to hide it. When you talked, she listened. She seldom said Never Mind Dear. She liked peanut butter. She got a kick out of the sounds of rain and leaves and the odors of grass and earth and spilt gasoline. She washed her face with Swan soap because she liked the name. She rooted for the Indians. She bought bubble bath for Sandra. She believed in God.

But that had been a long time ago. Almost three years ago. And now she was dying. And now she wept. And now she monkeyed around with no one.

But there had been a time . . .

An autumn morning in 1945, a gray and crisp autumn morning, and the taxicab stood waiting at the curb. Morris Bird III and his father carried her suitcases to the cab. She was returning to Paradise Falls. She stood on the front porch with Morris Bird III's mother, and their faces were tight. Sandra sat on the porch steps and stared up at them. They had been arguing for more than an hour. It had begun in the kitchen, had continued in the living-room and now it was ending on the porch.

You *want* to go home, said Morris Bird III's mother. You *want* to go away. You don't care about me.

Alice, said the grandmother, please. Let it lie.

A lot *you* care, said the mother.

I do care.

You could have fooled *me!*

Please, Alice. Please. The children.

Let them hear. It'll do them some good. It'll show them the truth about their beloved grandmother.

Alice, don't you *want* to be a mother?

What? What did you say?

You heard me.

That's the worst thing I ever heard in my life.

The grandmother sighed. You don't need me. You need to be a mother. All you want is a housekeeper. I love them, but *you're* their mother. The war's over. You got to get back to being one.

But we *need* you. We *do too* need you.

No, said the grandmother, shaking her head.

Morris Bird III and his father labored with the suitcases. Sandra stared. A big Schlitz truck went past. The cabdriver filed his nails and looked at the trees. The meter was running. The grandmother turned away. She bent over and hugged Sandra. She kissed Sandra on a cheek. Sandra hugged the grandmother's knees. Then the grandmother hugged Morris Bird III. He was perspiring. The mother stood with her hands on her hips. Her nostrils were wide, and she was wheezing. After loading the last suitcase into the taxicab, Morris Bird III's father stood with his hands in his pockets. He shook hands with the grandmother when she came down off the porch. Morris Bird III's mother did not come off the porch. This is the worst thing you've ever done! she hollered. The grandmother smiled at Morris Bird III's father. He smiled back. It wasn't much of a smile. The grandmother looked at Morris Bird III and said: Be brave. Morris Bird III nodded.

She got into the taxicab, and the taxicab went away, and Morris Bird III and Sandra waved at it. Their father stood with his hands in his pockets.

The mother ran inside the house, and she was sniffling. It occurred to Morris Bird III that she surely must have been monkeyed around with good. He breathed deeply, and the air didn't taste half bad at all.

Morris Bird III's grandmother had had seven children, and except for his mother they all lived in Paradise Falls, and he didn't have much use for any of them. He hadn't always felt this way, but things forever changed, and a person got older, saw more, discovered Fake. Oh, a *couple* of his aunts and uncles were *all right,* which meant they were weak instead of downright evil, and any port in a storm: his aunts and his uncles on his mother's side were all the family he had. No one was left on the Bird side. So Morris Bird III, a beggar who could not afford to be a chooser, at least tolerated the weak ones (his Uncle Alan and his Aunt Pauline) and sometimes even was able to love them. At least they didn't go *out of their way* to behave like Fred C. Dobbs.

It all was real tough. As a little kid, he had spent part of his summers in Paradise Falls, and back in those days his aunts and uncles had been giants. And of course there had been his grandmother, and she had been in good health, and the days had been sunny and green and fragrant. Paradise Falls was a great little town, no doubt about it. The air there almost always smelled good, and everywhere were brick sidewalks with humps. He often got to ride in a police cruiser with his Uncle Jim, the old football hero. Uncle Jim was beefy, and he had a loud redfaced way of talking, and people almost always grinned when they were with him. They said he didn't have a mean bone in his body. He liked to clap people on the back, and they almost always winced. Sometimes, when Uncle Jim was chasing a speeder, Morris Bird III got to crank the siren. Those were the best times of all. The police cruiser got up to speeds of 70 and 75 miles an hour, and Morris Bird III just about had all the breath sucked out of him. Grinning, both hands tight on the steeringwheel, Uncle Jim always caught the speeders, and it was fun watching the speeders hem and haw and make weak fibby little excuses. (To this day, Morris Bird III had great respect for cars with the word POLICE written on them. Back on October 20, 1944, the day he and Sandra had gone on their trip to see Stanley Chaloupka, they had played hookey from school. Several times that day they had seen cars with the word POLICE written on them, and Morris Bird III had been more than a little scared. The Law was The Law, and you didn't mess with it. You always got caught, and your weak fibby little excuses were useless.) And back in those days Uncle Jim hadn't been such a drinker. Or maybe Morris Bird III hadn't noticed it. But no matter. The point was: Morris Bird III noticed it *now,* and he didn't like it. It made his mouth all gummy and his eyes hot. It was one of the things that had taken the shine off Paradise Falls for him. And this was a big shame. There were a lot of good things to be said for Paradise Falls. For instance, now when he was in Paradise Falls he got to ride his cousin Pete's bicycle. And he was allowed to roam anywhere he wanted. He liked to walk on the humpy sidewalks and listen to leaves. And, on Main Street, there was a place called Becker's Confectionery, and Mr. Becker allowed him to read funnybooks without having to buy them. And, out at the edge of town, there was a great big Chesapeake & Ohio Railway yard that always had a great smell of coalsmoke and creosote and earth and splinters. His Uncle Alan was a telegrapher at this yard, and once he arranged it so Morris Bird III could take a ride in a yard engine. The engineer's name was John T. Clift, and everyone called him John T., and he had a wart over his left eyebrow, and he was about six and a half feet tall, and he called his locomotive a hog, which was (Morris Bird III later learned) a real railroad man's term of endearment. The cab of John T. Clift's hog had been very hot and noisy, and Morris Bird III had never been so happy-scared in his whole entire life. But that had been a long time ago (Morris Bird III had been no more than six), and John T. Clift was dead now, and Uncle Alan had a sinus condition and never took Morris Bird III to the yards. As a matter of fact, since the end of the war Morris Bird III had had very little to do with his adult relatives in Paradise Falls. Before the war, his family had spent the greater part of its summers down there. But now this was all changed. His mother didn't get along very well with her brothers and sisters, and so the visits were brief. And Morris Bird III more or less messed around by himself. He rode around a great deal on his cousin Pete's bicycle. This was due to no great generosity on the part of his cousin Pete. It just so happened that Pete was in the Army. (Morris Bird III had never owned a bicycle, and so he probably rode cousin Pete's bicycle more than he would have under ordinary circumstances.) Pete was stationed in a camp in South Carolina, where he was a chaplain's assistant, and trust *him*. It was not difficult to picture him passing out prayer books and arranging games of checkers. He was tall and blond (the only son of Uncle Jim, the police chief), and he had been valedictorian of his class at Paradise Falls High School. He'd also been a secondstring halfback on the football team, and this hadn't made his father very happy. But Pete endured it. He was a real endurer, was Pete. He almost always smiled, and he called his classmates "fellows and girls," and any minute you expected him to launch into a commercial for Wheaties, The Breakfast of Champions. His ambition was to go into politics after doing his Army time and graduating from college, and no one with any sense would have bet against his eventually becoming President of the United States. Votes were to him what touchdowns had been to his father, and at Paradise Falls High School he had been elected president of the student council, president of the senior class, president of the National Honor Society, president of the French Club, president of the Hi-Y and president of the Boosters Club. He wasn't exactly one of Morris Bird III's favorite people. He showed too many teeth. Morris Bird III didn't trust people who showed too many teeth. Oh well, at least Pete *had* owned a bicycle, and it was kind of good to know that it was available whenever Morris Bird III wanted it. For this, if nothing else, he was grateful to his cousin Pete.

Morris Bird III's mother was the oldest of his grandmother's seven children. She was also the smallest, the skinniest and the shriekiest. The others, in order of age, were:

UNCLE JIM, the police chief, who had played football at Ohio University, who drank too much, whose face always was too red, who never smelled particularly good. His home was on South High Street in not a very good section of town. It was only two blocks (or "squares," as the people down there called them) from Mineral Avenue, where most of Paradise Falls' colored people lived. His wife's name was Emily, and she was blond, and a long time ago she had been pretty. She had married Uncle Jim the winter before their graduation from Ohio U., or so Morris Bird III had been told. He had now and again heard talk that their only child, the saintly Pete, had been born just three months after the marriage. He didn't know whether this was true, but he had done some interesting figuring. The year of Uncle Jim's birth had been 1908. He knew this because it was a sort of family joke. His mother had been born in January of that year, his Uncle Jim in December, and Morris Bird III's grandmother had once told him that that particular year had been the most trying of her life. She had married Morris Bird III's grandfather at the age of fifteen, shades of Barney Google by cracky, and exactly ten months later she'd given birth to her first child. Then, eleven months after *that*, along came Uncle Jim. My stars, she told Morris Bird III, I felt as though I'd been given the responsibility for the future of the entire human race, and your grandfather and I used to laugh like the dickens about it. Well, getting back to the probability of the saintly Pete being an extremely premature baby, the fact of the matter was that he'd been born in 1930. (Morris Bird III knew this as the absolute truth because of the Bible in the parlor. All the family births—even his own and Sandra's—had been recorded in that Bible. The list went all the way back to 1821, the year his grandfather's progenitors, the Joneses, had come to Ohio from parts unknown.) All right, the Bible listed Pete's date of birth as May 23, 1930. There was no record of exactly when Uncle Jim and Aunt Emily had been married. All Morris Bird III knew was that he'd been *told* the marriage had taken place the winter before their graduation. For some reason, the year of the graduation hadn't ever been revealed to him. But, given Uncle Jim's birthday as December of 1908, then he was only twentyone when Pete was born. Suppose, for the sake of argument, Uncle Jim was graduated from Ohio U. in June of 1930. He was only twentyone that year. More than likely, he was graduated in June of 1931. Most people graduate from college when they are twentytwo, and Morris Bird III didn't think his Uncle Jim was the type to take extra work and get himself graduated early. In June of 1931, cousin Pete was a year and a month old. Thus, if his father and mother were married the previous winter, he already had been alive and kicking for more than six months. Which meant that, unless Morris Bird III's figuring was really away offbase, his dear cousin Pete was a genuine blueribbon 300% proven out by mathematical logic bastard.

UNCLE ALAN, the telegrapher, who was a bachelor, who had a suite of rooms in the town's only hotel, the Acterhof House, who played hearts for money, who spent an average of five dollars a week on sinus remedies, who always sent Morris Bird III expensive Christmas presents. Uncle Alan read a great deal, mostly sciencefiction and detective novels. His favorite authors were H. G. Wells and Raymond Chandler. In the summer of 1947, he gave Morris Bird III a number of paperback volumes by these two writers. Morris Bird III read every one of the Chandler books, but the H. G. Wells stuff left him cold. Raymond Chandler, though, was a horse of a different complexion. Next to President Truman and Manager Lou Boudreau of the Indians, Philip Marlowe was maybe the greatest man in the whole entire world. Philip Marlowe was like that old guy Howard from the movie. He had balance. He was able to laugh. He had little use for Fake. Morris Bird III had discussed Philip Marlowe a couple of times with his Uncle Alan, and his Uncle Alan had agreed with him. I wish I was half the man Marlowe is, Uncle Alan had said. What I mean is, he doesn't sit around. You know what I mean? And Morris Bird III knew what his Uncle Alan had meant. Skinny, a smoker of cheap cigars and a reader of nevernever books (including the Philip Marlowe books, which after all were *fiction;* as much as you wished there were a Philip Marlowe, there really wasn't, and this was a fact you had to face or else start cutting dolls), poor Uncle Alan was a silent driedup victim of something or other, and not even he really knew what the something or other was, which of course made the situation so terrible it just about tore out your heart.

AUNT PHYLLIS, who was in her thirties, who was rather heavy, who had red hair and an immense mouth, whose rump stuck out, who had five children (Kenny, Kitty, Kristine, Karen and Karl, all of them about as pleasant as snot in your eye), who was married to a man named Harry B. Dana, secretary and treasurer of the Paradise Falls Clay Products Co. Aunt Phyllis took singing lessons, and she played bridge but never for money, and she was a dear friend of Mrs. Norma Westfall Estes, clubwoman and wife of the Honorable Dwight F. Estes, mayor of Paradise Falls. (Their daughter, Rose, was the one who had, on June 24, 1946, shown Morris Bird III everything she had had, such as it had been.) Aunt Phyllis always smelled of bath salts; she always gave big hugs; she always sent cheap Christmas presents.

UNCLE HOWARD, who was about thirty, who taught geography and coached the basketball team at Paradise Falls High School (1947–48 record: 7–12), who wore a hearing aid that had kept him out of the war, who was married to a woman whose maiden name had been Edythe Breitenbach (she played the harp, and she had no chest worth mentioning). Uncle Howard and Aunt Edythe had four children. Their names were Tom, Larry, Jane and Howard Jr., and they weren't quite as unpleasant as the drippy Kenny, Kitty, Kristine, Karen and Karl. At least a person could talk with them without being made to feel like something the cat scraped up off the pavement.

UNCLE WALTER, who drove a bus for the Paradise Valley Traction Co., who never tired of talking about what a hero he had been in the war, who belonged to the American Legion, the Veterans of Foreign Wars, the AMVETS, the Disabled American Veterans and the Paradise Falls Gun Club, who in 1946 ran unsuccessfully for the Ohio House of Representatives on the Democratic ticket, who was a little fellow with no meat on him, who always wore his Ruptured Duck, who had served as a Pfc with the 99th Infantry Division in the Battle of the Bulge (he had been a BAR man, a position of no little responsibility), who called everyone Buddy and Chief and Old Timer, whose shrillish voice was like feeding time in a parrot cage. Uncle Walter was married to a plump girl whose maiden name had been Iris Schmidlapp. They had no children. Aunt Iris was one of three Paradise Falls girls who had served in the WACs in the war, and she had thick hairy legs.

AUNT PAULINE, the youngest, who was just twentythree, who worked as a clerk in the sportswear department of Steinfelder's Department Store, who was just about beautiful (what with her long black hair, her moist and trembly mouth, her huge brown eyes, her narrow little figure and her good, even if maybe they were a shade skinny, legs), who never spoke in more than a whisper, who was engaged to a young man named Lloyd Sherman, a fussy little fellow who spoke with a slight lisp and was in charge of the shoe department at Steinfelder's. (Lloyd Sherman knew exactly one joke, and it had to do with his line of work. There's no business like shoe business, he was forever saying, and it made you want to curl up like a piece of bacon that has remained too long in the skillet.) Aunt Pauline was the artistic member of the family. She painted. On Sunday afternoons, when the weather was decent, she and Lloyd Sherman took trips into the country in his 1947 Hudson. They had picnics, and she set up her easel, and she painted cows and trees and hills and barns and meadows and covered bridges and such, while Lloyd Sherman lay quietly on the grass and read the latest selection that had been sent to him by the Book-of-the-Month-Club. Morris Bird III could remember his Aunt Pauline when she had been a child. Back when he'd been about seven, they had played endless silent games of tic-tac-toe and Pit and Touring. He often wondered what it was she had let get away.

Naturally, the best member of Morris Bird III's family had been the first to die. His grandfather, the late James N. Jones Sr., dead since the summer of 1943, had for some reason chosen Morris Bird III as his favorite grandchild. He had been a good deal older than Morris Bird III's grandmother, but no one ever had accused him of being feeble: he was, people said, something of a rip and a heller, and there was no one who did not admire him for those qualities. He talked a lot, and he liked to take Morris Bird III for walks, and he never failed to buy Morris Bird III something delicious and extravagant to eat. He was a retired salesman (he had traveled in ladies' readytowear, was the way he put it, grinning), and he honestly believed there was little in the world he had not really and truly enjoyed. He had been employed by a Columbus firm, and it would have been more convenient for him to have lived up there, but Paradise Falls had always been his home, and he'd never abandoned it. I love this town, he told Morris Bird III, really love it. Maybe it's because I spent so much of my life on the road, or maybe it's because I'm just an old stickinthemud, but no matter. The point is: I wouldn't trade the least of this town for the best of Paris or Rome or London or New York City or what have you. I can't understand it when people say they're bored with this town. I could spend a hundred lifetimes here and still not get to know everything about the place. We got a population of six thousand, give or take a couple hundred either way, and that's a lot of people, and they're all different, and I could just stare at them night and day. They make me laugh, and they make me want to flush myself down the toilet, and they make me warm and sort of weepy, and maybe I ought to be ashamed of myself, but I'm not. I don't really have the *time*. There's too much to *see*. Ah, you poor kid. Why is it old people feel they got to make speeches to kids? What do the kids care? They got their lives to lead. They don't want to listen to a lot of fool *talk*. So please accept from the bottom of my heart my apologies. Come on. Let's take us a nice walk.

Morris Bird III and his parents attended the funeral of James N. Jones Sr. Morris Bird III was made to look at whatever it was that lay in the coffin. It was thin and white, and people told him it was his grandfather, and okay, if they said so, let them. But he knew different. That *thing*, that *whatever it was*, was just an old *corpse*, a *nothing*. It wasn't his grandfather. It wasn't *anybody*. His grandfather had had dimension and breath; he had made sounds; he had done more than occupy space. Okay, so his heart had stopped beating, but that didn't mean he was a *corpse*. It just meant he was living somewhere else. Oh sure, Morris Bird III knew this belief sounded dumb and churchy as anything, but so what? It was *his* belief, and it kept the winds at night from becoming too cold. It helped dim his mind to questions about such people as Stanley Chaloupka and Benny Goodman.

(Oh, his grandfather's funeral had been really something. His Aunt Phyllis, she of the rump that stuck out, hired a man to take color movies. About the only good thing that could be said for it was the trainrides down and back. Also, Sandra was left in Cleveland in care of a couple named Wysocki, who lived next door. In those days, Morris Bird III had had little use for Sandra.

Such a puler and whiner the world never had seen. Now, though, she was older and quieter, not half hard to get along with. He counted it as a great day in the history of mankind when she found that copy of *Appleton's Cyclopaedia of American Biography*, the 1887 edition, Volume III, GRIN through LOC. It kept her quiet, and glory be. But five years ago she'd seldom been quiet, and if she'd come along on those trainrides they would have been disasters. Morris Bird III loved trainrides. He didn't want anything to distract him from the enjoyment. He especially liked the smell of daycoaches. To get from Cleveland to Paradise Falls by train, you changed at Columbus from the New York Central to the Chesapeake & Ohio. The layover was an hour and a half, but who cared? The waiting room was directly over the tracks, and there were plenty of immense windows through which you could see all the trains arriving and departing. The windowsills were large enough for you to sit on. You actually were able to look down the smokestacks of the locomotives. Ah, such a time . . . such delight . . . so okay, so his Aunt Phyllis had hired a man to take color movies, so the folding chairs in the undertaking parlor had had splinters, so Morris Bird III had had to wear a *suit* and stare down at a *corpse* as though it *meant* something . . . so okay, you had to take the bitter with the sweet . . . and anyway, none of it mattered. His grandfather was no *corpse*, and never would be.)

His grandfather had taken Morris Bird III to the trotting races at the Paradise County Fair, where the horses ran stately and erect, where wiry middleaged men laid spidery fastidious whips on their hindquarters, where the rich itchy odor of horse mess made you grimace and hold your breath. His grandfather had taken Morris Bird III to the Sportsmen's Tap Room, which smelled of beer and pretzels and damp mahogany, where men draped themselves over each other's shoulders and sang songs and discussed the price of feed and told each other great wild stories about women, where all the men greeted Morris Bird III's grandfather by his first name, where Morris Bird III ate limburger cheese (he *loved* it, and forget the smell) and drank Nehi and occasionally was given minute sips of beer. His grandfather had taken Morris Bird III to Becker's Confectionery to play the Iron Claw machine (once he actually got something *out* of the machine—a little clicky tin thing in the shape of a frog; each time you squeezed it, it went *gik*) and eat doubledip chocolate ice cream cones. His grandfather had taken Morris Bird III to visit the Paradise Falls Coal & Ice Co. plant, where Morris Bird III was allowed to suck all the ice slivers he wanted, where the floor trembled from the vigor of the great rumbling ice-making machine, where the walls sweated, where the owner, a man named Scofield, never failed to complain about taxes and those insane Democrats in Washington. His grandfather had taken Morris Bird III to the Elysian Theater to see Abbott & Costello movies and eat Hershey bars and drink Orange Crush. His grandfather had taken Morris Bird III walking along the edge of the river, pointing out to him the place where a farmer, his wife, his three children, a wagon and a team of horses had careened off a road and vanished into the waters without a trace—*to this very day*. His grandfather had taken Morris Bird III walking through the colored section, where everyone was addressed by first name, where now and then they were taken into fragrant homes and fed gigantic sandwiches of mysteriously hot and tasty meats, where everybody grinned a lot and had pictures of President Roosevelt hanging over the mantel. His grandfather had taken

Morris Bird III up a long green hill to the Oak Grove Cemetery, where they never looked at graves but instead went to a secret place that had a majestic view of the town and, more specifically, the softball diamond where the Paradise Falls Clay Products Co. team played its home games in the Southeastern Ohio AAA Fast-Pitch League.

Yeah, this had been a great man, and no great man ever is a corpse, and all the color movies in the whole entire world can't change *that*.

Or so Morris Bird III believed. And would continue to believe. Until maybe he learned different. And maybe even after that. Honest to God.

Fine. Great. If you took a survey of the human race, Morris Bird III's grandmother and late grandfather would wind up classified among the Goods. But one was dying and the other was dead, and Morris Bird III was left surrounded by people who, for the most part, put a taste of rat fur in his mouth. This had nothing to do with love. He loved his mother, and he loved his father. He honestly and genuinely *did*. (He had a lot of dreams about them. In the dreams they were happy and smiling, and they weren't afraid to hug a person, and big joke. Ha ha.) But *loving* someone and *looking up* to someone were so different it wasn't even funny. His father was The Voice of Cleveland & Northeastern Ohio and his mother was a lover of china owls and dayold bread, and why wasn't there a key somewhere? Why wasn't there some sort of magic set of words? Like maybe: *Come on out where the air is. Smile awhile, let a song be your style, and you won't need Fitch Shampoo. Don't despair, use your head, breathe the air; it's great; it makes you grin.* Ah, fooey. Bushwah. Horse apples. Wishing was dumb. You had to take the sum and total of your personal now, and go on from there. Eventually that thing called Maturity would come. You would achieve balance, like that old fellow Howard, like Benny Goodman's father, like your grandmother, like your late grandfather.

Fine. Great. But how come did she have to cry?

Did it hurt *that* much?

How could *she* have been hurt by *anything* that much?

She wasn't just the average person you met on the street. She was his *grandmother*, and she was braver than the sky.

Yeah, sonny, but you keep forgetting that things forever and relentlessly change. And Fred C. Dobbs keeps banging at the door.

The year was 1948, and the month was August, and it was five weeks since Morris Bird III and his mother and Sandra had visited his grandmother, his poor pale old grandmother, lying there in that big brass bed in that house in Paradise Falls.

They had once again journeyed to Paradise Falls by train. It was maybe the tenth time Morris Bird III had made the trip (not counting the little kid times before his memory began), and he still enjoyed it immensely. (Which was a blessing, since his parents were too cheap to buy a car.)

But the visit itself had been altogether another cup of Ovaltine.

Uncle Jim met them at the depot. It was late in the afternoon, and he was driving a police cruiser. He embraced all three of them, and his breath was bad. It was a hot day, clear and brilliant, and Morris Bird III got to feeling a little funny in the stomach. Uncle Jim drove them in the police cruiser to his home on South High Street. Morris Bird III and Sandra sat in the back seat. There were no inside handles on the doors back there. This was because prisoners sometimes rode in the back seat. It was a great feeling.

As he drove, Uncle Jim told Morris Bird III's mother about the old dying lady. "The pain," he said, "is getting worse and worse. I tell you the truth, it's tough for me to go upstairs and look at her."

"Jim," said Morris Bird III's mother, "the *children*." She made a hushing noise.

"Oh," said Uncle Jim. "Yeah. Sure."

Morris Bird III expelled his breath in a slow gasp. Sandra, next to him, said nothing.

"Sure is hot," said Uncle Jim. "Been dry, too."

"Yes," said Morris Bird III's mother.

"Got to ninetynine two days ago."

"Well, this always has been a warm place."

"Doc Hendrickson got her some pills. They seem to help."

"Pills?"

"Yeah. Pain pills. I don't know what they're called, but I guess they take away the edge of the pain."

"That's good," said Morris Bird III's mother.

"Sometimes I wish we would of left her in the hospital."

"At thirty dollars a *day*? When it's *terminal*?"

"No," said Uncle Jim. He sighed. "You're right. You're always right. One thing about you, Alice—you got good sense."

Morris Bird III's mother didn't say anything. All around them, warm leaves made dry abrupt sounds. Morris Bird III was sweating. He wiped his forehead. It felt bumpy. His good old forehead. The police cruiser pulled into the driveway next to the house on South High Street. Morris Bird III reached through the open window and opened his door from the outside. He helped Sandra out of the car. He and Uncle Jim carried the suitcases into the house. Uncle Jim's wife, the blond Aunt Emily, met them in the front room. They went into the kitchen, and Aunt Emily served them glasses of cold water from an old milk bottle kept in the refrigerator. Uncle Jim examined his glass of cold water with some suspicion, but he made no comment.

"Pauline's upstairs with Mother," said Uncle Jim.

"Oh?" said Morris Bird III's mother. "And how is dear Pauline?"

"Fine, I guess. She's still going around with that pansy, and she keeps saying she's going to marry him. I tell you, anything in this world I can't stand, it's a pansy."

"Well," said Morris Bird III's mother, "I don't know if I'd go so far as to call Lloyd Sherman a *pansy* . . ."

"Mommy?" said Sandra.

"Yes?"

"Can we go see Grandma now?"

"In a minute. Let me finish my glass of water."

Sandra nodded.

Aunt Emily spoke up. "Got a letter from Pete yesterday."

"He doing all right?" Morris Bird III's mother wanted to know. She sipped her water, and she really was interested a whole lot in how Pete was doing. Sure she was.

"His basic training will be finished in two weeks," said Aunt

Emily. "And then he'll stay on at the post chapel. It's all been arranged. The chaplain likes him a lot."

"Who doesn't?" said Morris Bird III's mother.

"Now," said Uncle Jim.

Morris Bird III turned his head and looked out a window. That way, no one could see his grin. His mother and Aunt Emily had never gotten along. It was a big Family thing that had been going on for years.

"A lot of people going to stop by tonight," said Uncle Jim.

"Oh?" said Morris Bird III's mother. "Who?"

"Phyllis and Harry. Howard and Edythe. Walter and Iris. And Pauline's staying for supper. Alan's working second trick, and so he won't be able to make it, but all the rest'll be here."

"The whole zoo," said Morris Bird III's mother.

"Yeah," said Uncle Jim, and he just about grinned.

Morris Bird III stared at his hands.

"I suppose," said Morris Bird III's mother, "the principal item on the agenda will be the barn."

"Yeah," said Uncle Jim.

"Phyllis and Iris still fighting over the dishes?"

"Yeah. Among other things."

Morris Bird III's mother sighed. "I can hardly wait."

"Alice?" said Uncle Jim.

"Yes?"

"You want to know something?"

"What's that?"

"You enjoy it."

"Well, don't *you?*"

"No."

"Hypocrite," said Morris Bird III's mother, grinning.

Uncle Jim opened his mouth to say something, then thought better of it.

"Don't answer back," Aunt Emily said to Uncle Jim. "She's just trying to get your dander up."

"I know," said Uncle Jim. "I *know*."

Morris Bird III's mother kept grinning.

The barn: oh that blessed barn. As far as Morris Bird III could tell, his relatives never thought of anything else. All his grandmother's possessions were in that barn. They'd been stored there after she'd sold her house. Tables, chairs, dishes, rugs, pictures, beds, chests, a sewing machine, baby cribs and even the porch furniture and several trunks full of old dresses and suits and coats and underclothing—all were piled in that old barn. It faced on an alley behind Morris Bird III's grandmother's old house over on Mulberry Street, about halfadozen blocks from Uncle Jim's place here on South High Street. When she sold her home in 1943, she retained title to the barn and stored all her stuff there. Then she went to Cleveland for two years to live with Morris Bird III's family. On her return to Paradise Falls, she had just begun to look for a new place to live when she became ill. She had about fifteen thousand dollars in the Paradise County National Bank—her savings, plus her late husband's insurance money, plus the proceeds from the sale of her house—but she went to the hospital, and there was an operation on her stomach, and then there were radium treatments at the Ohio State University Medical Center in Columbus (every Tuesday for more than a year, Uncle Jim drove her there in a police cruiser), and then there was another operation, and there were hospital fees, plus special care fees, plus the cost of her pills and medicines, and now just about all her money was gone, and now she

134

lay in that big brass bed in an upstairs rear bedroom of Uncle Jim's house. And all that stuff was still in that barn. Morris Bird III's parents and aunts and uncles talked about it all the time. They were like alleycats tugging at a dead fish. And apparently they didn't care who knew it. After all, how else would Morris Bird III have known so much about his grandmother's finances? They openly discussed his grandmother's money in front of him, and they openly argued over who was to get what from the barn, and talk about your Fred C. Dobbs.

And his poor grandmother wasn't deaf. Sometimes, when Morris Bird III's parents and aunts and uncles gathered in the kitchen of Uncle Jim's house, their arguments became mighty loud. But a lot they cared if his grandmother heard. A lot they cared about anything other than Gimme. The only exceptions were Uncle Alan, who just naturally kept his mouth shut as a private rule, and Aunt Pauline, who just naturally was a mouse.

The biggest aggravation, as far as the shouters in the kitchen were concerned, was the fact that Morris Bird III's grandmother wouldn't give them any of her possessions *now*. They would have to wait until she died. Why? Because she was an extremely foolish woman. She insisted she would recover. According to her, there still were such things as miracles, and *really*, she was just too *blind* and *childish* for *words*.

And so why didn't she hurry up and die and stop causing so much trouble?

Sitting in that kitchen, sitting there and sipping at his glass of cold water, listening to his mother and his Uncle Jim and his Aunt Emily discuss the dishes and the porch furniture and whatever, Morris Bird III felt his poor offending forehead dampen. He got to wondering how come these people never *heard* themselves.

Wasn't there any time when they really understood what they were doing? Was Maturity a thing of blinders and earplugs? How absolutely 197% Fake could people get?

He licked the outside of his glass. He made moist sounds, but no one paid him any mind. Finally his mother stood up and allowed as how it was time to go upstairs. She led the way. Morris Bird III and Sandra followed. They all walked slowly. Uncle Jim and Aunt Emily did not accompany them. Uncle Jim went out to his car and drove away, and Aunt Emily started fussing with supper. Morris Bird III's mother preceded the children into the room where the grandmother lay. Aunt Pauline sat on a chair at the foot of the bed. The grandmother was skinnier than Morris Bird III had remembered her. She lay with her hands clasped on her chest. Her eyes were closed. Aunt Pauline rose, smiled at the visitors. She went to Morris Bird III's mother and whispered: "I think she's dozed off."

"No," said the grandmother, opening her eyes. "No, I haven't." She blinked. "Who's there?"

"It's me," said Morris Bird III's mother. "Alice."

The grandmother braced herself on her elbows. "Those two great big people you got with you—aren't they Morris and Sandra?"

"Yes," said Morris Bird III's mother.

"Well, bring them here. I don't want to have to shout across the room at them."

Morris Bird III's mother took the children across the room.

The grandmother was smiling. She was quite white. The room was very warm, and she was covered by only a single sheet.

"Hello, Grandma," said Morris Bird III.

"Morris," said the grandmother.

"Hello, Grandma," said Sandra.

"Sandra," said the grandmother.

Then, simultaneously, Morris Bird III and Sandra bent over their grandmother and hugged and kissed her. She smelled funny, almost like milk. She kissed him on both cheeks, and her mouth was scratchy. She squeezed one of Sandra's arms so tightly that Sandra gave a little squeal. *"Well,"* she said. "Well *now* you two. *Well."*

Then her daughter—Morris Bird III's mother—came to the bed. Morris Bird III and Sandra disengaged themselves from their grandmother and stepped back.

The grandmother looked at Morris Bird III's mother, and Morris Bird III's mother looked at the grandmother. Added together, the sum and total of the expressions on their faces came to a clear fat zero.

"Mother," said Morris Bird III's mother.

"Alice," said the grandmother.

The mother bent over the grandmother. A dry smacking sound.

Straightening, the mother said: "You look fine. A lot better."

"Doesn't she though?" said Aunt Pauline, still whispering. "I was just telling her that this afternoon."

The grandmother smiled. "Thank you."

"I *mean* it," said Morris Bird III's mother.

"You don't *hurt,"* said the grandmother.

"Now, *Mother,* I understand you have *pills* . . ."

"Yes," said Aunt Pauline. "She has nice pills."

"Let me talk with the children," said the grandmother.

Morris Bird III and Sandra looked at their mother.

"Go ahead," she said, sighing. She backed away from the bed.

Morris Bird III and Sandra advanced on the bed. He bathed the roof of his mouth with spit. Behind him, his mother was breathing in a sort of rasp.

"You still eating your oatmeal for breakfast?" the grandmother asked him.

"Uh huh," he said.

"*All* of it?"

"Uh huh."

"Sandra, is he telling the truth?"

"Far as I know," said Sandra.

"He used to fuss about it," said the grandmother. "He used to put it on his spoon and just play with it and *play* with it."

"Well," said Morris Bird III, "I guess I still do *that*."

The grandmother looked past the children. "Do you take them to church?" she asked their mother.

"Uh . . . yes. Not . . . uh . . . not every Sunday, but I *do* take them."

Morris Bird III inspected the wallpaper. It had a design of what appeared to be bells and butterflies and chains of daisies.

"Is Mr. Pallister still the minister?" the grandmother wanted to know.

"Yes," said the mother.

"Do you like going?" the grandmother asked Morris Bird III.

"Me?" said Morris Bird III.

The grandmother nodded.

"I like it fine," said Morris Bird III. He hadn't been to church in almost three years. With his mother or anyone else.

"Sandra, how about you?"

"Oh. Well. *Fine*," said Sandra.

"Good," said the grandmother. "Mr. Pallister is a good person. A good *parson* too, for that matter." A smile.

Morris Bird III also smiled. He rubbed his forehead, and just smiled like anything.

"The last week or so, I've been feeling a lot better," said the grandmother.

Morris Bird III and Sandra nodded.

"It still hurts, but when it isn't hurting I *do* feel better."

More nodding by Morris Bird III and Sandra.

"I'm only fiftysix," said the grandmother. "I bet I have oh a good twenty years to go. I always thought I looked young for my age, didn't you?"

"Yes," said Morris Bird III.

"Uh huh," said Sandra.

The grandmother's face turned all wrinkled and yellowish. She started to cry. She put her hands over her face. She made no noise, but she did tremble. Her shoulders made shrugging movements.

"*Mother,*" whispered Aunt Pauline. She pushed past the children, bent over the grandmother and patted her on a shoulder and an arm.

The grandmother's hands did not come away from her face.

Morris Bird III and Sandra were ushered out of the room by their mother. They did not look back. He wished he knew why he felt so angry.

That night, after Aunt Emily served a supper of fish cakes, mashed potatoes and peas, the guests arrived—Aunt Phyllis and

Uncle Harry, Uncle Howard and Aunt Edythe, Uncle Walter and Aunt Iris. Uncle Harry was full of the good news that this would be a record year for the Paradise Falls Clay Products Co., what with the enormous postwar demand for sewer tile. He lit a Prince Edward and allowed as how he hadn't felt so chipper in he didn't know when. Aunt Phyllis fussed a great deal over Morris Bird III and Sandra, hugging them and telling them oh goodness, how *big* they were growing, how *fast* time was passing. Aunt Emily told everyone all the latest news about her Pete. Uncle Jim broke open a bottle of something called Jack Daniel's Green. He poured a generous glass, then asked if anyone cared to indulge with him. No one did. Aunt Pauline came down from the grandmother's bedroom. She went into the kitchen and had herself a glass of milk and a piece of bread and blackberry jam. She'd not eaten supper with the rest of them. She wasn't hungry, she told Aunt Emily. She said she'd given the grandmother another of the pain pills, and now the grandmother was asleep. Morris Bird III's mother sat on a high-backed straight chair in the parlor. Morris Bird III and Sandra sat crosslegged on the floor next to her. They didn't know what else to do. Aunt Phyllis and Uncle Harry sat on the love seat. Uncle Howard and Aunt Edythe sat in a couple of easy chairs. Kitchen chairs were brought in for Uncle Jim and Uncle Walter and Aunt Iris. Aunt Emily brought in a chair from the diningroom. Aunt Pauline sat on an ottoman. Outside of the Cleveland Stadium and the Loew's State Theater, Morris Bird III had never seen so many chairs in his whole entire life. Aunt Pauline, who lived alone in an apartment over Hoffmeyer's Restaurant, said she couldn't stay long. Laughing, Uncle Jim asked her did she have a secret meeting arranged with her big brave handsome Lloyd Sherman. Aunt Pauline looked away from him and said nothing. Aunt Emily told him for heaven's sake to be *still.* Aunt Iris scratched a hairy knee and said something about the weather. Uncle Harry allowed as how it had cooled off quite a bit since sunset. Everyone nodded. Big deal. Uncle Walter said the weather reminded him of Camp Polk down in Louisiana. He had taken his basic training there. He told of doing a closeorder drill in the middle of a field where the temperature was 114 degrees. Aunt Phyllis fluffed her red hair and said she'd changed her underwear twice already today. Uncle Harry gave her a dirty look. It occurred to Morris Bird III that this wasn't exactly the way the wife of the secretary and treasurer of the Paradise Falls Clay Products Co. should talk. Huh. Sure was funny. A woman who put on such airs talking that way. He bet she would hear about it later, once Uncle Harry got her alone. Boy, there surely was no telling about people. Aunt Phyllis, old la de da Aunt Phyllis, saying a thing like *that.* Well, maybe it was the heat. Next to Morris Bird III, Sandra lay flat and closed her eyes. No one noticed. Uncle Walter and Uncle Howard began discussing the way the Russians were stirring up so much trouble in Berlin. Uncle Walter (he was wearing a suitcoat, and in the lapel was his trusty Ruptured Duck) said those Russkys had damn well better watch their step. Uncle Howard nodded, but his heart really didn't seem in it. It was just a pale nod, a nod for the sake of nodding. Aunt Phyllis said she couldn't *wait* for the election. Uncle Jim asked her why. She told him she was very anxious to see that awful little Truman get his just deserts. She smiled, announced that election night would give her a great deal of pleasure. (Aunt Phyllis and her dear friend, Mrs. Norma Westfall Estes, wife of the Honorable Dwight F. Estes, mayor of Paradise Falls, were cochairmen of The Paradise

County Women Volunteers for Dewey-Warren.) Aunt Phyllis said she personally would have been happier if the Republican Party had nominated Ohio's favorite son, U. S. Sen. Robert A. Taft. But, mind you, she wasn't complaining. Dewey was a fine man, she was sure, and anyway, *anyone* was preferable to that poisonous little Truman. Uncle Walter disagreed. He told Aunt Phyllis that Truman was doing a good job. He suggested that the only reason she didn't like Truman was because his first name was Harry. Everyone except Aunt Phyllis laughed. She cast a quick glance at her husband, Uncle Harry. He was laughing along with all the rest of them. He was laughing so hard he was biting his cigar. He shook his head at Aunt Phyllis and told her to stop behaving like the Queen Mother. That was the end of the political discussion. Aunt Pauline rose from the ottoman and whispered her goodnights. She suggested that someone look in on the grandmother in an hour or so. Aunt Emily became a little angry. She told Aunt Pauline not to *worry*; she—Aunt Emily—would look in on the grandmother *personally*. She told Aunt Pauline she loved her husband's mother just as much as Aunt Pauline or *anyone* did. Aunt Pauline nodded, apologized. She said she hadn't meant any offense. Aunt Emily told Aunt Pauline well, all *right*. Smiling palely, hunching forward her shoulders a little, Aunt Pauline left. As soon as she was safely out the door and down the street, everyone got to talking about her and that little nambypamby Lloyd Sherman. Uncle Jim suggested that maybe she didn't want a man. Uncle Howard said he certainly didn't think Lloyd Sherman was the marrying kind, ahem, and that was putting it *mildly*. Uncle Walter commented on Lloyd Sherman's 4-F draft status in the war. He said he didn't believe the classification had been made because of flat feet or a punctured eardrum. He said he thought he saw the picture quite clearly. He lisped as he spoke, and he held out a limp wrist, and Uncle Jim and Uncle Harry laughed the loudest. Uncle Howard and the women also laughed, but not as loudly as Uncle Jim and Uncle Harry. Morris Bird III didn't laugh. He saw nothing to laugh *about*. Sandra didn't laugh either. She was asleep. Aunt Phyllis asked Aunt Emily if Dr. Hendrickson had paid a visit today. Aunt Emily nodded. She said Dr. Hendrickson had told her the grandmother's decline was beginning to accelerate. According to the doctor, the grandmother probably would be dead within two or three months. Aunt Phyllis sniffled. Uncle Harry looked at her. Aunt Edythe announced that it would be a blessing. Morris Bird III supposed she was talking about his grandmother's death. He wished he had the nerve to walk across the room and whack Aunt Edythe a good one across the face. They all got to talking about the diningroom suite that was stored in the barn. Morris Bird III's mother held out for the sideboard. She said the only things she *really* wanted *badly* were the sideboard and maybe one of the bedroom suites. Aunt Phyllis immediately asked her *which* bedroom suite. It turned out that both Morris Bird III's mother and Aunt Phyllis wanted the same bedroom suite. Aunt Phyllis was redecorating one of her guest rooms, and she had been *counting* on it. Uncle Howard and Aunt Edythe got into a conversation with Aunt Emily about the porch furniture. Aunt Emily said she had no objection to their getting the porch furniture. She said she had all the porch furniture she ever would need. Uncle Walter and Aunt Iris put in their bid for the dishes. Aunt Emily allowed as how some of the late James N. Jones Sr.'s suits could be tailored for her saintly Pete after his discharge from the Army. Pete would be going to college, and a young man who wanted to get ahead certainly had to dress well. The material in the late James N. Jones Sr.'s suits was excellent (after all, the man had been a *salesman*, and a salesman had to dress well so he made a good impression on his customers), and a great deal of money would be saved by Uncle Jim and Aunt Emily if they had the suits for Pete. Aunt Iris told Aunt Edythe she'd always been very fond of the dishes. Aunt Phyllis spoke up, telling Aunt Iris that *she'd* told the grandmother many years ago she would like to have the dishes. Uncle Walter asked Aunt Phyllis what did that have to do with the price of Grape-Nuts. Uncle Jim poured himself another glass of Jack Daniel's Green. He told Uncle Harry he'd received the bottle that day from an attorney named Jim Walter. Seems Uncle Jim had testified for the attorney's client in a personal injury suit that had come out of an automobile accident Uncle Jim had investigated. Aunt Iris told Aunt Phyllis she'd trade her the dishes for the bedroom suite. Aunt Phyllis laughed, told Aunt Iris she couldn't possibly be *serious*. Morris Bird III's mother asked Uncle Jim if he'd made any headway in his attempts to persuade the grandmother to make out a will. Uncle Jim shook his head no. He told Morris Bird III's mother the grandmother absolutely *refused* to make out a will. He said the grandmother still was convinced she would recover. Morris Bird III's mother shook her head. She told Uncle Jim there certainly would be quite a battle royal as soon as the grandmother died. Uncle Jim nodded, drank some more Jack Daniel's Green. Uncle Howard and Uncle Harry got to talking about baseball. They agreed that the New York Yankees probably would win the pennant again. The Cleveland club certainly was *interesting*, but it surely couldn't last. Morris Bird III started to say something but then shut his mouth. A lot of good an argument would do. Aunt Phyllis and Aunt Emily got to discussing the linens in the barn. Aunt Iris joined in. They agreed that the linens were lovely, and then they gave each other narrow looks, like leopards edging toward a piece of raw meat. Uncle Jim pursed his lips, rolled some of the Jack Daniel's Green on his tongue. Uncle Howard told Uncle Harry that the prospects for the 1948–49 Paradise Falls High School basketball team were extremely promising. He spoke glowingly of a boy named Arthur Potter, a transfer pupil from New Straitsville, over in Perry County. According to Uncle Howard, this Arthur Potter was six-five and could make all the shots there were. Unless the kid had a heart attack and dropped dead, he would be the team's starting center. And, best news of all, he was only a junior. Uncle Howard admitted that Arthur Potter probably wasn't the brightest kid he'd ever encountered, but so what? Arthur Potter would pass all his subjects. Uncle Howard would see to it. There was an outside chance, said Uncle Howard, that PFHS might make it to the sectional Class A finals. Uncle Walter told Aunt Phyllis that nothing had been settled about the dishes. He wanted that made perfectly clear. Aunt Emily fixed some iced tea and served it to everyone except Sandra, who was asleep, and Uncle Jim, who didn't believe he cared for any. Morris Bird III thanked her for his iced tea, and she took the time to give him a smile. He decided it might be a good thing if he got hold of a calendar and drew a red circle around the date. Aunt Emily asked Morris Bird III's mother if she wanted to take Sandra to bed. Morris Bird III's mother told Aunt Emily that Sandra was just fine where she was. Later would be soon enough to put Sandra to bed, she said. Uncle Jim was humming to himself. Morris Bird III's mother told Aunt Emily that Sandra was always grumpy when she was awakened from a sound sleep. Uncle Howard and Aunt Edythe said they needed a kitchen table. Smiling, Uncle Howard looked around the room and asked if anyone else had put in a claim for the grandmother's kitchen table. All heads were shaken no. Uncle Howard nodded, leaned back, crossed his legs. Aunt Phyllis suggested that it might be a good thing if a list were drawn up. She said she *knew* she sounded awfully *callous,* but, well, facts were facts. Uncle Jim blinked at her and told her yes, she surely was being awfully callous. Aunt Emily told Uncle Jim to hush, for pity's sake. That did it for Morris Bird III. He stood up. Pity's sake, huh? *Pity's sake?* Yeah, pity's sake. Such experts on pity. Oh boy. You *bet.* Aunt Emily asked him was he tired. He told her yes, he sure was tired. She told him there were folding cots for him and Sandra in the upstairs guest room next to where his mother would be sleeping. She said he could go upstairs any time. He looked at his mother. She was talking with Aunt Phyllis. She was telling Aunt Phyllis about *The Early Bird Show* and the success with it that The Voice of Cleveland & Northeastern Ohio was having. She spoke at some length on the subject of Listener Surveys, and she smiled and nodded at Aunt Phyllis, smiled and nodded, just smiled and nodded away as though her life were a great big platter of chocolate layer cake with whipped cream on top and probably a maraschino cherry. Not to mention maybe nuts. Morris Bird III stood quietly and waited for her to stop smiling and nodding. He wanted to say good night. It was all he wanted. But his mother kept talking. She told Aunt Phyllis that The Voice of Cleveland & Northeastern Ohio couldn't be spared from his program, which was why he hadn't accompanied her on this trip to Paradise Falls. Aunt Phyllis smiled and allowed as how The Voice of Cleveland & Northeastern Ohio had always been a good one with the vocal chords. She said she remembered, as a little teeny girl, hearing Morris Bird II sing in the Paradise Falls High School A Capella Choir. A really marvelous bass voice it had been, and she was happy he'd not lost it. Morris Bird III's mother went back to smiling and nodding, and she told Aunt Phyllis that it was about *time* The Voice of Cleveland & Northeastern Ohio had a program of his own. When she thought of all the untalented *clods* who had pushed themselves past him, well, it simply made her blood *boil*. By this time, Morris Bird III had become tired of waiting for his mother to acknowledge his presence. He told her he was going to bed. She waved a hand, told him to go right ahead. As he made his way out of the room, his aunts and uncles all bade him good night. He mumbled something to them. He didn't know what he mumbled. He wasn't listening. Just as he was about to climb the stairs, he hesitated. He went back to the parlor, bent down over Sandra and shook one of her shoulders. She blinked up at him. He told her come on, it was time for bed. Rubbing her eyes, she stood up. She wasn't a bit cranky. She looked at her mother and said good night. Another wave of a hand from the mother. She was discussing food prices with Aunt Edythe. Again Morris Bird III made his way out of the parlor, but this time he was leading Sandra by the hand. They climbed the stairs. He looked in on his grandmother. The room was dark, and he heard nothing, so he supposed she was asleep. He could make out the shape of the brass bedposts. Sandra went into the bathroom to wash her face and brush her teeth. Morris Bird III didn't bother. He knew he really should wash his face—especially his forehead—but he was too tired. Sandra came into the bedroom and fetched her nightie. Then, very properly, she repaired to the bathroom to change clothes. Morris Bird III took off his shoes and socks and trousers and shirt and lay down in his underwear. He pulled a sheet up to his neck. Earlier, he had hung his pajamas in the closet, but he was just absolutely too pooped to fuss with them. He stared at the ceiling, and eventually Sandra came in and lay down on the other cot, and they did not speak to each other. She was asleep in maybe ten seconds. He listened to the heavy sound of her breath. He listened to the sound of tree frogs outside. He listened to the thick unintelligible sounds of the voices downstairs. He listened to his pulse. He rubbed his teeth with his tongue. He got out of his cot, went to the closet and took his pajamas off their hook. He went to the bathroom and washed his face and brushed his teeth. The toothpaste was Pebeco, and he tried not to splatter. He took off his underwear and put on his pajamas. He returned to the bedroom and hung his underwear on the hook where the pajamas had been. Then he picked up his pants and shirt (they'd originally been dropped on the floor) and hung them up, too. He returned to his cot. Sandra snorted in her sleep. He lay down and closed his eyes. He saw Fred C. Dobbs, but he was not afraid. Next to his family, Fred C. Dobbs was about as frightening as the Easter Bunny. Fooey on you, small change, he told Fred C. Dobbs, and a little later he fell asleep. He imagined he heard his grandmother weeping. Or maybe he didn't imagine it. He never did find out which.

One afternoon a week or so later, when they were back in the house on Edmunds Avenue, Morris Bird III sat on the porch steps for a couple of hours and stared out at the little he could see of the world. Sandra sat next to him, and they talked. Usually he didn't like to talk with Sandra, but that afternoon he almost kind of wanted to.

Her copy of *Appleton's Cyclopaedia of American Biography,* the 1887 edition, Volume III, GRIN through LOC, was open on her lap.

"How far along are you?" he asked her.

"Page 195."

"Who you reading about?"

"Hickenlooper, Andrew."

"Who was he?"

"He was an engineer and a soldier and lieutenant governor of Ohio."

"Oh? When was that?"

"Back a long time ago. He was born in 1837." Sandra consulted the book. "And he wrote something called *Competition in the Manufacture and Delivery of Gas.*"

"Gas, huh? I guess people will compete for anything."

"You're being *nasty.* It doesn't mean *that kind* of gas."

"I manufacture gas all the time. Did it in English class once last year."

"Now be *nice,*" said Sandra.

"Huh?" said Morris Bird III, innocent as soapsuds.

"*You,*" said Sandra, and she put a hand over her mouth and giggled.

"Did it in a swimming pool once, too."

"*Now . . .*"

"And the bathtub. Blub. Blub. Like a motorboat."

"Nasty . . ."

Morris Bird III grinned. "Some world. Hickenlooper and his gas. Great day in the morning."

"Well, *somebody's* got to worry about gas. Do something about it, I mean."

Morris Bird III nodded. His grin started to go away. He cupped his chin in his palms, leaned forward. He stared across the street. A family named Pisani had lived in one of the houses over there—until 1945. That was the year Mr. Pisani had died. He had had cancer, and he had screamed a lot. The week after his death, the rest of the Pisani family had moved away. Now a bunch of Lithuanian DP's lived in that house, but Morris Bird III couldn't look at the place without thinking of Mr. Pisani's screams.

Sandra studied her book.

"I bet Grandma's got what Mr. Pisani had," said Morris Bird III.

Sandra looked up. "Who?"

"You don't remember Mr. Pisani?"

"No."

"He lived here, and then he died."

"Where? *Here?*"

"Not *here.* Across the street. The house where the Katalinases live."

"Oh. The Katalinases. Poo on them. That Yvonne Katalinas, she's the biggest stuckup in the neighborhood."

"Yeah. But anyway, a long time ago this Mr. Pisani lived there, and he screamed a whole lot, and now he's dead, and I bet Grandma's got what he had."

"No," said Sandra.

"What do *you* know about it?"

"I got a right to talk."

"Sure, but what do you *know?* We saw how Grandma was, and I remember how Mr. Pisani was, and I'm just putting two and two together."

"Big deal," said Sandra.

"I don't *want* her to die. I don't *want* her to scream."

"Morris, please . . . please stop talking about it. Please . . ."

"Okay. Don't cry."

"I'm not going to cry. How come you think I'm going to cry? That's for *little* kids. I'm just sitting here trying to read my book."

"Sure," said Morris Bird III, nodding.

Silence from Sandra. Her head was averted. She seemed very interested in the sky and the treetops.

"I wish there was someone," said Morris Bird III.

"Someone for what?" Sandra asked him. Her eyes came back from the sky and the treetops.

"Someone who would get it all straight."

"Get all *what* straight?"

"I don't know."

"You're talking funny."

"Yeah. I suppose what I ought to do is go into an alley somewhere and kick a can."

"What?"

"And call me a dog: Here, Spot! Here, Spot old boy old fellow old friend loyal and true!"

"Are you crazy?"

"No. I just think too much."

"Huh," said Sandra. "Maybe that's the same like being crazy."

Morris Bird III grinned.

"You get real awful funny and *morbid*," said Sandra.

Morris Bird III nodded.

"You didn't use to be that way."

"Well," said Morris Bird III, "things change."

"Morris?"

"Yeah?"

"You shouldn't ought to feel so bad."

"About what?"

"Gas," said Sandra, giggling.

"Gas?"

"Uh huh. I make gas in the bathtub too."

Morris Bird III looked at his sister. Then he closed his eyes, threw back his head and whooped.

The year was 1948, and the month was August, and Morris Bird III wanted more than anything to flush his grandmother out of his mind. She was nothing anymore. Her face was wrinkled and yellowish. She wept. She was a dying old lady who owned a barn, and her children were fighting over the things in that barn, and the terrible Fake spectacle of it made small itchy creatures crawl across Morris Bird III's heart. The sum and total of his personal now had become all wormy and sour, and that was the truth, and it made him angry. The days were long, and they were warm, and they abounded with distractions (the American League pennant race, his gallery of Slaves, his battle with his complexion, his pushups and his deep knee bends), and yet he kept thinking about his grandmother. Not so long ago, she had been The One, but now she was dying, and now she betrayed him with her weeping, and he knew of no one large enough to replace her as The One. She had made him to understand Virtue; she had made him to understand Love and Courage. There, in the kitchen of that house on Edmunds Avenue, she had said to him: Do what has to be done. Don't hold back. Forget what the people down the street will say. If a thing is right, it is right. Don't turn your back on it. Don't put comfort ahead of duty. Sure, Morris Bird III had heard similar words from other people, but none of them had been The One. So now what was he supposed to do? Go at things on his own? Draw on the sum and total of his personal now? But how *could* he? It wasn't large enough, and there were too many parts that didn't make much sense.

But then came August 21, 1948, and he saw a baseball game, and he saw Julie Sutton, and he rode on a train, and he rode on a bus, and he saw his grandmother, and she *hurt*, and she asked him to help her, and he made a decision, and . . . well, the upshot was that a lightbulb got turned on.

A big lightbulb.

And, blinking, throwing his hands over his eyes, Fred C. Dobbs staggered away and hid. Forever.

August 21, 1948, was a Saturday, and Mickey Jones, the Dynamic Eyeful, was at the Roxy Burlesk. The featured presentation at the Loew's State Theater was *Abbott & Costello Meet Frankenstein*. President Truman announced he was exempting husbands and fathers from the draft. The American League standings that morning were:

	Won	Lost	Percentage	Games Behind
CLEVELAND	70	42	.625	
Boston	68	46	.593	3
Philadelphia	68	47	.591	3½
New York	65	46	.586	4½
Detroit	53	56	.486	15½
St. Louis	44	66	.400	25
Washington	44	70	.386	27
Chicago	36	75	.324	33½

The Indians had won eight straight games, the last four by shutouts, which tied the league record. Last night, before 78,382 whooping maniacs who jammed Cleveland Stadium (the largest night game crowd in baseball history), the Indians edged past the enfeebled Chicago White Sox, 1–0. The Indians' good old Satchel Paige got the best of a Chicago lefthander named Bill Wight. Boy, if ever a team was *hot*, it was the Indians. It was a great time to be playing the sadsack White Sox. Ah, this *had* to be the year. Last night Morris Bird III hadn't even left his radio to go to the bathroom. It was 0–0 until the fourth inning, and then the Indians got three singles off Bill Wight for their one run, and from that moment to the finish Morris Bird III sat on the edge of his bed and writhed and gasped, holding his breath, crossing his fingers, dying with every pitch. But old Satchel did in the White Sox, and the 78,382 whooping maniacs tore back the night with the volume of their yells, and Morris Bird III sprinted into the bathroom and had himself just about the greatest #2 in the history of the American Republic. (He had been putting it off for more than an hour, and if the White Sox had tied the score and sent the game into extra innings he probably would have exploded, *baroom*, like the atom bomb or something.) He didn't sleep very well. He kept hearing the whoops of the 78,382. And he kept thinking of the game he would be seeing today. He hoped it wouldn't rain. Today the Indians would be going after their ninth straight victory—and their *fifth straight shutout*. If they got the shutout, they would set a record for all of baseball, and Morris Bird III would be able to tell people for the rest of his life that he had seen *that* game. Not any old game, but *that* one. Mr. Wysocki, the man who lived next door, was taking Morris Bird III to today's game. It would start at 2 o'clock this afternoon. Morris Bird III hoped he could hold out that long. He didn't want to have a stroke or anything like that. Going to baseball games was a big thing with him. It always had been—or at least as far back as his memory went. Over the years, Mr. Wysocki had taken him to maybe two dozen games. Mr. Wysocki was a fine man. He had no thumb on his right hand. Instead of a thumb, there was a shiny nub. Morris Bird III hadn't ever gotten up the nerve to ask Mr. Wysocki how the thumb had been lost. Which probably was just as well. It would have been a very rude question, and Morris Bird III had no desire at all to be rude with Mr. Wysocki. This was too fine a man. You treated him with re-spect, even if he *was* an auditor for the Internal Revenue and people sometimes kidded him about it. The thing was—*somebody* had to be an auditor for the Internal Revenue, and better Mr. Wysocki than a lot of people Morris Bird III could have named. Mr. Wysocki drove a majestic 1936 Packard that was as shiny and powerful as it had been the day it had come from the factory. It was Morris Bird III's favorite car in the whole entire world. He never rode in it except when Mr. Wysocki was taking him to baseball games, and so naturally he had to prefer it above all

others. There were four members of the Wysocki family—
Mr. Wysocki, Mrs. Wysocki, their son Frank, and their daughter
Suzanne. Another son, Ralph, had been killed in 1945 while serv-
ing with the Marines on Iwo Jima. Mrs. Wysocki was fat and
talked a lot, but she had nothing against smiling. And she was a
good cook. Morris Bird III's mother had gone back down to Paradise Falls the previous Tuesday (the grandmother's condition
was a good deal worse), and Morris Bird III and Sandra had been
taking their meals with the Wysockis since then. Suzanne
Wysocki, who was twelve and blond and beautiful, scared Morris Bird III half to death. A few years back, he'd thought he'd
loved her, but now she was too much for him, and he had as
little to do with her as he could get away with. She was almost
always silent, and she walked with her eyes turned toward
heaven, and she attended parochial school now (for her first six
years of school, she'd gone to plain dirty old Hough Elementary,
but now she was Beyond All That), and when you were in her
presence you talked in a whisper. She seemed all the time to be
holding private conversations with saints and angels. Seated, she
always folded her hands and placed them in her lap. Standing,
she always had her head cocked to one side, as though she were
awaiting some silent secret signal from the Almighty. She said
she wanted to become a nun, and she made Morris Bird III's
bones rattle. But Suzanne provided the only uncomfortable mo-
ments when he visited the Wysockis. Mr. Wysocki was great, and
Mrs. Wysocki was great, and their son Frank was absolutey top-
notch. He was a great big guy with arms and a chest that were
hairier than a grizzlybear's backside, and he had more girlfriends
than the Loree A. Wells Funeral Home had folding chairs. He
also had served with the Marines in the Pacific, and now he was

a policeman (he rode in a zone car in the Central Area, where a great many colored people lived), and he never laughed when he could roar, never roared when he could stamp his feet and whomp people massively on the back. He often made his pious little Miss Priss of a sister gasp and blanch, and of course this delighted Morris Bird III. (It was no particular secret that Frank Wysocki went out with Mrs. Mary Ellen Mossler, the War Widow who lived across the street and had an honored place in Morris Bird III's gallery of Slaves. He was a good fifteen years younger than Mrs. Mossler, but he didn't seem to mind, and no one had heard *her* complaining. They made a goodlooking couple—Mrs. Mossler with her Lauren Bacall walk, Frank Wysocki with his epic laughter and his immense build. They looked as though they really knew what the world was all about, which meant that the difference in their ages didn't have the significance of a hill of dried beans.) Suzanne aside, Morris Bird III envied the Wysockis. They seemed to know *a lot* of what the world was all about. And, if *they* didn't have balance, then *no one* did. It was great being with them, and today—August 21, 1948—would be a great day.

It began with a dream, which was not unusual.

Last night, baseball had kept him from going to sleep right away. This morning, Julie Sutton was keeping him from coming awake right away.

She was smiling. Oh yes. She always smiled. She was smiling, and she wore these veils, and she was snapping little clicky things, and she was dancing to the music of an oboe, and she

157

was softly crooning to him a song that had something to do with a desire she had to make his slightest wish her command. Everywhere were perfume and colored lights, and her lips were moist, and her little chest went in and out, in and out, *in* and *out*, and he got to thinking that maybe he would have to fall down and chew on an elbow.

His trusted aide, Turhan Bey, sat crosslegged at his feet. Turhan Bey's lips had spread themselves into an oily smile. Does this one please you, sire? he murmured.

A nod from Morris Bird III. He had no strength for words.

Excellent, said Turhan Bey. I am pleased to be of service to my master.

Another nod from Morris Bird III. He kept his eyes on Julie Sutton's chest.

Turhan Bey clapped his hands. Just once.

Julie Sutton hesitated, looked at Turhan Bey.

The master finds you desirable, said Turhan Bey.

A shy smile from Julie Sutton.

You may come forward, said Turhan Bey.

Julie Sutton nodded. She moved forward.

Morris Bird III scrunched back a little.

Forward came Julie Sutton. She moistened her lips with her darling little tongue. Master, she said, I am so flattered . . .

Morris Bird III made a sound like a chicken with its neck caught in a picket fence.

Onward came Julie Sutton. She plucked at her veils.

An oleaginous smile from Turhan Bey.

Love, said Julie Sutton. *Desire*. She held out her arms.

Ah, said Turhan Bey, how sublime.

Onward came Julie Sutton, still plucking.

Morris Bird III let out a squealing sound.

Love, she said. *Desire.* I shall feed you pomegranates, and each night will be an eternity of delight.

Morris Bird III's blood was about to squirt from his ears.

Kisses, said Julie Sutton, gentle kisses . . .

Morris Bird III groaned.

She lowered herself on his lap.

Oh *my,* said Morris Bird III.

She stroked his cheeks, his ears.

Master is pleased. Ah, my heart rejoices, said Turhan Bey.

Her arms encircled Morris Bird III's neck. She wriggled on his lap. A long sigh, and then she said: How would my master care to begin?

Oh splendid, said Turhan Bey. The ecstasy on master's face is a joy to behold.

Love, said Julie Sutton. *Desire.*

Ah, master, prepare yourself for such transports as are experienced by only a select and valiant few, said Turhan Bey.

That did it. Waving an enervated hand, Morris Bird III buried his face in Julie Sutton's hair (it abounded with an odor of priceless ancient perfumes) and mumbled, addressing himself to Turhan Bey: Would you please get out of

". . . here?" said Morris Bird III, groaning. He flopped over on his stomach. Sunlight had insinuated itself through his eyelids, and now he knew what was happening. He pressed his face against his pillow. He squeezed his eyes tightly shut. Sometimes, if he concentrated hard enough, he was able to resume his dreams. But this time his heart was pumping too violently, and he was sweating too much, and something painful was happening in his belly. He thrashed a little, almost listlessly, and then he kicked his legs wide apart. Grunting, he rolled over on his back. He opened his eyes. Now all he had to do was keep his hands above his waist. There was a trick he employed. It had been quite successful. He blinked toward the sunlight, stared at his hands. He decided that now was a good time to employ his trick. He raised his arms until they were vertical. Then he let them fall behind his head. He grasped the bedposts. He squeezed the bedposts very tightly. He breathed slowly, deeply. He kept squeezing the bedposts. As long as he kept his hands above his waist, he was all right. He forced himself to look directly into the sunlight. Then he filled his mind with visions of the Swiss Alps, buckets of ice water, blizzards, polar bears, igloos. He squeezed the bedposts like mad. Gradually, the odor of priceless ancient perfumes went away. Bowing and scraping, Turhan Bey withdrew behind a curtain. Julie Sutton skittered off, her veils swirling. Morris Bird III kept his legs wide apart. He squeezed the bedposts until his hands hurt. Sweat ran down his nose. It itched. It itched awful. But he knew he could not afford to scratch. If he scratched, he would have to let go of one of the bedposts, and this he could not afford. At this particular moment, a free hand could have meant catastrophe.

He lay that way for perhaps five minutes. Finally, when conditions in his belly were more or less normal, he took a chance and released the bedposts. He busily scratched the sweat off his nose and forehead. Then, grunting, he got out of bed and lay facedown on the floor. He did twenty pushups. Then he rolled over and lifted himself into a squatting position. He did twenty deep knee bends.

Gasping, he flopped on the edge of his bed. He glanced at the alarmclock on the dresser. He leaned toward the nightstand at the head of the bed and turned on the radio. He changed the station from WJW, which carried the broadcasts of the Indians' games, to WCCC and *The Early Bird Show*. He listened to his father discuss the bargains that could be obtained at a place called the Bizzy-B Department Store on Prospect Avenue. This was some department store. It was to real department stores what the Gordon Park Berardinos were to baseball. Frowning, Morris Bird III listened to his father introduce the Peggy Lee record, "Mañana." His father sounded so much *different* on the radio. Almost as though he had nothing for the world but friendship. Huh, it sure was peculiar. Back in the days when his father had been just a plain old announcer, his deep voice had reflected him exactly as Morris Bird III thought of him—a big man with one foot who never was hardly anything but solemn. But now Morris Bird III's father sounded different. *The Early Bird Show* had made him almost buttery. He called himself *Morrie Bird*, and now and then he actually *chuckled*, like maybe he was *Arthur Godfrey* or somebody, and oh boy, how Fake could one person get? Sure, when he did a station break he still *sounded* like The Voice of Cleveland & Northeastern Ohio, but something new and somehow Fake lay behind the sound, and it made Morris Bird III feel like a worm in a skillet. He guessed maybe his father just wasn't cut out to be a Personality Kid, and he supposed it was a shame. Oh well. It was too early in the day to be feeling sorry for his father. And besides, there was something big and happy on the agenda—the baseball game. Thinking too much about his father would take the joy out of it.

Humming along with Peggy Lee, Morris Bird III shucked himself out of his pajamas and put on his underwear, socks, a sweatshirt, his trousers and his shoes. He hung up his pajamas in the closet. His father said a few words about Chesterfields. He heard Sandra potting around in the bathroom. He looked at the alarmclock: 7:15. He hollered at Sandra to get a wiggle on. Breakfast at the Wysockis was served at 7:30 on the old noseroo. He and Sandra took all three of their meals at the Wysockis. His father, who got off work early in the afternoon, joined them there for the evening meal. Except for that evening meal, Morris Bird III and Sandra saw very little of their father these days. With their mother down in Paradise Falls, their father had been going out nights on what he said were visits to friends. He came home quite late, and Morris Bird III wondered how he did it. With his show going on the air at 5 A.M., he had to get up at 4 in order to catch the 4:38 Hough Avenue owl trackless trolley that took him downtown to the studio. The bus stop, at Hough and East 90th, was a good fiveminute walk from the house on Edmunds Avenue. Huh. In a way, it was sort of mysterious. The past three or four nights, Morris Bird III's father had come home after Morris Bird III and Sandra were asleep. And he'd left home before they were awake. If it weren't for the mussed bedclothes in his bedroom and the dirty coffee cup he left on the kitchen table every morning, there would have been no proof that Morris Bird III's father had come home *at all.* It almost made Morris Bird III feel like the laziest person on the face of the earth, sleeping his life away while his tireless father came and went, night after night, silently and spookily, like maybe Lamont Cranston, known to his intimates as The Shadow.

Oh for crying out loud.

Another frown. A cluck. A sigh. Morris Bird III stood up and cocked his head. His father was giving the weather forecast. The day would be warm and sunny, and hot *dog*. More music came on, this time "You Can't Be True, Dear." Morris Bird III's head still was cocked. He was listening for sounds from the bathroom. He heard none. He went into the hall. He called to Sandra. A muffled noise came from the other side of her bedroom door. Ah, the Crown Princess had completed her duties in the bawthroom. Sometimes she took hours, or at least so it seemed. Whistling through the openings between his teeth, Morris Bird III went into the bathroom. It had a warm thick Ivory Soap smell. The first thing he did was take a damp washrag and dig the boogers out of the corners of his eyes. Then he examined his forehead in the mirror. Nothing had changed. It still looked like the surface of the moon. He wondered how his grandmother was doing. He shook his head, filled the basin with hot water. *Really* hot water. It steamed. It just about bubbled. He dipped the washrag in the water, then rubbed Ivory Soap into the washrag. His palms turned pink. Squealing, he slapped the washrag on his face. He rubbed. He rinsed. He washed. He rubbed his forehead so hard that it got to feeling as though someone had doused it with gasoline and then had lit a match. He rubbed away the heads of exactly three pimples. Then he took a census. Counting his cheeks, his chin and his forehead, his face had exactly seventeen pimples. He exhaled heavily, dried his face, pulled the plug from the drain. The water rushed out of the basin. It made a heavy hasty sound that was something like gas in the bathtub. Then he brushed his teeth with Pebeco. He splattered the mirror. He wiped away the splatters, then returned the Pebeco to the medicine cabinet over the basin. He put the cap on the Pebeco. He'd always been pretty good about remembering. He combed his hair. The part was very straight. He was as skillful a parter of hair as just about anyone he knew. Lately he'd taken some pride in his hair. He couldn't quite understand why. Up until about three or four months ago, he'd never given a whoop about it one way or another. But ah yes, things forever and relentlessly changed, and that was Life. Which was a magazine. Which cost 15 cents. And, if you didn't have 15 cents, it was tough. What was tough? Life. What was Life? A magazine. How much did it cost? 15 cents? What if you didn't have 15 cents? That was tough. What was tough? Life. What was—*oh forget it!* Talk about your mice running on treadmills.

Sandra was waiting for him in the hall. Her copy of *Appleton's Cyclopaedia of American Biography*, the 1887 edition, Volume III, GRIN through LOC, was hugged to her chest.

"Come on," said Morris Bird III. He started down the stairs ahead of her.

She followed silently.

They left the house, crossed the front lawn, crossed the Wysocki driveway, crossed the Wysocki front lawn, then climbed the front steps of the Wysocki house. They let themselves in and marched straight back to the kitchen. It was exactly 7:30, and breakfast was waiting.

Mr. Wysocki sat at the table. He was digging into a couple of eggs that had their sunny sides showing. Mrs. Wysocki was at the stove. Suzanne, spotless and silent, was pouring milk. Morris

Bird III and Sandra took their places at the table. Everyone said good morning to everyone else. (Frank was upstairs, still in bed. He was working the four-to-midnight this month.) Mrs. Wysocki brought toast and eggs to Morris Bird III and Sandra. Glasses of orange juice already were on the table. Suzanne brought them glasses of milk, then seated herself across the table from them. Morris Bird III kept his eyes off her. Instead, he looked at Mr. Wysocki, who was reading the morning paper and grinning. Suzanne asked her father for the women's section. Grunting, Mr. Wysocki extracted it and handed it to her. She thanked him. Her voice was very proper. Morris Bird III's tongue made a dry sound against his teeth. No one noticed. He set to work on his eggs. They were just right. They had paprika on them. He took a couple of bites, washed them down with orange juice. Then he used his boardinghouse reach and speared a piece of toast with his fork. He spread it with butter and Welch's Grape Jelly. Ah, such breakfasts Mrs. Wysocki served. They had to be the greatest breakfasts in the world. They never included oatmeal. (At home, he had oatmeal every morning. Oatmeal, juice and milk—the routine never varied. There never was toast. There never were eggs. The oatmeal and the juice and the milk were like the moon and the stars and the evolution of the seasons: they were always the same. He'd never been in a poorhouse, but he had an idea poorhouse food was a good deal similar to the hateful little breakfasts his mother served.) Mr. Wysocki still was grinning over the paper. Mrs. Wysocki scraped two eggs from the skillet, turned off the stove, went to the table and seated herself next to her husband. She nudged him in the ribs. "All right," she said, "what's so funny?"

A pleased little snort from Mr. Wysocki. "Nothing's funny,"

he said. "I'm just feeling good. My ball club won again last night." He looked at Morris Bird III. "We're making our move. We're only four and a half games behind *your* people."

"It'll never last," said Morris Bird III. "And anyway, your team didn't pick up an inch last night. Old Satchel Paige did in the White Sox, so who cares what the Yankees did?"

"The *White Sox*," said Mr. Wysocki. "*Those* humptydumpties? What are they in? Sixteenth place?"

"A victory over them counts as much as a victory over anybody," said Morris Bird III.

"Yeah? So how come, if the Indians are so great, they win by 1–0 against the *White Sox*? How come they don't *kill* the White Sox?"

"One run's as good as a hundred," said Morris Bird III.

"Sure. But against *that* team, it's almost like losing." Here Mr. Wysocki consulted his paper. "Thirtysix victories and seventy-five defeats—now *there*'s a team."

Morris Bird III grinned, shook his head.

"Come on now, kid," said Mr. Wysocki. "Admit it. Don't you think *your* Indians are getting a little nervous about the hot breath of *my* Yankees on their necks?"

"*Worried?* How come, if they're so worried, they've won eight straight games?"

"Baseball," said Mrs. Wysocki, sighing. "My *Lord*."

Suzanne fastidiously scraped up egg yolk with a piece of toast.

Mr. Wysocki ignored his wife. "Eight straight victories, sure. But over who? The White Sox? The St. Louis Browns? You call such a thing an *accomplishment?*"

Suzanne rattled the women's section.

Mr. Wysocki glanced at her briefly but said nothing.

"Well, there's one thing you got to admit," Morris Bird III told Mr. Wysocki.

"And what's that?" said Mr. Wysocki.

"The crowd last night. It was some crowd."

"That I'll admit," said Mr. Wysocki. "Seven, eight, three, eight, two is some crowd. That old Satchel. You got to give him credit. He brings in the people." But then a moist deprecating sound came from Mr. Wysocki's lips, and he said: "All those people. And all the people in this town who're rooting for their beloved Indians. It sure is a shame to think of them listening to the World Series on the radio—with the Yanks playing, I mean."

"Don't be too sure of that," said Morris Bird III.

"Ah Morris my boy, you are very young. Don't you know the Yankees always win?"

"Always?"

"Well, almost always."

"Almost isn't always," said Morris Bird III. He didn't quite know the meaning of what he'd said, but the words surely had *sounded* good.

A grin from Mr. Wysocki. "Ah," he said, "this is some debater I got sitting at my kitchen table."

Morris Bird III smiled. He had to. Mr. Wysocki never said things he didn't mean. He wasn't the type. He was, as far as Morris Bird III was concerned, a wholly admirable man. Maybe somewhere there were Fake parts in him, but they'd not been discovered by Morris Bird III, and gloryosky, hot dog, hooray, hooray. So okay. So Mr. Wysocki didn't have much use for the Indians. So he rooted for the hated New York Yankees. At least he made no bones about it. At least he was consistent. Morris Bird III knew a lot of people who *said* they were Indian fans when they really weren't. Sure, they rooted like mad for the Indians when the Indians were winning. But, let the Indians lose a game or two, and those same people sneered and booed and made disparaging remarks. So, Morris Bird III would take a Mr. Wysocki any day of the week in preference to *those* people. At least he knew where Mr. Wysocki stood. At least he knew Mr. Wysocki was no loudmouthed fairweather Fake. Mr. Wysocki honestly & genuinely preferred the New York Yankees, and *that* was *that*, and how could it be knocked?

Except for chewing sounds, the table was silent. When Suzanne broke the silence, it came almost as a shock to Morris Bird III. But there was nothing unusual in being surprised. Old Suzanne had never really been the blabbermouth type. And now, what with her holiness and all, she was most of the time as quiet as a grain of sand. But this morning she chose to do the world a favor and *say* something. Looking at her mother, she said: "Betty May Moneypenny is getting married to Lindsley dodd Van der Veer."

"How's that again?" said Mrs. Wysocki.

"It says so in the paper."

"It says *what* in the paper?"

"It *says:* Betty May Moneypenny is getting married to Lindsley dodd Van der Veer."

Sandra giggled. "Moneypenny," she said.

"Her picture's in the paper," said Suzanne. "She's pretty."

"Oh?" said Mrs. Wysocki. "Let's see."

Suzanne folded the paper and showed her mother the picture.

"Mm," said Mrs. Wysocki, "yes indeed, she's very pretty."

The picture was passed around. Betty May Moneypenny was blond, and yes, you honestly had to say she was pretty.

Sandra giggled. "Moneypenny," she said.

"Lindsley dodd Van der Veer's quite a mouthful too," said Morris Bird III. He looked at Sandra, and her giggling got him to giggling too.

Mrs. Wysocki smiled at Morris Bird III. "Shhh," she said.

He blinked at her.

"They're probably very nice people," said Mrs. Wysocki. "You shouldn't laugh just because their names are a little different from the runofthemill names you run across every day—like Wysocki and Bird, I mean."

Morris Bird III nodded. He had stopped giggling.

So had Sandra.

"She's pretty," said Mrs. Wysocki, "and she's getting married, and I bet she's very happy, and we really shouldn't laugh."

Morris Bird III nodded.

So did Sandra.

"Yes," said Suzanne, glancing toward heaven.

"Yes *what?*" Mrs. Wysocki wanted to know.

"Yes they shouldn't laugh."

Mrs. Wysocki sighed.

Mr. Wysocki spoke up. "Suzanne, it's *their* private conversation. They don't need your nickel's worth."

"Yes, Daddy," said Suzanne. "I'm sorry." She buttered herself a piece of toast. She chewed silently, and she appeared about as *sorry* as the Japanese had been *sorry* for bombing Pearl Harbor.

Mr. Wysocki rolled his eyes, withdrew behind the paper.

Mrs. Wysocki changed the subject. "Heard from your mother yet?" she asked Morris Bird III.

"No."

"It certainly is a shame. About your grandmother, I mean."

Morris Bird III nodded.

"She was such a good neighbor."

Morris Bird III nodded.

"She was so friendly."

"Was?" said Morris Bird III.

Mrs. Wysocki cleared her throat. "Well . . . ah, all I meant was—"

Mr. Wysocki emerged from behind his paper. He looked straight at Morris Bird III. "You know what she means."

Morris Bird III stood up. His face was warm. "Excuse me," he said. He went out of the kitchen. Everyone stared at him. His face got warmer and warmer. He went out of the Wysocki house. He went next door to his own house. Upstairs, his radio still was playing. He could hear his father's voice. Oh *Lord*, he had forgotten all about it. If his mother had been home, she would have skinned him alive. A low electric bill was one of the great loves of her life. Grunting, he ran upstairs and switched off the radio, silencing his father smack in the middle of a commercial for a hemorrhoid unguent. He sat on the edge of his bed and rubbed his fists in his eyes. Oh, why did *she* have to be The One? Why couldn't The One have been someone who wasn't about to die? He snuffled. He rubbed his poor forehead. Then he heard someone coming up the stairs. It was Sandra. She looked in on him for a moment, but did not enter his room. Both her arms were tight around her copy of *Appleton's Cyclopaedia of American Biography,* the 1887 edition, Volume III, GRIN through LOC. Without saying anything, she backed out of the doorway and moved on down the hall to her own room.

A little later, Morris Bird III went back next door and told Mrs. Wysocki he was sorry. She smiled at him, told him he was getting to be quite a man. She did not try to pat him or hug him or do anything else that would have ruined what was happening. She told him lunch would be served at noon sharp. Kielbasa, she said, and they both smiled. He loved kielbasa. She was washing dishes. Mr. Wysocki still sat at the kitchen table. He told Morris Bird III they would leave for the game immediately after lunch. Nodding, Morris Bird III said he would be back at noon with bells on. His eyes were tingly.

The rest of the morning he sort of pooped around the house. He made his bed, read part of a story called "Nevada Gas" from a book entitled *Spanish Blood* that had been given to him earlier that summer by his Uncle Alan, the telegrapher and sufferer from bad sinuses. The author of this book, a collection of stories, was good old Raymond Chandler. A girl in the story "Nevada Gas" was named Francine Ley, and Morris Bird III saw this as being one of the great names of all time. A little after 10, the telephone rang. Morris Bird III answered. It was his father. He told Morris Bird III he wouldn't be joining them at the Wysockis' for lunch. He said he had more friends he wanted to visit. Okay, said Morris Bird III, and that was the end of the conversation. They both hung up. Great day in the morning, he had no idea his father had so many friends. He wondered how come he'd met so few of them. Ah nuts. Bushwah. The ways of his father were too mysterious to comprehend. If he wasn't coming for lunch, he wasn't coming for lunch. End of thought.

He wandered into Sandra's room. She was on Page 441 of *Appleton's Cyclopaedia of American Biography*, the 1887 edition,

Volume III, GRIN through LOC. She was reading about a man named Cave Johnson, born in Robertson County, Tennessee, on January 11, 1793, died in Clarksville, Tennessee, on November 23, 1866. He was appointed Postmaster General of the United States in 1845 by President James K. Polk. Later, he was president of the Bank of Tennessee. Sandra read all this information to Morris Bird III, and he nodded gravely, squeezing his chin. He told her their father wouldn't be joining them for lunch. She grunted, did not bother to look up from her book. He told her to be sure to let him know how it came out. She giggled. He went back to his own room, resumed reading "Nevada Gas," immersing himself in a passage that began: *Francine Ley sat in a low red chair beside a small table on which there was an alabaster bowl. Smoke from the cigarette she had just discarded into the bowl floated up and made patterns in the still, warm air. Her hands were clasped behind her head and her smoke-blue eyes were lazy, inviting. She had dark auburn hair set in loose waves. There were bluish shadows in the troughs of the waves.*

He was lying on the bed. He closed the book. Sighing, he reached up and seized the bedposts. He squeezed them and squeezed them and squeezed them, and eventually he was all right.

Lunch was great. The kielbasa was so rich it just about made Morris Bird III burp. It was a wonder to him that everyone in the Wysocki family didn't weigh at least three hundred pounds. The kielbasa was augmented by dumplings, sauerkraut, head-lettuce salad and cherry strudel. When he was finished, he barely was able to rise from the table. His face was warm, and he could feel the action of his heart, and on any other day he would have hidden himself somewhere for a nap. But not *today*. Today was the day he and Mr. Wysocki were going to the ballgame. All during the meal, he and Mr. Wysocki kept up their argument over the merits of his Indians and Mr. Wysocki's New York Yankees. Frank Wysocki, up and about by now, also participated in the discussion. He took up Morris Bird III's side. He accused Mr. Wysocki of being a traitor to the city of Cleveland. This made Mr. Wysocki laugh. He told Frank he wished he had a nickel for every time he had been told that. Frank also laughed. He accused his father of being a hopeless old reprobate. To which Mr. Wysocki said: Look who's talking. You and all the girls you chase after. You and your redhot mama, that Mossler woman across the street. Ah, Pop, said Frank Wysocki, jealousy will get you nowhere. Suzanne and Sandra took in all of this, but they said nothing. At one point, Suzanne glanced sharply at her mother, but Mrs. Wysocki was too busy grinning to notice. Suzanne looked briefly up toward God or Whomever, then sighed, fluttered her eyelids, folded her hands in her lap. Boy oh boy, Morris Bird III said to himself, I bet *she* never made gas in the bathtub. Or, as far as that goes, anywhere else. (A Crucifix hung over the mantel in the Wysocki parlor. Below it, squarely in the middle of the mantel, stood a creamcolored plaster Madonna. Suzanne crossed herself whenever she passed the mantel. Honest.) After baseball and Frank's love life, the Wysockis briefly discussed politics. Mr. and Mrs. Wysocki and Frank all intended to vote for President Truman. They liked him very much. They admired the fierce brave way he stood up for what he thought was right, and the devil take the Republicans and the newspapers. (About the Crucifix and the Madonna: Mr. and Mrs. Wysocki were quite religious, and they attended Mass every Sunday morning, but they didn't make a big federal case out of religion the way Suzanne, all pious and pale and prissy, did. Which was why they sort of smiled whenever they saw her cross herself in front of the mantel. They seemed to understand that she was being sort of dishonest, using religion as an instrument to make herself seem better than they were. Not that they were angered by it. They weren't. It was just that sometimes they had to smile.) Mrs. Wysocki got to talking with Sandra about *Appleton's Cyclopaedia of American Biography*, the 1887 edition, Volume III, GRIN through LOC. She asked Sandra why the great interest in such a big fat book. Sandra said something to the effect that, well, *somebody* should read it. It hadn't ever been read, she told Mrs. Wysocki. She knew this, she said, because most of the pages had been uncut. And anyway, she liked information. In the past year or two, she had been a great one for reading almanacs and informing people of the average annual rainfall in Kuwait and El Salvador, the sheep population of Bhutan, the exchange rate of the dollar and the pound sterling, and so on and so forth and so on. (About the Crucifix and the Madonna: Morris Bird III didn't think it was right that Suzanne looked on her religion as something that made her better than everyone else. It seemed to him that religion was what you *made* of it. By itself, it was nothing. It was one thing to cross yourself and go around looking all pious and pale and prissy. It was quite another thing to live your life according to His groundrules. Morris Bird III's grandmother had taught him that much. As far as he could tell, any other sort of behavior was outandout Fake.) Mrs. Wysocki asked Morris Bird III if The Voice of Cleveland & Northeastern Ohio would be honoring them with his presence for dinner. Morris Bird III said he didn't know. His father hadn't bothered to clue him in. Apparently he was very busy taking advantage of the opportunity to visit his multitude of friends. (Morris Bird III didn't say *that* to Mrs. Wysocki, but then he didn't suppose he had to.) A little before 1 o'clock, Mr. Wysocki rose from the table and suggested to Morris Bird III that it was getting along about That Time. A nod from Morris Bird III. A quick nod. A vigorous nod. A happy nod. A few minutes later, he and Mr. Wysocki were inside Mr. Wysocki's majestic 1936 Packard, and its engine was making sleek thrumming sounds, and they were on their hot dog whoopee hooray for Mr. Wysocki and all people who were generous way.

The Cleveland Stadium was perched on the edge of Lake Erie just north of the city's downtown business area. It had been built in 1931, and from that year through 1946 the Indians had played about half their home games there and half in an old place called League Park, located at Lexington Avenue and East 66th Street, not too far from Morris Bird III's home on Edmunds Avenue. But, in 1947, shortly after the purchase of the Indians by the flamboyant Bill Veeck, the club shifted all its games to Cleveland Stadium. The reason for this was no particular mystery. The seating capacity of Cleveland Stadium was about 80,000, as compared with League Park's 29,000. The team was a good one, and it was drawing the people, and League Park had become simply altogether too small. In a way, this was a shame—at least as far as Morris Bird III was concerned. At League Park, you just about sat on top of the players. You could hear their shouts to each other, and you almost were able to reach out and touch them. It was an old wooden and concrete ballpark, and it didn't even have lights for night games, and it was about as modern as Rutherford B. Hayes, and yet . . . and yet . . . well, it had a *humanness* to it, a feeling of sweat and leather and splinters and vivid green paint and earth and grass and muscle . . . and none of these things could be felt in the great cavernous Stadium. Morris Bird III had seen games in League Park, and he had seen games in the Stadium, and for him League Park had been at least 2,000% better. But Bill Veeck and the Stadium represented Progress, and he supposed he was a stickinthemud for thinking the way he did. And anyway, baseball was baseball, and there never had been a game like it, and there never would be. Oh sure, Morris Bird III *enjoyed* other sports, but baseball he *loved.* It was a team game, and it was an individual game, and thus it was unique (think of the odds: nine men trying to dispose of just one), and there was nothing in the whole entire world that had such a power to grab him by the throat.

So now, sitting next to Mr. Wysocki in that splendid thrumming old Packard, Morris Bird III almost sort of grinned at the world, and—for *now* at least, for a few thin hours of noise and sunshine and the odor of peanut shells—maybe he would be able to push away all his frets and aches, his thoughts of Fred C. Dobbs and his parents and his aunts and his uncles and his complexion and Julie Sutton and Czerny the lizard and raindrop races and his grandmother, his *dying* grandmother, his wrinkled and yellowish and weepy grandmother who just happened to be The One, no matter how hard he told himself he wished she would hurry up and get the dying over with, yeah, *over* with and *done* with and *forgotten,* but who just happened to be The One, whose dying just happened to be chewing up his heart. Who just happened to be The One. Dear God. The One.

"Hey, pal," said Mr. Wysocki, "you all right?"

Morris Bird III blinked. He looked out his window. They were moving west along Hough Avenue not far from East 55th Street.

Mr. Wysocki repeated his question. "You all right?"

Morris Bird III nodded. "Um. I'm sorry. I guess my mind was a million miles away."

"That's the kind of mind you've got, isn't it?"

"Huh?"

"I didn't mean that as an insult," said Mr. Wysocki. "All I meant was, you're sort of a thinker."

Morris Bird III shrugged.

Mr. Wysocki slowed for the light at East 55th. The great old car came smoothly to a stop. He looked at Morris Bird III, smiled a little and said: "Was it about your grandmother?"

"Yes," said Morris Bird III. He didn't see any reason to lie.

"You going down there to Paradise Falls before she dies?"

"I don't know. I mean, my mother didn't want Sandra and me to go down with her."

"How come? Didn't she think you and Sandra would be able to take it?"

"She didn't say. She didn't give any reason. She just went."

"Oh," said Mr. Wysocki. The light changed. The car moved forward. There was no jerk when the gears shifted.

Morris Bird III glanced at the sky. It was white and blue. Clouds ran in thin swift streaks.

The car moved easily. Mr. Wysocki drummed his fingers on the steeringwheel.

At Hough and East 49th Street, they passed a pie bakery. Morris Bird III leaned out his window and took a deep breath of Piesmell.

"Your grandmother and my wife used to have great conversations," said Mr. Wysocki.

Morris Bird III nodded. He glanced at an old frame house. A man and a little boy were playing catch on the sidewalk in front of the old frame house. The little boy couldn't have been more than six or seven. The man threw him the ball underhand. For some reason, Morris Bird III had to close his eyes for a couple of seconds. They were warm, and oh was he forever and a day *dumb*. When he opened his eyes, Mr. Wysocki was looking at him funny. He said nothing. Neither did Mr. Wysocki. The car turned north on East 40th Street, then west on Payne Avenue. It was following the downtown route of the Hough Avenue trackless trolleys. The sidewalks along Payne Avenue were filled with old women who wore babushkas. This was a Serbian neighborhood. Or maybe Croatian. Something like that. The sunlight was really great.

"Should be a great day for a game," said Mr. Wysocki.

"Yes," said Morris Bird III.

"I hope Seerey gets in the game."

"So do I," said Morris Bird III. They were referring to Pat Seerey, a pudgy outfielder who had been traded by the Indians to Chicago early in the season. Seerey and a pitcher named Al Gettel had been sent to the White Sox for an outfielder named Bob Kennedy. Seerey was quite some colorful character all right. He had been with the Indians since 1944, and the fans loved to boo him. This was because he struck out so often. When it came to striking out, Pat Seerey was the absolute champion of the universe. He also hit a lot of home runs, but his strikeouts far outnumbered his home runs. Still, when Pat Seerey got ahold of the ball, it really went. Earlier this year, he had hit four home runs in an 11-inning game against Philadelphia. It would be good to be seeing old Pat Seerey again, and Morris Bird III hoped he got in the game.

"I always liked Seerey," said Mr. Wysocki.

"Me, too."

"He's always been interesting to watch. Home run or strikeout, you're never bored."

"Yes."

"And, you know something? I got a hunch he takes it all in his stride."

"Uh huh."

"Anyone who strikes out as much as *he* does would *have* to."

"Uh huh."

"Otherwise he'd go out of his mind."

"Uh huh."

The car turned north on East 30th Street. It passed scrubby trees and tiny frame houses. The sunlight made golden shadows in the trees. At St. Clair Avenue, the car turned west again. St. Clair Avenue was very wide. It was lined by old warehouses and business establishments. Here and there, winos sat in doorways. A lot of loose paper flapped and skidded in the wind. They passed a number of gypsy fortunetelling places. They were in old storefronts. Plump dark women sat behind dirty windows and beckoned to passersby. Now the automobile traffic was heavier. Mounted policemen were helping direct the traffic. Their horses were immense and beautiful. At East 9th Street, Mr. Wysocki maneuvered the Packard into a line of cars that was turning right. Now, on the sidewalk, stood men who were selling pennants and balloons and peanuts and little fuzzy windup bears and kittens and puppydogs. The Packard moved north on East 9th Street. Up ahead, to the left, vast and stolid, was the Stadium. Beyond it was the lake. The water of the lake glistened, and here and there were tiny specky sailboats. Staying in line, the Packard crossed the bridge that took East 9th Street over the Memorial Shoreway. The Stadium parking lot lay just west of the place where East 9th deadened at the lake. A pier fingered out into the lake. An old steamer was tied up to the pier. Its name was *City of Conneaut*, and it looked sort of forlorn and dilapidated, and Morris Bird III couldn't help but feel sorry for it. Its paint was all cracked and dull, and along the waterline it displayed a great deal of rust. Mr. Wysocki guided the Packard into the parking lot. He gave a colored man half a dollar. Other colored men waved and yelled at him, pointing out the place where he was to park. Morris Bird III looked around. Cars were everywhere. Obeying instructions, Mr. Wysocki parked the Packard in a line with about a million other cars. He shut off the ignition, then detached a pair of sunglasses that had been clipped to the sunshade on the driver's side. He put on the sunglasses. Then he rooted around in the back seat and came up with an old straw hat. He put it on his head. Okay, he told Morris Bird III, let's go. They got out of the car, walked across the gravel parking lot, threading their way through the rows and rows and rows and *rows* of parked cars. Mr. Wysocki wore a pair of old khaki trousers and a sport shirt that was decorated with a design of surf and sand and palm trees. These things, along with his sunglasses and his old straw hat, gave Mr. Wysocki the appearance of a benign old gangster overlord, sort of a softhearted

Howard DaSilva or Sheldon Leonard, and Morris Bird III was a little proud to be walking alongside such an impressive figure of a man. Mr. Wysocki moved briskly, and Morris Bird III almost had to trot to keep up with him. They made their way into the crowds that were advancing on the gates to the Stadium. Everywhere were voices, and almost everyone was grinning: kids wearing baseball caps, kids wearing baseball gloves, kids wearing baseball caps *and* baseball gloves, men in sportshirts, women in loose print dresses, guffawing Negroes, skinny hawkers with dirty necks, stolid policemen, young men holding hands with their girls. Morris Bird III grimaced at all these people, and a gentle and surpassingly pleasant burp came up to remind him of the kielbasa. They entered the Stadium at Gate D. Morris Bird III went through the turnstile ahead of Mr. Wysocki, who gave the tickets to a small redfaced fellow with blue veins on his nose. The small redfaced fellow tore the tickets in half, directed Mr. Wysocki to a tunnel that went off to the left. Now all the world smelled of mustard and peanuts. Shouts echoed. Mr. Wysocki moved as briskly as a drum major. He stopped only once—to buy a scorecard from a small Negro boy. Consulting the ticket stubs, he led Morris Bird III up a ramp that opened onto the thirdbase side of the field, just behind the Chicago dugout. The greenness of the field astounded Morris Bird III. No matter how many times he saw it, it always just about sucked the breath out of him. It was almost *too* green. It almost hurt his eyes. An usher came and took Mr. Wysocki's ticket stubs. He led Mr. Wysocki and Morris Bird III down a long sequence of shallow cement steps, past rows and rows and rows of seats. He marched them straight to the very first row, squarely behind the Chicago dugout. Morris Bird III hadn't ever sat up *this* close before—not even at intimate little League Park. He looked at Mr. Wysocki, and Mr. Wysocki grinned and asked him were these good seats or were these good seats. He told Mr. Wysocki he'd never seen such good seats. Good, said Mr. Wysocki. He gave the usher a quarter. The usher thanked him and went away. Mr. Wysocki and Morris Bird III sat down. Directly in front of them, the Chicago pitcher was warming up. Over on the firstbase side, the Cleveland pitcher was warming up. Morris Bird III examined the clock on the scoreboard out in center field. It said 1:50. Ten minutes to go. The Chicago pitcher was righthanded. Morris Bird III asked Mr. Wysocki who the fellow was. Randy Gumpert, said Mr. Wysocki. He used to be with the Yankees. When he's good, he's very very good, and when he's bad he's awful. Like the little girl with the little curl right down the middle of her forehead. You ever heard that poem? Morris Bird III shook his head no, and Mr. Wysocki told him oh well, it didn't matter. Morris Bird III squinted over toward the Indians' side of the field. The Cleveland pitcher today would be Bob Lemon, who probably was the best pitcher in the American League. Morris Bird III and Mr. Wysocki got to discussing Bob Lemon, and even Mr. Wysocki had to admit Bob Lemon was pretty good out there on the old mound. A couple of months ago, Bob Lemon had thrown a no-hitter against the Detroit Tigers, and he'd already won sixteen games, and if anyone was money in the bank to continue the Indians' winning and shutout streaks, it was this guy. A former outfielder and infielder, Bob Lemon was only in his second season as a pitcher, but already he had the best sinker in the league, which made him awful tough to hit. Mr. Wysocki shook his head and said it wasn't hardly fair, using a man like Lemon against such a feeble team as the White Sox. Then they turned to the subject of the Indians' shutout streak. The four straight shutouts tied a league record. The 1903 Cleveland team had performed the same feat. Actually, that 1903 team had rolled up 41 consecutive scoreless innings. So far, counting the last three innings of the game that had preceded the streak, the Indians had blanked the opposition for 39 straight innings. So, if they held the White Sox through the third inning of today's game, they would at least set a new *inning* record. Morris Bird III grinned, watched Bob Lemon very closely. Old Bob Lemon would do it. Good old Bob Lemon. In the Cleveland dugout, the players were moving around, pounding their gloves, hefting their bats. Morris Bird III spotted Lou Boudreau, Number 5, the manager and short-stop. He was looking at a slip of paper in his hand. Then he emerged from the dugout. At the same time, a stout man emerged from the Chicago dugout. The stout man was, said Mr. Wysocki, poor old Ted Lyons, the White Sox manager. Ted Lyons and Lou Boudreau and the umpires met at home plate. The managers exchanged slips of paper, gave copies to the home plate umpire. Then an enormous voice came over the publicaddress system. Quickly Mr. Wysocki reached into a shirt pocket and came up with a pencil. The lineups were announced:

CHICAGO	CLEVELAND
Hodgin, rf	Mitchell, lf
Lupien, 1b	Peck, rf
Appling, 3b	Boudreau, ss
Seerey, lf	E. Robinson, 1b
A. Robinson, c	Doby, cf
Philley, cf	Keltner, 3b
Kolloway, 2b	Berardino, 2b

Michaels, ss	Hegan, c
Gumpert, p	Lemon, p

The Indians' names—especially Lou Boudreau's—were met with cheering that just about took off the top of Morris Bird III's head. But he couldn't really complain, since he cheered right along with everyone else. Except Mr. Wysocki, that is. Mr. Wysocki was too busy scribbling the lineups in his scorecard. And besides, it would be a cold day in the warmest place of all when Mr. Wysocki cheered for the Indians. Ah, but no matter. Mr. Wysocki had brought Morris Bird III to all this magnificence, and so had a right to cheer or not to cheer just as he pleased. Then the publicaddress voice asked everyone to stand up for Our National Anthem. At the same time, the Indians ran out of their dugout. The players all paused, took off their caps, placed them over their hearts. The National Anthem came from the publicaddress system. All over the park, everyone stood motionless. Morris Bird III looked out at the flag that hung from the centerfield pole. It flapped, and its colors were very bright. He stood very straight. At the conclusion of the National Anthem, everyone cheered and clapped. The home plate umpire tossed a baseball to Bob Lemon, who kicked at the mound and looked around at the outfielders. The Chicago leadoff hitter, a fellow named Ralph Hodgin, stepped up to the plate. He hit lefthanded. According to Mr. Wysocki, Ralph Hodgin was fast and a good outfielder but a very weak hitter. Bob Lemon's first pitch was a strike. Everyone whooped. Another strike. More whoops. Then Ralph Hodgin struck out. *Loud* whoops. The next Chicago hitter was the first baseman, Ulysses (Tony) Lupien. He was a fine defensive player, but not much of a hitter either. At one time, he'd played for the Boston Red Sox. He was the only graduate of Harvard University who'd ever played in the major leagues. He also was a left-handed hitter. Mr. Wysocki told Morris Bird III to watch Bob Lemon's sinker. It looks like it's working well today, he said. The words were no sooner out of his mouth when Lupien grounded weakly to Eddie Robinson at first base. Two out. More whoops. The next hitter, old Luke Appling, the Chicago third baseman, was about two thousand years old. It was said he could punch foul balls for hours. He'd been the Chicago shortstop since the beginning of time, but now in his declining years he'd been moved to third base, where the action supposedly wasn't so strenuous. He was having a good year. His average was above .300, and he was just about the only bona fide hitter in the entire Chicago lineup. He batted right-handed. Bob Lemon kept the ball low and got old Luke to ground to Ken Keltner at third. The White Sox were out in the first inning. No runs, no hits, no errors. The Indians' string of shutout innings now had reached 40! The scoreboard showed:

CHICAGO   0
CLEVELAND

A hotdog vendor came along. Mr. Wysocki asked Morris Bird III if he wanted one. Morris Bird III shook his head no and said something about the kielbasa. Mr. Wysocki smiled. The first Cleveland batter was Dale Mitchell, the left fielder and a lefthanded hitter. Dale Mitchell was the fastest man on the team. He was hitting over .300, and he owed his good batting average to all the infield hits his speed gave him. He received a splendid ovation. He flied to Philley in center. The next hitter, also lefthanded, was Hal Peck, the right fielder. Mr. Wysocki grinned as he watched Hal Peck come to the plate. This fellow plays pretty well for a cripple, he said. Morris Bird III asked Mr. Wysocki what he meant. Well, according to Mr. Wysocki, Hal Peck had shot off a couple of toes a few years back. A hunting accident. Oh, said Morris Bird III, and he glanced briefly at the place where Mr. Wysocki's thumb should have been. Hal Peck chopped a Gumpert pitch toward the second baseman, Kolloway. The ball rolled very slowly, and Hal Peck beat Kolloway's throw to first. The first hit of the game, and up to the plate—amid great cheers—stepped Lou Boudreau, shortstop and manager extraordinary. A beer vendor came along. Mr. Wysocki bought a bottle. The vendor poured it into a paper cup. Lou Boudreau, batting righthanded, crouching over the plate, the bat held out from his body and almost over his head, lined a single to right field. When Hodgin fumbled the ball, Peck went to third and Boudreau to second. Mr. Wysocki took a deep mournful swallow of beer. Morris Bird III was on his feet. So was just about everyone else. He could feel the earth shake from the volume of the yelling. He looked around. The Stadium wasn't filled to capacity, but it was a good crowd, and right now there was a great deal of armwaving and backslapping going on. Runners on second and third and only one out! Ah, poor Randy Gumpert! He wouldn't even get through the first inning! The next Cleveland hitter was the big handsome first baseman, Eddie Robinson. He batted lefthanded. Girls were said to be wild for him. Gumpert discussed the situation with his catcher, Aaron Robinson, no relation to Eddie. Gumpert nodded, and then Aaron Robinson patted him on the rump and returned to home plate. Aaron Robinson also was a former Yankee, Mr. Wysocki told Morris

Bird III. Gumpert worked carefully and slowly, and big Eddie Robinson hit the ball straight in the air. It was foul. Aaron Robinson settled under it. Two out. Everyone groaned. Except Mr. Wysocki. He simply sat there and sipped his beer. Up to the plate stepped Larry Doby, the center fielder, a lefthanded hitter and one of two Negro players on the Indians' roster. (The other was old Satchel Paige.) They were, as a matter of fact, the only Negro players in the American League. Morris Bird III had heard a lot of talk about these Negro players, and some of the talk hadn't been particularly pleasant. Ah, but he didn't care one way or the other. All he wanted was for Larry Doby to get a hit. Larry Doby dug in. Gumpert stared at him. Again Gumpert worked deliberately. He ignored the baserunners. He got Doby to go for an outside pitch. Doby hit it into left field, a routine chance for pudgy Pat Seerey. Side out. No runs, two hits, one error. Now the scoreboard showed:

CHICAGO	0
CLEVELAND	0

Pudgy Pat Seerey, a righthanded hitter, led off for Chicago in the second. The crowd, still making deep growly disappointed sounds because of the Indians' failure to score, let Seerey know exactly what it thought of him—with boos, boos that were so loud they shook the foundations of the Stadium. Mr. Wysocki grinned. So did Morris Bird III. Seerey almost tore the cover off the ball, but he lined it straight to Ken Keltner at third base. One out. Next up was the catcher, Aaron Robinson, a big lefthanded hitter. Lemon kept the ball low, and Aaron Robinson lifted a weak fly to Mitchell in left. Two out. One more out, and the Indians would tie the scoreless inning record. The next Chicago batter was the center fielder, a stocky young fellow named Dave Philley. A switch hitter, he batted lefthanded against the right-handed Lemon. He beat a low pitch into the dirt, grounding out to Eddie Robinson, unassisted. The Indians had tied the record of 41 consecutive scoreless innings! No runs, no hits, no errors. Now the scoreboard showed:

> CHICAGO   00
> CLEVELAND   0

First up for the Indians was Ken Keltner, third baseman and a righthanded hitter. He was generally conceded to be the best fielding third baseman in the league, and he hit a lot of home runs, too. He tore into a Gumpert pitch. Everyone stood up and hollered. The ball sailed out to left field. But Seerey was there when it came down. One out. Next up was Benny Goodman's old pal, Johnny Berardino, a righthanded hitter. He was filling in for the regular second baseman, Joe Gordon, who had a sprained ankle. It's too bad this guy doesn't hit as good as he looks, said Mr. Wysocki. (Johnny Berardino had, according to Mr. Wysocki, ambitions to become an actor once his baseball days were finished. A Hollywood actor, a profile type.) Gumpert had no trouble with Johnny Berardino, getting him to pop to Kolloway, the second baseman. The next Cleveland batter was Jim Hegan, the big Irish catcher who was absolute Death on foul balls but couldn't hit very well. He hit righthanded. Gumpert got him to fly to Seerey. No runs, no hits, no errors. Now the scoreboard showed:

CHICAGO	00
CLEVELAND	00

Mr. Wysocki bought Morris Bird III a bag of peanuts. This was the big inning. If the White Sox were kept from scoring, the Indians would break the 1903 record. The first Chicago batter was Don Kolloway, a righthanded hitter who scared no one. Lemon kept the ball low, and Kolloway grounded to Boudreau. Next up was Cass Michaels, the shortstop and also a right-handed hitter. Morris Bird III offered some peanuts to Mr. Wysocki. They were declined with thanks. Mr. Wysocki grinned, told Morris Bird III that Cass Michaels' real name was Casimir Kwieteniewski, or something like that. He said he could understand why it had been changed. Lemon worked easily on Michaels, striking him out. He also struck out Gumpert, the pitcher. Gumpert, who hit righthanded, swung at Lemon's sinkers like someone's aged Aunt Maud. The Indians had set the new record—42 consecutive scoreless innings! Lemon had retired the first nine Chicago hitters in order. No runs, no hits, no errors. Now the scoreboard showed:

CHICAGO	000
CLEVELAND	00

Everyone hollered and whooped and clapped. Morris Bird III asked Mr. Wysocki what did he think of *that*. Mr. Wysocki shrugged. The cheering became louder as Lemon, a lefthanded hitter and not a bad one for a pitcher, stepped up to lead off for the Indians in the third. He took a good cut at the ball, flied to

Philley in center. Next came Dale Mitchell, and he got one of his patented infield hits. His liner bounced off Gumpert's glove for a single. Hal Peck, the toeless wonder, was next. He fouled to Tony Lupien near the Cleveland dugout. With Boudreau at bat, Mitchell tried to steal second base. He was thrown out, Aaron Robinson to Michaels. No runs, one hit, no errors. Now the scoreboard showed:

CHICAGO	000
CLEVELAND	000

It had been a close play at second base, but Mitchell clearly had been out. Still, the umpire's decision was booed. Mr. Wysocki looked around and said something about most people being Stupes. Morris Bird III, who had been booing right along with almost everyone else, closed his mouth. Up stepped Hodgin, the Chicago right fielder who was supposed to be such a weak hitter. He promptly lined a single to center. That's the way of the world, said Mr. Wysocki. It's always the lumpy who gets the first hit. There were groans from the stands, but they changed to cheers when Lupien flied to Peck for the first out. The next hitter, old Luke Appling, fouled off a number of Lemon's pitches, finally worked him for a walk. Now there were two men on base and only one out, and pudgy Pat Seerey was the hitter. Mr. Wysocki leaned forward. So did Morris Bird III. Hegan and Lemon had a conference. The crowd booed Seerey. They'd better be careful with this guy, said Mr. Wysocki. He'd like nothing better than to park one. Morris Bird III nodded. Lemon hitched up his belt, looked in to Hegan for the sign. Seerey swung mightily. Strike one. A great appreciative roar from the crowd. On the next pitch, Seerey again swung mightily. The ball went straight up. When it came down, Keltner caught it in foul territory. Morris Bird III leaned back and sighed. All around him, people were shrieking delightedly. Up stepped Aaron Robinson, the big Chicago catcher. Lemon's sinker worked beautifully, and Aaron Robinson grounded out, Eddie Robinson to Lemon covering first. Now the streak stood at 43 consecutive scoreless innings! No runs, one hit, no errors. Now the scoreboard showed:

CHICAGO	000 0
CLEVELAND	000

Mr. Wysocki brought Morris Bird III a Coke to go with the peanuts. Smiling, he pointed to the scoreboard and called Morris Bird III's attention to the progress of the game between the Yankees and the Philadelphia Athletics. It showed:

NEW YORK	010 000
PHILADELPHIA	000 00

Morris Bird III nodded, but pointed out to Mr. Wysocki that a 1–0 lead wasn't exactly overwhelming. And anyway, he said, as long as the Indians kept winning, the Yankees could win until they were blue in the face and it wouldn't do them a bit of good. Lou Boudreau led off for the Indians, and he almost beheaded poor old Luke Appling with a line drive down the left field line. It went for a double. Again Morris Bird III and all the rest of Mr. Wysocki's Stupes were on their feet. Okay, okay, *now* the rally would start! Goodbye, bye, Randy Gumpert! So long, it's been good to know you! Goodbye, bye, Randy old buddy old sock! Your time has come! Lou Boudreau stood on second base and waited for Gumpert to pitch to Eddie Robinson. Everyone was leaning forward again. Mr. Wysocki said something that had to do with counting chickens before they were in the pot. Morris Bird III paid him no mind. Gumpert took a deep breath, went into his stretch, checked Boudreau on second base, pitched to Eddie Robinson. A strike. Then a ball. Then another strike. Then Eddie Robinson swung. The ball went almost straight up in the air. Tony Lupien drifted over into foul territory and caught it. One down. Groans. Doby stepped to the plate. He hit a grounder to second and was out, Kolloway to Lupien. Two down, with Boudreau advancing to third on the play. Now it all was up to Keltner. Strike one. Ball one. Ball two. Foul, strike two. On the next pitch, Keltner struck out. Three down. No runs, one hit, no errors. Keltner slammed down the bat. Now the scoreboard showed:

CHICAGO	000 0
CLEVELAND	000 0

Morris Bird III made a wet flapping sound with his lips. All through the park, there was a general grumbling sound as everyone settled back. The White Sox were hanging sort of tough today, especially that guy Gumpert. This was pointed out to Morris Bird III by Mr. Wysocki, but Morris Bird III said nothing. Philley, leading off, grounded out, Eddie Robinson to Lemon. Well, at least that Eddie Robinson could *field*. Kolloway hit a slow grounder to Boudreau, who easily threw him out. Michaels, or Kwieteniewski or whatever his name was, worked Lemon for a walk. That's kind of an important walk, said Mr. Wysocki. It keeps the White Sox from having the pitcher lead off next inning. Huh. An interesting thought. Mr. Wysocki surely did know his baseball. Gumpert grounded to Boudreau, who threw to Berardino, forcing Michaels. The scoreless streak was at 44! No runs, no hits, no errors. Through the first five innings, Lemon had allowed just one hit and two walks. Now the scoreboard showed:

| CHICAGO | 000 00 |
| CLEVELAND | 000 0 |

Morris Bird III finished his Coke. The first Cleveland batter was Johnny Berardino, the profile. He walked. Morris Bird III and his fellow Stupes began a rhythmic clapping. Gumpert and Aaron Robinson held a conference on the mound. Hegan laid down a perfect sacrifice bunt and was out, Lupien to Kolloway covering first. Berardino took second. Another conference between Gumpert and Aaron Robinson. Bob Lemon was really quite a good hitter, and they couldn't afford to take him lightly. Gumpert nodded. Aaron Robinson patted him on the rump. The Stupes' rhythmic clapping was louder. Mr. Wysocki's face was expressionless. Lemon belted a double to deep center, scoring Berardino easily. The Indians had scored! They were ahead! Morris Bird III was on his feet, and so was everyone else. He was whistling and clapping and screaming. Goodbye Gumpert! he hollered. Goodbye! Goodbye! The rhythmic clapping continued. He was barely settled back in his seat when Mitchell hit one deep to center. But Philley caught it, and there were two out. Up came Hal Peck, but the best he could do was send a fly to Hodgin. One run, one hit, no errors. When Gumpert came off the mound, he appeared tired. Disgustedly he threw his glove into the dugout. Morris Bird III waved his arms at Gumpert and made faces. Now the scoreboard showed:

CHICAGO	000 00
CLEVELAND	000 01

Mr. Wysocki sighed. Another hotdog vendor came along. Mr. Wysocki asked Morris Bird III whether the kielbasa had settled. Yes, said Morris Bird III, and so Mr. Wysocki bought him a hotdog. Hodgin grounded out to Boudreau. The hotdog was very hot, and the mustard was very sharp, and it was maybe the best hotdog Morris Bird III ever had had in his whole entire life. Lupien popped a single to center, the ball falling just in front of Doby. Morris Bird III thanked Mr. Wysocki for the magnificent hotdog. You're welcome, said Mr. Wysocki, and he allowed as how the White Sox might try the hitandrun in this situation. Sure enough, they did. Old Luke Appling nudged a single to right, and Lupien dashed to third. Two on and only one out, and Pat Seerey stepped to the plate. Lemon hitched up his belt. The crowd was making very little noise. Lemon threw a strike. A big cheer. Seerey fouled off the next pitch. Then, taking a tremendous cut, Seerey swung and missed. Two out, and everyone whooped and shrieked and whistled. Aaron Robinson hit Lemon's first pitch deep to center, but the ball was caught by Doby. The scoreless inning streak had reached 45! No runs, two hits, no errors. Now the scoreboard showed:

CHICAGO	000 000
CLEVELAND	000 01

Boudreau hit the first pitch deep to left. It brought everyone to his feet. But Seerey ranged back and caught the ball. Eddie Robinson popped to Kolloway. Morris Bird III finished his hotdog. Behind him, two colored men were arguing about whether Doby should have caught Lupien's pop single the inning before. Doby hit a long foul into the right field stands, then grounded to Kolloway. This time, when Gumpert returned to the dugout, he did not throw his glove. No runs, no hits, no errors. Now the scoreboard showed:

CHICAGO	000 000
CLEVELAND	000 010

Mr. Wysocki called Morris Bird III's attention to the progress of the Yankee game. The scoreboard showed:

NEW YORK	010 000 4
PHILADELPHIA	000 000

My boys really broke it open, said Mr. Wysocki. Looks like the class of this league is finally beginning to tell. To which Morris Bird III grinned and said: Don't count your chickens yet. The game's never over until the last man's out. To which Mr. Wysocki also grinned and said: And don't *you* go counting *yours*. After all, 1–0 isn't much of a lead. As he spoke, Philley hit a grounder that took a bad hop and bounced over Eddie Robinson's shoulder for a single. But, on the next pitch, Kolloway fouled to Hegan. Then Michaels grounded into a forceout, Boudreau to Berardino. Up stepped Gumpert, and he got a pretty good hand. He tapped weakly to the mound, and Lemon threw him out. Now the streak was at 46! No runs, one hit, no errors. Now the scoreboard showed:

CHICAGO	000 000 0
CLEVELAND	000 010

Mr. Wysocki again called Morris Bird III's attention to the scoreboard, this time to the game between the second place Boston Red Sox and the Washington team. The scoreboard showed:

WASHINGTON	300 00
BOSTON	011 4

Yes, said Mr. Wysocki, it looks as though your team would be welladvised to win this one. Otherwise, a lot of ground could be lost. Morris Bird III nodded, concentrated on the game. He had just stood up to take his seventhinning stretch. It had felt kind of good, what with the kielbasa, the dumplings, the sauerkraut, the headluttuce salad, the cherry strudel, the peanuts, the Coke and the hotdog. Keltner began the Indians' seventh with a line single to left. The Stupes' rhythmic clapping resumed. It was accompanied by some footstomping. Berardino laid down a nice sacrifice bunt and was out, Appling to Kolloway covering first. Appling and Aaron Robinson held a conference with Gumpert. This time it was Appling's turn to pat Gumpert on the rump. Out in the Chicago bullpen beyond the leftcenter field fence, a lefthander was warming up. Hegan hit the ball back to the mound. Gumpert grabbed it, wheeled, threw to Appling. Now Keltner was trapped in a rundown between second and third. Appling threw to

Michaels, who tagged Keltner. Mr. Wysocki said something to the effect that the White Sox weren't playing like a lastplace club today. Morris Bird III had to agree. Gumpert struck out Lemon. No runs, one hit, no errors. Now the scoreboard showed:

CHICAGO	000 000 0
CLEVELAND	000 010 0

The Yankees were cleaning up on Philadelphia:

NEW YORK	010 000 40
PHILADELPHIA	000 000 00

But the Washington club had rallied to tie the score against the Red Sox:

WASHINGTON	300 003
BOSTON	011 40

Hodgin grounded to Berardino to begin the Chicago eighth. Then a Lemon pitch stayed high, and Lupien flied deep to Doby. Very interesting, said Mr. Wysocki. Seems our friend Lemon's sinker isn't working quite so well. Maybe he's getting a little tired. It could be interesting if Appling gets on base, what with our buddy Seerey coming up next. But old Appling didn't get on. He was called out on strikes. Morris Bird III clapped Mr. Wysocki on the back, and Mr. Wysocki grinned and shrugged. The streak was at 47 innings! One more inning, just three more outs, and the Indians would have their fifth straight shutout! No runs, no hits, no errors. Now the scoreboard showed:

CHICAGO	000 000 00
CLEVELAND	000 010 0

When Gumpert came out of the Chicago dugout, the back of his uniform shirt was dark with sweat. He walked slowly to the mound. The rhythmic clapping began again. He wiped his pitching hand across his shirtfront. This inning he would have to face the top of the Cleveland batting order. Mitchell stepped to the plate. Gumpert worked deliberately, but Mitchell got hold of one and lined a double to leftcenter. The clapping was augmented by a jubilant roar. A couple rows behind Morris Bird III and to his right, a girl of about fourteen was jumping up and down. She reminded him a little of Julie Sutton, and she also for some reason made him think of Francine Ley, the "Nevada Gas" girl. She wore a pink dress, and parts of her went in several directions. Blinking, he looked away from her, again concentrated on the game. Peck hit a sharp grounder to Kolloway, who threw him out, Mitchell taking third. Now, with just one out, the Indians had an insurance run on third base—and Lou Boudreau was coming to bat! And Lou Boudreau didn't disappoint the crowd. He got around on a Gumpert fast ball and flied to Philley, Mitchell scoring after the catch. The insurance run had been delivered! When Lou Boudreau returned to the bench, the crowd gave him a mighty hand. The people seated behind the dugout even stood up. After going down the steps into the dugout, Boudreau went to Mitchell and slapped him on the back. The next hitter, Eddie Robinson, popped to Kolloway, but no one particularly cared. Dale Mitchell and Lou Boudreau surely had put the game out of reach of the poor sad-sack White Sox. One run, one hit, no errors. Now the scoreboard showed:

CHICAGO	000 000 00
CLEVELAND	000 010 01

Gumpert's head was down as he came back to the dugout. Morris Bird III couldn't help but almost feel sorry for him. It surely couldn't be much fun to pitch for the White Sox. He wondered what Julie Sutton was doing this afternoon. He glanced back over a shoulder at the girl who had reminded him of Julie Sutton. He'd only seen Julie a couple of times this summer, and then not to talk to. Such a blabbermouth she had been that day of the lizard and the ducks, but apparently that had been a very unusual day. Manager Lou Boudreau sent Bob Kennedy to right field in place of Hal Peck. Bob Kennedy was a fine defensive outfielder, had a great arm. Seerey led off for the White Sox. Lemon's first pitch to him was high. Morris Bird III had arranged it a couple of times so that he walked past the Red Arrow Restaurant when Julie was having supper with her mother. From what he could see of the mother, she was a thick squat woman with dark hair. She wore a white waitress' uniform. Lemon's second pitch to Seerey was high. Morris Bird III wondered if maybe some evening he could just sort of *drop in* on Julie. He wondered if this would make her angry. Lemon's third pitch to Seerey was high. Mr. Wysocki told Morris Bird III that Lemon's sinker *definitely* wasn't working. This game's far from over, he said. You just wait. Lemon threw a strike to Seerey, then a fourth ball. Man on first, nobody out. Lou Boudreau came in from his shortstop position and conferred briefly with Lemon and Hegan. Out in the Cleveland bullpen, a righthander named Ed Klieman was warming up. Aaron Robinson stepped into the batter's box. Mr. Wysocki was leaning forward. The White Sox coaches were clapping their hands. Several of the White Sox players had moved to the top of the dugout steps. Morris Bird III could see the backs of their heads. Lemon threw his first pitch to Aaron Robinson. Foul, back to the screen. The next pitch was a ball. Lemon sighed, hitched up his pants. Aaron Robinson took a level cut at the next pitch. As soon as the bat met the ball, Mr. Wysocki was on his feet. *Look out!* he hollered. *There it goes!* The ball took off on a high arch toward right field. Bob Kennedy backtracked. He backtracked all the way to the fence, but the ball kept going. It cleared the fence easily. Preceded by Seerey, Aaron Robinson trotted around the bases. At home plate, Seerey shook his hand. So did Philley, the next batter. Directly in front of Morris Bird III, the White Sox players in the dugout were whooping and clapping. The stands were silent. At the dugout, Aaron Robinson was met by shouts and more handshakes. The stands were very silent indeed. The home plate umpire tossed a new ball to Bob Lemon. Mr. Wysocki asked Morris Bird III what he thought of *that*. Morris Bird III said nothing. What he *wanted* to say was so what, the score only was tied, wasn't it? The Indians still would win the game in the last of the ninth or extra innings. But he kept quiet. Philley hit a high fly out toward Bob Kennedy in right. Bob Kennedy drifted back. He drifted back and he drifted back. *Uh oh!* hollered Mr. Wysocki, and again he was on his feet. Bob Kennedy drifted back and drifted back. Then he was leaning against the fence. The ball sailed over his head and over the fence. Another home run. More whoops and claps from the White Sox dugout. Philley trotted around the bases. At home plate, Kolloway shook Philley's hand. All the Chicago players clustered on the top step of the dugout to greet Philley. Mr. Wysocki was standing and clapping. *At a way to go, Dave boy!* he hollered. Morris Bird III sat silently. His shoulders were hunched. Except for Mr. Wysocki and maybe three or four other people, everyone in the stands was absolutely dead silent. Lou Boudreau walked to the mound and held another conversation with Bob Lemon. He took the ball from Bob Lemon and waved to the bullpen. Mr. Wysocki sat down. I guess your manager wants Klieman, he said to Morris Bird III. A nod from Morris Bird III. Ed Klieman stepped through the bullpen gate and walked across right field toward the mound. Bob Lemon started trudging toward the Cleveland dugout. The fans gave him a good hand. Even Mr. Wysocki applauded. This was sort of strange. In past years, Mr. Wysocki had booed the Indians with great spirit. Now, even though he didn't root for them, he never booed them either. Frowning, Morris Bird III asked Mr. Wysocki how come. Easy, said Mr. Wysocki. *This* team I got *respect* for. Oh, said Morris Bird III, and he was silent again. He hurt. His belly felt heavy. The Indians' scoreless inning streak was down the drain, and their shutout streak was down the drain, and maybe their winning streak would go down the drain too. It sure was some big drain. For some reason or other, he rubbed his arms. He glanced at the sky and the sun, and the sky and the sun were warm, and so why was he rubbing his arms? Ed Klieman began his warmup pitches. He was a thinnish fellow, and he wore glasses. He was righthanded. Well, said Mr. Wysocki, my team did it again. Morris Bird III looked toward the scoreboard. The final score of the Yankee game had been posted:

NEW YORK	010 000 401——6
PHILADELPHIA	000 000 000——0

201

Mr. Wysocki was smiling. He fanned himself with his straw hat. Yes sir, he said, this might just turn out to be a good day. Yes sir, it might just. Morris Bird III rubbed his arms. How come so much of the time things turned out wrong? He got to thinking about his grandmother, and then he got to thinking about his grandmother's barn and her possessions and the way his aunts and his uncles talked about them, and then he got to thinking about Fred C. Dobbs, and then he told himself: Come *on* now, it's only a *game*. Klieman finished his warmups. Kolloway popped to Boudreau. Michaels stepped to the plate. He swung hard, but he also popped to Boudreau. The stands were quiet. Gumpert came to bat, and here and there a few people applauded— including Mr. Wysocki and, a little reluctantly, Morris Bird III. Gumpert grounded to Boudreau, and the side was out, and Klieman had done a good job of relief pitching, but it had been one run too late. Three runs, two hits, no errors. Now the scoreboard showed:

CHICAGO	000 000 003
CLEVELAND	000 010 01

Morris Bird III and all the other Stupes began their rhythmic clapping. Doby was up, and Doby could hit the ball a long way. The clapping became louder. Doby swung and missed. The clapping died for a moment, then swelled up again. Gumpert kept the ball inside and low to Doby and struck him out. The clapping vanished. As Doby walked back to the dugout, there were some boos. Keltner got under a Gumpert pitch and popped to Michaels. Berardino was called back from the ondeck circle, and Walt Judnich, an outfielder who hit lefthanded, was sent up to bat for him. Like Doby, Walt Judnich also was capable of hitting the long ball that would tie the score. The clapping resumed. Gumpert took his time. The clapping became louder. Morris Bird III was just about *praying,* and no fooling. Gumpert kept the ball low. Judnich banged it into the dirt and grounded to Lupien, who made the putout unassisted. The game was over. Gumpert and Aaron Robinson met along the thirdbase foul line and shook hands. Somewhere in the stands, some idiot stomped on a paper cup. It made an explosive sound. The grinning Chicago players disappeared into their dugout. The final score, as posted on the scoreboard, looked like this:

	R	H	E
CHICAGO	000 000 003——3	6	1
CLEVELAND	000 010 010——2	7	0

And the Red Sox had rallied in the eighth inning to defeat Washington:

WASHINGTON	300 003 000——6
BOSTON	011 400 04x——10

Now the Indians led the Red Sox by just two games, the Yankees and Athletics by just three and a half. In other words, the day had been a calamity. Randy Gumpert! Aaron Robinson! Dave Philley! *Some* heroes! Huh! Boy oh boy, the world sure was a peculiar and hateful place. Morris Bird III said nothing as he and Mr. Wysocki made their way up an aisle and through a tunnel and out of the Stadium. No one was making much noise. The fans filed out of the park like mourners. The only people whose voices were loud were the vendors who were trying to get in some lastminute sales at the exits. Now the popcorn smell was rancid, and Morris Bird III's belly felt as though it were full of about 279.6 gallons of crankcase sludge. He patted it and tried to burp, but nothing happened. Mr. Wysocki smiled at the world but said nothing. He was a good man, this Mr. Wysocki. He'd never been one for rubbing it in. Randy Gumpert! Aaron Robinson! Dave Philley! *Bah! Humbug!*

Back in the Packard, Mr. Wysocki said: "Come on. Cheer up. Tomorrow's another day. You can't win them all. Not even from the White Sox."

Morris Bird III nodded, stared at his lap. He rubbed his forehead.

Mr. Wysocki started the great old car. He eased it into the line of traffic leaving the parking lot.

Morris Bird III rubbed his forehead and rubbed it and rubbed it.

Mr. Wysocki hummed something tuneless.

Morris Bird III's palms were sweaty. He rubbed them on his thighs.

"Morris?"

"Yes?"

"Things don't always turn out the way we want them to."

"I know *that*."

"Then stop sitting there looking like your pet canary died."

Morris Bird III had to grin.

"If you want to see her that badly, I'll finance the trip."

"Huh?"

"Your grandmother."

"No!"

Mr. Wysocki made a clucking noise. It came from the roof of his mouth. "It's more than just being sad because she's dying, isn't it?"

Morris Bird III let the air out of his lungs. Heavily. "Yes," he said.

"You think maybe you owe her something?"

"Maybe . . ."

Now they were out on St. Clair Avenue. Mr. Wysocki drove carefully. In the storewindows, the gypsy women beckoned. "You got it straight in your mind?"

"No," said Morris Bird III.

"You know what duty means?"

"I think so."

"I bet your grandmother's talked to you about duty." A hesitation. "Hasn't she?"

Morris Bird III nodded.

"What's the matter? Is watching her die too much for you?"

Morris Bird III nodded.

"How old are you now? Thirteen? Fourteen?"

"Thirteen."

"And you think she's playing a dirty trick on you, don't you?"

Morris Bird III looked sharply at Mr. Wysocki.

Mr. Wysocki's eyes were anonymous behind his sunglasses. "You're too old to be thinking something like that." Another hesitation, then: "She loves you. Dying's hard. If she had her choice, she wouldn't be dying. That makes sense?"

Morris Bird III nodded.

"Now then, if she loves you doesn't it stand to reason that she would want to see you before she dies?"

"I . . . I guess so."

"You *know* so."

Morris Bird III nodded.

"You owe it to her. It's your duty."

Morris Bird III nodded.

"It's that simple."

Morris Bird III nodded.

"You got the guts for it?"

No answer from Morris Bird III.

"You're old enough to travel on a train by yourself, aren't you?"

"I guess so."

"Don't worry about your father. I'll fix it with him. If you want to go, you can. I was in Pittsburgh when my mother died. I was visiting a girl there. My mother was in Scranton. All my brothers and sisters were with her when she died, but *me,* I was in Pittsburgh visiting a girl. I didn't care enough. Or I didn't have the guts. Or something. I wouldn't want you to act the same way. And, like I said, I'll finance the trip."

"You don't have to do that. I got seventeen dollars. Saved it up from my job at the Addison library."

"It's none of my business, is it?"

Morris Bird III shrugged, said nothing.

"You probably think I shouldn't have brought it up."

"No. It's okay."

"I loved my mother. I should have gone to see her. But oh *no,* Big Shot had to go chasing after some girl. And, the thing is—I don't even remember her name."

"Mr. Wysocki?"

"Yeah?"

"Once I read somewhere, a poem I think it was, and it had to do with someone who went off in all directions at the same time."

"So?"

"That's me."

"It's not *you*. It's just the age you're at."

"That's what people all the time say."

"Well, it just happens to be true."

"My father would never go for it."

"Don't worry about your father. I'll take care of him."

"But, I mean, what do I say to her?"

"You don't have to *say* anything. You just *go* there."

Morris Bird III shook his head. "I don't know . . ."

"What's there to know? Just *do* it."

Morris Bird III was silent. He looked out the window on his side. The Packard was headed south on East 40th Street back toward Hough Avenue. He thought about his mother. He figured she would sure as anything have a hissy fit if he went down to Paradise Falls. "Mr. Wysocki?"

"Yes?"

"Down in Paradise Falls, Grandma's got this barn full of stuff."

"Oh?"

"And they bicker about the stuff. My mother and my aunts and my uncles. Grandma's not even dead yet, but all they can think of to do is bicker."

The Packard turned left onto Hough Avenue. "Well," said Mr. Wysocki, "all the more reason you should go down there."

"Huh?"

"She'll have somebody to talk to."

"Oh."

"Your father's not a bad guy. I'll explain it to him."

"No."

"What?"

"If I go, *I'll* explain it to him."

Mr. Wysocki grinned. "Hey," he said, "at a way. Good for you."

Funny Mr. Wysocki being so interested. Funny Mr. Wysocki caring so much. Funny Mr. Wysocki volunteering all that about Pittsburgh and the girl and his mother. Frowning, Morris Bird III tried to sort out all the things that were clamoring in his head. He told himself: So okay. So the Indians lost. So tomorrow is another day. So things don't always turn out the way a person wants. So what does all that have to do with Grandma? Come *on* now. Stop kidding yourself. It has *everything* to do with Grandma.

"Mr. Wysocki?"

"Yes?"

"You'll really talk to him?"

"Yes."

"I mean, I don't want him to think I've run off."

"I'll take care of it."

"I like riding in trains."

"Good."

"It's okay to admit something like that, isn't it?"

"Sure."

"I mean, if part of the trip is fun, I don't have to feel bad about it, do I?"

"No. Of course not."

"If he's home when we get there, I'll talk to him. But I don't think he's going to be there. He's been away a lot the past couple days. Visiting friends."

"Yes. Friends."

"I mean, if he *is* there, *I'll* tell him. If he isn't, then you'll have to."

"Fair enough."

"I just don't want you to get the idea I'm scared to tell him."

"Farthest thing from my mind."

"I meant it when I said I would."

"I know you did."

"And I *will*—if he's home."

"Sure."

"But, if I go, I got to do it now."

"Yes."

"Before I lose my nerve."

"Don't worry about a thing. You just go on and you go. I'll tell your father. I know what it is to hurry up and do a thing before you lose your nerve. It happens to most of us all the time. Adults, I mean. And don't think I'll be thinking you're afraid to tell your father."

"Mr. Wysocki?"

"Yes?"

"Maybe I make too much of a federal case out of things."

"Maybe—but it's better to be that way than the other."

"Thank you for taking me to the game."

"Ah, but your team lost."

"That's not what I mean."

At the corner of Hough Avenue and East 71st Street, Morris Bird III saw a clock in the front window of a fillingstation. It said, as close as he could make out, 4:28. Now he and Mr. Wysocki were silent. There wasn't anything left to say. His palms again were damp, and again he wiped them on his thighs. He breathed slowly, almost in grunts. He watched a blind colored man cross East 71st. The blind colored man wore an orange jacket and tapped on the pavement with a cane that had a crimson tip. Now *there*, Morris Bird III told himself, is somebody who has a right to make a federal case out of things. He blinked, rubbed his forehead. He would wash up real good before he left. He decided the thing he should have been feeling right now was relief. But he felt no relief. Instead, he felt scared. Good and scared. But not scared because of the trip, not scared because he would take it alone. Scared because he didn't know whether he was doing the right thing. He wanted to see his grandmother and he didn't want to see his grandmother. He wished he were about five years younger. Then things would be simple, and he wouldn't have this stupid desire to run off in all directions at the same time. Good Russians and bad Russians. Things that were Fake. People who didn't have anything better to do with their time than play raindrop race. People who behaved like Fred C. Dobbs. People who betrayed you by dying. People and things that forever and relentlessly changed. Tight hands on bedposts, warm dreams of Slaves and obsequious Turhan Beys. Oh *brother*, what a life—and please, no mention of that magazine. Sleek and thrumming, the Packard moved east on Hough Avenue, past Addison Junior High and all the places Morris Bird III saw every day nine months of the year on his way to and from school. Apartment windows were open, and he heard music and voices. Dogs prowled. Little kids chased each other. A girl leaned out a thirdfloor window and watered some geraniums in a windowbox. She wore a chemise, and her boobies were immense. Women, moving in quick lurching steps, embracing great bulgy bags of groceries, crowded the sidewalks. The front doors of the saloons were open, and the signs in the windows of these saloons said *Schlitz* and *Liquor* and *Television*. Somewhere was a thin tight odor of garbage that had remained too long in the sunlight. He really and truly had no idea whether he was doing the right thing. But, right or wrong, he supposed he had to do it. His grandmother had been The One for a long time, and she had done so much for him, and maybe now he could do something for her. The word was Love, and he guessed the Rev. Gar P. Pallister probably would have understood. At Hough and Crawford, a little girl got off a trackless trolley. Her skirt was torn in the back. She was alone, and she was eating what appeared to be a pretzel, and he supposed she was a Hillbilly. She was terribly skinny. Gnawing on the pretzel, she skipped away from the trackless trolley. Actually *skipped*. Big deal. Poor skinny Hillbilly girl. Poop. The Packard passed East 87th Street, East 88th Place.

Now it was in front of the apartment building where Julie Sutton lived. She was sitting on the stoop. She was alone. She wore a white blouse and a pair of blue jeans. Her hands rested against her knees, and she didn't appear to be looking at anything in particular. Well, since this was Morris Bird III's day for *doing* things . . .

She smiled. "Hi," she said.

"Hi," said Morris Bird III, advancing up the walk toward her.

Her little tongue came out and ran along her bottom lip. She slid over a little, making room for him. "You want to sit down?"

He nodded. Then, for some reason, he cleared his throat. Then he sat down.

She did not look at him.

He checked the distance between them. There was no immediate danger that their rear ends would touch.

"Nice to see you," she said, not looking at him.

"You, too."

"I was just sitting here."

"Uh huh."

"Looking at the world. Kind of."

"Sure."

"You ever look at the world?"

"I guess so."

She smiled, but she still wasn't looking at him. "You mad at me?"

"No."

She turned her face to him. Her eyes were quite large. "I saw you get out of that car up at the corner."

"Oh? Well, I saw you too. I was with a man, and I asked him to stop."

"Just so you could get out and come see *me*?"

"Uh huh."

"Thank you."

"No. You don't have to say that. I did it because I wanted to."

"Um," said Julie, and she was silent.

Again Morris Bird III cleared his throat. Then he said: "You been having a good summer?"

"Uh huh. You?"

"Fine."

"I went to Toledo."

"Toledo?"

"Yes. To see my daddy."

"Oh. Sure. How was the trip?"

"Fine. You want to know something?"

"What's that?"

"Nancy Turpin was very sweet."

"Who?"

"Nancy *Tur*pin. She's the girl who married my daddy."

"Oh. Yeah. That's right."

"We went riding in my daddy's boat almost every day. He caught a lot of fish. Whitefish. And we talked a lot. Nancy's very pretty. Big blue eyes and all."

"Um."

"I told them about you."

"*Me?*"

"Uh huh. I told them you're the nicest person I know. I told them about the rainy day and how silly you were with the ducks. Everything. They seemed very pleased."

"Well. Well now. That's good."

"I told them I only wished I had the nerve to talk to you in school."

"That's okay."

"No it isn't. I ought to get *out* of myself more."

"Well, for some people that's harder than for others. You know, it takes all kinds to make the world."

"Yes. But I don't want to be the Me kind anymore. I want to be the Other kind. My daddy said it'd be good for me."

"Well, maybe so."

"You're the only person I ever talk about me with."

"I got good ears."

A small laugh. "I guess you *do*." A fluttery movement with a hand, and her chest went in and out, *in* and *out*. "You'd have to, to put up with *me*."

"That's a lot of bushwah. There's nothing wrong with you. Except maybe you knock yourself too much."

"I wanted to talk to you in school. I really did. A couple times I almost got up the nerve, but then . . . oh I don't know. I just didn't."

"Don't worry about it."

"Morris?"

"Yes?"

"I been thinking about you all summer."

"Me?"

"Yes. And I watch for you all the time. I sit at the window."

"Watch for me?"

"Uh huh. I sort of scrunch around behind the curtain so you can't see. You go past here a lot. A couple of times you looked up toward the window.

"Yes."

"I hid. I shouldn't have. People shouldn't hide. That's what my daddy says. Nancy Turpin, too."

"Julie, I dreamed about you this morning."

"About *me?*"

"Yes. You were in a long white dress, and you had a crown on your head. And there was sort of a golden cloud around you, and I called you Golden Princess."

Julie put her fists in her eyes.

"Hey!" said Morris Bird III.

The fists came away from Julie's eyes. She blinked. "Don't mind me. I'm *dumb.*"

"It was a fine dream."

Julie blinked at her lap.

"Best dream I ever had."

Julie didn't say anything.

The hurt had returned to Morris Bird III's belly, but now it took in more than just that part of him. It had spread below his belly, and he knew he didn't dare stand up. He wanted to cry and he wanted to shout and he wanted to go to the bathroom. His breath was like a cactus that had gone down his gullet sideways. "Julie?"

She looked at him. "A dream? A dream about *me?*"

"Yes," said Morris Bird III, and then he embellished his sweet lie a little more. "You were, uh, being coronated. It was a big room you were in, and it was full of bishops and lords and ladies and footmen and soldiers and I don't know who all."

215

"I see. And I was in a white dress?"

"Yes. Prettiest white dress in the world. Uh, but wait a minute. There's something I want you to promise me."

"What's that?" said Julie, and she drew back her head.

"Nothing to be ascared of. I just want you to promise me you'll speak to me after school starts. *In* school, I mean."

"I'll *try*."

"I want more than that. I want you to *promise*."

"All right."

"Promise?"

"Yes."

"And you mean it?"

"Yes."

Morris Bird III grinned. "I'll hold you to it."

"Okay."

Morris Bird III leaned forward until his elbows were on his knees. He stared straight ahead. His forehead itched with moisture, but he didn't bother with it. "Uh," he said, and then he hesitated. He didn't quite know how to put what it was he wanted to say. It wasn't that he was *shy* or anything like *that;* it was just that he was having a hard time finding words. "Uh, Julie, I'm . . . I'm going out of town for a couple of days. My grandmother—she lives in a little town down below Columbus—my grandmother is real sick. Dying, I guess."

"Oh," said Julie, "I'm sorry."

"Yeah. So am I. And, the thing is, I got to go see her."

"You love her?"

"Yes."

"Then you *ought* to go see her."

Morris Bird III nodded.

"Look at me."

He looked at her.

She was frowning. "Love is a big thing. I don't know much about *dying* and all *that*, but if you love her, and maybe she's dying, then you got no choice."

Morris Bird III nodded.

Julie's frown went away. "My daddy and Nancy Turpin, I love *them*, and I want to go see them every chance I get, and they're not even dying."

Morris Bird III nodded.

"They're out there on the lake, and they're in all that sunshine, and they *talk* to me, and I love them."

"Uh huh."

"I like you very much."

"I'm glad."

"I'm glad you're glad."

"I'm glad you're glad I'm glad."

"I'm glad you're glad I'm glad you're glad."

"Dalg," said Morris Bird III.

"Now you stop that, you old Teddy Karam you."

"Julie?"

"Yes?"

"Do you like to go to the movies?"

"Yes."

"Would you like to go with me sometime?"

"Yes."

"Honest?"

"I *said* yes. I *said* it and I *meant* it."

"Well," said Morris Bird III. "*Well* now."

"You," said Julie, grinning, "are an absolute *nut*."

217

Morris Bird III nodded. What else was he supposed to do? Stand on his head and spit elephants?

A little later, he said goodbye to Julie and went on home. He walked sort of hunched over.

Well, now that he had made up his mind, now that he was such a man of *action,* there was a great deal to be done. As soon as he got home, he telephoned the ticket office of the New York Central. The next train for Columbus left at 7 P.M., arriving there at 9:17, Columbus time. Cleveland was on Eastern Daylight Time, and Columbus was on Eastern Standard, which meant the trip actually took three hours and seventeen minutes. Morris Bird III wrote down the times, then asked the man about connections on the Chesapeake & Ohio for Paradise Falls. There was a long pause while the man consulted the Chesapeake & Ohio timetable. He finally came back on the line to say that there was no connection at that time of night. The last train for Paradise Falls left Columbus at 5:55, he said. Morris Bird III thanked the man and hung up. He then telephoned the Greyhound people. A girl told him the last bus for Paradise Falls left Columbus at 10:30 P.M., Columbus time, arriving in Paradise Falls at 11:56. Paradise Falls was on the same time as Columbus. He thanked the girl and hung up. He went upstairs to his bedroom. First, though, he looked in Sandra's bedroom, but she wasn't there. The copy of *Appleton's Cyclopaedia of American Biography,* the 1887 edition, Volume III, GRIN through LOC, lay on her bed, but old Sandra was nowhere to be seen. He shrugged, went on into his own room. The $17 was in a box in his dresser. It consisted of a ten, a five and two ones. They were folded inside a paperback copy of *Two Years Before the Mast*, by someone named Dana. He had crooked this book last summer from Albrecht's Drug Store. It hadn't been worth the bother. He had crooked the book thinking it had something to do with flogging, but it had turned out to be duller than ditchwater. He removed the ten, the five and the two ones and shoved them in a pants pocket. Then he dragged a small suitcase from his closet. He filled it with socks, underwear, shirts, a pair of pajamas. He went into the bathroom and washed his face and hands and brushed his teeth. He washed his face with great vigor. He gave his forehead special attention. He rubbed and rubbed and rubbed. Returning to the bedroom, he removed his only suit from the closet. Carefully he folded the suit and put it in his suitcase. He knew he'd probably be needing it. For his grandmother's funeral. Then, snapping his fingers, he returned to the bathroom and fetched his toothbrush and toothpaste. He dried the toothbrush with a towel, made sure the top of the toothpaste tube was screwed on securely. He went back to his bedroom with the toothbrush and toothpaste. He dropped them into the suitcase. He checked the contents of the suitcase. He'd forgotten handkerchiefs. Oh, and a necktie for the funeral. He got the handkerchiefs from the bureau, a couple of neckties from the closet. The pain from his encounter with Julie Sutton was almost gone now. He was able to walk erectly. He dropped the handkerchiefs and the neckties into the suitcase. Then he slammed shut the suitcase and snapped the catches. Grunting, he lifted the suitcase and lugged it downstairs and next door to the Wysockis'. The clock in the Wysocki front room said 5:57. He set down the suitcase in the front room, then went into the kitchen. Mrs. Wysocki served supper at 6 o'clock sharp, and

219

he supposed his father would be waiting for him there. He didn't feel particularly afraid. His mouth was a little dry, but that was about it. His father was not waiting in the Wysocki kitchen, however. This afternoon, while Morris Bird III and Mr. Wysocki had been at the Stadium, The Voice of Cleveland & Northeastern Ohio had telephoned Mrs. Wysocki to inform her that he had some more *friends* to see and wouldn't be joining them for supper. (NEWS FLASH—*Morris Bird II, wellknown Cleveland radio personality, has been judged The Most Popular Person in all of Cleveland & Northeastern Ohio, drawing more votes than Harry S. Truman, Thomas E. Dewey, Lou Boudreau, Bob Feller, Mrs. Eleanor Roosevelt and God combined.*) Sandra, Suzanne and Mr. Wysocki were seated at the table. Mr. Wysocki asked Morris Bird III if everything was all right. Yes, said Morris Bird III, my bag's packed; I'm ready to go. He looked at Sandra. She knows, said Mr. Wysocki. Uh huh, said Sandra, and it's okay with me. I'm sleeping here tonight. Mrs. Wysocki asked Morris Bird III if he wanted something to eat. She had made some nice BLT sandwiches (bacon, lettuce and tomato). No, said Morris Bird III, I'm not hungry, thank you. I had a lot to eat and drink at the game. Mrs. Wysocki smiled. She told Morris Bird III she thought he was doing the right thing. He nodded, said he hoped so. Mr. Wysocki again promised to explain the situation to The Voice of Cleveland & Northeastern Ohio. Suzanne promised to pray for Morris Bird III's grandmother. He looked at her. She almost was smiling. He decided maybe she wasn't quite so awful after all. Maybe the religion thing with her wasn't so bad. After all, everybody had to have *something* that made them feel superior. Mrs. Wysocki asked Morris Bird III did he want her to pack him a lunch. He shook his head no. He told her he'd get something on the train if he became hungry. Then, briefly, he discussed the baseball game with Mr. Wysocki. He reminded Mr. Wysocki that, even though the Indians had lost, they still were in first place. He also reminded Mr. Wysocki that the new record of holding the opposition scoreless for 47 consecutive innings wasn't anything to be sneezed at. Mr. Wysocki smiled, said: Sure, kid. You're absolutely right. Morris Bird III gave Sandra his house key. He told her she'd better lock up the place before she went to bed at the Wysockis'. She nodded. He looked at the kitchen clock. It showed 6:10. I guess I better get the show on the road, he said. They all accompanied him to the front room. Mr. Wysocki asked him did he want a ride to the bus stop. No, said Morris Bird III, I can make it. Another smile from Mr. Wysocki. I just bet you can, he said. Then, as an afterthought, he asked Morris Bird III whether the visit with the girl had been pleasant. What girl? said Sandra. None of your beeswax, said Morris Bird III. Oh *ho!* said Sandra, grinning. Morris Bird III's face became warm. We had a nice little talk, he said to Mr. Wysocki. Fine, said Mr. Wysocki. Morris Bird III picked up the suitcase. They ushered him to the door and out onto the front porch. He shook hands with Mr. Wysocki. Sandra asked him to kiss her. He did, on the forehead. Suzanne looked at him but said nothing. Mrs. Wysocki hugged him, told him to be careful. He nodded, reminded Mrs. Wysocki he wasn't exactly journeying to the end of the world. Lugging the suitcase, staggering a little, he went down the porch steps and out onto the sidewalk. Leaves hissed in the wind. The people on the Wysocki porch all waved at him. He waved back. He had taken about a dozen steps when he remembered something. He set down the suitcase. Keep an eye on it for me a second, okay? he hollered to the people on the Wysocki porch. He ran inside his own house, dashed up to his bedroom, taking the stairs two at a time. He removed the copy of *Spanish Blood* from the nightstand next to his bed. He ran downstairs and out of the house. He waved the book toward the people who still stood on the Wysocki porch. Thought I'd take along something to read! he hollered to the people on the Wysocki porch. They all nodded and waved. Mrs. Wysocki hollered to him to watch the streets. He nodded, picked up the suitcase, staggered on up Edmunds Avenue. He did not look back. Looking back was corny. He made his way up East 90th Street, past the Goodman house with its genuine *television aerial* and past the house where lived Teddy Karam, he of the punchboards and the criminal interest rates. At the corner of East 90th and Hough, he set down the suitcase and waited for a trackless trolley. He seated himself on a rail made of pipe. The rail was part of a fence, but it was bent in a shallow U from all the rumps of all the people who had sat there while waiting for the Hough Avenue trackless trolley. When the trackless trolley came along, he lurched a little as he hauled the suitcase aboard. The copy of *Spanish Blood* was tucked under an arm. After paying his fare, he sat on the side of the bus that was on Julie Sutton's side of the street. But now the front stoop of her apartment building was deserted. He supposed she'd gone off to supper with her mother. When the bus passed the Red Arrow, he saw her sitting inside the place with her mother. He cleared his throat. He didn't have to be hit on the head with the Soldiers' & Sailors' Monument; he *knew* he'd taken a big step today with Julie Sutton. He was frightened, and he was ashamed, and he was jubilant, and he got to wondering whether she preferred westerns or musicals or comedies or romances or what. He supposed she preferred romances. Girls usually did, or at least so he had been led to believe. He closed his eyes. She wore a white dress, and a bishop was coronating her, and the golden cloud spun delicate lights around her darling head. Oh boy. Oh Lordy. Oh such a life. His chest hurt. He opened his eyes. The trackless trolley was pulling away from the East 75th Street stop. Not too many other people were aboard. He looked at the driver, who was a colored man with a mustache. He got to wondering how come so many colored men wore mustaches. Then he got to wondering how come he had got to wondering something as dumb as *that*. He asked himself why he was afraid of Julie Sutton. He decided there was no reason. He decided he would no longer be afraid of her. And he decided he would no longer be ashamed. The next person who called her Gunboats he would personally smash. Yeah, Killer, he said to himself, ain't you something. Two tall skinny Hillbilly men boarded the trackless trolley at East 66th Street. They sat down and talked about someone named Barbara. They discussed all the various ways this Barbara would consent to do It. They guffawed, nudged each other. Morris Bird III felt warmth in his cheeks. His forehead was damp. He rubbed it. He glared out his window. The two tall skinny Hillbilly men were sitting directly in front of Morris Bird III. The way they said Dayumm reminded him of Estelle Bunning, her and her horizontal stripes and her odious Don Schwamb. The two tall skinny Hillbilly men got off the bus at East 40th Street, and good riddance. Morris Bird III sighed. He heard someone else sigh. He looked around. Two seats behind him, a thin middleaged woman in a flowered hat was making prissy sounds through lips that were puckered and bloodless. She gave Morris Bird III a dirty look. Quickly he faced forward again. The bus went north on East 40th Street, then west on Payne Avenue. It stopped at East 36th Street to admit a young fellow and his girl. They were about sixteen, as close as Morris Bird III could tell. They sat facing the center aisle. The girl wore a flowered dress. She was a redhead, and she had a big chest. Her legs were thick, and she kept her knees close together. Her escort wore a suit but no tie. They sat silently, and they held hands. They said not a word. They held hands so tightly, however, that their knuckles were white. They looked as though they were on their way to face some enemy. The guy was chunky, and he perspired a great deal, but he just let it run down his face. Apparently reaching for a handkerchief would have meant releasing the girl's hand. Morris Bird III watched them from the corner of an eye. The girl's shoes had high heels. Her toes stuck out. Her toenails were an off pink. At East 17th Street, they rose and got off the bus. Morris Bird III supposed they would walk up East 17th to one of the movie houses on Euclid Avenue. He watched them as they stood at the curb and waited for the light to change. They were very brave. He hoped they would get what they wanted, defeat the enemy or whatever. He loved them. He really did. The bus moved away from the handholders. Their faces were expressionless. Morris Bird III wanted to wave to them, but that much nerve he did not possess. The colored bus driver was humming and fingering his mustache. What is a colored bus driver? Morris Bird III asked himself. Is he a bus driver who is colored? Or is he someone who drives a colored bus? Then Morris Bird III made a small timid face and shook his head, but almost imperceptibly. He didn't want anyone to notice that a crazy person was sitting in this bus. At East 13th Street, the bus turned north a short block to Superior Avenue. Then it turned west on Superior. A minute or two more and it would be at the Public Square, end of the line. The

Public Square marked the center of Cleveland. Two of the biggest department stores faced on the Public Square. So did the luxurious Hotel Cleveland, and so did the Terminal Tower. The railroad station was in the lower level of the Terminal Tower. Ah, the Terminal Tower, the good old Terminal Tower. Everyone in Cleveland was very proud of the Terminal Tower. It was the tallest building in the city. A long time ago, Morris Bird III had heard someone say that the Terminal Tower was the tallest building in the United States—outside of New York City. He didn't know whether this was true, and he didn't exactly stay awake nights worrying about it. The bus looped around the public library building and the Old Post Office, and then it was on the Public Square. Morris Bird III took a deep breath, grunted, lifted his suitcase. He went clattering down the bus steps and out onto the Public Square. Pigeons abounded. They swooped, flapped, strutted. They came in gusts. Morris Bird III tucked his chin against his chest. He drew a bead on the Terminal Tower. It was caddie-cornered across the Public Square from the place where he'd gotten off the bus. He squeezed tight on the handle of his suitcase. *Spanish Blood* was snug against an armpit. He crossed a roadway, and then he was in front of the Soldiers' & Sailors' Monument. He paused for a moment, set down his suitcase and stared at the Soldiers' & Sailors' Monument. It was something to stare at all right, and besides, he wanted a break from lugging the suitcase. The Soldiers' & Sailors' Monument was covered with greenish statues that appeared to be made of cast iron. They showed Civil War fighting men in various poses. They all looked very intrepid, and a great many of them wore beards. They seemed terribly determined, and Morris Bird III thought it was sort of a shame they were all of them so greenish. It occurred to him that the Soldiers' & Sailors' Monument probably at one time had been very important to a lot of people. But now most of those people probably were dead, and so now the statues were greenish (and white, too, what with the abundance of pigeons), and it seemed to him that a shameful thing had been allowed to happen. The Soldiers' & Sailors' Monument spread over an entire quadrant of the Public Square. The base was made of rock, and inside the base there was a big echoing room that contained more statues, plus the names of hundreds and hundreds of men, names written on the stone walls, names of men who had served in the Civil War. Morris Bird III had visited that big echoing room several times (one of his heroes a few years back had been old Ulysses S. Grant), but he knew that most people thought the Soldiers' & Sailors' Monument was a Monstrosity. There had been many articles about it in the papers, and every other week or so some bigdeal civic group made a public announcement urging that it be torn down. Sure. Fine. So maybe it *was* a Monstrosity. But what about the feelings and wishes of the people who had placed it there back before the turn of the century? They had built this thing as a symbol of respect, to honor the men who had fought in that old war. Were such emotions monstrous? Respect was respect. Honor was honor. They did not change with architectural fashion. Sighing, Morris Bird III shook his head. There you go again, old buddy, he told himself. There you go rushing off in all directions at the same time. You are The Prize Dumbhead of the World. All the things you got to be worrying about, and now you get yourself all steamed up over a *monument*. Come on. Worry about the monument some other time. Tote that barge. Lift that suitcase. You got a train to catch. Grinning a little, Morris Bird III winked in the direction of the

Soldiers' & Sailors' Monument, then trudged off toward the Terminal Tower. He pushed through pigeons, and he pushed through the Saturdaynight crowds of people on their way to the movies and whatever, and the sun, courtesy of Daylight Saving Time, still was high and white and warm, and the sweat worked across his forehead in fat salty dribbles. He tried not to think about the sweat. Grunting, he staggered forward, onward, ever onward, toward the Terminal Tower. He bumped into an elderly woman, and she said something about These Brats A Person Meets Nowadays. He paid no attention to her. Life was too short. The entrance to the Terminal Tower was a series of doors topped by a line of windows. Above the windows was a clock, and above the clock was the tower, and a million windows, fingering toward God. It was all very impressive, but the clock said 6:41, and Morris Bird III had to hurry. He nudged open one of the doors, then trotted down a wide ramp to the lower level where the railroad station was. It was very crowded. He scuttled across the waiting room to the row of ticket windows. He went to a window that said COACH PASSENGERS ONLY. The window was quite high. He barely could see over the sill. A man with a hearing aid peered down at him. He asked the man for a oneway ticket to Columbus. The man frowned. It's okay, said Morris Bird III, I know I don't look it, but I'm thirteen. The man twisted something in his hearing aid. What? he said. A ONEWAY TICKET TO COLUMBUS! shouted Morris Bird III. Yes sir, said the man. He produced a ticket, stamped it, told Morris Bird III the charge was $4.97. Morris Bird III fumbled in his wallet and came up with the five. The man reached in a drawer and gave him his change, pushing the three cents under the window's iron grillwork. In a loud voice, he told Morris Bird III the train was departing from Track 16. Morris Bird III nodded, thanked the man. Lurching away from the ticket window, he almost had to grin. Sometimes, and this was one of those times, he was entirely too sensitive about his size. Sure the old man had frowned, but not because of Morris Bird III's *size.* The frown had been caused by an outofkilter hearing aid. Huh. It surely was remarkable the way some people always jumped right straight toward the wrong conclusions. Well, who was perfect? And ányway, this had been kind of a hectic day. Quickly he glanced toward a clock on a far wall. It said 6:52. He looked for Gate 16. It was almost directly in front of him. A lot of people were clustered around it. They were moving forward and down a flight of stairs. Morris Bird III hurried across the waiting room. The sign over Gate 16 said:

TRAIN NO. 301
DEPARTS 7 P.M.
LINNDALE
WELLINGTON
CRESTLINE
GALION
DELAWARE
COLUMBUS
SPRINGFIELD
DAYTON
MIDDLETOWN
WINTON PLACE
CINCINNATI

Grunting, he got into line and passed through the gate and descended the stairs. Down on the track level, everything was cool and damp. His face itched. He had to stop, set down the suitcase and wipe his face. Ah, better. Much better. He picked up the suitcase, moved forward again. Track 16 was to his right. The passenger cars were enormous. Little strings and dribbles of steam escaped from underneath them. There was an odor of coaldust and stale tar. Baring his teeth, he breathed it in, and it was delicious. Ahead of him, behind him, the passengers for Train No. 301 marched in hurried and straggly formation. Men, women, small trotting children, all scuttled along the darkened platform toward a tall trainman who stood at the entrance to one of the cars. He was grinning, and the letters NYC were on his cap and jacket. This is Train Number 301! he hollered. Columbus and Cincinnati train! Don't get on this train if you want to go to Walla Walla or Mexico City or Timbuctoo! The best we can offer is Columbus and Cincinnati, not to mention Wellington, Crestline, Galion, Delaware, Springfield, Dayton, Middletown and Winton Place! Sorry, folks, if you want to go anywhere else, you're out of luck! Morris Bird III grinned. Behind him, a woman said: Oh, *well* now, isn't *this* fellow the one. The tall trainman helped the passengers up the steps into the coach. Smoker forward! he shouted. Addicts of the filthy weed please turn to your left! When Morris Bird III got to where the tall trainman stood, the tall trainman grabbed hold of the suitcase and swung it up into the vestibule. There you go, buddy, he said. Morris Bird III grinned, thanked him. We aim to please, said the tall trainman. In the vestibule, Morris Bird III looked to the left, then to the right. More seats were available in the coach to the left, the smoker. Apparently a lot of cleanliving types were traveling on Train No. 301 tonight. He picked up the suitcase and entered the smoker. He found himself a seat about halfway up the coach.

229

He'd learned a long time ago that, when a choice presented itself, it was wise not to sit at the end of a coach. The ride was rougher when you sat directly over the wheels. Standing next to his seat, he looked up. The baggagerack was awfully high up in the air. He frowned. Oh well, he said to himself, faint heart never won anybody nothing. Grimacing, he grabbed hold of the suitcase and climbed up on the seat. He dropped *Spanish Blood* onto the floor. Then he placed his feet wide apart, lifted the suitcase over his head and tried to hurl it into the rack. He did not succeed. It struck the edge of the rack and bounced back into his face. He was knocked off the seat, and the suitcase fell on top of him. He hit his head on the armrest of the seat across the aisle. The suitcase wound up down by his knees. He gasped, shuddered, closed his eyes. He almost kind of wished he were dead. Then he felt the weight of the suitcase come off his knees. You all right? someone wanted to know. He opened his eyes. A plump man with eyes like olives was bent over him. Behind the plump man stood a man who was even plumper. This man had a pink horizontal scar directly under his mouth. Morris Bird III nodded, tried to grin. Sure, he said, I'm okay. Good, said Olive Eyes. He handed the suitcase to Scarface. Here, you idiot, make yourself useful, he said. A grin from Scarface, who with no effort at all slid the suitcase up on the baggagerack. Morris Bird III got to his feet. He brushed at his rump. Thank you, he said to Olive Eyes. A nod from Olive Eyes. Think nothing of it, he said. With my brains and this idiot's brawn, we're forever going around the country doing good deeds. He nudged Scarface. Isn't that right, Spaghetti Brain? A nod from Scarface, and another grin. You bet, he said. Morris Bird III nodded. He didn't think it was his place really to make any comment. If these two men wanted to be insane, that was their right—as long as they didn't do anyone any physical harm. He moved around the two men and seated himself under his suitcase. He picked up *Spanish Blood* and held it in his lap. The two men camped across the aisle from him. They had two enormous suitcases, but Scarface had no trouble with them. He lifted them to the baggagerack without even grunting. Then he and Olive Eyes sat down and began discussing someone named Sam Stayman. Morris Bird III looked around. The car was filling up. Directly behind him sat a fat blond woman who held a skinny sack upright in her lap. Her face was damp, and there were great dark circles at her armpits. She did not notice Morris Bird III stare at her. She apparently wasn't noticing much of anything. The car was beginning to fill with smoke. Morris Bird III rubbed his eyes, stared out the window. He couldn't see much. The reflected light from inside the car was too bright. A little boy of about five came running down the aisle. He was yelling, evidently just for the sake of yelling. He ran to the forward end of the car, turned, butted a shoulder against a wall, then ran back. He still was yelling, and somewhere behind Morris Bird III a female voice said: Billy, if you don't stop that I'm going to have your father whip you as soon as we get home! The words were followed by a gasping noise, presumably from Billy. Then some whines. Then silence. Morris Bird III wondered how long it would last. Across the aisle, Olive Eyes and Scarface were arguing with some heat over something called a Jump Two Response Vulnerable. A man wearing a Palm Beach suit seated himself directly in front of Morris Bird III. He was a skinny fellow. Sighing, he settled back and made gas. Morris Bird III made a face. A couple of seconds later, Olive Eyes looked across the aisle at Morris Bird III. Not me, said Morris Bird III. He inclined his head forward. Oh, said Olive Eyes, and then it was his turn to make a face. Next to him, Scarface chuckled. Morris Bird III took his handkerchief from a pocket and spread it over his nose. After a time, the smell went away. Then the train began to move. Morris Bird III took a deep, sort of shuddery, breath. The train slid out of the station and across a long bridge over The Flats, where were steel mills and factories and railroad yards and piles of iron ore and the snaky filthy Cuyahoga River. The car rocked gently, and across the aisle Olive Eyes and Scarface lit themselves a couple of long fat cigars. They had a smell to them that was almost like the gas that had come from the skinny fellow in the Palm Beach suit. Again Morris Bird III reached for his handkerchief. The train picked up speed. As inconspicuously as he could, Morris Bird III covered his nose. Behind him, the blond woman said something unintelligible. Morris Bird III studied boxcars and sidings and factories. He saw a boxcar that said MONON, and he saw one that said NORTHERN PACIFIC. A little later, he didn't particularly notice the smell of the cigars. He put away the handkerchief. He was sitting on the lefthand side of the coach. Since the train was headed south, he figured the setting sun wouldn't bother him. He looked down at *Spanish Blood*, then placed it on the seat next to him. He wouldn't be reading. He never read on trains. There was too much to see. The wheels went *dicka dicka, dicka dicka, dicka dicka, dicka dick*. He grinned. He still didn't quite know whether this trip was a good idea (his mother probably would have him boiled alive when he showed up in Paradise Falls), but now was too late to be worrying about it. Done was done, and so he might as well enjoy it. He saw a yard engine pushing a string of boxcars onto a siding next to a warehouse. The yard engine reminded him of the late John T. Clift's hog. Morris Bird III loved steam locomotives. To him, they were more than machinery. So many different parts went in so many different directions. He could not really explain why he loved steam engines (and didn't particularly see that he *had* to), but love them he did, and they were one of the principal reasons why he enjoyed himself so much when he rode in a train. The wheels went *dicka dicka, dicka dicka, dicka dicka, dicka dick,* and then behind him someone opened the door to the vestibule, and the wheels went *dicka DICKA, DICKA, DICKA, DICka dicka, dicka dick,* and presently he heard the cheerful voice of the tall trainman. Tickets plizz! shouted the tall trainman. Have your tickets ready plizz! And we don't mean parking tickets! Next to Morris Bird III, old Olive Eyes twisted around in his seat and looked back toward where the voice had come from. Ah, he said to Scarface, we got us a regular Jack Benny. Scarface nodded, then said something about Responding With Four Of A Minor Suit Over An Opening Bid Of One In A Major Suit Not Vulnerable.

Biting hard on his cigar, Olive Eyes told Scarface there was nothing to it, you just . . . and Morris Bird III filtered out the words, returned his attention to his window. The train was slowing. This was Linndale. All trains stopped at Linndale. A big yard was there, and it was the end of the line for the electric locomotives that took the passenger trains in and out of the terminal downtown. Except in extreme emergencies, steam locomotives weren't allowed in the terminal. The people who'd built the terminal hadn't wanted it dirtied by smoke. So, at Linndale to the southwest and in the Collinwood yards to the northeast, the New York Central had elaborate facilities for exchanging electric locomotives for steam, and vice versa. Morris Bird III felt the brakes grab, and very smoothly the train came to a stop. Rows and rows and rows of sidings stretched off beyond his window. He counted four yard engines moving about, pushing and pulling freight cars. One came by right on the next track. He waved at the engineer, and the engineer waved at him. It was great how engineers almost always waved at you when you waved at them. The tall trainman poked Morris Bird III on a shoulder. Morris Bird III jumped a little. The tall trainman was smiling. You a railfan or something? he wanted to know. Yes, said Morris Bird III. Good. So am I, said the tall trainman. Morris Bird III smiled, handed the trainman his ticket. Ah, said the trainman, Columbus. A good city. Capital of our fair state. You planning on seeing the governor? Morris Bird III shook his head no. Ah, too bad, said the tall trainman. He punched the ticket. Handing it back to Morris Bird III, he said: Do you know who our governor is? Yes, said Morris Bird III, his name is Thomas H. Herbert. A grin and a nod from the tall trainman. I have a hunch, he said, that you are not an unintelligent boy. Morris Bird III shrugged. Well, said the tall trainman, wherever you're going, God be with you. Still grinning, he stuck a little red tab in a slot in the seatback directly in front of Morris Bird III. Keep an eye on that, he said. I know it doesn't look as impressive as the ticket, but it'll get you to Columbus. Doesn't seem like much for $4.97 I know, but, well, that's the way of the world. With that, the tall trainman turned and collected the tickets of Olive Eyes and Scarface. Whoo, he said to Olive Eyes and Scarface, what a couple of cigars. Ah, so you gentlemen are going to Columbus too? Are you by any chance in the political game? A negative nod from Olive Eyes. We should live so long, he said. The tall trainman laughed, punched their tickets, moved on down the aisle. Olive Eyes grinned at Morris Bird III. Well, friend, it takes all kinds, he said. Morris Bird III managed a nod. He looked out the window. There was a gentle bump. He supposed the new locomotive was being attached. He wrinkled his nose. The smell of the cigars really & truly was *something.* Then, slowly, the train began moving forward again. Up ahead, a woman laughed at something the tall trainman had said. Behind Morris Bird III, the blond woman said something that sounded like rumblefiltafrash. He shook his head, grinned, told himself the name of this train had to be The Lunatic Special. The train picked up speed. The Linndale yards fell behind. The land was flat, crisscrossed by roads and lines of trees. Now the factories and warehouses were spread farther apart. Morris Bird III sneezed. He supposed it was from the cigars. He wiped his nose with his handkerchief. He was glad he'd brought along his handkerchief. It really was getting a workout. The train slowed a little, clattered over a great many switchpoints. He looked across the aisle. Tracks trailed off to the right. They were the main line of the New York Central. They went clear to Chicago. He saw a watertower, and on the watertower in black letters was written the word BEREA. The train now was on the Big Four division of the New York Central. At one time this division had been a separate railroad called the Cleveland, Columbus, Cincinnati & St. Louis, hence the nickname Big Four. (Morris Bird III had obtained all this railroad information from his late buddy, Stanley Chaloupka, the fellow who had owned such a magnificent layout of Lionel O Gauge trains. Stanley Chaloupka had been the greatest railfan west of the Alleghenies, and there hadn't been a thing about trains and railroads he'd not known. He'd really been quite a buddy, this Stanley Chaloupka, and even now, almost four years after his death, Morris Bird III missed him a whole lot.) The train again picked up speed. Now the factories and warehouses were gone. Telegraphpoles went past. They made urgent whispery sounds. *Dicka dicka, dicka dicka, dicka dicka, dicka dick,* went the wheels, and Morris Bird III took a deep happy breath, and never mind the cigars, never mind the gas from the man in the Palm Beach suit. He looked out the window, and he saw a little girl. She was maybe five, and she was standing on a pile of gravel. She waved at the train. Morris Bird III waved back. He hoped she saw him. Darkness was rushing toward the train. It hung, gray and thick, beyond a line of trees that crowded against the horizon. He supposed that in half an hour or so his looking time would be up. He decided that night trains weren't as much fun as day trains. He wondered if Julie Sutton liked mysteries. He wondered if she would have liked *The Treasure of the Sierra Madre.* Maybe she'd seen it. He'd ask her, next time he saw her. If there was enough left out of the $17, maybe he'd be able to take her *downtown* to the movies. They would ride the Hough Avenue trackless trolley and get off at East 17th Street just like the handholders. The walk up East 17th was only three blocks, and it went through Chinatown, and on the door of one of the buildings there were the words HIP SING ASSOCIATION, and every time he saw them he thought of hula dancers. There were a lot of movie houses downtown along Euclid Avenue—the Warner's Lake, the RKO Palace (which also offered vaudeville), the Loew's State, the Loew's Ohio, the Warner's Allen, the Loew's Stillman, the Hippodrome. Oh they were plentiful all right, and at night the dazzle of their lights was all warm and crackly, and maybe he would hold her hand, and maybe a sidewalk photographer would take their picture, and just let *anybody* call her Gunboats within *his* hearing. Anybody at all. Whoever was so foolish would be smashed to a bloody quivering pulp. No fooling. Honest to God Almighty. STATION STOP IS WELLINGTON! shouted the tall trainman, lurching down the aisle and grinning at everyone. REAR DOOR OUT! STATION STOP IS WELLINGTON! ALL THOSE WHO ARE MORE INTERESTED IN VISITING WELLINGTON THAN STAYING ABOARD THIS GREAT TRAIN OF ALL TRAINS, PLEASE USE THE REAR DOOR, AND IF WELLINGTON DOESN'T LIVE UP TO YOUR EXPECTATIONS, DON'T COME WHIMPERING TO US AND SAY YOU WEREN'T WARNED! From one end of the car to the other, people giggled and guffawed. From across the aisle, Olive Eyes looked at Morris Bird III and said: This guy may be the greatest thing that's happened to the railroad business since the invention of the Westinghouse Air Brake. Morris Bird III laughed. This really was turning out to be quite a trip. Quite a day, too, what with his talk with Julie Sutton, not to mention the villainy of Randy Gumpert, Aaron Robinson and Dave Philley. He would have a great deal to tell his grandmother, and maybe some of his words would make her laugh, or at least smile a little. Just as long as she didn't *bawl*. The train was slowing. He saw little frame houses and big trees. The darkness had made the green of the grass almost black. A yard engine went by on the next track. It came in a great black smoky rush, and Morris Bird III drew back from the window for a moment. A couple of seats in front of him, an old woman got up and came back down the aisle. Olive Eyes looked up at her and said: Ah, too bad you're leaving us. You'll never know what you'll be missing. Surprisingly (at least to Morris Bird III), the old woman grinned, smote Olive Eyes on a shoulder and said: Oh *you*. Then, cackling, she moved on. She was carrying a shoppingbag, but she was rather a big and fat old woman, and she had no trouble with it. Behind Morris Bird III, the blond woman snorted and said ellarampleshush. Huh. This was some train all right. All it needed was Fred C. Dobbs to lead everyone in a nice hearty community sing. Yeah, and everybody *would* sing, too. Morris Bird III could hear the words, the slow threatening *If you know what's good for you, you won't monkey around with*

Fred
C.
Dobbs.

Morris Bird III grimaced. What a way to be thinking. He was as crazy as all the rest of the people aboard The Lunatic Special. Oh well. Didn't cost anything. And, the truth was, it almost kind of felt good. He wouldn't have been surprised if a brass band had come marching down the aisle. A brass band with plenty of drums. The train stopped briefly, then began moving again, and so much for Wellington. His attention returned to his window. Now the world was all gray. The darkness clamored like a fog, all swirly and inexorable. The windowpane reflected his forehead. He rubbed his forehead. He scratched at a hicky with a fingernail. He looked around. To the rear of the car was a sign that said MEN. He debated going back there and washing his face. He decided against it. What with all the things that had been happening in this goofy train, he might have missed something. Now the train really was moving. Outside his window were the faint outlines of flat fields, punctuated here and there by skinny lonely trees. And here and there were tiny solitary lights, very white and almost forlorn. Behind him, the blond woman rustled her bag. She did not, however, deliver any comments. The train was moving so fast that now the wheels went *dickadicka, dickadicka, dickadicka, dickadick*. If the tall trainman's behavior was any clue to the personality of the engineer, Morris Bird III almost kind of wished he were a Catholic. At least Catholics had beads and things at times like this. Then Morris Bird III's shoulders began to shake. He laughed silently, but his laughter was desperate, breathless. It brought tears to his eyes. He couldn't remember *when* he'd felt so funny. Not funny-peculiar, though. And not funny-ha-ha. Just funny-good, and of course funny-good was the best funny of them all. For some reason, he remembered something Benny Goodman had said to him a year or so ago. He'd asked Benny: You like it that your name's the same as that clarinet player's? Benny's reply: You got it wrong, old pal. My name's not the same as his. *His* is the same as *mine*. Maybe a lot of people would have called this a wiseguy answer. Morris Bird III, though, didn't see it that way. The way *he* saw it, the reply had meant Benny was a special sort of human being, brave and funny (funny-good, to be sure) and full of balance up to his eyeballs. Another time, while speaking of his mother, Benny had said: She's a funny mother for somebody like me to be having. Now, don't get me wrong. I'm not knocking her. I wouldn't do that for a hundred thousand shares of God. All I mean is, she's all the time going around talking like that Mrs. Nussbaum on the Fred Allen program, making with the *oy* with every other word coming out Yiddish, and here she is the wife of a *college professor,* with a degree of her *own,* from the University of Chicago no less, and yet to listen to her you'd say to yourself: Boy, here's one who got off the boat a week ago last Thursday.

You know, for a long time it got under my skin. Until I thought it out. And you know old Benny when he thinks a thing out. He usually comes up with the right answer. And you know what the answer to my old lady is? Simple. She talks the way she does because that way she doesn't sort of fake out my old man. You know what I mean? One doubledome parent is enough. Morris Bird III had frowned at the time. He'd told Benny he *thought* he understood. Well, that's enough, Benny had said. Just keep thinking about it. It'll get through to you one of these days. Now, staring out into the flat gloom, sitting and rocking and pitching, worrying a little about the engineer and the urgent clacking *dickadicka, dickadicka, dickadicka, dickadick* of the wheels, Morris Bird III saw what Benny Goodman had meant. He thought of Benny Goodman's mother, and he thought of love, and yes you bet, he told himself, I am *too* doing the right thing. Love is love. You don't push it away. You do your duty by it. I remember how one time I told myself it was awful Grandma was getting the life squeezed out of her real slow. I told myself God was evil not to squash her, put her out of her misery. But *Benny* was squashed, wasn't he? And Stanley Chaloupka, too. Did the squashing make it any easier? No! Dying is dying, and squeezing or squashing, what's the difference? So, the thing is, I got to do my duty by the love and forget the dying. It'll come soon enough. *Dickadicka, dickadicka, dickadicka, dickadick,* and Morris Bird III's cheeks were tight from holding back the tears. He rubbed his forehead, made a face, awaited further developments here in The Lunatic Special. They weren't long in coming. At the rear of the car, the vestibule door opened. Then someone back there began grunting and gasping. Morris Bird III looked around. A very small man carrying a very large tray came waddling up the aisle. If someone had thrown a bucket of water at him, his face couldn't have been wetter. He had a very long nose, and somehow most of it had been pushed to one side. His eyes were immense and he had no hair. His stomach stuck out, and his legs were bowed. In profile, his shape had the appearance of a shallow C. The tray rested against his stomach. A heavy cloth belt ran up from the tray around his neck and back down again. He wore khaki trousers, a white shirt (not very clean) and a green cap (not clean at all). He was grinning, and he didn't have enough teeth to fill a thimble, and he was saying: Pop get your soda pop here grape orange ginger ale Coke and root beer sandwiches tunafish salad ham chicken roast beef candybars Mars Oh Henry Hershey Nestlé's Mounds Almond Joy Beeman's Pepsin Gum Wrigley's Spearmint Gum Camel Lucky Strike Chesterfield and Old Gold cigarettes coffee doughnuts cookies Lance peanut butter & cracker sandwiches get them now folks it's a long long way to Galion and points south not to mention Tipperary coddle The Inner Man and he will reward you with the blessings of good health an alert mind and godly habits coffee? yes sir cream & sugar? black? yes sir that'll be 15 cents please the Union News Co. expects a reasonable return on its investment a ham sandwich? by all means would you care for mustard? no mustard all right sir that'll be an additional 35 cents *thank you* yes and who's next now for pop candy sandwiches gum coffee and so forth and so on? yes sir? a Mars Bar? by all means *there* you are 15 cents please *thank you* and you little miss? a Mounds? yes indeed 15 cents please *thank you* always remember that the free exchange of money for goods is one of the bulwarks of the American economic system so who now for a chicken sandwich? a chicken sandwich of a delicacy unparalleled I personally knew this chicken and she was of a disposition sweet and gentle a *tunafish salad* sandwich sir? by all means *there* you are 35 cents *thank you* now then who's for some nice cooling Dad's Old-Fashioned Root Beer? remember folks Thomas Alva Edison got his start this way when he was a boy with a bum ear and please you don't have to remind me that I'm fiftysix years old and hardly a boy within my bosom there yet beats a heart abrim with ambition so let us please hear your gentle voices calling for pop sandwiches gum candy cigarettes coffee cookies doughnuts and Lance peanut butter & cracker sandwiches today's baseball scores were I regret to report Chicago 3 Cleveland 2 alack & alas New York 6 Philadelphia 0 and Boston 10 Washington 6 *thank you all very much* and until we meet again don't let the bedbugs bite. With that, the little man grunted his way through the door at the forward end of the car, and everybody looked at everybody else, and then the laughter came, and it was just about general. Across the aisle, Olive Eyes nudged Scarface and said: What next? Dancing bears maybe? Unicycle riders? A chuckle from Scarface, and then he said something about That Board Last Week When I Led Toward The Bare King In My Hand And Levine Didn't Go Up With His Ace, Which Gave Us A Top On The Board. A nod from Olive Eyes, and he said: Yes sir, you're a genius. Morris Bird III supposed Olive Eyes and Scarface were talking about some sort of card game. Apparently they really were interested in that card game, whatever it was. It was all they'd discussed since getting aboard the train. He bet they were as good at it as Benny Goodman had been at Electric Football. People who talked that much about a game just about had to be. Otherwise, they would have given it up. The door opened at the forward end of the car. In came the tall trainman. STATION STOP IS CRESTLINE! he hol-

lered. REAR DOOR OUT! FOR THOSE OF YOU WHO ARE
GOING ONLY THIS FAR, THE NEW YORK CENTRAL SYS-
TEM HAS EMPOWERED ME TO WISH YOU GODSPEED!
STATION STOP IS CRESTLINE! A FINE LITTLE RAILROAD
TOWN, AS LONG AS YOU DON'T MIND A LITTLE SMOKE!
REAR DOOR OUT PLEASE! WHEN IN CRESTLINE, BE SURE
TO VISIT THE WAYNE & BRANDON BURIAL VAULT COM-
PANY, THE WESTERN PIPE COMPANY AND CHARLES
EDMONDSON & SONS BUILDERS SUPPLY COMPANY, ALL
FINE LOCAL BUSINESS ESTABLISHMENTS THAT DESERVE
YOUR PATRONAGE! REAR DOOR OUT IF YOU PLEASE! The
tall trainman slammed out through the rear door, and the train
began to slow. Morris Bird III saw a liverish dog lying at the base
of a streetlight. Its chin rested on its forepaws, and it surveyed
the train with no particular interest. The air brakes grabbed hold,
and the train came to a stop. Morris Bird III looked around. Apparently no one in this car wanted to get off at Crestline. The car
was really quite full. People were jabbering away to beat the
band, and some of them were eating anonymous little goodies
from paper bags. There was a good deal of laughter, too. He
supposed the behavior of the tall trainman and the little
sweaty news butcher had had an effect. He certainly hoped
so. It was good not to be sour, and the people in this car didn't
appear to be sour hardly at all, and so God bless the tall trainman, God bless the little sweaty news butcher. The train began
to move. A yard engine went past. It was pushing a string of
gondola cars. The train went by a factory that had an immense
neon sign on its roof. The neon was crimson and it said WAYNE &
BRANDON BURIAL VAULT CO. FOUNDED 1901 HOME OF THE W&B
NON-SEEP VAULT. Morris Bird III shuddered a little. The darkness

was complete. He sighed, reached for *Spanish Blood*. Maybe now was as good a time as any to finish "Nevada Gas." The W&B Non-seep Vault had kind of gotten him into the mood. The train was moving quite fast now: *dickadicka, dickadicka, dickadicka, dickadick.* He'd just opened the book when someone sat down next to him. How we doing? said the tall trainman, grinning. Morris Bird III placed the book on his lap. Fine, he said. The initial is R., said the tall trainman. Huh? said Morris Bird III. And the tall trainman said: The middle initial of our governor. It's R., not H. And Morris Bird III said: Oh. And the tall trainman said: But you knew his name, and that's the important thing. He's our governor, but you'd be surprised how many people don't know his name. Thomas R. Herbert, and he's a Cleveland man at that. Went to East High School. And Morris Bird III said: East High's in my neighborhood. In a couple of years, I'll be going there. And the tall trainman said: Good. Maybe some day you'll be governor. And Morris Bird III said: I doubt *that.* And the tall trainman said: What do you want to be? And Morris Bird III said: I don't know. And the tall trainman said: Well, no matter. You got time to decide. And Morris Bird III said: Uh huh. And the tall trainman said: You like traveling alone? And Morris Bird III said: I don't know. This is my first time. And the tall trainman said: You don't look as though you're afraid. And Morris Bird III said: I'm not. And the tall trainman said: You seeing someone in Columbus? And Morris Bird III said: No. I'm going on to a place called Paradise Falls. And the tall trainman said: I know the town. It's on the C&O. And Morris Bird III said: Yes. But I'm going to take a bus from Columbus. No trains are running. And the tall trainman said: Well, you certainly seem in control of the situation. Uh, you don't have to tell me if you don't want to, and please pardon my long nose, but how come you're going to Paradise Falls? And Morris Bird III said: To see my grandmother. She's dying. And the tall trainman said: Oh. I'm sorry. And Morris Bird III said: So am I. And the tall trainman said: You love her? And Morris Bird III said: Yes. And the tall trainman said: Love is good. Love is spontaneous. Love is the best Giving thing there is. And Morris Bird III said: Mister, don't get mad, but can I ask you a question? And the tall trainman said: Sure. And I promise I won't get mad. And Morris Bird III said: Mister, how come you talk so much? And, laughing, the tall trainman slapped Morris Bird III on a knee and said: I don't know. I suppose I missed my calling. Maybe I should have been a minister. And Morris Bird III said: I bet you'd have been a good one. And the tall trainman said: Thank you. And Morris Bird III said: Don't *thank* me. I *meant* it. And the tall trainman said: Do you believe in God? And Morris Bird III said: Yes. And the tall trainman said: And what do you think of Him? And Morris Bird III said: I don't know. Sometimes I think He's all right. And then sometimes I think He maybe doesn't care enough. And the tall trainman said: You must always remember to have faith. And Morris Bird III said: I try. And the tall trainman said: There are a lot of good people in the world. You don't hear much from them, but they're all around you all the time. And, remember, they are creatures of God. And Morris Bird III said: Uh huh. And the tall trainman said: You like to fish? And Morris Bird III said: I don't know. I've never been. And the tall trainman said: Fishing is my hobby. You should try it some time. It is a very quiet thing to occupy your time with. It gives your mind tranquillity. Your grandmother, I expect she has tranquillity. And Morris Bird III said: Yes. Or at least she did. Now she hurts. How come God takes it out on her that way? And the tall trainman said: Pain is nothing. And Morris Bird III said: Huh? And the tall trainman said: It doesn't last. Eternity lasts. And there is no pain in the Kingdom of God. Pain is of the earth, earthy. It simply serves as a step to the Kingdom of God. And Morris Bird III said: I thought pain was a punishment. My grandmother never did anything to anybody. And the tall trainman said: I wish I could explain more fully, but I can't. I've read a great many books in my time, and all they've ever really shown me is the rightness of acceptance. Do you follow me? And Morris Bird III said: I think so. And the tall trainman said: You're really quite a remarkable young man. And Morris Bird III said: No. I'm nothing. And the tall trainman said: That's not true. Nobody's nothing. And Morris Bird III said: I hope you're right. And the tall trainman said: I *am* right. You can count on it. And Morris Bird III nodded, made a puffing sound with his lips. Then the forward door opened, and in came the little sweaty news butcher. You care for a little snack? the tall trainman wanted to know. Don't mind if I do, said Morris Bird III. Hey, Paul! shouted the tall trainman. Right this way! My friend and I want to put on the old feed bag! A grin from the little sweaty news butcher. He came lurching down the aisle to their seat. And what'll it be? he asked them. Pop candy coffee sandwiches cookies doughnuts Lance peanut butter & cracker sandwiches? Morris Bird III and the tall trainman settled for grape soda and Lance peanut butter & cracker sandwiches. The tall trainman insisted on paying for all of it. Morris Bird III tried to pay for his share, but the tall trainman would hear none of it. I insist, he said. This is my treat. The New York Central System appreciates your patronage. And Morris Bird III said: Thank you. And the tall trainman said: My pleasure. And Paul the little sweaty news butcher said: Friendship. Ah, friendship. Sixty cents is indeed a niggardly sum to pay for such a treasure. And the tall trainman said: Yes, Paul my friend, you have hit upon a glorious truth. He gave Paul a dollar bill, and Paul gave him a quarter, a dime and a nickel. Then, head tilted back, throat working, Paul proceeded down the aisle, throwing his spiel in a breathless rush to the other inmates—er, *passengers*. The grape soda was in little paper cups. It was good and cold. The tall trainman lifted his paper cup and said: Your very good health. And Morris Bird III said: Same to you. They drank. Then they broke open their Lance peanut butter & cracker sandwiches. They munched silently. The tall trainman's jaws worked slowly, with great dignity. Ah, he said, hits the spot. Morris Bird III nodded. Behind them, the blond woman said frammerapitoid. The tall trainman winked at Morris Bird III. Joy to the world, he said, lifting his paper cup and finishing off his grape soda. Merry Christmas, said Morris Bird III, finishing off his own grape soda. Then Morris Bird III grinned, and so did the tall trainman. Quietly they did away with their Lance peanut butter & cracker sandwiches. Then Morris Bird III sort of yawned. He rubbed his forehead. The tall trainman was smiling, but he said nothing. Another yawn from Morris Bird III. He blinked. He closed his eyes, and the first thing he saw was Dave Philley's home run sailing over the fence. Quickly he opened his eyes. Be in Galion in about ten minutes, said the tall trainman. Morris Bird III nodded. The Gordon Park Berardinos had a 2–0 lead over the Chicago White Sox with play in the last half of the ninth. Morris Bird III and Teddy Karam stood on the pitcher's mound and discussed how Teddy should pitch to Pat Seerey. On the bench, Manager Benny Goodman was yelling at everyone to hang in there. Morris Bird III rubbed up the ball for Teddy Karam, only it wasn't a ball; it was a china owl. Laughing, Don Schwamb pointed at Julie Sutton's feet and said: That's quite a pair you got there, Gunboats old kid. Pat Seerey hit the china owl squarely on the nose. A great crash resounded, and the china owl went in 1,948 directions simultaneously. Snickering, Fred C. Dobbs said to Julie Sutton: You got nothing to worry about, kid, not with Gunboats like *those.* You can always get yourself a good job at a winery. Trampling the grapes. Grandma smiled and said: It doesn't matter that I hurt. The hurt is of the earth, earthy. Morris Bird III smashed Don Schwamb with his right hand and Fred C. Dobbs with his left. They shrieked and bleated. Smiling, Julie Sutton went to her hero and gave him a stuffed duck as a token of her esteem. GALION! somebody hollered. It was a familiar voice, almost. STATION STOP IS GALION! REAR DOOR OUT! A FINE LITTLE TOWN! GOOD FARM COUNTRY HEREABOUTS! FARM COUNTRY IS GOD'S COUNTRY! AH, THE PEACEFULNESS OF THE ARBOREAL DELL! THE SMELL OF NEWMOWN HAY AND CORN ON THE HUSK! STATION STOP IS GALION! REAR DOOR OUT, IF YOU PLEASE! If you want to, said Julie Sutton, you can kiss me. I am of the earth, earthy, and you shouldn't be forgetting that little point. I smile good, and you said yourself I'm not half badlooking, even if maybe I do have big feet. You can have the silverware, said Aunt Phyllis to Aunt Iris, if I can have the jewelry. You can have the porch furniture, said Uncle Howard to Aunt Emily, if I can have the sheets and pillowcases and bedspreads. I'll trade you my heart, said Morris Bird III's mother to God, for six loaves of day-old bread. Don't worry, said Julie Sutton. I won't break. Hang in there, old pal, said Benny Goodman. I'll tell you what. If it makes you feel better, go ahead and steal a shovel and come out to the cemetery some night. I won't mind. I mean, what difference does it make to *me?* Just because I'm *in* the earth, that doesn't mean I'm *of* the earth. You go ahead and make all the gas you want to, said Sandra. I'll take color movies. Grandma said, smiling: do what's right. It may cost you something, but it won't cost you as much as doing wrong will. March brave, and stop rubbing your forehead all the time! Along came the Ohio State University marching band, and the drum majorettes were carrying an immense banner, and on the banner was written THE SUM AND TOTAL OF THE NOW OF MORRIS BIRD III COMES TO A NICE COZY $#*&Ç%?@#*#! (How's that again? Did it read $#*&Ç%?@#*#!? Yeah, that's correct. You got it exactly right. Every syllable.) Francine Ley stroked his head and said: If Julie Sutton fails you, come up and see *me* some time. STATION STOP IS DELAWARE! the familiar voice yelled. FOR THOSE OF YOU OF THE METHODIST PERSUASION, THIS FINE TOWN IS THE HOME OF OHIO WESLEYAN UNIVERSITY, FOUNDED IN 1842 WITH A PRESENT STUDENT ENROLLMENT OF MORE THAN 2,000! ITS PRESIDENT IS THAT NOTED EDUCATOR, ARTHUR S. FLEMMING! STATION STOP IS DELAWARE, FOR ALL THOSE ABOARD OF AN INTELLECTUAL BENT! REAR DOOR OUT, IF YOU PLEASE! I won't have words for Grandma, said Morris Bird III. I hope they aren't needed. I hope just being there is enough. If she's counting on me for words, she's going to be in bad shape. A thin smile from Suzanne Wysocki. I am praying, she said. I honestly & truly am. I was in Pittsburgh when I should have been in Scranton, said Mr. Wysocki. The worst thing in the world is to be in Pittsburgh when you should be in Scranton. Believe me. I know. So, if she is The One as you know she is, you got no choice. You got to go be with her. Shrieking, flapping his arms, clutching a handgrenade, Wright M. Ludwigson, principal of Addison Junior High School, advanced on the Soldiers' & Sailors' Monument. But then along came Morris Bird III, and he felled Wright M. Ludwigson with a flying tackle. He wrested the handgrenade from Wright M. Ludwigson's feverish grasp. Smiling, he stood up, walked to the nearest sewer and dropped the handgrenade down into all the guck and slop and mess. It landed with an enervated and harmless plash. Turning, he saw that Wright M. Ludwigson was beating his head against the ground. Oh *come* now, he told Wright M. Ludwigson, you're Abusing Yourself. Off beyond the horizon, a chorus of ten thousand was singing "The Battle Hymn of the Republic." Smiling, acknowledging the cheers of the multitude, our hero said: *If you know what's good for you, ye forces of evil, you won't monkey around with*

> *Morris*
> *Bird*
> *III.*

Then someone was tugging at his shoulder. Rise and shine, said the familiar voice. We'll be in Columbus in a few minutes. Morris Bird III opened his eyes. The tall trainman was smiling down at him. Huh? said Morris Bird III. Columbus—we're almost in Columbus, said the tall trainman. Oh, said Morris Bird III. Blinking, he thanked the tall trainman. Our motto is service, said the tall trainman, and then he turned to Olive Eyes and Scarface across the aisle. He asked them would they mind telling him where they were going in Columbus. A shrug from Olive

Eyes. It's no military secret, he said. We're going to the Deshler. A nod from the tall trainman. Are you going there by cab? he wanted to know. Uh huh, said Olive Eyes, frowning a little. The tall trainman smiled. Then perhaps you wouldn't mind dropping our friend here at the bus station, he said, nodding in the direction of Morris Bird III. No, not a bit, said Olive Eyes. He looked at Scarface and said: That all right with you, Jack? Scarface nodded. Sure, he said, if the kid can fit in with us and all our bulk, I got no objections. The tall trainman thanked Olive Eyes and Scarface. I also want to wish you good luck in the tournament, he said. Thanks, said Olive Eyes. With this idiot I got here for a partner, we'll need it. Then Olive Eyes gave the tall trainman a sharp look. How did you know we're playing in the tournament? he asked the tall trainman. I have ears, said the tall trainman. Then he turned to Morris Bird III. It's all arranged, he said. These two gentlemen will take you to the bus station. It's not far from their hotel. A nod from Morris Bird III. Again he thanked the tall trainman. Then he nodded toward Olive Eyes and Scarface and thanked *them* too. Olive Eyes made a deprecating movement with a hand. It's nothing, he said. Then he looked up at the tall trainman and said: How long you been with the New York Central? And the tall trainman said: Oh, about two thousand years. And Olive Eyes said: Well, pal, I think you're crazier than a goonybird, but the railroad's lucky to have you. And the tall trainman said: You're very kind. And Olive Eyes shook his head. Just simply shook his head. The tall trainman grinned. Now the train was slowing down again. Morris Bird III looked out his window and saw lots of lights. STATION STOP IS COLUMBUS! shouted the tall trainman. HOME OF OHIO STATE UNIVERSITY, THE COLUMBUS RED BIRDS, BENNY

251

KLEIN'S STEAK HOUSE, THE DESHLER-WALLACK HOTEL, THE NEIL HOUSE, THE OHIO PENITENTIARY AND THE OHIO SCHOOL OF THE DEAF! THIS IS THE CAPITAL CITY OF OUR STATE! REAR DOOR OUT PLEASE! BE SURE, IF YOU HAVE A CHANCE, TO DROP IN TO SEE OUR GOVERNOR, THOMAS R. HERBERT! WHAT WITH THIS BEING AN ELECTION YEAR AND ALL, I'M SURE HE'LL BE HAPPY TO SEE YOU! STATION STOP IS COLUMBUS! GLAD TO HAVE HAD YOU WITH US! KINDLY USE THE REAR DOOR! Just as the tall trainman was about to push his way out through the rear door, almost everyone in the car began applauding. The tall trainman smiled, then hollered: THANK YOU! THANK YOU! GOD BLESS YOU ALL! The applause followed him out of the car. Morris Bird III and Olive Eyes and Scarface were among the loudest of the applauders. Morris Bird III even allowed himself to yell YAYYY! Then he grinned at Olive Eyes and Scarface, and they grinned at him. He looked up and down the aisle. Except for the blond woman, everyone was smiling. Even the man in the Palm Beach suit was smiling. Olive Eyes leaned across the aisle. My name is Goodwin, he said. He held out a hand. Morris Bird III took hold of it. Mr. Goodwin's grip was gentle. Then, nodding back over a shoulder, Mr. Goodwin said: My stupid friend here is named Pearl. That's his *last* name. Be friendly toward him. He's very rich. Grinning, Mr. Pearl reached around Mr. Goodwin and shook Morris Bird III's hand. And who might you be? Mr. Goodwin wanted to know. My name is Morris Bird, said Morris Bird III. *Oh?* said Mr. Goodwin. *Oh?* said Mr. Pearl. Are you by any chance a Jewish boy? said Mr. Goodwin. No sir, said Morris Bird III. Um, said Mr. Goodwin, I thought maybe because your first name is Morris. Ah, but I should have known. After all, you don't *look* Jewish. Then Mr. Goodwin got to laughing, and so did Mr. Pearl. They had a lot of teeth to show, and they showed just about all of them. Mr. Goodwin's laughter came in a keen. Mr. Pearl's came in a roar. They clapped each other on the back. Morris Bird III looked blank. He didn't have the slightest idea what was so funny. Oh well. This was that kind of a day. He glanced out his window. The train was barely moving. Then the station platform slid into view. Well, said Mr. Goodwin, it's about that time. He stood up. Mr. Pearl followed him out into the aisle. Morris Bird III tucked *Spanish Blood* under an arm. The train stopped. The tall trainman appeared at the rear door. COLUM-BUS! THIS WAY OUT! he yelled. Quickly, easily, Mr. Pearl brought his and Mr. Goodwin's suitcases down from the bag-gagerack. Then, just as quickly and easily, he brought down Morris Bird III's. Thank you, said Morris Bird III, sliding out into the aisle. You don't have to thank him, said Mr. Goodwin. It's the one thing in this life he can do with skill. A mock frown from Mr. Pearl. You, he said to Mr. Goodwin, are all lip, and lip is the only thing *you* can do with skill, so please do me a favor and don't make cracks about your physical superior. A groan from Mr. Goodwin. Oh *brother!* he said. The *gall* of this man! A line had formed in the aisle. It began slowly to move toward the rear of the car. Morris Bird III and Mr. Goodwin and Mr. Pearl picked up their suitcases. Then somebody made a snarly noise. Morris Bird III looked down. So did Mr. Goodwin and Mr. Pearl. The blond woman was glaring up at them. Waringlopagas, she said. Same to you, madam, said Mr. Goodwin solemnly, and twice on holy days. A grunt from the blond woman. Her face relaxed a little. Apparently now she was mollified. Itsamunteralliblatch, she said. Oh yes. Yes indeed, said Mr. Goodwin. You just better

believe it. The blond woman nodded. Morris Bird III and Mr.
Goodwin and Mr. Pearl moved on. They went out the rear door
and down the vestibule steps. The tall trainman helped them
onto the platform. Keep the faith, he said to Morris Bird III. And
thank you gentlemen for giving our friend an assist to the bus
station, he said to Mr. Goodwin and Mr. Pearl. Think nothing of
it, said Mr. Goodwin. Then, as an afterthought: You make sure
that blonde makes it to wherever she's going, okay? The tall
trainman smiled. It'll be taken care of, he said. Good, said Mr.
Goodwin, and he and Mr. Pearl and Morris Bird III moved away.
They climbed a flight of stairs to the waiting room. Mr. Goodwin
and Morris Bird III puffed. There were no sounds at all from
Mr. Pearl. The light in the waiting room was brilliant. A train
passed below the station, and the floor trembled a little. Footsteps
made hollow echoing sounds. A voice came over the publicaddress system. It was quite loud, and not a word could be
understood. Morris Bird III glanced up at a clock. It showed 9:21.
Well, the train had been on time, Lunatic Special or no. Morris
Bird III by now was staggering a little, but he tried not to let on
that anything was wrong. Then somebody grabbed the handle
of his suitcase. I'll take over for awhile, said Mr. Pearl, smiling.
Morris Bird III opened his mouth to say something, but Mr. Pearl
cut him off: No arguments, please. I hate arguments. They upset
my lower digestive tract. Whereupon Mr. Goodwin chipped in
with: And, Morris my friend, you got to admit that he's got a lot
of lower digestive tract to *get* upset. I mean, when it comes to
lower digestive tracts, my great buddy here, the one and only
Jack K. Pearl, is a man seriously to be reckoned with. To all this,
Morris Bird III could only nod. He rubbed the arm that had been
carrying the suitcase, and he nodded away for all he was worth.

Flanked by Mr. Goodwin and Mr. Pearl, he made his way toward a door that had hanging over it a neon sign that said TAXI. The station was really quite crowded, and they had to make several detours around clusters and straggly little lines of people. Little kids were everywhere, and you had to be careful to keep from stepping on them, or at the very least kicking them in the chest. But, fortunately, there were plenty of cabs outside. Morris Bird III and Mr. Goodwin and Mr. Pearl went to the head of the line. The driver was a tall fellow of Hillybillyish appearance. He opened the rear door for them and piled their suitcases on the front seat. Morris Bird III found himself squeezed between Mr. Goodwin and Mr. Pearl. It was a real cozy fit. Mr. Goodwin told the driver to take them to the Deshler-Wallack Hotel by way of the bus station. Yes *sah*, said the driver, and now Morris Bird III's suspicions had been verified. As soon as the cab got going, Mr. Pearl said to Mr. Goodwin: I'm serious, Harvey. I don't want you giving a jump response in my suit when you've only got ten points. I don't care how effective it is in blocking out the opposition. I'd like for us to play a nice conservative *winning* game for a change. And Mr. Goodwin said: Now, look, champ, if you *know* my style of play, you can make *allowances*. And Morris Bird III said: Excuse me? And Mr. Goodwin said: Yes? And Morris Bird III said: Excuse me for interrupting, but uh are you talking about some sort of game? This brought laughter from Mr. Goodwin and Mr. Pearl. Morris Bird III's face became red. He glared straight ahead at the traffic and the lights. A headshake from Mr. Goodwin. I'm sorry, he said, Jack and I are just a couple of screwballs. The game, my boy, is *bridge*. We are here in Columbus to participate in the summer championships of the Buckeye State Bridge Association. Jack and I are, and ahem, please pardon the bragging, the defending champions. We've been playing together since 1931, and all we do is argue, and I'm sorry. We haven't shown very good manners. And Morris Bird III said: No. No. I didn't mean to butt in. I was just interested, that's all. And Mr. Pearl said: A piece of advice, son. If you have your choice between being torn apart by a herd of lions and entering a bridge tournament, don't hesitate. Hold wide your arms and welcome the lions. Then Mr. Pearl chuckled, and so did Mr. Goodwin. After the chuckling had subsided, Mr. Goodwin said: Morris, I am, if I do say so myself, a successful attorney in Cleveland. And my friend Jack here has a scrap business that makes him so much money it's obscene. But do we enjoy the fruits of our labors? I should say *not*. We go all over the country playing this accursed game. A word of advice from a nice middleaged Jewish man: Morris Bird, under *no* circumstances take up this sport of the devil. Do something *important* with your life. Jack and I are doomed. We will be felled before our time. On my tombstone will be written: 'He took out his partner's penalty double.' And on Jack's will be written: 'He finessed the Jack the wrong way.' So, avoid this game as you would scurvy. Raise a family. Attend church regularly. Spend your spare time doing good works for the Epworth League. Or, for that matter, turn to a life of crime. Rob banks. Become a professional assassin. *But*, under *no* circumstances take up the game of bridge. Only ruin and despair can follow. Then Mr. Goodwin made an abrupt cackling sound. So much for bridge, he said. Morris Bird III nodded. He liked Mr. Goodwin and Mr. Pearl, but he felt a little sorry for them too. With all the things there were to do in this life, they spent their time running around playing a card game. And, if you could believe what Mr. Goodwin said, they didn't even *like* the card game. Ah, but did dope fiends like dope? Need and like were different, weren't they? Morris Bird III rubbed his forehead, decided he was again letting his mind get away from him. He looked around. He saw some large buildings. He saw lights, and he saw newspapers flapping on the sidewalks, and he saw some Saturdaynight people walking along. Some of them were young and holding hands. The cab bounced over a complex of streetcar tracks, made a right turn, headed down a narrow dark street. Then a left turn, and a large crimson

G
R
E
Y
H
O
U
N
D

sign came into view. The cab pulled up to the entrance to the bus station. First stawp, said the Hillbilly driver. Morris Bird III shook hands with Mr. Goodwin and Mr. Pearl. Remember now, said Mr. Goodwin, you stay away from the bridge table. Morris Bird III nodded, thanked Mr. Goodwin and Mr. Pearl for the lift. The driver reached over, opened the door on the passenger's side. Morris Bird III grabbed hold of his suitcase and pulled it out of the front seat. Then he set down the suitcase and slammed shut the door. The driver thanked him. As the cab pulled away, Morris Bird III heard Mr. Goodwin say something to Mr. Pearl about The Odds of Probability Involving A Four-One Break In Trumps. He grinned, shook his head, picked up his suitcase, lurched toward the door to the bus station. He suddenly felt very lonely, and almost sort of cold. He pushed open the door and entered the bus station. It didn't smell good. It was full of people, people who sat on benches, people who milled around, and the air was clammy, and he had some trouble with his breath. He looked at a clock on a wall. It said 9:36. He would have to wait almost an hour until the Paradise Falls bus left this awful place. Sighing, he marched across the waiting room to the ticket booth. The man behind the window had on a green eyeshade, and a fly was crawling along a ridge in one of his ears. Morris Bird III wanted to blow at it or something, but he managed to restrain himself. He asked the man for a oneway ticket to Paradise Falls. The man stamped the ticket, collected $1.03 from Morris Bird III, and during this transaction the fly tenaciously hung on to the man's ear. The man's movements were quite a bit jerky, but the fly would not let go. After pocketing the ticket and his change, Morris Bird III stood there and watched the fly. Now that the man's movements had subsided, the fly was washing its hands. The man frowned at Morris Bird III. Anything more I can do for you? he wanted to know. Quickly Morris Bird III shook his head no. He picked up his suitcase and staggered away. He picked his way toward an empty seat on one of the benches. It looked to be the only empty seat in the place. Out of a corner of an eye, he saw a stout man making for the same seat. He quickened his pace and beat the stout man to the seat. Sighing, he settled back.

The stout man gave him a filthy look, but he ignored it. He placed *Spanish Blood* on top of his suitcase, draped his legs over the suitcase. He cleared his throat, rubbed his forehead. He was sitting between a sailor and a colored fellow. The sailor was asleep. The colored fellow was reading *Action Comics*. A row of seats faced Morris Bird III. All the seats were occupied. For want of something better to do, he counted the seats. The total was twelve. Then he took inventory of their occupants. From left to right, it came to:

ONE old lady who wore a blue dress with white polkadots. A paper sack was in her lap. The word LAZARUS was printed on the sack in a flowing script.

ONE old man who wore overalls. From time to time he spoke quietly with the old lady, and Morris Bird III supposed he was her husband.

ONE rigid little girl, about six. She was blond, and she was eating a candied apple and making a little bit of a mess with it on the front of her dress, which was yellow and appeared kind of thin.

ONE motionless little boy, about three. He was slumped, and his mouth hung open, and he was either asleep or dead. He wore a T-shirt that said BUCKEYE LAKE. It was dirty. So were his pants. Morris Bird III assumed he was asleep.

ONE woman, maybe thirty years of age, maybe a little less. She had a mustache, and she wore a white sailor hat. She probably was the mother of the two children. She stared straight ahead, and she looked for all the world as though she'd been sitting there for about three thousand years.

ONE man, of approximately the same age as the woman. The children's father? The husband of the woman with the mustache? Suitcases were piled in front of him. They were made of cardboard, and they bulged. The man was thin, and his eyes were large and deep, and he wore a white shirt, khaki trousers and the double-breasted coat from an old blue pinstripe.

ONE soldier, ruddy and plump, fast asleep.

ONE old lady, very skinny, with frizzy red hair that peeked out from a hat that resembled a lampshade.

ONE girl of about sixteen or seventeen, very slender. She wore a white sweater and a pleated plaid skirt, and her legs were crossed. They were bare. Her mouth was large, and her eyes were set widely apart. She had dark hair. It was piled on top of her head, and she wore shoes that had high heels. Her mouth was moist and crimson.

ONE neat man in a gray business suit. His eyes also were gray, and so was his complexion. Sort of. He was reading *Official Detective.*

ONE woman of about forty. She was heavy in the chest and belly, and she wore a white dress decorated with a design of what appeared to be brown and yellow leaves. Two suitcases were in front of her, and she was chewing on a toothpick.

ONE *very* old man whose hands and head shook. A yellow cane was held upright between his knees. His mouth was wet. He was tiny and thin, and his face was about as smooth as a plowed field.

Next to Morris Bird III, the colored fellow grunted and turned a page in his *Action Comics.* The colored fellow's lips moved ever such a little bit. Morris Bird III fumbled in his pockets and came up with his bus ticket. It was orange, and printed across the top were the words PARADISE VALLEY TRACTION CO. Below these words was printed GOOD FOR FARE ONEWAY COLS., O. TO PARADISE FALLS, O.,

SUBJECT TO REGULATIONS PUBLIC UTILITIES COMMISSION OF OHIO (PUCO). GOOD FOR SIX MONTHS FROM DATE OF ISSUANCE. Puco, said Morris Bird III under his breath, pronouncing it pooko. He thought of his Uncle Walter, who drove a bus for the Paradise Valley Traction Co. Good old Uncle Walter. Him and his Battle of the Bulge and his Ruptured Duck. Better his name should have been Uncle Mouth. Ah now, Morris Bird III told himself, just you hold on. Who're you to be knocking other people? What did *you* ever do? Sighing, Morris Bird III adjusted his rear end. The seat was hard, and his rear end was perspiring a little. He wondered whether Uncle Walter would be driving the bus that would take him to Paradise Falls tonight. No. There was little chance of that. As Morris Bird III remembered it, Uncle Walter had the Paradise Falls-Portsmouth run. Well, good. Maybe Uncle Walter meant well, but he surely did talk a lot, and Morris Bird III already had had enough talk for one day, what with Mr. Wysocki and Julie Sutton and the tall trainman and Mr. Goodwin and Mr. Pearl, not to mention the little sweaty news butcher named Paul. If Uncle Walter were driving tonight's bus, he'd insist that Morris Bird III sit behind him and keep up a steady line of palaver all the way to Paradise Falls. And Morris Bird III simply didn't have the energy for it. Maybe, if he was lucky, he would be able to take a little nap in the bus. He cleared his throat, again rearranged his rear end. He rubbed his forehead, then concentrated on his twelve friends across the aisle. He paid particularly close attention to the girl in the white sweater and pleated plaid skirt. Now and then her tongue emerged to moisten her lips. She was directly across from Morris Bird III, and her knees were pink. Her legs were almost as good as the legs of Miss Gail (Legs) Beggs, the greatest librarian in the civilized

261

world. The only thing was, she was pouting, and she seemed to be pouting directly at *him*. Briefly he looked away. He wondered if his fly was unzipped. He folded his hands in his lap, fingered the edge of his fly. It was all right. He sighed, folded his arms across his chest. The girl uncrossed her legs. Then she recrossed them, and oh boy, didn't she ever recross them *good*. Her skirt somehow got itself hiked up, and he was able to see an edge of her panties. They were white. He cleared his throat and rubbed his forehead. Simultaneously. Then he looked at the man who was reading *Official Detective*. He looked at the woman who was chewing on the toothpick. He let his eyes flick clear to the other end of the row, where sat the old lady in the blue dress with the white polkadots. His head hurt. So did his stomach. So did just about everything. Breathing slowly, he gave up: he let his eyes return to the girl and her legs and the edge of her panties. She'd apparently done a lot of swimming this summer. Her thighs were brown. Smooth, too. Morris Bird III coughed, remembering to cover his mouth. The girl jiggled one of her highheeled shoes at the end of a toe. She shifted her position a little, and now Morris Bird III was able to see about 700% more of her panties. He rubbed his stomach. He closed his eyes and tried to think of blizzards and Swiss ski resorts. He opened his eyes. He didn't feel in the least little bit cold. He could see the way her panties hugged her thighs, and he could see this just as *clear*, and he didn't know whether he would blow up or spit elephants or die or what. He folded his hands, placed them in his lap. Quickly he took them away from his lap. The girl yawned. She threw back her head and just yawned and *yawned*, and naturally her skirt got itself hiked up higher. She still was jiggling the shoe, and it made *all* of her jiggle, and her legs and her thighs and the secret forbidden area up there by her panties were *so* brown and *so* smooth and *so* oh sort of Lord forgive him *yummy* that whistling noises began coming from his nostrils in urgent hurtful bursts. He knew what he had to do, and he hoped he had the strength for it, and so he looked around. Across the room was a neon sign that said MEN. He closed his eyes. He asked himself: Will I be able to stand up straight? He told himself he'd never know until he tried. He opened his eyes. The girl was staring at nothing in particular. She still was jiggling. Next to him, the sailor made a weak moaning sound but remained asleep. Poor guy. Morris Bird III reached down and picked up *Spanish Blood* from its place on top of the suitcase. Then, wheezing a little, he stood up. The girl looked at him, but with no interest. She still was pouting, but apparently she pouted like that all the time. Morris Bird III bent over to pick up the suitcase. He felt dizzy. He bit his tongue, seized the handle of the suitcase and straightened up. So far, so good, but it was a foolish farmer who counted his Rhode Island Reds prematurely. He did not look at the girl. For all he knew, she could have changed into a hamburger patty or something. He kept his eyes high. He took about three steps and then he tripped over the foot that was jiggling the shoe. *Whah!* he said, losing his balance. *Spanish Blood* went flying. He dropped the suitcase, pitched forward on his hands and knees. Someone had thrown kerosene in his face and set it afire. He wanted to die. *Die. Die. Die.* Then someone touched his shoulder. He trembled. Are you all right, sonny? someone said, and of course it had to be Her. He took a deep breath. He stood up. He wiped his hands on his trousers. I'm . . . uh, I'm *fine,* he said, not looking at Her. But She wasn't satisfied. She asked him was he sure. He nodded. Then She apologized. Me and my big feet, She said. Now he *had* to look at Her. In the name of decency, he had to face Her and tell Her everything was all right. And so he did. And then She smiled, and Her teeth were exquisite. Nodding, he picked up *Spanish Blood* and the suitcase. She had uncrossed her legs, and now there was nothing untoward to be seen, but now was almost too late. Down the line, the old woman in the blue polkadotted dress pursed her lips and gave him a look he supposed was meant to indicate concern. He smiled at her, and it made his lips hurt. As quickly as he could, he made his way toward the sign that said MEN. Once inside the washroom, he almost sort of gasped. A little kid, standing at a urinal, frowned at him. He paid the little kid no mind. The washroom smelled of pee and Boraxo. He staggered to a pay toilet. He inserted a nickel in the lock, turned the door handle and pushed his way inside. It was cramped, what with the suitcase. He placed the suitcase on the commode. Then he placed *Spanish Blood* on the suitcase. *Sonny,* he said. Are you all right, *sonny?* He made fists. Then, turning sideways so he'd have enough room, he thrust out his arms. *Sonny,* he said. Are you all right, you cute adorable little devil you? Grimacing, he began the deep knee bends. He did twentyfive. Then, for good measure, he did ten more. Then he removed *Spanish Blood* and the suitcase from the commode and sat down and attended to a couple of matters. He was breathing hard, but at least he was all right in that place where he had no right *not* being all right. He closed his eyes and looked at Her (all except Her legs and all the et cetera), and he heard Her call him Sonny, and oh boy, oh boy, sometimes life was very long. Sometimes it was altogether *too* long. Yes *sir.* Hot *dog.* She had called him Sonny. Big fat hot *deal.* After a time, the matters had been attended to. He stood up, adjusted his shorts and trousers, emerged from the pay toilet. Carrying *Spanish Blood* and the suitcase, he went to a sink and washed his face and hands. He used Boraxo, and he didn't care that it stung his face. Sonny, he muttered. Sonny. Sonny. Fifteen paper towels were used up before his face and hands were dried to his satisfaction. Then he tucked *Spanish Blood* under an arm and lifted the suitcase. When he reentered the waiting room, he did not look in Her direction. He glanced at the clock. It said 10:08. He went to the ticket booth and asked a man where the Paradise Falls bus was leaving from. This was the same man who'd sold him his ticket. The man still wore the eyeshade, but the fly was gone from his ear. Gate 11, said the man, not looking up. Morris Bird III thanked the man, then looked around for Gate 11. It was clear at the other side of the waiting room. Sighing, he lugged the suitcase to the gate. A line already had begun to form. He hoped to God that She wasn't taking this bus. He examined the line, and She wasn't in it. A bus driver came to the gate. It was not Uncle Walter. This was a fat bus driver, and his gray shirt was dark with sweat. Bus for Groveport, Canal Winchester, Lancaster, Egypt, Paradise Falls, MacArthur, Wellston and Jackson! shouted the driver, and then he began collecting tickets. Slowly the line moved forward. It wasn't much of a line, and maybe Morris Bird III would be able to get the seat directly behind the driver. It was far and away his favorite seat in a bus. When he gave the driver his ticket, all the driver did was grunt. Clearly, this driver was nothing at all like the tall trainman, which was probably just as well. Wheezing again, Morris Bird III climbed the steps to the bus. The seat directly behind the driver was unoccupied. Morris Bird III braced himself and hurled the suitcase up toward the baggagerack. This time it made it all the way. It teetered on the brink for one awful second, but then it slid back behind the little ropes that prevented the baggage from falling out. Morris Bird III sat down. The view was great. As long as he scrunched himself far enough to the left, he would have no trouble seeing around the driver. There were two signs over the driver's seat. One said:

YOUR OPERATOR
B. B. GRASS
SAFE—DEPENDABLE—COURTEOUS

The other said:

Please do not speak to operator while coach is moving

Well, good. If that was the way the Paradise Valley Traction Co. wanted it, fine. Maybe Morris Bird III would be able to catch another nap. Only this time he hoped he wouldn't dream. He stared at the name B.B. GRASS. He decided it was a shame the man's name wasn't GUNN. The nameplate was detachable. To the best of his recollection, this was the first time he'd ever seen one of these nameplates. Usually, bus drivers didn't bother with them. The space was left blank, and you could amuse yourself for hours speculating on the driver's name. You usually came up with names like Sauer and Crabb. Morris Bird III settled back, placed *Spanish Blood* on the seat next to him. Only about half the seats in the bus were taken. There was little talk from the passengers. The interior of the bus was dark, and it was in every way a contrast to The Lunatic Special. Which was perfectly all right. A person needed peace and quiet *too.* Morris Bird III sighed, stretched his legs. A little later, B.B. Grass came aboard. He sat down behind the wheel, fiddled with his seat for a moment or two, adjusting it, then pulled a big lever that closed the front door. It went *pishhh*. He started the engine. It made a good deal of racket. The bus glided away from the station and entered the Columbus traffic. Yawning, Morris Bird III looked over the driver's shoulder at neon signs and streetlights and automobiles and streetcars and pedestrians and stray dogs and parked cars and apartment buildings and lawns and whatall. B.B. Grass hummed a little, but he offered no conversation. It looked to be a peaceful trip. Hooray. Briefly, Morris Bird III thought back on the incident involving Her. If only She hadn't called him *sonny*. Who did She think She was? She couldn't have been more than seventeen, and what right did She have to call him names? Ah, now, now, he told himself, you just hold on. She didn't *mean* anything. It's just that you're so dadblasted dingbusted allfired glory and tarnation *short*, as Walter Brennan would put it. B.B. Grass worked the gears smoothly. The bus made a number of turns, and then it was out on the open highway. The white line was straight and bright. Morris Bird III watched the speedometer. B.B. Grass got it up to 50 and held it there. From time to time, he jockeyed the bus around automobiles that were moving too slowly. This was interesting to watch, especially in view of the rather heavy traffic that was coming in the opposite direction. Morris Bird III got to leaning with B.B. Grass as the bus changed lanes. After awhile, he began feeling *he* was driving the bus. He supposed there were worse ways to make a living than driving a bus. The open road and all. The challenge of passing. The feeling of power, of speed. And so forth. There was a good moon, and he could see a great deal of the countryside. It was flat countryside, dark and plump, with neat fields, plain little farmhouses, immense barns. Morris Bird III's window was open a little, and he was able to smell the thick sweet conglomerate odor of earth and fertilizer and grass and trees and growing things. He saw signs that said 666 COLD TABLETS, and he saw signs that said CLABBER GIRL, and he saw billboards that advertised Sohio X-70 Gasoline and Omar Bread and Coca-Cola and Dewey for President, and across the front of some of the immense barns were the words CHEW MAIL POUCH TREAT YOURSELF TO THE BEST and THE MAY CO. WATCH US GROW, and the great bus made a level heavy whirring sound as it walloped along the highway at its steady 50 miles an hour, and now and then Morris Bird III dozed off, and the dreams were all out of him, and the bus nudged through Groveport and Canal Winchester (neat little towns, both of them, neat and quiet, with spindly houses and a warm nighttime dampness that lay on trees and grass), and people got on the bus and people got off, and from time to time Morris Bird III sat up straight and wiped boogers from the corners of his eyes, and with each mile more tenseness went out of him, and so what if his mouth did taste a little furry? So what if his head was heavy and thick? It wouldn't be long now until he would be with his grandmother, and this was what was important; this was what the entire day had turned out to be all about. Lancaster was sort of a big town, a very old town, with deep lawns and tall pointed houses, wide lawns and thick squatty houses, and the dampness here was so thick and warm and green that you almost believed you could reach out with a spoon and scoop it out of the air. The bus stayed in the Lancaster bus station for about ten minutes. A lot of people got off. Not so many got on. Whistling through his teeth, alternating it with his humming, B.B. Grass took the new passengers' tickets, consulted his watch, then pulled shut the door and steered the bus out of the tiny Lancaster station. Now the bus moved south and east, following Ohio US 33-A, and almost immediately the country became hillier. Fifteen minutes out of Lancaster, the bus crossed into Paradise County. The hills blotted some of the moonlight. Morris Bird III dozed off. When he came out of it, the bus was just leaving a little town called Egypt, which was on the south bank of the Paradise River. He saw a sign that said PARADISE FALLS 6. To his left, the river was a pale moist glitter in the moonlight. Now the highway and the river ran parallel to each other, and it wouldn't be long now; it wouldn't be long now at all, at all. Morris Bird III bathed the inside of his mouth with saliva, and some of the furry taste went away. He saw lights from summer cottages along the river. Now the highway was lined by little fillingstations and hotdog stands, dark at this hour. Then the bus climbed a long hill, followed a gentle curve to the right, and there, spread out due ahead and a little below them, was Paradise Falls.

It wasn't quite midnight, but Paradise Falls was just about all tucked in for the night, Saturday or no Saturday. Morris Bird III leaned forward and asked B.B. Grass to let him off at South High Street, and B.B. Grass nodded.

Coming into Paradise Falls from the northwest, Ohio US 33-A followed along Grainger Street to South High Street, then made a brief dogleg one block north to Main Street, which ran east-and-west through the center of town. As the bus passed the corner of Grainger Street and Ruple Avenue (with still ten blocks or so to go before it got to Grainger and High), Morris Bird III stood up and began wrestling with his suitcase. The movement of the bus didn't help. He had to stand on the seat. Finally, after a great deal of tugging and twisting, he got the suitcase out of the rack. He also managed to keep it from falling on his head.

The bus pulled to the curb at Grainger and High. Morris Bird III thanked B.B. Grass. Another nod from gabby old B.B. Grass, and then he pushed the lever that opened the door. Tucking *Spanish Blood* under an arm, Morris Bird III dragged his suitcase off the bus. *Pishhh*, and the bus pulled away from the curb. He watched it turn north on High Street. He set down the suitcase for a moment. He rubbed his hands together, looked around. Grainger and High was what the people down here called a *good* corner. People of means lived here. The houses were large, and so were the lawns, and a couple of the houses even had gazebos in their backyards. He stood very quietly, and he could hear tree frogs. The sidewalks were of brick, and most of the lawns were guarded by iron picket fences. A dog barked. Then another dog barked. They were quite a distance off. The barking was brief, though. It ended after just the one exchange. Maybe, for all Morris Bird III knew, they'd simply been saying good night to each other.

He picked up the suitcase, began walking south on High Street. All streets that ran south from Main Street were called South, so this actually was *South* High Street. And . . . surprise, surprise . . . all streets that ran north from Main Street were called North. Ah, the complexities of the human mind.

You moron, said Morris Bird III to himself. Julie was right. You *are* a nut.

His footsteps were louder than he would have liked them. He shifted the suitcase from his right hand to his left. A white cat came out of some bushes, stared at Morris Bird III for a moment, then ran off like the devil.

"Well," Morris Bird III said aloud, "glad to see *you* too."

The big houses along this part of South High Street were almost all dark. One of them (he couldn't remember exactly which one) was occupied by Mayor and Mrs. Dwight F. Estes and their daughter, Rose. He wondered if she'd filled out any. Maybe, in a day or two, he would try to find out. With his luck, though, if she *had* filled out, she'd probably no longer be interested in showing him all she had. Yeah, the luck of the Irish. Only Morris Bird III wasn't Irish.

He lurched across First Street, then Second Street, and the houses were getting smaller. Now he was out of the *good* part of South High Street. Up ahead on the left, just beyond the intersection of South High Street and Meridian Avenue, was the little house where lived his Uncle Jim and Aunt Emily, the house where Morris Bird III's grandmother lay dying in that big brass bed.

He crossed Meridian Avenue. Several cars were parked in front of the house. He recognized them. They belonged to Uncle Harry, Uncle Walter, Uncle Howard and Uncle Alan. Lights were on in the rear of the house, and he supposed they all were sitting around holding one of their councils of war about the porch furniture and whatever.

He shook his head.

He went to the back of the house and let himself in the kitchen

271

door, and his mother and his aunts and his uncles just about fell out of their chairs.

Uncle Jim was wearing his police uniform. It was tight around his middle. A glass of something dark was on the kitchen table in front of him. "Well, my God," he said, blinking.

Morris Bird III's mother jumped to her feet. "Morris!"

"That's my name," said Morris Bird III, setting down his suitcase.

"Don't get smart with *me!* Where's your father?"

"He's not here."

"What?"

"I came down by myself."

"You did *what?*"

"I *said:* I came down by myself." Morris Bird III was standing by the door. They all were sitting there in the kitchen, his mother and his aunts and uncles, the entire Cast of Thousands—Uncle Jim and Aunt Emily, Aunt Phyllis and Uncle Harry, Uncle Howard and Aunt Edythe, Uncle Walter and Aunt Iris, plus Uncle Alan, plus Aunt Pauline. Their faces were blank. He supposed he could understand why.

"Your father *let* you come down?" the mother wanted to know.

"He wasn't home."

"Wasn't home? What do you mean?"

"He was out visiting friends."

"Friends?"

"Yes. That's what he said. He telephoned Mrs. Wysocki."

"You mean you just up and left?"

"Yes."

The mother's eyes became squinty. "Where'd you get the money?"

"I had it. From when I worked at the library."

"What do you *want*?"

"I want to see Grandma before she dies."

"And you came all the way down here all by yourself just to do that?"

"Yes."

"How'd you come? On the train?"

"Train to Columbus. Bus the rest of the way."

"Oh, Lord," said the mother. She rolled her eyes. "Shades of that Chaloupka business. You're a great one for running off, aren't you?"

"I didn't run off. I told Mr. Wysocki. He said it was okay."

"Oh. He did, did he?"

Aunt Phyllis spoke up. "Now, Alice," she said, "there's no sense you getting all wrought up." She rose, went to Morris Bird III and hugged him. "How are you? Was it a nice trip?"

"Fine," said Morris Bird III.

"Phyllis," said Morris Bird III's mother, "please don't interfere."

Aunt Phyllis drew back. At the table, Aunt Emily opened her mouth to say something, but then thought better of it. The others simply stared at Morris Bird III. Uncle Jim sipped at his dark stuff, and there were no sounds other than breath and tree frogs.

Morris Bird III's mother put her hands on her hips. "You just come and go as you please, don't you?"

"I just wanted to see Grandma."

"And so you asked *Mr. Wysocki*, and *Mr. Wysocki* said go ahead."

"No."

"What do you mean?"

"Well, it was sort of his idea. He said if I love her, I ought to go."

"His idea. Oh great."

"Okay, Alice," said Uncle Jim, *"okay.* We got room. He's got a right. Relax."

Morris Bird III's mother moistened her lips. She gave Uncle Jim a hard look and said: "He's my son. You mind your own business."

Uncle Jim sighed. "All right. Fine. Go on. Beat the poor kid to death with a club. Do whatever you want."

"Oh, you're very funny," Morris Bird III's mother said to Uncle Jim. "You're just a barrel of I don't know what." Then, turning again to Morris Bird III, she said: "All right. Go upstairs. We'll talk about it in the morning." A hesitation. More moistening of lips. Then: "But don't think you've gotten away with anything."

Morris Bird III nodded. None of this had particularly surprised him. "Can I see Grandma?"

"She's asleep."

"Can I see her in the morning?"

Uncle Jim spoke up. "Sure you can."

"I told you to stay out of this, Jim!" shrieked Morris Bird III's mother.

"It happens to be my house," said Uncle Jim.

"Thank you, Uncle Jim," said Morris Bird III. He picked up his suitcase.

"You always have to be smart, don't you?" said the mother.

Morris Bird III didn't say anything. He started toward the door that led into the front of the house.

"Answer me!" shrieked the mother.

"Alice, please shut up," said Uncle Alan. His voice was quiet and calm. He was sipping from a cup of coffee.

Morris Bird III's mother was shaking. She looked at Uncle Alan. Then she looked at each of the others. Their faces still were blank. Uncle Jim and Aunt Emily were looking at each other. Aunt Phyllis and Uncle Harry were inspecting their hands. Aunt Pauline was biting her lower lip. Uncle Howard and Aunt Edythe were staring at the table. Uncle Walter and Aunt Iris were examining their laps. The room was very white, and it *looked* cool, but it actually was quite warm, what with the Cast of Thousands plus the yelling and all.

Morris Bird III took a step forward. Nothing happened. "Well," he said, "good night."

"Morris?" said Aunt Emily.

"Yes?"

"Would you like a glass of milk or something?"

"No. Uh, no thank you. I ate on the train."

"All right," said Aunt Emily. "The cots are still in the guest bedroom. Have a nice sleep."

"Yes," said Uncle Harry, "you do that."

"Be sure to open a window," said Uncle Howard. "Otherwise, you'll get too warm."

"Yeah," said Uncle Alan, "and tomorrow drop around at the hotel. I see you got my *Spanish Blood* with you. We can talk about the stories."

Morris Bird III nodded.

"Go to bed!" said his mother. "We'll talk in the *morning*."

He nodded.

Dragging the suitcase, he left the kitchen.

He was not surprised.

His mother was not that difficult to figure out.

He went upstairs, and his bones ached.

He unpacked his suitcase and hung up his clothes. Downstairs, his mother and his aunts and his uncles were talking in loud voices. He was very careful in hanging up his clothes. Then he went to the bathroom and brushed his teeth and washed his face and hands. He was especially diligent with his forehead. He found places for his toothbrush and toothpaste in the medicine cabinet. After closing the medicine cabinet, he inspected the mirror to make sure he hadn't splattered it. Then he carefully cleaned out the sink. He returned to the room where his cot was. He took off his shoes. His eyes were warm. Blinking, he walked in his stockingfeet down the hall to his grandmother's room. The door was open. He looked inside.

"That you, Pauline?" said the voice from the big brass bed. It was a ramshackle voice, weak and scrapy and torn.

"Grandma?" said Morris Bird III, whispering.

"Who's that?"

"Morris."

"Morris?"

"Morris Bird."

"The Second?"

"No. The Third."

"*My* Morris? My grandson?"

"Yes."

"I can't *see* you . . ."

"Can I come in?"

"Yes. Come in. Please . . . please come in and talk to your grandmother. There's a . . . a light by the bed. Turn . . . turn it on."

He padded across the room and turned on the light. He shouldn't have. He should have left it off. He shouldn't have come here at all. He should have shot himself first. He should have fallen on his sword.

He blinked, and his throat was full of pebbles and hair.

It had been five weeks since he'd last seen her. Just five weeks, but in that time something had devoured her by about half. Oh she was really dying now. She was really good and dying. She was just about as dying as a person could be. Her cheeks had fallen in. Her neck was nothing but old strings. Her hands and arms were outside the covers. They were white and purple. The white was the color of something dead. The purple was the color of old veins. "Morris . . . oh Morris," she said. One of her arms stirred.

He bent over her and kissed her on a cheek. It was dry. Her breath was sour.

One of her hands patted the back of his head.

He straightened up, cleared his throat.

"I . . . I look terrible," said the grandmother, "don't I?"

"No. You look fine."

"Don't lie . . ."

Morris Bird III was silent.

Now the grandmother's breath came in a shudder. "You . . . you caught me at the right time . . ."

He didn't say anything.

"My . . . uh, my pills . . . Pauline gave me one a little bit ago. Half of one. The . . . the dosage. She has to be very careful with the . . . dosage . . ."

He nodded.

"Morphine sulfate," said the grandmother. "You ever heard of it?"

"No."

"God bless morphine sulfate . . ."

He cleared his throat.

"Morris?"

"Yes?"

"I've . . . given up. There's not going to be any miracle. No. The hurt's too much. It makes me cry. Please . . . please don't come around when I cry . . ."

He nodded.

"Morris. Please hug me."

He bent over the bed. He hugged her. He was crying, but at least he was making no noise about it.

Her bony arms came around his neck.

He closed his eyes. Her breath was awful.

She again patted him. Then her arms relaxed.

He straightened up. He opened his eyes.

"Don't go," she said.

"No," said Morris Bird III. "I'm right here."

"I wish there was something I could say to you. Some . . . words of wisdom."

"No. No. That's okay."

She looked at the far wall. "I don't suppose you'd do it."

"Do what?"

"Get the pills. They're in the medicine cabinet in the bathroom. Get them and bring them to me."

"I'll call Aunt Pauline."

"No . . ."

"Why?"

She spoke slowly. "Dr. Hendrickson . . . you know Dr. Hendrickson, don't you?"

He nodded.

"I . . . had a . . . talk . . . with him last week. He told me the truth. All . . . of it. He said: Elizabeth, about all I can do is keep the pain away . . ."

Morris Bird III wiped at his eyes.

"But I . . . I *hurt*. Every day the hurt gets worse . . . and the pills do less. God bless morphine sulfate, yes, but only . . . up to a . . . point. If you get them for me, if you . . . bring them here . . . with a nice little glass of water, then I can—"

"No," said Morris Bird III.

"It's a little pink bottle. You can't miss it—"

"No."

"I *hurt*."

"*No.*"

"I asked him. I said: Harold, if I should die and maybe more pills are missing than . . . than should be, would you say anything about . . . about it? And he said: No, Elizabeth. I . . . I wouldn't say a word—"

"No. Grandma, don't talk. Please don't talk."

"You don't *know*."

"I can't do it. I can't kill you."

"It's not killing. It's helping."

Morris Bird III shook his head no.

"It's helping. Helping. *Helping.* I'm going to die no matter what. I can either die now . . . and not feel anything . . . or die later and feel it all . . ."

"Grandma?"

"Yes?"

"Remember how you used to talk to me about being brave no matter what?"

"Yes. I expect I do."

"Well . . ." Morris Bird III let his voice peter away.

"This . . . this isn't the same . . ."

"Brave is brave."

"This isn't the *same.*"

"Aunt Pauline won't do it, will she? How come you expect me to do it?"

"You're brave. She isn't."

"Brave doesn't mean killing."

"Morris . . . Morris Morris Morris . . . *please* . . ."

"Grandma?"

"Yes?"

"A man said to me tonight: Pain is of the earth, earthy."

"That's taken from Paul."

"Paul?" said Morris Bird III, thinking of the little sweaty news butcher.

"One of the Epistles to the Corinthians in the . . . Bible . . ."

"Oh."

"But this man, I wonder . . . how much . . . he knows about . . . pain . . ."

280

"He seemed like a good man."

"*Talk* is . . . one thing. *Knowing* is another." Now the grandmother was sort of picking at the sheet. Her eyes were pink and wet. "Please, Morris. Please . . . *please* oh dear Morris please do it . . ."

He didn't say anything.

"I'll take them out of the bottle, and you can . . . return the bottle to the . . . bathroom . . . and you won't even have to . . . watch . . ."

Weeping, he turned off the light and ran out of the room. She called after him, but he did not look back.

He flopped down on his cot. He did not bother to take off his clothes. He put his fists in his eyes. What *right* did she have? Who did she think he *was?* How large could love get? Could it include killing? He folded his arms over his eyes. Downstairs, the Cast of Thousands still was at it. He trembled. If living required bravery, didn't *dying?* His grandmother wasn't an old horse to be led out behind the barn and shot between the eyes. Okay, so she hurt. So a lot of people hurt. But they didn't gulp down pills. You didn't lead *people* out behind the barn to be shot between the eyes. You did what you could for them, but that was it.

You did what you could for them.

Morris Bird III bit at a mouthful of knuckles.

But all a human being could do was of the earth, earthy.

Right away, socko bam. He was no sooner in the room but what she was putting it up to him.

281

And he had refused. And she was The One.
Morris Bird III wept.

A little later, he got up and went to the bathroom and washed his face. Passing his grandmother's room, he heard nothing. He did not look in. After drying his face and hands, he went to the head of the stairs and sat down. He could hear his mother and his aunts and his uncles very clearly. Naturally, they were discussing the contents of the barn. Morris Bird III's mother was doing most of the talking. ". . . and my dear husband and I, all we want are the sideboard and the bedroom suite," she said. "Daddy and Mommy's bedroom suite?" said Aunt Phyllis. "Yes. You know that. I've told you a thousand times," said Morris Bird III's mother. "But . . . well, I'm sorry, but I don't quite think it's fair. When Mommy was in better health, she told me I could have it—the bedroom suite," said Aunt Phyllis. "But you got no witnesses, do you?" said Morris Bird III's mother. "If we can just have the *clothes* . . ." said Aunt Emily, whining a little. "You can have them. Anyone want to argue with her about them?" said Morris Bird III's mother. No answer, and so she continued: "As far as I can tell, everything has been settled except this matter of the bedroom suite. Right?" Still no answer, and so on she went: "Phyllis, how about flipping a coin?" A murmurous sound from the Cast of Thousands. "Oh, you really are *it*," said Uncle Alan. "Why? This is the only way it's ever going to be settled," said Morris Bird III's mother. No one had any answer to that. Morris Bird III's chest hurt. He stood up, ran back to the room where his cot was. This time he took off his clothes, put on his pajamas and got into the cot. He pulled the sheet up to his neck. He wiped his eyes with a corner of the sheet. He lay very still. He had seen *The Treasure of the Sierra Madre* ten times (twice at the Hippodrome, twice at the Warner's Allen, three times at the Keith's East 105th Street, three times at the Astor), and he shouldn't have bothered. *The Treasure of the Sierra Madre* was taking place right down there in the kitchen, and his mother was the ultimate Fred C. Dobbs of the world, and so who needed to go see a *movie?* They wouldn't even wait until she died. They had to get it all settled *now*. He'd heard his mother's explanation for this. It's just good common sense, she'd told the other members of the Cast of Thousands. If we wait until *after* she's dead, then we'll all be under a terrible strain, and we'll *never* be able to agree on anything. Morris Bird III covered his mouth with the sheet. He cleared his throat. Oh, the world forever and relentlessly changed, and Fake and pain (things that were forever and relentlessly of the earth, earthy) kept winning, kept getting the best of balance and tranquillity.

Oh yeah?

Then how explain Benny Goodman?

How about the tall trainman?

How about good old Mr. Wysocki? Mrs. Wysocki?

How about the Golden Princess of the World, Julie Sutton?

And what was so terrible about Sandra?

Had Stanley Chaloupka meant anyone any harm?

Those two kids holding hands on the Hough Avenue trackless trolley, had they been representatives of Fu Manchu?

Grandma had said it.

Endure, Grandma had said.

And Grandma was The One.

The sickness and the pain and the dying changed nothing.

283

If you loved people, you did what you could for them.

You did what you could for them.

Morris Bird III suddenly sat up. It was so simple. He shook his head. All the ingredients of the sum and total of his personal now fell into place with an easy gentle click. The lightbulb was turned on. A big lightbulb.

Something finally had emerged from that poor uck of a mess. It dazzled.

He lay back. Now all he had to do was wait. He stared at the ceiling. All the tiredness had gone out of him, and his bones no longer ached.

He lay quietly. All the tears were out of him. An hour or so later, he heard the Cast of Thousands dispersing. Doors slammed. Automobile engines started up. He heard his mother and his Uncle Jim and his Aunt Emily come up the stairs. He closed his eyes. The door opened. He supposed his mother was looking in on him. He made his breath thick and slow and heavy. The door closed. He opened his eyes. He listened to his mother and his Uncle Jim and his Aunt Emily move up and down the hall, in and out of the bathroom and their bedrooms. His Uncle Jim said something about the business of flipping the coin. He evidently was speaking to Morris Bird III's mother. "Alice," he said, "you are the absolute limit." And Morris Bird III's mother said: "Let me by. I got to go brush my teeth." And Uncle Jim said: "Just wait a minute." And Morris Bird III's mother said: "Careful, Morris might hear you." And Uncle Jim said: "I don't care. It might do him some good." And then Aunt Emily's voice joined in the conversation. "Jim," she said, "let's just go to bed, all right?" And Uncle Jim said: "In a minute. First I got to say something to this sister of mine. About flipping coins." And, sighing, Morris Bird III's mother said: "All right, Jim. Get it out." (Now Morris Bird III could hear every word just as clear as anything. He glanced toward the door. His mother hadn't closed it securely.) And then Uncle Jim said: "She's *your* mother, too. I mean, okay, so I'm not so much and I know it, but I'd never think to do such a thing as flip a coin over a dying woman's bedroom suite." And Morris Bird III's mother said: "What are you making such a fuss about? Phyllis didn't agree to it. No harm was done. Your dear precious conscience didn't get itself injured." And Uncle Jim said: "But you got what you wanted, didn't you?" And Morris Bird III's mother said: "But I *paid* for it. I gave her fifty dollars, didn't I?" And Uncle Jim said: "Oh, God." And Morris Bird III's mother said: "You'll *thank* me for it." And Uncle Jim said: "What?" And Morris Bird III's mother said: "It's all settled, isn't it? After she dies, nothing will be messy. A year from now, you'll come to me and tell me I was right all the time." And Uncle Jim said: "Never." A hesitation, and then he continued: "I drink. You don't drink. I got nothing in my life to aim towards anymore. You do—money. I never won any brain prizes. You, on the other hand, got a mind like a fox. But there's one thing I got going for me that you don't even understand. Namely, and to wit: *I* know *I* stink." A snort from Morris Bird III's mother. She followed it with a short laugh. Then: "Go to bed. Sober up. You're going to feel awful in the morning." Then there were clacking sounds, and a sort of wheeze from Uncle Jim. The bathroom door slammed. "Jim," said Aunt Emily, "come to bed. I just checked on your mother. She's all right. She's sound asleep. But, *honestly,* I don't really think the *boy* should be hearing all this." Heavy footsteps, and a moment later another door slammed. Toothbrushing sounds came from the bathroom. Then silence. Then a door opened and closed. Footsteps. Clacking footsteps. They paused at the door to the room where Morris Bird III was sleeping. A short gasp. He closed his eyes. The door was pulled shut. Now the clacking footsteps were less loud. Another door was closed, and then there was silence. Morris Bird III opened his eyes. He heard tree frogs and his own heart and breath. He wiggled his toes. Then he began to count. He counted to a thousand. Then, just to be on the safe side, he counted to five hundred. There were sixty seconds to a minute. He had counted slowly, trying to make one number count for one second. Six hundred seconds were ten minutes. Twelve hundred were twenty minutes. Fifteen hundred were twentyfive minutes. It had been twentyfive minutes, more or less, since the door to his mother's bedroom had been closed. Not long enough. Grimacing, Morris Bird III again counted to a thousand. Then he again counted to five hundred. Now the total was three thousand—fifty minutes all told. Almost an hour, and certainly enough time for all of them to fall asleep. He threw back the sheet and sat up. He rose, shucked himself out of his pajamas, got dressed again. He picked up his shoes but did not put them on. He tiptoed to the door and peeked out into the hall. Silence. Darkness. He entered the hall. He was as high on the balls of his feet as he could get. He moved cautiously. He made no sounds, and no sounds came from any of the bedrooms. His heart was loud, but he suspected it was loud only to him, and so he tried not to worry about it. Silently he descended the stairs. He kept waiting for one of the steps to squeak, like in the Abbott & Costello haunted house movies, but none did. He padded across the parlor and the diningroom into the kitchen. Aunt Emily kept her kitchen matches in a box on a shelf behind the stove. He could see the box quite clearly. There was a lot of moonlight here in the kitchen. He went to the box and helped himself to a handful of matches. Then he let himself out the back door. It was unlocked. People in Paradise Falls didn't lock their doors at night. He ran in his stockingfeet across the back yard. The grass was damp and cool. He loved his grandmother. She was The One, no doubt about it. He loved her, and this all was for her, and it was so very simple. He squeezed through an opening in a fence. Now he was in an alley. He paused to put on his shoes. The matches made loose dry sounds in his pants pocket. He began to run. He ran up the alley three blocks. Then he ran up another alley two blocks. He saw no one. Here and there were lightpoles, and bugs and moths danced around the lights, but he saw not a single human being. The barn was really more of a shed than a barn. It was very old. The front doors were locked. They were immense double doors, like the doors to a garage. They were held together by a big padlock. He didn't bother with it. He'd remembered that there was a smaller door to the rear of the barn. He went around to the rear. Sure enough, the door was as he had remembered it. He looked up, and the stars were very clear. This door was held shut by a much smaller padlock. He pushed against it. Nothing happened. Again he pushed against it, and this time there was a tearing sound. He lit a match. The hasp was rotten at the hinge. He grabbed it, twisted it. Another tearing sound, only louder. He paused. He heard nothing. He resumed his twisting. A minute or so later, he had torn loose the hasp. He pushed open the door. Ahhh, he said to himself, me strong like bool. Me Charles Atlas. He entered the barn. Almost immediately he sneezed. Then the dust and the warm airlessness made his eyes run. He blinked, rubbed his eyes. Then he waited for them to become accustomed to the darkness. Furniture and boxes were piled to the eaves. There were trunks, cartons, stacks of newspapers. Everything he touched gave off dust. He saw the bedroom suite his mother had been talking about. He went to the bed and touched it. He made a long trailing fingermark in the dust on the bed. He opened a trunk. It was full of old letters and postcards. He found several photographs of his grandmother and grandfather. They looked very young. He lit several matches while examining the photographs. One of the photographs had a date written on the back: October 11, 1913. *You did what you could for them.* He picked up some newspapers off a pile. He carried them to the front of the barn. He looked at the floor. It was covered with a thin layer of straw. It appeared to be quite dry. Good. Backing toward the rear of the barn, he spread the newspapers on the floor. The straw made small crackling sounds. After spreading the newspapers over just about all the floor space, he began looking around for something. There had been a bellows in front of the fireplace in his grandparents' old house on Mulberry Street. He rooted around for it. He even climbed up on several boxes. He searched for it for maybe fifteen minutes. Then, shrugging, he gave up. Standing at the front of the barn, he knelt and lit a match. *You did what you could for them.* He held the match to the corner of a newspaper. Retreating, he lit another match. He held it to the corner of another newspaper. He did this three more times, and then he was at the rear door. The newspapers were burning well. So was the straw. Then the cartons caught fire. Then the boxes. Then the smaller pieces of furniture—the wicker porch furniture, for example. *You did what you could for them.* For your grandmother and your late grandfather both. And, for that matter, your mother and your father and your aunts and your uncles. Now Morris Bird III was sweating. One of the rafters caught fire. He ducked out the rear door. He ran all the way back to the house on South High Street, and no one saw him.

The year was 1948, and the month was September, and on the first day of that month Morris Bird III's grandmother died. It was a quiet death. She was full of pills. The barn and its contents—both uninsured—had been a total loss. Fred V. Lillis, Paradise Falls fire chief, listed the cause as spontaneous combustion probably brought on by the long dry spell. A lot of people showed up for the funeral, and there were a great many flowers. She was laid out in a place called the Charles Palmer Light House of Rest. Morris Bird III and his Uncle Alan held several long discussions having to do with the works of Raymond Chandler. At the funeral, the same man took color movies for Aunt Phyllis. Morris Bird III found himself thinking less and less about Fred C. Dobbs. And his gallery of Slaves sort of faded away, too. He escorted Julie Sutton to the movies for the first time on the evening of

Saturday, September 24. They saw *Johnny Belinda*, starring Jane Wyman and Lew Ayres. Julie enjoyed it a great deal. She held his hand, and after the show he bought her a strawberry milkshake in the Royal Castle at Chester Avenue and East 13th Street. The Indians went on to win the American League championship, and they defeated the Boston Braves in the World Series, four games to two.